THE GULES OF
August

THE GULES OF
August

REVELATIONS 1

NOEL MURPHY

authorHOUSE®

AuthorHouse™ UK
1663 Liberty Drive
Bloomington, IN 47403 USA
www.authorhouse.co.uk
Phone: 0800.197.4150

Published by AuthorHouse 10/15/2015

ISBN: 978-1-5049-9025-7 (sc)
ISBN: 978-1-5049-9024-0 (hc)
ISBN: 978-1-5049-9026-4 (e)

Print information available on the last page.

The Gules of August
+ R E V E L A T I O N S   I +

The account of how six siblings meticulously reveal a series
of links that connect them to an Incredible Trinity;

The Greatest Story Ever Told,
The Greatest Mystery of all Time,
and…
….The Greatest Evil that Ever Existed.

Contents

ANTE ADMONITIO

(Forewarning)

THIS ACCOUNT IS founded on real persons, incidents, locations, artefacts, myths, legends, maps, dates, and historic facts.

THAT WHICH MAY be proven, the vast majority, is substanciated at the end of this book.....for that which cannot be proven, it may equally not be possible to disprove. It may not be possible to provide full and final evidence of myths and legends but one can go far to prove that these same myths and legends exist.

For the purposes of this account, person names and place names have been changed, although place names are only slightly varied so that their true meaning is not lost.

People whose names which are important to the deeper meaning of this account have not been changed and therefore remain their true names.

All of the locations, their descriptions, their importance and their proximities to each other are real. The manner in which they are linked has never previously been explored and identified...until now.

In this series of events, no one could have predicted that six school children, brothers and sisters, could have peeled back centuries of history, that they could reach back into the time of the ancients, into the timeless conflict between Pagans and Christians, and that they could ultimately unearth a power beyond which anyone could have anticipated. A power that could potentially threaten the Christianity of Northern Europe, or further.

That such a dark power exists just below the surface of our day to day life is almost... unbelievable, yet we accept the power of Christianity and the Saints, we know the Evil that Exists everyday and we are aware of the age old battle of good and evil.

Often we take for granted the security of the ground we walk upon every day, the same ground that our ancestors walked and the same ground that has been fought for over the years by generations and civilisations.

It is said that you are only three links away from anyone in the world, famous or otherwise, similarly you may only be three links away from histories most important and powerful figures...... and their dark equals.

This was written approximately 7 years ago......

I

INCEPTUM

(Beginning)

SOMEONE IS GOING to die......

Christian shot upright in his bed like he'd been struck from head to toe by a lightening bolt. He gasped a deep breath and held it tight, staring ahead and listening. He could see nothing, hear nothing.... yet he knew he was not alone in his own room. He had been awoken by a whisper inside his own head.

It was dark, too dark, but for a single sliver of moonlight which like a ghostly pencil drew a slim white glowing traceline down the contours of his face. He focused, wide eyed, straight ahead, waiting and forcing his eyes to adjust to the gloom. The hairs on his neck prickled like a thousand tiny warriors raising their spears; his heart pounded desperately against the inside of his chest rising almost to his throat and thumping loudly in his ears like some ancient drum beating out an urgent warning. *Stop pounding!* he urged, and then, as his eyes slowly came into focus, it did just that, the drumming stopped... his heart stood still.

He could see something, *someone*, at the end of his room. It wasn't quite ... someone, more like a *shadow* of someone, just....standing there. It was too dark to distinguish any features, but he knew that it could only be a man. It was no-one from his family, not Dad, the figure was too tall, too lean, and his peripheral vision told him that the bedroom door was still closed, the way he had left it. He attempted to shout at the intruder, to raise an alarm, but the voice that emerged from his own throat was nothing more than a mere whisper. *'Who are you?'* The whispered words seemed to echo before evaporating into nothing. The shadow did not move.

'What do you want?' his wispy words barely reached the end of the bed, but they did it. He could see, no, he could feel the shadow move; it appeared to be slowly, deliberately, raising its arms. In an instant Christian felt a tightening grip snake around his throat. He inhaled sharply, barely getting enough air into his lungs. But it was a familiar feeling, one he had felt before; his hands went to his own neck in a vain attempt to relieve his obstructed airflow. He forced the air out of his lungs and tried to inhale again but the airway was tighter, he was fighting for his very breath. The shadowy intruder was still at the other end of his room, yet the grip was tightening around his throat. With his eyes still on the shadow he grasped blindly at the collection of clutter on his bedside locker feeling for the one item that he knew would save him, the one thing that would be his salvation. His fingers rattled around, seeking the familiar shape, knocking things to the floor, he would not die here, not today.

Now a new feeling engulfed him, he felt his vision blurring, his body weakening. This was not familiar, this was new. He could barely see the presence in the room, but he could feel that it was still there, its arms now extended fully, raised slightly above shoulder height, he knew that its actions were causing what was happening to him. He willed it to go away, to leave him alone. His hand clasped something hard from the locker and he gripped it; it wasn't the right shape, it wasn't what he so badly wanted, what he so badly needed…that item had fallen to the floor and lay uselessly out of reach.

He gripped tightly and gasped out one last whisper. *'Get out of my house!'* It was his last moment of conciousness before all reality faded away into a black swirling vortex and his body collapsed lifelessly back onto the bed.

'Glad you're still alive to tell the tale.' Dad eyed Christian with gravitas the next morning having listened in full to what had occurred during the hours of darkness.

Christian was hunched over the breakfast table, listless and trying to make sense of the nocturnal events. Mom was diligently checking his temperature, his tongue, his eyes, his pulse …and she was taking particular note of the state of his unkemp fingernails. He was glad to be alive to tell the tale too, to have awoken this morning still breathing after the traumatic visitation. Around the table five siblings sat perplexed by this strange and worrying tale.

'Perhaps he came to give you a warning.' said Dad.

'What do you mean a warning?' Taymi flung a look at Dad. She was eldest of the siblings but at sixteen she was still the one who would be least happy left alone in the dark. Christian was second eldest, followed hot on his heels by Sophia, then Mols, then the other brother Morgen and then the youngest, Lila. At seven she was the infant of the family.

'Well I don't know.….Have you been upsetting anyone lately?' Dad answered Taymi's question and directed one to Christian, 'Perhaps someone… from beyond the grave?' Dad intoned in a somewhat evil voice arching his eyebrow pointedly. He flicked a dark hair back from his eye and plucked a little at his slim beard completing the demonic effect.

Mom interjected, 'I still think what you saw could be described as just a very realistic dream.' She wasn't interested in hearing suggestions about a supernatural visitor or anything that couldn't be practically explained. 'A weak spell like this is not unusual for Christian,' she continued, '…and he does occasionally have asthmatic attacks, so lets put it down to a combination of both those things happening simultaneously… a coincidence.' She concluded.

'No such thing as coincidence.' Dad countered. 'Every occurance forms part of..'

'…the design of perfection, yes we know!' Mom had heard Dads theory before. She looked into Christian's eyes, 'You're not going to die, Ok,' she gave a sideways glance at Dad for having insinuated such, '...but this is the second time this has happened in as many days, So, I think that the best thing is that you need to take more care of yourself. And keep out of stressful situations. Ok?'

'...Ok.'

It was so that Christian had been suffering from occasional weak spells; these had remained an unexplained phenomenon despite doctors' visits, special investigations and inconclusive medical tests. These debilitating spells could strike like a viper at any time and in any place; their sequence or cause was not yet understood by the medics or him. Mom was convinced it was stress related and had become watchful over him. First time it happened was just four months ago, the day of his fourteenth birthday. He had felt a weakening wave wash over him and sweeping him into the nearest seat where he held his head in confusion and dizzyness ...but there was something else there too, something he wasn't sure of then but was now.

It was so also that he had suffered from asthma since a child although it was mild and occassional and he hadn't had one in a long, *long* time, in fact he had hoped that it was completely gone but kept his inhaler at his bedside nonetheless. He has never ever suffered both ailments simultaneously. He held his inhaler now, rolling it around in his right hand..... his salvation? Last night it had fallen to the floor, out of reach, useless. What *was* it that saved him then?

Mom said it was a dream, he might have believed that but no, it confirmed something to him. He was sure of something now that he wasn't before on the day he turned fourteen. Back then, in his weakness he'd had a fleeting glimpse of something, a shadow; he wasn't sure, a presence? When he raised his head there was nothing to be seen, nothing physical at least, but there was a distint presence lingering, where the air seemed thinner than normal. Now he knew that this shadowy visitor, this dark intruder had been before, he knew the shadow brought the weakness, the breathlessness, and he knew that it was very, very real....not a dream.

As the chatter, clatter and argument around the breakfast table returned to its normal clankiness, Christian could not help but think that Dad may just have, inadvertently, put his finger on it. *Someone from beyond the grave?* He knew now that this mysterious visitor may have had something to do with what happended yesterday morning, the fall, the message.

Christian's left hand rested on his knee. He slowly unfurled it revealing a small carved object tied onto a fine cord so he could hang it about his neck, an artefact given to him by his parents as a confirmation gift just two years ago. 'It's a family heirloom, it will keep you safe.' Dad had said. It certainly looked old enough. Last night Christian had clutched it in a stricken panic and it remained in his hand even now, its coarse whittling having left replica marks embedded in his skin. Could *it* have been his salvation? This tiny Crucifix carved out of a little square of wood? As he stared at it his mind warped back over all that had happened in the last twenty four hours.

II

NEGOTIUM

(Task)

It had begun by Mom calling everyone together for some sort of announcement, Dad took a backseat.

'Your father and I have a suggestion for all of you.' …it was an ominous beginning, '…we think that it would be good for you to undertake a summer project, something that you can focus on over the school holidays.' Morgens groan said; *I thought school was out for summer.* Mom continued 'It will be a project that you can work on as a team or independently, a project you can learn from and which *should* help to save you from being bored.' She paused, scanning faces and noting the mixture of trepidation and anticipation. Around the table they were stepping stones of height, age, colour and character, alike yet uniquely individual. Three dark hairs, three blond, not a small family. Taymi, Mols and Lila shared the same thick dark wavy hair and it's accompanying often stubborn temprament. They took after Dad in both regards though none of them quite had his darkness. He was proud of how he had so far evaded the inevitable invasion of grey specles, it was his boast that he had kept grey at bay using mind over matter…..grey matter.

Taymi was the darkest of all the siblings, in her colour and her behaviour and she had little patience. She lightly tapped the pencil in her left hand whilst nibbling on her right thumb nail, impatiently awaiting more information on this apparent project theme, description and deadline. She had an inquisitive and analytical mind and she enjoyed…actually *enjoyed* preparing for exams. With little interest in household chores she found that when she had no academic focus in her life, such as now, during the summer holidays, she could be become lackadaisical, moody and bored, saved only by her interest in art. 'Oh that's just typical teenage behaviour.' Dad had pointed out, endlessly defending her silent broodiness.

Lila's innocent seven year old face belied her penchant for causing trouble for her brothers and sisters; nonetheless she had both her parents twisted tactfully around her finger so that she could get away with just about anything. As usual she was hastily scribbling into a notepad and just as quickly dispatching the pages, trying to ignore everything that didn't exist within her own little world….her own vast little world of fascinations, imaginations and a limitless belief of infinite possibilities. If it could be imagined, then it could be true, if it could be visualised, then it *was* true. For Lila there was a very thin line, if any line at all, between existence and imagination, truth and figment, reality and unreality. She argued convincingly that she had seen Fairies in her room at night, *Tooth Fairies* she said. They had wings but they were big, like us, not small like in storybooks and they spoke to her, they told her things.

'What things?' Taymi probed, somewhat spooked by Lila's description of these large as life beings.

'Secrets' Lila whispered. Taymi dismissed it. 'Remember before, you told us that Foxy spoke to you…..I think its time to grow up little Lila!' Lila clutched her tatty old soft toy more tightly and breathed its comforting fragrance. She glowered at Taymi, a menacing, malicious, malevolent glare, a disturbing thought circling behind that look. *All I have to do is ask them to sort you out..*

Mols was much more attentive; her deep brown eyes watching unblinkingly. She had a Bambiesque demeanour, something she had acquired from her love of animals. Her studious observance of many doe eyed creatures had almost made her into one. Mols made careful studies of animal behaviours and habits and she relished living surrounded by habitats which danced with wildlife. Their surroundings were resplendent with woods, marshes, lagoons and grasslands where creatures crept and crawled, sniffed, scurried and nestled, most times unaware of the slim surveyor, slunk stealthlike in the scutch grass. Mols was a predator of habits and nuances, examining every creatures movements, wondering.... *Are they acting on instinct or intelligence? What they would do if I were to startle them? Would they retreat or would they attack?* Even though she was the greater beast, she knew that some animals would leap into attack against a larger foe; they would thrust themselves even to certain death in an attempt to protect their own colony. It was an instinct that humans don't have and it interested her.

That and their sixth sense! It was as though within the animal kingdom you could smell danger, hear it or taste it on the wind. How did they do it? Could sixth sense be learned? She had heard that humans posess the power but very few have been able to develop it. A sense of otherworld, an unfelt touch, a connection to some sort of spiritual ....something or other. The closer she got to animals, the closer she felt she was to these answers.

Morgen flicked his head at repeditive intervals so that he could peep out between tangles of blonde curls inherited from Mom which draped onto his shoulder. Despite his angelic face, Morgen at ten years old considered himself more of a ninja warrior. He conducted his duties with stealth and energy, stealth that sprung surprises, energy that got up early, stayed up late, got bored easily and rested little. He was funny haha, popular in class and flitted around like a restless spirit, his trademark locks whipped up in the breeze, a real life wil'o'the'wisp. Morgen viewed life as a series of conquests, every encounter was a battle and if it was'nt, then he could make it one. He saw past the mundanity of everyday life to the adventure that swirled beneath the surface. To him the supernatural was never far away, if you looked closely enough you could see it, beyond the ordinary, supernatural superpowers existed, he believed that. This project that Mom was on about sounded like it might be boring, but actually if he thought about it perhaps it could be the great adventure he had always dreamed about.

Sophia shared Morgens hue of blonde, but in contrast to his curls, her hair was long, straight and billowy. She leafed absentmindedly at a tabletop calendar, one lavishly decorated with images of Angels and their messages. Every single morning Sophia flicked over a new leaf of this calendar and quietly read the daily message. Actually she did more that read, she breathed these words into the core of her inner being, brooding over the meaning. '*What you set your heart upon must come about*', was what she read today. Sophia loved these divine words; she loved all words, especially when they were expressed through poetry. And more importantly, she believed in Angels; she had always felt that her own Guardian Angel hovered somewhere nearby, protecting, guiding, watching over her. Each morning she inhaled the calendar message into her heart as though it was a message from her own Guardian Angel and she wished that her heavenly protector would someday, in some way, reveal himself.....or herself!

Christian stared intently. His demeanour gave the impression that he was trying to find something, to figure out something, and he was, he was trying to figure out himself. Despite being relatively popular, good at school, happy at home, Christian sometimes felt lost. He was pretty good with a guitar, not bad at art, but he had never felt a calling towards any particular goal and he did not have the first clue in what direction he wanted to take his life. He enjoyed history, delving deep into touching distance of the past, but often wondered if what he was reading was entirely true or just some stories coloured by a flamboyant historian's fanciful imaginations. He enjoyed the sciences, proven belief in how things worked, how we exist, and often wondered whether he should ever believe anything which couldn't be proven scientifically. Sometimes he found himself tormented by runaway thoughts and big questions, *Is this all there is...to the world...to life?* Or was there more, another layer, another dimension, a place that he hadn't learned to tap into yet, a world where everything made sense, a world of clarity, a world of vision, a world of purpose. He had almost died once, so he concluded that there must be a purpose, a reason for life, a goal, a target, a grand plan......but what? He was staring at Mom and just realised she was looking at him too. 'Whats the project?' he asked.

'How to paint the shed and mend the fence.' It was Dads typical jibe which Mom typically ignored.

'We thought that a suitable project would be an exploration ....and a study of ......' Mom picked her words carefully and paused effectually before delivering the *Tada* moment. '...Your Woods!' She gestured with a sweep of her hands and a nod of her head in the direction of the hearty green woods, the magnificent leafy woods, the familiar and nostalgic woods at the western edge of which they lived their entire lives. Christian followed the gestures flow and gazed through the window into the thick tranch of trees which began at the end of their garden and beyond which lay an ancient and beautiful, one hundred and fifty acre, tree world.

'Since you'll be spending so much of your time in the Woods during summertime anyway, as you have always done,' Mom continued, 'it would be really great for you to find out something of its history, its wildlife, its plant life, its stories, the river, the castle, the mysteries....all of it!.'

'Yep, all of it.' Said Dad smugly.

Truth was, the Woods of Castle-Hanes had abundances of history, wildlife and plant life and it was the place that they spent much of their spare time. Deep in the Woods was a historic castle ruins, a crumbly bell tower, a winding river, a ferocious waterfall and multitudinal timeless and secluded glades and nooks. There were copious slopes and valleys and inaccessible dark hollows that presented challenge and intrigue. The Woods teemed with birds and wildlife and all sorts of chirping and nattering, scratching insecty crawly creatures and most inspiringly the Woods were lorded over by two majestic soaring Buzzards.

'And you can use the opportunity to improve your sketching and writing skills.' Mom glanced from Taymi to Sophia. 'Perhaps some still life studies, or poetic descriptions?'

'How bout some wildlife research.....or collecting flowers.' Dad glanced from Mols to Lila.

'History and adventure.' Mom nodded towards the boys.

'I can help if you need finding out about the design of the Castle,' Dad started, 'it's the name of my game,' he was referring to his profession, an Architect 'So just let me know if you need a good looking advisor.' He specifically tailored this latter part of his comment for Mom, who in response, raised her eyes to the Angels in a silent cry for help before continuing.

'We thought that the best starting point would be for you to visit your Grandparents, especially to talk to your Grandfather, his family have lived here for generations, I can set it up for this afternoon and you can pick his brains.' In the background Dad pointed to himself by way of including himself in the ongoing generations of Grandas family. Their Grandparents lived just a skip away and in a winding country lane south of the Woods. They were pretty certain that Granda would know much about the history of the area since he appeared to still live in it. A man of another era they considered him, rooted firmly in bygone times, puffing on his pipe, not like some of their friends grandfathers who were bang up to date with the technologies of the modern world.....like Granny.

And so it was wholly agreed that they would undertake this summer project, a fact finding exercise, an arts exercise, a learning experiment, a historical enquiry, an adventure based in, on and around that which was always there, and always will be there, the Woods. On the whole it seemed to please everyone. Though Taymi indicated towards Christian through some lazy eye contact, that at least they could idle away countless hours in the Woods under the pretence of project research; in a way it would be a perfect 'get out of work' clause.

'And who knows, perhaps you might even find the Hidden Fort.' Dad said, reminding them of one of the mysteries of the Woods, a supposed location suggested as being an ancient and sacred place swallowed up somewhere deep in the depths of the clambouring undergrowth. It was one of those whisperings which seemed to add mistique to the idea of the Woods; they had heard it trotted out alongside other murmurings such as Treasures, Ghosts, Beasts, sinister, strange and apparently inexplicable happenings. The only thing that seemed inexplicable to them was that they had not encountered any of these things despite having bobbled about the Woods since infancy.

'You hav'nt gone looking for them.' Dad would say by way of reasoning.

It was true, they had'nt, but now they very much would be looking for this and any other gems of interest and as Christian was soon to find out, it appeared that a Ghost would come looking for him.

That very same morning, all six brothers and sisters set off for the Woods, what better way to start off the project than to delve straight into the subject matter …and to hang out there for a while of course. Mom was right to say they would be spending a lot of time in the Woods, they had always done so, it was their world, their domaine and they christened areas of special importance with their own pet names. Today they ambled down to their most favourite haunt. Some years ago they had discovered a secluded spot among the trees, a place where a valley tumbled deep down to the rivers edge and haunched up against a banked platform where they could hang out and watch the river streaming by. It had an added attraction of an old swingrope dangling over the river. Despite Morgens petition to christen this Hangmans Noose, the others decided it too macabre and opted to simply call it The Rope. It was where they were going now; it was where it would all begin.

As Mols stepped out into the bright and breezy morning, the sun was already at its most brilliant and cotton wool clouds billowed across an azure sky like balloons chasing the wind. With school out for months, summer, like the infinite sky, stretched endlessly into the future.

A sudden piercing scream grabbed her and she snapped her head skywards. Again, a shriek from high above echoed from the sky, like a murdered soul dropping from heaven. Mols held her breath tight. '*Peeeeuuuuu!*' She knew what it was and narrowed her eyes against the bright sky, scanning the skyzone and eventually picking out, very high up, two tiny black dots, circling, hunting, catching the wind funnels, being propelled higher and higher, touching Heaven, her friends, the Buzzards. Her heart soared. Mols had always felt that the Buzzards were calling out to her. Were they saying hello? Sometimes it felt a little more urgent than that, were they trying to tell her something? Sometimes their cry seemed like a cross between a cry for help and and a warning shriek, sometimes it seemed like a prayer from the edge of heaven. 'Speak to me.' she whispered and then flashed them a secretive wave. She often watched them, mesmerised, as they hovered high above the edge of the Woods, wavering like a kite on a string, holding an exact spot, before folding back their wings and swooping at breaktaking speed to snatch up some tiny vermin spied with telescopic precision from cloudlevel. A week ago one Buzzard had swooped so low across the garden, right in front of her, that Mols was able to see its back, a fleeting collage of red and brown, she caught a glimpse of its grey belly feathers and most impressively its ring of subtle white feathers encircling the neck. This ghostly choker was known by a name usually associated with Angels and Saints, a spiritual name,

'It's called a halo.' Mols had informed Taymi.

'More like a slipped halo.' came the retort.

In that close encounter, the swooping buzzard had swept her breath away and as it did so, she had the absolute conviction that this grandious manoeuvre was especially devised for her. That the bird has somehow wanted to make a connection, to come within touching distance and she was fairly sure that it was looking at her up close, just as inquisitively as she was looking at it.

They had not always been here; the Buzzards, they had arrived only about a year ago. Mols wondered where they had come from and why they had made this their home now. Somehow she felt there was resonance, a deepness with their arrival, a message in them coming, but she couldn't quite put her finger on it. This project might be the chance to look into it a bit more deeply, for sure it would be the perfect opportunity to try and discover where in the Woods they had built their nesting place, it would be a sacred location she was sure of it and maybe if she found it, it would reveal some of their secrets.....

Lila skipped along the avenue, taken, as usual, with the delight of their garden, burgeoning with wildflowers, daisies, buttercups, dandelions and primroses. At the end of the garden was a towering tranche of tall woodland trees, their abundant leafiness swishing in the morning breeze, a living wall of sound and motion, shimmering with green energy. For Lila it was where the magic of the Woods began on a sunny day like this. Unlike winter when the trees morphed into a foreboding slew of soldiers braced against biting winds who repelled the disturbing dark Wood shadows and who made Lila worry about what was really out there and what would happen if it, whatever it was likely to be, escaped......But today was a sunny day.

Taymi and Sophia wandered after Lila, leaving behind their sandy coloured home, its red roman roof tiles and deep eaves reminiscense of a French cottage farmhouse. It was stamped on the wall with the name *Westwoods* cast in white ceramic onto a black wrought iron nameplate which bore an image of an Oak tree. An Oak tree was a symbol of strength but it also had a more mysterious meaning.

'Oak was used to make doors...' Dad had explained the symbology behind the image, '...and in Celtic mythology it was understood to create a doorway between different worlds.' In a way this made sense, this was the door that led them to the Woods, that altogether otherworld. The nameplate too gave them the name by which they most often referred to themselves; *Westwooders*.

Taymi clutched her sketchbook and pencils hoping to scribble some still life sketches down by the bank of the river. Sophia brought her notepad, her constant companion. She was fond of jotting prose and poetry and found the Woods to be a place of creative inspiration. It was as though words hung in the air there, like whispers, like a mist with a message, but from where…. the past? Heaven? Was the whispered silences she often felt the voice of the Angels?

The boys had already raced ahead, past the cranky wooden gate with its one broken rail, under the canopy of branches that arched across the sleepy country booreen to the West Wood Gate just around the bend. The West Wood Gate announced one of the once formal passages to the Woods, curved cut stone walls had once made it a grand entryway to the Castle Estate. Now, time and decay had taken their toll on the old wall and it was barely fit to hold back the grappling overgrowth and clawing branches; and the once grand avenue was little more than a grassy track. They could have entered the Woods from any of a multitude of approaches, holes in the ditch or hopping over fences, but the West Wood Gate was the most convenient and they had passed this way more than a thousand times. From here the remnants of the estate avenue carved and swayed in rolling descent until it eventually plunged into the river before rising anew on the opposite side. Once a sturdy stone bridge here carried carriages and carts and ladies and gentry gallantly o'er the gurgling gushes. Now a modern metal footbridge, a spindly spine of a thing, did the same trick but in a pathetic way.

To get to The Rope, they didn't have to go as far as the metal bridge, instead ducking off to the right, slipping between trees and scuttling down a steep valley drop to the river. When the girls reached the top of this valley they could see the boys already far below, at rivers edge, their shouts swirling up in echos. They were trying to splash each other. 'Boys will be boys will be boys.' Sighed Sophia. Lila followed closely, picking her steps precisely and gripping tightly to branches for balance. She had slipped down this slope more than enough times before, even when trying to make her way up. Mols followed next and Taymi completed the descending troupe, she loved this part of the woods with its subdued colours and dusty earth, a haven to spend hours sketching and thinking, '*A place to engage with the spirit*', she liked to say.

'Spirits.' Lila had replied once.

'What?'

'Spirits! You can talk to the Woodland Spirits!'

Taymi had decided not to reply to this strange statement from her seven year old sister.

Morgen had wanted to call this Hangmans Noose because of how the long length of tough rope suspended from a high overhead branch dangled directly over the centre of the river. The Westwooders had no idea who had put the rope there, or when, or how anyone had managed to have it tied at such an extraordinary height. Even as it swung loose in the wind they could hear the creak of the weight of the heavy tether and the branch combine eerily.

'It's the sound of a man hanging.' Morgen insisted.

'It's the sound of the old tree moaning at the sight of you.' Admonished Taymi.

With such a long pendulum, the rope could swing a very long lazy arc, the entire way across the river from one embankment to the other and back in a slow drawl. They had fashioned a seat out of a thick stick wound into the plait of the rope and they took turns in loping over and back and taking a diagonal run at it to create a circling motion. Even Lila, who looked like a little doll on the great swing, was an expert at negotiating her way over the river on the rope.

A logjam of river debris and branches had accumulated just downriver from The Rope creating a dammed up hulk. They used the dam as a dry crossing to the East River bank which was their favourite side, a shallower slope attracting more sun. To get the end of the rope which dangled above the water, someone had to wade in, retrieve and bring it to the bank; this task usually fell to Christian and could be quite tricky if the river was swelled. Still there was more of a thrill swinging over the river when it was flowing faster and higher and stronger.

Today the river flowed serenely and sunlight shafts bathed the East River bank. Taymi sketched diligently and Lila sifted through interesting pebbles at the rivers edge. Sophia pondered over words, pursing her lips and squinting in concentration. Mols scoured the treetops knowing that the Buzzards nest would be positioned in the tallest of trees .....*Just not any of these ones*, she thought. They chatted about the project, skimmed flat stones off the surface of the water, drew a map of the Woods noting all their favourite haunts and stretched out in the lazy sunspots. Taymi kept a check on her watch and after a few hours she called out to the others. 'Almost time for lunch, time to go home.'

Christian clung to the rope, swinging lackadaisically over and back. Leaning backwards he let the ends of his hair trail in the water one last time and gazed skyward. A steady draught of clouds formed and reformed, linking and breaking. *Clouds; a mass of tiny droplets, frozen crystals suspended in the atmosphere, chasing the breeze, forming creations.....* He blinked... a mass of tiny droplets, crystals suspended in the atmosphere, appearing right before his eyes, splintering the panorama...*What?*

Morgen had been watching patiently and waiting for his moment to strike. He saw Christian leaning back gracefully on the swing unable to defend himself, Morgen stole to the waters edge and juked down. Cupping his hands he swept up some cold, sparkling water and in a flash of crystalline flung it at his brother.

Christian saw the scattering of droplets just a split second before he felt the shock of cold water smack him in the face. The jolt knocked him off his perch. His feet splashed into the flowing river and with a shout he scrambled quickly to the embankment but it was too late, he looked at his soaking footwear. Morgen, wildeyed, whooped with joy at his triumph.

'I'm going to trounce you.' Christian roared at his assailant.

'Not today brother!' Morgen screamed, whizzing away with the teenager tearing after him fixated on executing his threat. They disappeared off into the trees on the East River side.

'Okay...., I think we'll be going home this way then.' Taymi gathering her equipment, resigning herself to not taking the shortcut home but following the boys instead. This way would take them to the metal footbridge where they could rejoin the estate avenue back to the West Wood Gate.

The girls walked together through the shaded tree grove; the stabs of sunlight petereing out eventually by the masses of leaves. Suddenly, crashing through branches, Morgen came bounding back, his face flushed with panic.

'What happened?' Taymi shouted as he raced towards them.

Between breathes Morgen squeezed out his message.

'It's Christian!' he cried, 'He can't move...he's collapsed! He can't breathe!"

III

EPISTULA

(Message)

THEY RAN QUICKLY with Morgen and when they approached Christian they found him on his knees crunched over, striken. Taymi assisted him, 'Are you ok?'

'..feel weak,' he gasped, '… barely breathe…' His face was deathly pale and beads of cold sweat sat out on his forehead.

'Breathe slowly, let me help.' She moved him into a sitting position and sought a water bottle from her bag which she brought up to his mouth. He sipped slowly, gaining back his breath and composure.

'He'll be fine everyone.' Taymi reassured them, 'Let's just wait here for a few minutes until he recovers.' She had witnessed his asthma attacks before but not of this violence.

'What happened?' she murmured to him.

'Not sure,' he wheezed, 'I was just running along, then I just felt weak, like someone hit me, I just fell on my knees, then my breath started to go.' Some colour was beginning to creep back to Christians face and Taymi could sense his appreciation for more regular breathing.

Mols had wandered off a little way, she had noticed that this was a particularly dark nook slightly off the beaten track and she couldn't remember having been here before. She listened. It was abnormally quiet, eerie. She spotted Sophia a short distance away similarly preoccupied, but staring intently at a tree trunk. Sophia called out softly. 'Guys, come and have a look at this.' Christian lay where he was while the others wandered over.

'Look here.' Bemused, Sophia pointed out a rather unusual sight. In the wide trunk of this tree was what appeared to be an unusual carving, a series of rudimentary vertical lines with other notches laid out in rows. 'It looks like someone carved some sort of …symbols.'

Taymi examined the carving more closely. 'Must have been done a long time ago…' she ran her finger over the grooves slowly and eyed them intently, '...because the carving has grown into the bark of the tree. It could have been done a hundred years ago.' The strange linear arrangement puzzled them.

'Aliens.' Said Morgen.

'It *could* be some sort of foreign language.' Sophia said wondering therefore how and why a foreign lanuage would have been scribed here a hundred years ago. Intrigued by what little he could hear of the conversation, Christian gathered himself up, ambled over and pushed past to see.

'I think…I think I might know what this is.' He mused, his eyes scanning the strange scratchings. The others all turned to look at him, *how could Christian know what these olde symbols were,* they waited for what they assumed would be a devine enlightenment.

'Ooaaamm.' He said.

…. did Christian really make that noise.

'Do you need to sit down again?' Taymi asked.

'No, it's pronounced 'Oam' spelled O-g-h-a-m. If I'm right, and I think I am, this is an old Celtic language…a *line* language,' he offered. They continued to look at Christian, somewhat amazed and rather interested by this revelation.

'I learned about it in history class.' He spoke carefully, concentrating on what he could remember. 'It's very ancient, more than a thousand years old. See here, look, each set of lines and strokes represents a letter of the alphabet. I have the full translation in my text book at home. Sophia, If you copy these symbols into your notebook, then I think I could work it out at home…' he said, then muttering '… if I can find my history book.' Christian knew that the difficulty may not be in working out the translation but in finding his hastily discarded school books. Sophia set about carefully transcribed the symbols and where they were difficult to see clearly, she guessed.

'But this wasn't carved more than a thousand years ago.' Taymi pored over the cuttings again. 'Else they would have been grown out, and this tree isn't as old as that.'

'How come we didn't see this before?' Lila asked.

'Don't normally walk this way.' Taymi explained looking around. 'It's a coincidence that Christian fell down just here.'

'No such thing as coincidence,' Mols advised, 'Dad always says there is no good luck, bad luck or coincidence, its all part of..'

'..the design of perfection.' Taymi sighed, she had heard this enough times already and still did not agree with it.

Christian gazed at the carved lines, he raised his hand to touch, but then drew back his hand to massage his throat again, his breath ever so slightly catching. He felt the lines of the carving morph and wave, they looked ancient at first but the more he looked the more fresh they appeared. He stood back somewhat unsteadily.

'Let's just go.' He whispered, and turning his back he walked away and somehow felt his breath ease up with every step.

They made their way to the footbridge, catching just a fleeting glimpse of the imposing remnants of tall Castle walls staring vacantly between trees. Christian sauntering slowly behind, thought that its sad windows implored him to come and visit. No-one had looked out those windows since the fateful day decades and decades before when the living beast of a Castle had met its catastrophic demise plunging to death amid a fiery inferno. In its death throes the majority of the hulk had collapsed in a ragged pile, except for one section of the walls which remained standing, old and craggy, still defiantly holding back the rains and the winds, in some way holding on to a second chance of life, a rebirth. But this second life was a desolate, twisted thing, a lifeless life, a life not worth living, a life without joy. Christian saw that these remaining walls could collapse at any moment, time the healer was time the destroyer, pick picking at the bricks, the joints, the plaster until that moment when perhaps a single grain brushed away by the wind would bring them to their knees and then to the ground. Yet he felt that these bricks and plaster would never give way on their own, so long as they can stand they will stay alive, they will never throw themselves on their sword, never cast themselves to the ground in defeat, never give up. Alive yet dead. Dead yet alive, the Woods was a contradiction of meanings, Seasons, Death, Rebirth. But carvings? by who? Alive? Dead? Its meaning? There was a darkness to them, he could feel it, there was a darkness that said *Death*, but there were words, words passed over generations, words which said *Alive*.

The clanky rattle of the others crossing the bridge brought Christian swirling back into the present and he turned to join them in making their way home carrying his thoughts like a heavy bag of black demons on his shoulders.

IV

AVUS

(Grandfather)

LATER, AFTER LUNCH, helping out with some laundry, avoiding other chores and trying to catch a quick look at TV, the Westwooders walked the well worn half mile to their Grandparents house, crossing the self same river which slashed a divide in townlands at Brockrady Bridge, to talk to Granda about the Woods; its history and mystery. They had decided to hold back on mentioning the ancient script carvings to anyone until they had at least tried to decipher them later. Nonetheless they had reported on Christians near collapse and he had been forced to go lie down for a half hour, remonstrating unsuccessfully until he recognised it as a get out of laundry clause and suffered a sudden relapse before bouncing back again post chores.

Their Grandparents farmhouse and outbuildings were hollowed out of a high hill, far in from the road, a seculded little fortress with a view over the Woods. The door stood open by way of welcome and inside Granda seemed particularly keen to contribute to their study project, parked in his most comfortable chair and contemplating his choice of words.

Henry James had lived here on the edge of the Woods his entire life as had generations of his family before him, he could recite breed, seed and generation going back over a hundred years and knew every rood of the surrounding land. He considered himself keeper of the ancestral James holdings which marched the Woods to the South and

West. Westwoods was built on part of the holdings, fortifying the stronghold even more with James' blood. He had hunted amongst the trees as a child himself and plunged in the dark pool at the base of the waterfall deep in the heart of the Woods. He had oft told them of *The King of the Woods*, an exceptionally tall tree, visible from high hills surrounding the Woods but impossible to find from within. They had considered this and some of his other stories a little bit of a tall tale, a tall tree tale this one, until he had actually taken them one day to nearby Carney Hill and pointed it out.

'You can see it from here,' he had said, 'but in there,..' he pointed at the Woods with his pipe, '.....it doesn't exist.' This mysterious revelation baffled them.

Henry James' pipe was never far from his mouth whether lit or not. He reminded them of the Seanchai, the storyteller from the olden generations sitting in a mist of his own smoke. If you weren't listening attentively, he would poke you with a shillelagh, a lean strong lean stick which he had hewn out from the bushes by his own hands. He was a man of another time, Christian thought, and had the appearance of someone who had been here before and could easily have passed as a remnant of the 1800's. Granny, as grannys do, was on her feet, tending the stove, biscuit arranging and texting obsessively to persons unknown. She kept a watchful eye over Granda, assuming the mantle of keeper of the keeper.

Granda spoke of the Castle as though he was familiar with it, although it had lain in ruins a good many years before he was born. His own mother Katie James who previously lived in this house had recounted stories of visiting the Castle whilst a child herself.

'It belonged to the Lucas family.' He told them, 'They were wealthy landowners, and highly respected for it, but they were kind to the local people. Each year Lady Lucas would host a party in the gardens, these were great sweeping gardens mind, and she would invite the local children to come play in the gardens and enjoy the food.' He looked at the faces of his grandchildren. 'My mother was one of those children, she told me about how grand the building and gardens were. To her, it was a different world.'

'What happened to it?' Mols asked.

'The Castle burned down, oh, over 90 years ago, razed to the ground…except for some of the old walls, but you've seen those yourself.' He considered the matter wistfully. 'I've walked among those old walls many a time.'

Must've been a long time ago, thought Christian, he couldn't imagine Granda making his way deep into the Woods now hobbling on that old stick.

'How did it catch fire?' asked Morgen, he already had the image of a meteoric fireball crashing through his mind and smack into the Castle, destroying it.

'That's never been explained,' said Granda 'The whole thing was somewhat mysterious really and there were many theories. It caused a tremendous commotion when it happened though, people came from all around to lay eyes on the burnt out heap of carcass of a great house.' Granda spoke gently, picturing the scene in his mind, as though he was there himself. 'Smoke rose out from the trees for long and many a day after. People came to pick about and see if they could find treasure. They found no treasure. The estate, in time, grew into ruins.'

'Can I presume then that Lucas Castle is the reason that the area is called Castle-Hanes.' Taymi queried. The district of Castle-Hanes encompasses the Woods and stretched several miles in each direction harbouring numerous townlands and a sprinkling of homes. It was a rural area with a small row of houses and a shop passing off as a village, buried deep in the folds of the county five miles from the nearby town. Both the town and county name was Monaghan, which pared back to its celtic origins translated to *Land of the little Hills*, for it was here that ancient glacial flows created a phenomenon of rolling Drumlins. An undulating and mysterious landscape where mists settled in the hollows and secrecy hid around every corner, a land rich for bandits and ripe for illusion, where anything, including the truth, could be concealed.

Granda tapped his pipe on his knee to loosen the caked tobacco that might infringe on his fresh smoke later. 'Not necessarily.' He said in response to Taymi, still tapping. 'It's said a castle or suchlike existed even before that. Some say that's where the name came from.' He looked up now and took a few pulls of the empty pipe to satisfy himself that it was clean right through. 'You should look into it when you are doing your project.'

'Could that be the hidden Fort that is talked about.' Sophia put it to him.

'Legend has it that theres something in there, yes,' he told her, 'a Fort, a Castle, a Ringfort or Fairy Fort, it could be any of these. I searched for it many a time myself. My brothers and my sister and I all did. But we never were able to find anything. We combed those Woods top to bottom, we *owned* them. The generation of James's before us did the same, the generation after us too, your Father that is. Its whereabouts is still a mystery to me.' He deliberated. 'It wasn't ours to find...ours wasn't the time, perhaps yours will be.'

Taymi looked at Granda and considered his cryptic conundrum. It was less likely in her opinion that they would find it so many years later than him as it was sure to be more overgrown and hidden than ever. Nonetheless they would certainly give it a try. She counted up Grandas brothers, four, and his sister, altogether six of them looking, seeking out the secrets of the Woods, history repeating history.

'What's a Fairy Fort?' asked Lila, her interest piqued.

'It's the remains of an ancient settlement,' he explained '...a large circle was cut into the top of a hill, and fenced around. A medieval village safe from intruders.' He could see that this answer disappointed her. 'But later after the people left,' he went on, 'the Fairies came and that's where they live now.' He nodded solemnly to assure her that this was so and was rewarded by a warm glow from her face at the thought of a fairys home nearby. He paused before continuing. 'It makes sense too. You see, this legend has it that, from what I've been told, assuming it exists, which I know it does, the Fort is hidden from view from mere mortals because it holds a secret.' He pursed his face as though unhappy with how he had worded this.

'Not just a secret, but a very powerful secret.' He chose these words more carefully. 'The secret to unimaginable wealth and power.' He pointed at them with the stem of his pipe and spoke very deliberately. 'So if I were you, I would make the primary focus of your project about trying to find it.'

Morgens jaw was about to drop open.

'What exact legend is this?' asked Taymi somewhat more sceptical as ever, 'and how do you know what you've been told isn't just an old wives tale?

'Because what I've been told was from my Grandfathers, Grandfathers, Grandfather.'

Now Morgens jaw did drop open to think that his Grandfather has been talking to his Grandfathers, Grandfathers, Grandfather.

'Not directly of course,' Granda clarified, '..but it was passed down the family through all the generations of James's that lived here. And they go back way further than even I know...so it's on good authority.'

Granda reveled in the esteem that his words raised but Granny was less impressed, in fact she looked somewhat concerned. 'You must be careful in the Woods,' she warned, 'it's not all safe in there and you really must be careful. There are dangerous drops and crevices, the waterfall is slippery and dangerous and you could just get lost wandering around in there.' She flustered. 'Too many things have happened in the Woods over the years.'

'What things?' asked Christian, thinking of the *thing* that had already happened to them that very morning in finding the carving.

Granny seemed slightly at a loss to describe the things, 'Well.... tree accidents, getting trapped in a crevice....or some other malady.' She hastily wrapped up the subject. 'And don't mind too much what your Granda says about a Fort, it may not even exist.' she warned.

'Oh, it exists alright.' countered Granda strongly, 'It has been spoken about by generations, the Fort and its secret. They said it and I believe it. There is no smoke without a fire you know.' He hovered on these words, allowing the connection to the castle to sink in before continuing. 'But your Grandmother is right about the dangers; stay safe and watch out for each other.'

They got the distinct impression that they should park that conversation there, so Mols asked instead what animals Granda had seen in the Woods over the years and he ran through a list of all the types that she was already familiar with,…. except one. 'There used to be deer roaming the Woods.' He said, 'Until just a few years ago, you had to drive past carefully in case one bolted out from the trees. Until recently, they're all gone now….they just seemed to fade away.' There was melancholy in his voice.

Morgen pictured a deer; its image fading slowly until it finally disappeared.

'Where did they fade away to?' asked Mols.

Granda frowned four furrows into his weathered brow, deep as the poughed ridges he pulled through the earth in his heyday but not quite as straight. The look he fed Mols was menacing. 'Maybe it had something to do with the Beast.' He bit onto his pipe.

'Beast?' said Morgen.

'The Black Panther.' Said Granda.

'Come on?' Morgen sputtered.

'Tellin me you didn't know about the Black Panther that roams the Drumlins?' Granda retorted.

This was news to Morgen…good news!

Mols shook her hear in disbelief, No, this is one creature she didn't count on being around and frankly she somewhat doubted it.

'I know about this!' Taymi burst out animatedly. 'I remember it was on the news… a few years ago.' She turned to the others to inform them of the strange story. 'A Black Panther was spotted roaming around the Drumlins, it was in the newspapers, someone caught it on video and then it was shown on TV but it was a bit blurry.' She seemed bemused at the thought now. 'Everyone was talking about it at the time, afraid to go walking alone.'

Granda broke into a hearty laugh at the thought of it and at the look on both Mols and Morgens faces. But it was true; a Black

Panther had been reported roaming around open fields causing a widespread panic lasting weeks. The story gained national headlines and featured on the main TV news bulletin.

'Every so often this Black Panther story does the rounds,' Granda continued, 'it gets reported in the paper and mentioned on the telly.' His face darkened. 'A black beast, the disappearing deer, theres a mystery you should investigate.' It was a mystery indeed that Morgen was very interested in investigating.

'But, I can't remember this!' said Sophia still undecided whether this was a joke.

'Me too.' Said Lila.

'No wonder,' said Granda towards Lila, 'You were probably just born last time it was reported.'

'You should Google it.' suggested Granny helpfully and everyone looked at her. Christian remained quiet. Like Taymi he had some recollection of encountering this story before and he had the same feeling about it now as he had then…. the feeling of a cold finger running down the length of his spine. There was no way that a beast like that should even be capable of surviving in a climate like this. It was unnatural, yet despite this, something told him that there was a truth to this story. That a beast of some sort had come to visit. And if it had come before, then there was nothing to assume otherwise than it could come again.

———◆━◆◆◆━◆━———

Dad was pondering their replaying of their conversation with his parents. He concurred with Granda's recounting of the legend of the hidden Fort. 'Got lost in there myself looking for that Fort.' he complained, his face lamenting the lost time in pursuit of an unattainable prize. '…Not mine to find.' he concluded, before suddenly brightening up. '…But I did find something that I believe was left behind by the Beast…' he pointed at Taymi, '…You were there,' he told her much to her surprise, '…you too.' he gestured at Christian much to his shock.

'Where was I?' Morgen was aghast.

'Too small the rest of you.' Said Dad spearing Morgen with blunt disappointment. 'Lila was just born.' Dad continued, 'I took you two for a walk, there was snow on the ground, we went in the West Wood Gate, just along the path there we saw it.' Christian's chest tightened as Dad continued. 'I wasn't sure at first, because of the snow you know, had to go over and see.' Christian felt the cold finger drawing down his back and he remembered. He must only have been about seven years old but it was coming back to him now.

'It was the skeleton of a large deer.' Dad said and Christian was back on that path. Standing stiff as Dad approached the carcase.

'Completely stripped of every scrap...amazing.' Dad said. Christian remembered it as a brutal image. *White bones on white snow.* It had stayed there for days maybe weeks but when the snow thawed it seemed to thaw too and disappear into the ground.

'It was the last of the deer.' Dad said. 'Wasn't there the day before,' he continued, 'left out for all to see just like a cat leaves a dead mouse at the doorstep. That's why I think it was the beast.' It wasn't very much of a rational reasoning yet Christian couldn't agree more.

'Did you ever get to hear any stories from Katie James.'asked Sophia, wanting to get away from the macabre images being painted by Dad although *he* seemed to be revelling in them.

'I do remember my Grandmother Katie telling about the Castle gardens when I was young.' He said. 'Though, I'd have a much better conversation with her now about it if that was possible.' He said sadly.

'It's a pity that there is no one still alive who could remember back to that time.' said Sophia.

'Oh, but that is where you are wrong.' said Dad. 'There is someone very much alive who can remember exactly what happened back then, and you should know better actually.' He said flicking a look of disgust at Sophia.

'What? Who could remember that far back? And how would I know?' she exclaimed simultaneously amazed and confused.

Dad looked at her. 'Try to recall, maybe about a year ago, you and I visited the opening of an exhibition of bygone times, in the museum.' Sophia thought back, trying to recollect. '..and we met a very old, very tall gentleman...' Dad prompted her further, '....a gentleman with a feather in his hat and a spring in his step.' Dad continued.

'Oh, yes!' Now she remembered, indeed this was a character it would be hard to forget.

'Where was I?' interjected Morgen.

'At home.' Stabbed Dad, 'Well that gentleman was the esteemed Sir.Jack Leslie of Castle Leslie. If you remember, I introduced us both to him and told him that we lived close by Castle-Hanes Castle, I knew he would be familiar with it being of acendency himself. But what he told me astonished me;' Dad saw that he had a captive audience and deliberated purposefully before continuing. 'He said that he *remembered* the day that the Castle burned down. He actually could *remember* it.' Dad was just as astonished recounting the story as hearing it for the first time. 'Sir.Jack told me that Lady Lucas came to stay in Castle Leslie following the fire that very day and stayed for a several days until they found new accommodation. He was very small at the time, maybe only four or five years old but the event caused such a stir that it is still clear in his mind.....So what do you think of that!'

What they thought of that was that it was barely believable to them that someone could have been there at that time...and remember it to this day. 'That's over ninety years ago!' Taymi quoted Granda.

Dad nodded. 'You know I am sure we could arrange a visit with Sir.Jack and you can ask him yourselves about what happened back then so you can include it in your project, straight from the horses mouth so to speak. Castle Leslie is not too far away, only about 10 miles.'

'Horse?' said Morgen.

'Are we going to see a real Castle?' said Lila. 'Sure Lila,' smiled Dad, 'We are going to see a real live Castle.'

'Do you think he might know more about what caused the burning of the Castle.' Asked Christian.

'This is a man who is a link through the generations' right back to that day.' Said Dad, 'If any man could shed a light on that mystery, I am sure Sir.Jack is that man.'

√

SENTENTIA

(Meaning)

AFTER SUPPER CHRISTIAN rooted around for his history textbook, which he eventually found jammed in a cupboard with some of his other schoolbooks. He flapped through the pages, found the translation notes for Ogham, laid these out beside Sophia's transcribed markings and sat down pencil in hand to begin the translation. It was a simple procedure; a key outlined the alphabetical letter opposite the Ogham symbol. Very quickly he had spelled out what he believed to be the first word and sat back to look at it. *BURNTH*. He wasn't sure if this was an actual word, but it seemed a close relative of *burn* or *burnt* so he continued with the remainder of the translation which disappointingly did not make full sense as it revealed itself, yet appeared to have some sort of a ring to it. Frowning he rechecked his translation before looking again at the confusing script.

BURNTH HOUF F ORIEL

'Whats it mean?' Taymi cast her eye over his findings having followed him to the study.

Christian screwed up his face in thought studying the script. She gave him time to consider his words. 'As far as I remember and it's in here somewhere' he tapped his history book, 'in olden times the letter *F* was sometimes used instead of the letter *S*. Except if it was still needed to be an *F*....if you know what I mean.' She didn't but let him continue, 'So if that's the case, then it means it reads slightly differently.'

He rewrote it as; *BURNTH HOUS F ORIEL*. 'It makes more sense like this but I think what it actually should say is...' and he wrote; *BURNT HOUSE OF ORIEL*.

Taymi was looking at the last word. 'Oriel.' she breathed as something dawned within. She stared fixidly at Christian. 'Oriel!'

'Oriel.' he said in reply, blinking blankly, 'Just remind me again about that.'

'The *Kingdom* of Oriel.' She said. 'Ireland was divided into seven ancient kingdoms. Oriel was one of them. See I listened in history class too.' She said and he was at once reminded.

'Oriel was this kingdom,' Christian circled his finger in the air, 'the one we're in right now.' He recalled now the ancient land divisions and where they were situated within them. They were actually sitting bang in the middle of the former Kingdom of Oriel and he remembered now that the name Oriel was still used in some local place names to this day. A street, some businesses, even a festival carried the name Oriel.

'So does that mean that the Castle is the 'Burnt House of Oriel''. Said Christian, 'Someone carved this after the Castle was destroyed?'

Taymi was thinking about the wording again, reconfiguring the letters in her head. 'I think that the first word *burnth* may not mean *burnt* as you say, but it could mean *burn-the*.That would make it, '*Burn the House of Oriel*.' She looked at him, 'It sounds like a warning, or even some sort of curse that the house of Oriel *will* be burnt... and of course this house was!' She tapped her finger repeatedly on the piece of paper and whispered darkly, 'I think someone carved this *before* the Castle was destroyed.'

They looked at each other now, each feeling a griptight feeling at the thought that the historic fire all those years ago might have actually been a deliberate act foretold or warned in ancient writings on a tree. Perhaps they had just stumbled on the answer to a mystery that had lasted almost a hundred years. But an even bigger mystery now revealed itself.

'Who would have done this?....and why?' Taymi spoke the question she presumed Christian was thinking. But he had gone beyond that. He was thinking something else entirely, something perhaps more sinister, something much more private and personal.

What power had these words that when I passed them I fell immediately to the ground? For he was convinced that there was a darkness in these words that had reached out from the wood of the tree, from many generations ago, through translation to touch him and to disempower him. Words that had lain in wait, concealed yet in plain view. He wondered if it was a conincidence that they had found it, or part of the grand design or what it was that Dad said. He recalled Grandas words, *'It wasn't ours to find'* and wondered if that somehow fit into the equation.

They decided to keep this strange message under wraps, withheld from parents and grandparents for the moment at least, to be revealed when they felt they had actually figured out what it revealed, perhaps at the conclusion of the project...and they began to wonder what it was that this project would lead them to conclude.

Now twelve hours later, Christian reflecting on his nighttime intrusion, wondered again about their finding of the ancient message and whether it was the catalyst for the intrusion and most of all whether he had found it because it was *his* to find.

VI

VISUM

(Vision)

OVER THE NEXT few days the Westwooders spent most of their time in the Woods, their own private adventure park with no queues, fees…or safety rails. They examined the carving again in much detail and searched for more scratches or scrapings or mysterious codes nearby but there were none. Nonetheless Taymi's sketch pad was filling up with drawings and details of unusual trunk formations and uprooted knotty tentacles of fallen trees in which she felt might lurk further decipherables. Sometimes her sketch of a twisted mess of vines conjoured up images that could be interpreted as distorted faces stuck in silent screams and some of her own work disturbed her.

Christian too brought paper and clipboard; he had begun to develop a map of the geographical and topographical layout of the Woods and areas of primary interest including their regular haunts. He studied the contoured ripples of the ground and how the river, through thousands of years, had worn a deep gorge into the fabric of the Woods, a cut straight to its bleeding heart. He tried to capture the rises and troughs on his map and wondered what dark secrets might be stowed among them.

He had also taken more interest in the formations and patterns of clouds and allowed these populate his mind with their imagery. He saw brilliant white plumes in slow motion, an impending avalanche, rolling over and devastating the landscape, suffocating all in its wake. Later in the evening hues, the dropping sun burnished the clouds an angry fiery red and he pictured the Horsemen of the Apocalypse cavalcading through the smouldering gloom and obliterating the lands with burning fire. Despite when and how he studied the clouds, he always seemed to perceive the same outcome; Devastation and Destruction. He wondered constantly about the carving, about the visitor, there had been no more strange activity since that day, since that night, yet his thoughts had taken a darker turn and he knew in the back of his mind that there was more to come.

Sophia had already exhausted one notebook and had moved onto her second one. She scribbled eloquently about that which she saw, describing the different Woodland areas in her best detail searching for the beauty in her surroundings and in her words. She had also begun to construct some poetry capturing her innermost thoughts on paper. Dad had introduced her to the work of Patrick Kavanagh, a great poet hewn from the same Drumlins as she. Though she found it tough at her age to understand all his writing, she had an appreciation for the pictures he brought to her mind through his words. She considered deeply the thought that though he was dead, his words continued to live. Dead yet alive, alive yet dead, words from beyond the grave, messages from another time. She thought about how in a way it showed that it was possible to live forever.

Mols made a compedium of the animals that made the Woods their home. One of the most common was the grey squirrel and she saw many of these, scurrying around the barky woodland floor and racing up the nearest tree whenever they sensed company. *Their sixth sense.* With her patient and quiet approach she managed to study her grey friends at close quarters and observe their peculiar habits. Another time she caught sight of a Fox who had slunk through the garden gate and crept along the bottom of the hedge. He was a magnificent creature and she saw him many more times and knew that he lived nearby. 'Look Lila,' she whispered to her sister, 'its Foxy, he's alive.'

Though she hated it, Mols understood the great circle of life, she cringed when she witnessed the Buzzard struggling to lift a heavy object from the ground which she was convinced was a rabbit.

'They're evil!' Taymi was constantly critizing the Buzzards; insisting that they were related to vultures because of the way they circled for prey. She felt that their presence cast a dark shadow over the entire area. Mols couldn't have felt more differently, to her the Buzzards were special, dignified and proud. There were so eminent soaring high and commanding the skies, majestic, royal and mysterious.

Morgen's main occupation on this summer project seemed to be the creation of a sense of energy and mayhem. He buzzed about energetically, getting up to mischief and flitting ahead of everyone else. He never tired of selecting small objects to flick at Christian and he always appeared to be headed towards the edge of danger or just to the edge of something, like his brothers temper. He has as much patience as an impatient knat and wanted action now, insisting on leading the motely group when they made their way through long grass or briars. He slashed a path through the undergrowth using a blackthorn stick, a rainforest explorer pursuing a hidden treasure, hacking aggressively through the barbed vegetation, eyes scanning for the slither of a poisonous snake, or a fearsome jungle beast, *dare they suggest that these creatures don't exist here…..they'll see!* If he really had his own way he would have been spending just as much more time on his X-box slashing through skateboard mutants, *dare they not allow me stack up more bonus points??* They, however had struck a deal with him and promised him a piece of technology which he could take outdoors into the wilderness, the perfect treasure seeker, something he felt sure would be the key that would unearth any secret wealth, something his ancestors didn't have to help them in their quest and he couldn't wait to try it out, yep, his own metal detector.

Lila was acquiring a burgeoning collection of naturalistic specimens including any and all things she found interesting: flowers, pebbles, leaves, ferns, grasses, tiny wild strawberries and raspberries which she brought home for Dad to taste since everyone else had politely declined.

'Dee-lish...' He said as he pursed his lips swallowing down the bitter little fruits. '...forbidden fruits of the forest. Make you live forever.' Lila popped one of the strawberries in her mouth and crushed it on her tongue. She winced somewhat but decided it was worth it to live forever as Dad had promised.

'See any fairies today?' Dad asked her.

'Yes.' She replied tasting a tiny raspberry.

'Where.'

'In the tree.' She said deciding infinite life wasn't worth this particularly berry.

'Which one.'

'All of them.'

Dad looked at her a long moment. 'Good girl.' He said.

The Westwooders often wandered up close to the Castle remains. Because of the instablity of the last few standing walls, a safety fence, which in itself was something of a safety hazard, kept wanderers, such as they, at bay. They pondered on how impressive the building must have looked before its sudden death, and how the gardens, now just an overgrown wilderness lurching about like a deranged buffalo had once been tended and manicured and sedate. The walls though old and cracked, still displayed some of their original ornate plasterwork all along their top and window surrounds; aka the parapet and opes; to use the architecturally correct terminology according to he who should know; aka their Dad.

They had asked Dad if he could find out more about the Castle and he had been able to produce a photograph of it in its halcyon days, a beautiful bright building shining in the sun, turrets and chimneys lancing the sky, pristine landscaping and sweeping steps. Technically he said, it wasn't actually a Castle, but simply a large grand and stately house occupied by the aristocracy.

'The proletariat called it The Big House.' He told them.

'The who now what now?' asked Morgen.

'The little people.' Said Dad.

'The fairies?' Said Morgen.

'They're big.' Said Lila.

'The commoners.' Said Dad. And he promised to dig up some more documentation about The Big House although he suddenly remembered something about it that seemed to have previously escaped him.

'There's something hidden in the Castle.' he said, ponderingly, 'It's still there, underneath.' He was building up the Morg-tension factor, nodding thoughtfully to himself, counting the seconds until Morgens head was about to explode off his shoulders with anticipation.

'*Dungeons!*' Dad blurted, with his eyes widening and gripping his hands as though he himself was going to use these dungeons to torture them all to death. Lila feigning a frightened face clung comically to Sophia. Morgens eyes already popping out of their sockets at this revelation, stayed so.

'Well they're not really dungeons,' Dad drew back somewhat; 'They may be wine vaults or suchlike running under the body of the main walls. But when we were kids, they were dungeons to us, we could go in there and follow their winding route for as far as we could go, before they disappeared... *into the dark nothingness.*

'Less drama already!' Taymi sighed.

'But you can't poke around in there any more because it's unsafe,' he reminded them, 'so stay out, else those dungeons might become your torture chamber.' He looked at Morgen, 'Especially *you.*'

Back in the woods, they took the route to the Waterfall they called the *Ledge Walk.* It was an cantankerous, contorting, path which twisted and narrowed and became more dangerous as they drew ever closer to its grand prize. It had steep slopes on either side; one falling rapidly to the valley below, the other rising jagged and foreboding above. Rotting black branches reached across in front of them like dead mens arms, slimy and twisted, trying to block the way. Morgen broke off the spindly ones and ducked past the rest. Newer fresh leafy twigs flicked at them like forest unchins trying to slap their cheeks. They bent these back without breaking them. Christian clambered over a rocky pile of rubble thrown there by a recent landslide. He glanced up at the steep slope above, if another landslide were to happen now it would easily knock him off the path and down to the valley below. He looked down the slippery slope into the chasm below, it would hurt, but he would be ok he reckoned. They called this bit *The Drop.* Nonetheless he picked his steps carefully, sunlight didn't much reach through the tall canopy in this part of the woods, everything was just a little dank and treacherous and uninviting; the dark before the dawn.

The end of the Ledge Walk led them to a pinnacle, the edge of the ledge, a pointy tip of branchy outcrop lurching over a precarious plunge. They crowded together and leaned over for a bird's eye view of the tumbling cascades. Swirls of misty vapour from thousands of gallons of raging river rose and damped their faces. Christian closed his eyes and breathed it in. Gigantic gushes of water roared over the edge and collapsed repeatedly onto the rapids below. Eventually it rippled outward more calmly into a large black pool, the one where Granda used to swim as a kid and many more before. The falls were not at their most dramatic today. No, for that it needed to rain, and rain hard; that would bring out the beast. The waterfall after a heavy rain became a tumultuous, uncontrollably raging monster sounding out a thunderous roar of power from the bowels of the woods through the hole in the roof of the trees for all around to hear, for all around to fear. Christian had seen the falls raging and from his house he had heard them roaring and he wondered what their full powers were truly capable of.

Lila, as the smallest, needed to lean out that little bit more to see. She held onto a wet branch and strained forward. She felt no fear whatsoever. Something snagged the back of her jumper as she leaned. She ignored it and stretched a little more until she could see fully. The others had been warned heavily to protect her; she knew that, and as she leaned forward just that extra little bit she could feel five hands grip her jumper just a little more tightly.

They were exploring more of the woods than ever before, searching into its darkest recesses, charting new territories, mapping new places. Rarely did they see anyone else in these woods, a figure in the distance perhaps, a woman making notes, a man walking a dog, but mostly it was quiet among the trees. Quiet, that is, in the normal scheme of things. Otherwise the woods were alive with noise, a cacophony of bird squacks and insect buzz, rustling leaves and creaking branches, tweeting, scurrying, trickling, swishing, bobbling, buzzing, humming, whistling and a million other vibrations creating an orchestration of nature. But apart from their own voices there was a ghostly absence of human beings. Taymi thought it strange. *Such a beautiful place and yet almost no-one comes here.*

They stumbled on some bizarre and incredible sights. They dubbed one the *Divided Tree*. Morgen insisted that it was a remnant of some malevolent superpower. A tree, still growing, still alive, had been split down its entirety to the base by another tree which remained lodged. Was it a freak of nature, caused by a ferocious lightning strike or a gale force wind or was it, as Morgen tried strenuously to justify, created by some another *un*-natural event. 'Look,' he gestured 'the tree that fell was complete ripped out of the ground.' Christian looked at the upturned roots, it would have taken a brutal storm to have heaved a tree of that size right out of the ground and split open another tree. Again he thought about the power that lurked here in these woods, a power that he could see now was capable of rising up in a violent rage and striking out.

Sophia found something else lodged in a tree, an old brown stout bottle. It looked like it had been discarded there many years ago and a young sapling had grown up, befriended it and moulded itself around the bottles shape raising it up from the ground as it grew. They took turns trying to twist the bottle free but the tree was mature now and he was not going to give up his lifetime friend, not for nobody, no how. They were intertwined and that was how it was going to stay. Sophia sullenly crossed her arms;

'You just can't give up the bottle can you?' she chided.

They witnessed much untamed beauty; rivulets running rapidly, shoots stretching strongly, wildflowers weaving wonderfully. It juxtapositioned sharply with old wood twisted into cantakerous carbuncles, murky mud puddles, leaves, dead and decayed. They knew that the woods looked entirely different in Autumn, Winter and Spring, it looked different with the changes in the weather as well as the seasons and they knew that the woods, like every other living thing could be moody and sulky as well as happy and light.

In a secluded clearing they discovered another strange occurrence. A sprinkling of thin trees had rooted and grown but only to about three feet high. Then it seemed as though they had lost their strength, they leaned over and flopped back down to the ground but continued to grow on top of the soil. Morgen examined them closely, 'It's like they had their spines ripped out.' he surmised. It made for an eerie sight, a network of stringy tree trunks creeping along the ground, looping over one another, extending like stretchy fingers, trying to clutch onto something vertical to prevent themselves drowning from lack of oxygen. It was like they were doomed to crawl on the ground forever, like the serpent from the Garden of Eden. What unearthly power could have cast them down to slither on their belly for all eternity.... and why? Christian marked the location onto his rudimentary map and named it *The Snakes*.

One of the most uninviting parts of the Woods he recorded was a dark and dreary place they called the *Dark Underworld*. It was so overgrown that it stopped the natural light penetrating through its canopy creating a murky and dark, damp tunnelling of trees and trunks and branches and briars.

Their search of the woods had reminded Christian that often not all was as it seemed. At first you saw beauty, but behind that there were scars, destruction, unexplainable and twisted things, good and bad, dark and light, mystery...mystery *and* he hoped, revelation.

Despite all of their mapping, investigating and searching, they had not yet identified anything even remotely resembling the supposed Fairy Fort.

Taymi, as they all knew, was sceptical about its existence anyway. 'I don't believe there is such a thing as a Fairy Fort, how come no-one has ever seen it, no-one has found it, Granda and all his family couldn't even find it.'

'It might be covered over.' Christians liked the idea of a Fort and its treasure, his eye was very much on the prize.

'If it's covered over then we will definitely never find it.' Scepticism becoming pessimism.

'I can see Faries.' said Lila out of the blue.

'Yes, Lila, just like you saw Foxy alive last night.' snapped Taymi.

'He could'nt sleep.' said Lila hurt; and then, 'I saw the Tooth Fairy.'

Taymi looked at her dismissively. 'Sure Lila, the Tooth Fairy and Foxy.'

Taymi was annoyed, they were making their way home and she wanted them to all stick together so no-one would get lost. Up ahead she saw long straight blonde hair going over the hill and out of sight. She called out sharply. 'Sophia, some back here or you're in trouble.'

'I'm right here' Sophia's soft voice came from behind her and Taymi swung around.

'I saw you up ahead. Did anyone else see that?' Taymi glanced round at the others, but no-one had seen neither what she saw nor anyone else around. Taymi jogged ahead quickly to the top of the slope and scanned around. There was no-one in sight amid the trees and she felt a slight shudder revertebrate through her. The Westwooders continued on their way home, Taymi dropped her claim about what she has seen and marched on yards ahead of the others who came chatting behind. She was convinced that she had seen Sophia ahead and felt that something was not quite right among the trees of the woods, no, something was very definitely wrong.

VII

CASTELLUM

(Castle)

NEXT DAY THE Westwooders were on their way to Castle Leslie, home of the ancestral Leslie family in the picture perfect stone cottage village of Glaslough. Its name translated to Glass Lake, the same lake over which the great castle gazed in endless thought, the same lake which serenely reflected a perfect mirror image of castle as though it was built down from the sky. They had made advance arrangements through a secretary to meet Sir Jack who perhaps might have found it peculiar that six kids had requested such an interview. On entering the grounds there was a parking area and a rustic lodge, stables and courtyards. A waft of rich coffee offered parental temptation, so they abandoned the car there so as to walk the remaining avenue to the actual Castle hidden beyond. The avenue wound around and about and on the sojourn they encountered a round tower and glimpsed a little church nestling in seclusion.

'It's where Paul McCartney got married.' pointed Mom. 'It was a huge media event, supposed to be a secret but Sir Jack told the press about it......... but he warned them to keep it a secret.'

'Who's Paul Mc *what* ? Cartwheel?' said Lila.

'He's very famous.' Mom explained, '....a Beatle.' She went on to explain to Lila about Paul, John, Ringo and George and how they weren't insects.

The castle began to reveal itself. 'Scottish Baronial architectural style.' Dads floated words over everyones elses heads. 'Sir Jack is a Baronet; it's a Royal title, it's why he's called Sir.'

It was a magnificent specimen of a castle; resplendent with turrets, tall windows, cut stone arches and an enormous wooden door. The building stood over them like a giant, coolly ignoring the insignificant visitors. When they reached the front porch Mols reached up and swung the cast iron knocker, rapping it on the door causing a loud echo in the outer porch and deep revertabrations inside the building. And they waited.

Eventually footsteps approached from within before a slow grating accompanied the rotating handle and the door began to slowly creak open. It was as dramatic as they could have hoped for and more. There in the doorway stood a very tall and gaunt figure wearing a hat with a striking feather plume. He looked ancient and historical in appearance and he was, unmistakably, Sir Jack.

'Hullo.' Sir Jack smiled a very wide welcome, putting them at ease straight away. Dad reintroduced himself and everyone and made arrangements for he and Mom to go have a hotly anticipated frothy coffee while the kids talked to Sir Jack on their project. When they stepped inside the castle door, Sir Jack swung it slowly shut causing a deep cavernous boom.

'Come through to the drawing room, and take a seat.' He instructed, leading them past oak panelling and tapestries into an enormous room burgeoning with antiquities. He gesturing them to sit and they all found themselves three in a row sitting on the edges of some gi-normous armchairs. Sir Jack sat on his own directly opposite; it seemed to fit him perfectly fine. He studiously observed each of them in turn.

'Now tell me young friends, what is it you want to know?'

'Can you tell us about the night that the Lucas Castle at Castle-Hanes burned down please.' said Taymi, speaking sheepishly on behalf of all.

There was a long pause and the clock ticked. 'Yes of Course.' Sir Jack said before pausing again. The clock tocked. 'From what I remember, the fire was a mysterious occurrence which to this day has never been fully explained.' They were already enraptured. 'Some say a maid accidently dropped a piece of burning coal on the floor, some say it was set alight on purpose,' he spoke carefully and precisely, 'and some say it was a Devils Curse put upon the Castle.' Taymi and Christian looked at each other at the mention of a curse.

'Do you think it was a Devils curse?' Sophie ventured.

'No, no, no.' laughed Sir Jack, 'That's how people explained all manner of odd things in those days, however the exact cause still remains a mystery and the occupants were lucky to escape with their lives.' His eyes were wistful as he stared off recalling times past. 'It was a miracle that they awoke as the fire started in the very early morning when everyone was still asleep. I believe it was the young girl who was awoken and raised the alarm. After escaping the fire they arrived here to Castle Leslie with horses and carriages and carts taking whatever belongings they could salvage. They stayed here for a short while before moving to more long term accommodation and eventually back to London. It was just the girl and her mother, all the others were maids, the older children had already left home. I still remember it well, playing with the little girl down by the lakeside, I was only about four years old myself.'

They were mesmerised by this man whose words could take them to another time, another world. 'I've gone back there many times since.' He said. 'To that time?' queried Morgen. 'No,' Sir Jack laughed again, 'to the scene of the crime, the castle ruins, many times, indeed I may pay it a visit again. You should know,' he continued, 'there was one other strange occurance which happened at that time.' His voice tailed off, the children leaned even further off the edge to hear. 'The Gatekeeper disappeared.' Morgen slipped off the couch and hurridly repositioned himself without Sir Jack noticing. 'After the fire at the big house, he was never seen again, it was suggested that perhaps he became trapped in the blaze but no body or remains were ever found. His gatelodge had since fallen into ruin.' Sir Jack reviewed his captive audience, 'Perhaps he had some connection to the burning of the Castle, or building incendiary devices for rebels. There's another theory for you for how the fire might have started, it was a troubled country in those days.' Taymi made hurried notes.

'You said the gatelodge is in ruins,' Christian said, 'but people still live in the gatelodge now Sir Jack.'

'No, you are thinking of the east gatelodge, a fine building no less, but I am talking about the west gatelodge, a tiny, tiny stone house.'

'But we've gone in and out of the West Wood Gate hundreds of times and we have never seen any remains of a stone house.' said Christian.

'I assure you young man, if you look *carefully*, you will find it.' Sir Jack was absolutely confident of that.

Sir Jack led them on a tour of Castle Leslie, showing them the many splendidly restored rooms and views over the lake. He took special delight on showing them into the haunted room, one in which it was said the bed would occasionally levitate. From an upper window they could see their parents returning along the avenue, Dad expounding magnamously about architectural merit and suchlike and so they made their way down towards the front door again. On the way there, Sir Jack stopped momentarily at a large glass frame which held within what appeared to be an infants white linen dress.

'This is the baptism gown of the great Winston Churchill.' Said Sir Jack referring to the historic British Prime Minister and Statesman. 'We were relations you know, cousins; he visited the castle here on several occasions.' He informed them much to Christians astonishment.

'In his youth,' Sir Jack continued, 'Winston had spoken with a lisp, *'It is cuthtomary to thtand up when the Kingth thpeech is read.'* They laughed at his gruff imitation.

'Thank You Sir Jack.' Taymi told him as the reached the Castle door. 'For everything.'

'You are most welcome.' Sir Jack replied and he looked kindly on all of them, especially Lila. 'What age are you?' He asked her.

'Seven.'

'You remind me of the little one, same age, same hair, same smile,...we played together, now what was that little girl called,... Oh yes, I remember now......her name was Oriel!'

VIII

INVENIO

(Discovery)

It was the name that blew them away. *Oriel*, the Castle was her house, the *House of Oriel*.

'Burn the House of Oriel, Why? Why would anyone want to burn down the house of a seven year old girl?' They had arrived home and were sitting around talking about it. Lila did not like the connection at all between her and this other seven year old girl who nearly met a fiery end.

'Very sinister.' Frowned Taymi trying to exact a meaning to this new found information.

'Sir Jack said that the young girl was the one who was awoken and raised the alarm.' Said Christian, pacing around. 'Did she sense something? How was she awoken?'

'From the noise of the fire?' Said Sophia.

'From the smoke? Said Mols.

'Her alarm clock? Said Morgen.

'Fairies?' Said Lila.

'Did someone wake her in the night?' Said Christian low enough so only he could hear; he thought of his own night awakening.

They didn't have much more time to discuss it, the girls had arrangements to spend the afternoon in town with Mom, leaving the boys, all three of them including Dad, at home. But Christian already had plans for how he and Morgen would be plying their time.

After the girls had gone on their expedition, the two brothers set off on theirs; heading off to West Wood Gate to look for the remains of a small stone cottage that Sir Jack assured them was there. For once they took a good look at the entryway as they approached and realised the tremendous amount of overgrowth burgeoning behind it. Morgen chose to search around and behind the left hand side wall. He had brought the most appropriate equipment he could think of; chocolate, a stick, water, a compass and a metal detector. Christian brought nothing except himself. 'Don't think you're going to need that.' Christian nodded at the detector. 'Walls ain't made of metal.' And he made off for the right side wall poaching among the scrabbly branches, brambles and briars, examining around for traces of a building. He picked his steps through decayed woody limbs fused with undergrowth, moving further under the dense canopy. Then he saw it! *If you look carefully you will find it.'* Sir Jack had said and sure enough there it was, barely. The outline of a small building, a clear definition made by a low stone wall reaching just inches out of the mossy floor.

'I found it!' He called out and his brother came hurtling through the prickly curtains to see.

It had been concealed by years of rambling wildness. The entire cottage could only have been one single room of about four metres long and two metres wide. There was a clear cut break in the wall in one place. 'That must be where the door was.' Christian pointed. Trees grew inside the building, some rooted in the stonework itself. Together they had a closer look, going 'inside' the cottage and poking around in the soft floor. They were astonished that a cottage really did exist, just like Sir Jack had said and its remains had lain here for decades overgrowing with its cut stone walls pickpocketed away over time.

'I found something too.' Morgen held a small piece of ceramic; white with decorative blue depictions. 'Its Willow pattern.' he said. *No help whatsoever* thought Christian yet he was forever amazed at the things which his brother knew. Morgen switched on his detector and began to scan it over the ground.

Christian looked around; the ruins of the cottage had remained hidden here for a long period of time, silent, secret, he tried to imagine it rebuilt; how small it would have been, surely it was only one room. At once he sensed a change of air, a presence. He stiffened as he felt as if someone had arrived, yet no-one had come through the undergrowth from any direction, no crunching twigs, no rustling branches. His conscience was drawn to the corner of the cottage, and just beyond Christian was certain he witnessed something. He could feel more than see it; an upright shadow, a shimmer, a tall figure, behind the leaves or in front of it? an illusion? As he looked he felt he was being looked at, the hairs on his neck bristled, goosebumps rose defensively on his arms, his heart beat like a fist, but strangely, he did not feel fear.

'Who are you?' he whispered, knowing his whisper could be heard. He felt this was the same presence that had appeared in his bedroom, here now to communicate, not to hurt him, not to warn him, but to warn him *of* something, to *tell* him something. Christians concentration wavered, he wasn't sure if he could see the shadow or not, as he continued to stare he realised that the shadow was gone and it was only the fixed image of it in his mind that he could see. What was there was now gone.

'I can't find anything.' Morgen's voice chirped beside him.

'Look over here.' Christian said quietly, directing Morgen and his detector towards the corner of the cottage where he had witnessed the vision. Morgen swept the detector over the rutty ground as instructed.

'Why here?..' Morgen began before a piercing beeping emitting from his machine stopped him in his tracks. beep...beep...beep... beepbeepbeeeeeeeeeee. The intensity of the signal told them it was a significant find and right at their feet. 'We in luck!' Morgen gasped. Christian got down on his knees and began scrabbling at the ground. Morgen proffered his stick and Christian used it to hoke out a hole, stub out stones and clear clods of clay.

'What do you think we got? Morgen's heart was pounding.

'I've no idea,' was the reply '..but there is something solid down here.' Christian has unearthed quite a sizable hole in the mud floor of the cottage, sweeping back handfuls of dusty soil. He grabbed the stick again and dug it into the hard object that was becoming revealed. There was a metallic clank! They looked at each other and then both grabbing sticks dug the hole wider until they were able to see more.

They were unearthing a metal box, they dug around it and discovered that it was contained within a small framed chamber. 'It's a safe hiding place, under the floor.' Christian said looking at the box which was now fully exposed but still in its hiding place. He picked it free from the chamber, carefully extracted it and laid it on the dusty clay pile. Perspiration sat out on his brow as he examined it. He reckoned it was about ten inches long by six inches wide and about three inches deep. Morgen waited; this was Christians find but he couldn't for the life of him understand how he had selected that exact spot to look.

There was a small latch on the box but no lock. Christian unlatched it and carefully hinged back the lid. It contained a book; an old book, pages tattered at the edges and many hanging loose, the cover with its bound edge ravelled. Christian took it up carefully and began to delicately leaf through it. The writing was joined script from an ink pen. The quality of the script was poor and some of the ink had faded making it difficult to read, on both counts. It appeared to be a record of comings and goings at the Castle gate, mostly names and dates spanning over several years.

'It's a register.' Christian explained. 'The gatekeeper used it to note who came and went to the Castle.' There were quite a few unused pages towards the end of the journal and he went to the last page of the book where there was a written entry. As he scanned over the words he felt a tingly sensation overcome him, a sense of eireeness.

A note was written there, in the same style, by the same hand albeit more scribbled or hurried. But the text was different to anything else in the book; it was strange, bizarre, cryptic.

'What is this?' Christian said, '...A prayer? A message?....' He pondered on this, '.....a *Message!*' he whispered, 'It's a *Message!*'

'A message?....to who?' Morgen whispered back daunted.

As Christian read quickly through the words once more, he felt that he knew why he had found this book, why this book had been *revealed* to him. He looked Morgen square in his frightened eyes with a sense of shock in his own.

'It's a message to me.'

IX

QUAESTIO

(Quest)

THE BOYS CLOSED the opening, carefully dusting earth over it and fixing mossy clumps to conceal that there was anything of interest there lest anyone came looking; which was unlikely since the place clearly hadn't been visited in many moons. They extricated themselves from the grapply quagmire with Christian taking care to guard the prize yet anxious to pore over the journals contents. Morgen scooted ahead throught the grand gateway keen for home to show and tell. Yet when Christian rounded the stocky pillar he saw that Morgen had stopped in his tracks frozen stiff in a stony stance. And then Christian too fell into a frozen state of fright.

It coursed by with the slow flow of polluted river; a reflection of distorted black branches concealed the black stare that bore into them with dark intonment. Morgen just stood and stared, Christian folded his arm more tightly about the box and its cargo. The cloud of darkness passed oh so slowly and they watched as it disappeared around the cruck of the road knowing that they were being watched in return.

It was the Dark One.

It was the name they had placed on him much time ago for his mysteriousness and the way he made them feel uneasy and most of all his darkness. When that dark car passed, they held their breath, it seemed to appear out of nowhere, silently, when least expected.

And they could never see the occupant but they knew who he was and were well familiar with his appearance. The Dark One always dressed in black and everything about him was black. They had seen him in the Woods on many occasions, in the distance, behaving mysteriously, searching dark shadows. And they knew where he lived, less than half a mile away, alone, reclusive, in a dark house high on a hill. But not a silent house, no, a house where dark music permeated, escaping through the thick walls and up the chimney to waft down on the houses below. Music to raise the demons. Someone said he had another life; someone said his closest friends were in other countries and that they were as dark as he. Someone said a lot of things but the Westwooders knew there was more to the Dark One than any someone would know. They had a suspicion that in the case of certain curious carrying ons that his influence was somehow brought to bear. That he was on the fringes of mistrust. And now just at this important, this mysterious moment, he appears as if by coincidence and Christian knew he betrayed himself by showing that he had just discovered this incredible and secret thing. And now the Dark One had seen him and would know; he would just know.

Morgen was looking at him, thinking the same thing but there was nothing they could do but walk on home.

It was much later when the girls arrived home and they agreed to head back to the woods where they would discuss this discovery, examine it in detail and see for themselves the remains of the gatelodge. On the way there, Christian described how he had felt a presence lead him to the concealed treasure but left out that the presence had been in the form of a shadow vision. He told how the Dark One had come along just as they emerged from the thickets exposed with the box in full view and how the Dark One had slowed almost to a stop when he passed right in front of them. Christian withdrew the box from his rucksack and made to open it.

'Not here,' said Taymi, 'It's too murky, take it to the beach and we'll look at it there.

The beach was a flat pebbly river shore at a wide swathe of river halfway between the waterfall and the rope. Because the river was so broad there and the trees so far back, the beach was a suntrap flooded with heat and light like it was sitting under a hole in the ozone. But taking the rivers edge to the beach wasn't as easy as a walk in the park. A tangleweed of branches caused constant disruption dipping into the river and causing them to duck and weave like a troope of featherweight boxer gymnasts. Bob up in the wrong place and you got a smack in the face. The cleanest way past all this tangley mess was to take to the water and wade up the centre of the river, which was an option sometimes taken. Today though they didn't want to risk dropping the carefully protected cargo in the river just as soon as they had discovered it; so they furrowed onwards until the last leafy lashes spat them out into their own private paradise. The secluded serenity always welcomed them. They had never seen another soul in this little pleasure spot and they set down the box on the rolly pebbles and gathered around. The waters did a little dance and a skip around small stones which peeped up to steal a look at their land-ho cousins.

Christian released the register again from the apparatus which had kept it concealed for generations and they pored over it deciphering names and dates which had been entered almost a hundred years ago. Christian turned the pages carefully ensuring no-one was going to damage it and controlling the pace at which they would reach the latter, most interesting pages where the most mysterious of all the entries resided.

'Now,' he said excitedly, 'take a look at this.' As he revealed a page of writing that were the final words that were to be written in the register by the hand of its author. Words that cast a sort of breathlessness on them but also drew down an invisible cloak of darkness about the bright rivers edge.

Together they read through the passage of mysterious words. Sophia saw immediately a poetic aspect to them. Taymi's mouth draped open as she re-read and frowned at the cryptic composition.

Morgen was somewhat smug that his seek and retrieve input had yielded such a great discovery. Mols was clearly spooked and Lila struggled in understanding the scrawly script.

'Read it to me.' She said.

Christian has already figured out the more difficultly scripted lines, and he had already mulled over it several times, so it was he who now read aloud. His voice exacting the significance and mysteriousness together with the excitment he felt even though the meaning eluded him.

The golden stone exists
Hidden in the circle
Macartans hiding place
Its power danger
Only the innocent can retrieve
My warning saved the child
Now I fear my sacrifice
At the holy place, the median
Macartans trinity
Buried at the forth point
To raise the fee
Angel peel of the coet
But I would again spare the infant
Of the seventh age, the end
Spirit of the child
To ban an drui
Banish by breaking the stone
By the pure hand

'Wow' whispered Sophie, 'What is that all about?'

'According to this,' Christian stabbed at the page, 'there is a treasure, a Golden Stone, and its hidden here somewhere,' he said; then concluding, 'in the circle.' as thought this explained precisely where they ought to go to find it. He examined the page again. 'See, it is buried at the forth point, I know that means the fort, there is a fort, and it's the circle.' he spotted Taymi's sceptic frown. 'The Fort exists and we are destined to find in.' Christian remonstrated, with Morgen in cahoots, nodding his approval.

'But what about this danger, the warning mentioned here.. and here' Taymi pointed out.

'I'm kinda worried about this,' said Mols, 'maybe we should talk to Mom and Dad about this.'

'Can't,' said Christian, 'Look were not going to do anything silly. Lets just wait to see where this goes. We can find out a bit more about it and then we can present it all to them as part of the project.'

'This book must have belonged to the Gatekeeper' said Sophia gravely, 'Do you remember Sir.Jack telling us that gatekeeper disappeared, maybe this tells us why.' They pored over the cryptic verse again and debated the meaning.

Christian was adamant that the name 'Macartan' was a reference to Saint Macartan. 'Its obvious.' he said. They were all fully aware of the name of St.Macartan, a famous saint from the region but Christian knew much more about Macartan than the others; and for very good reason; his school was named after the saint.

St.Macartans College was a famed boy's secondary school occupying a comandeering site above the town to which over 700 boys marched up the hill each school morning and down again after academic battle each day. The building itself was stately and imposing, a seventeen bay classical structure with bell tower and private chapel flanked by stacks of classrooms which sucked up eager students and then spilled them out full of knowledge. The school had a strong Christian tradition and it was a formidable physical presence.

Christian was proud of his school and its history and could quote the schools motto. 'Fortis et Fideles' he proclaimed, 'it means Strong and Faithful.' He went on to tell his siblings about how the saying was used by a onetime college priest teacher who died a captive of communists.'They were his last words.'

'You see, Macartan was the first Bishop of Clogher,' he went on to explain further, 'as decreed by St.Patrick himself, he was Patrick's right hand man and carried Pat over rock and rivers when the old man wasnt up to it any more. Clogher was Patricks gift to Macartan for standing by him."

'But there are lots of people named Macartan around here.' Taymi commented.

'But they are all named after *Saint* Macartan,' Christian was adamant and then another thought occurred to him. 'It's possible according to this, that Macartan might have even been right here in Castle-Hanes at one time, see here, '*Macartans hiding place, Macartans trinity*.' He read.

They were well familiar with Clogher; it was one of Irelands twenty six Christian dioceses, each one under the supervision of its own Bishop. Though each diocese came equipped with its own Cathedral, Clogher was an exception; it had three Cathedrals, each of them, somewhat confusingly, called 'St.Macartans Cathedral'. The most impressive of these was the one they were most familiar with, the one that towered over Monaghan town, towered over the people and even towered over St.Macartans College, its bell tower spire seemingly scraping a hole in the underbelly of passing clouds the way the iceberg tip ripped a hole in the Titanic. It was where they received their sacraments, baptism, communion, confirmation...so far; and each weekend they found themselves there in the dioceses most important building for mass. Could that be *the holy place, the median*, mentioned in the verse. It certainly seemed to have the power, often they had seen the rising sun light up the spire like a fiery golden sword, rising out of the dewy mists, pointing to the high heavens in magnificence.

Sophia wondered what was meant by *ban an drui* and *banish by breaking the stone*. 'What is a drui?... and does it mean that a drui will be banned or banished by breaking the stone, I take it its this Golden Stone?'

'*An* drui means '*the* drui' said Mols converting the meaning of the Irish work 'An', but no-one knew what a drui was so Taymi said she would try to find out. They had so many questions, 'What is the Golden Stone? Where did it come from? What is its power? How precious is it? If they found it could they sell it? Why would Macartan hide the stone? And from whom?'

Taymi had an instinctive feeling that the child mentioned could be Oriel. 'She was saved from the fire, wasn't she, it could have been the Gatekeeper that woke her, raising the alarm – it says here '*my warning saved the child* and it mentions age seven, and she was about seven years old, Sir. Jack said she was about the same age as Lila and Lila is seven. Here it says '*the infant of the seventh age, the end.*'

'It was the gatekeeper that I saw.' Christian said faintly staring into space, but they all heard him. 'In my room before and today at the cottage, I know who it was, it was the Gatekeeper.' His spooky revelation gave them all goose bumps. 'It wasn't a ghost,' he went on, 'it was his *spirit*, his spirit remains alive, I know I have a connection with him. I don't know if I can truly see him or if it's in my mind, but I know it is the Gatekeeper.' Christian looked up at them. 'He was giving me a message, *this* is the message and he was the messenger.' He pointed at the verse. 'Now we've just got to understand it, to figure it out.'

'Why,' Taymi began, drythroated, 'why would this message be meant for you?'

'I don't know,' he said, 'but I feel he is gone now, I feel I have seen him for the third and last time, I have received the message now, his message, his warning. I've received it now.'

'But why did the messenger try and strangle you?' said Morgen.

'It wasn't him, I can't explain it, it was something else that caused me to.......something that got in the way, trying to prevent the message..... ....' He looked up, failing in his efforts to explain, and if it was difficult to explain, it was even more difficult to understand. Knowing that the spirit was exclusive to Christian and that it wasn't necessarily a ghost but a spirit which may not return was not much comfort to the others. Had Christian really seen something? It couldn't be proven yet they couldn't dispute that he had accurately pinpointed where the register was hidden.

There were more and more questions, 'Why did the gatekeeper fear his sacrifice?' 'What is the median and Macartans trinity?' 'Is there a child spirit as well as a gatekeeper spirit?' The questions were endless.

'Maybe he through he would be turned in, or used as a scapegoat for the fire, that's how he thought he would be sacrificed.' Was Christian's plausible consideration.

'*The median*; A median is the middle number in a range of numbers.' Taymi scrutinised her maths memory. 'It's also the midpoint in a line.' Said Christian not to be outdone and dusting down his schoolhouse knowledge of technical graphics.

'Is that where the treasure is?' said Morgen, picturing it now, finding a golden trove with his detector and becoming the richest boy in the world, a fabled treasure seeker, setting off then to Peru to investigate the rumours of hidden Mayan treasure. Private jet and all that.

'Will there be a tiara?' Lila wanted to know.

'The age of innocence!' purred Taymi.

'I think there is a Golden Stone.' Mols explained to Lila, and noticing the little ones disappointment perked her up by clarifying, 'I think we're allowed to break it, so we can have a piece each.'

'We need to find out more.' said Christian, 'We need to do some research, I will see what more I can find out about Macartan if theres any trace that he visited here.'

'And I'll try to find out what a 'drui' is.' said Taymi plus she wanted to have a good read of the names and dates logged in the journal, there were some interesting ones from her first glance.

'I'm going to find out more about Fairy Forts' said Sophia, 'Especially where to find them.'

'I wanna find out about this Golden Stone' said Mols.

'What will we do?' said Morgen referring to himself and Lila.

'See if you can find out more about the 'spirit of the child" said Taymi, leaving the two looking at each other wondering how they were going to find out about something when they didn't even know what that something meant. 'Well then you can find out whats so important about being age seven.' said Taymi; this sounded to Lila like a much more suitable task.

'We were meant to find this, *I* was meant to find it.' said Christian closing up the book and causing a little plume of dust to disperse, 'and we are meant to find the Fort and its secret treasure.'

As he spoke he stood up and held the book aloft and moved into a golden shaft of hazy sunshine. And the glare that surrounded him caused them to see the book and he lit all around in a glorious halo and for that moment at least they all believed in his words.

X

STUDIO

(Study)

BACK HOME AFTER lunch, the boys were suckered into chores with Dad, Lila and Mols were dispatched on an errand to their grandparents, so Sophia and Taymi decamped to the Study, already having been renamed Project Woods Room. They were anxious to research Fariy Forts and the mysterious word 'Drui' and pulled out thick history schoolbooks dogeared and labled to death. Sophia quickly found some information about hillforts and began scan through it, telling little pieces to Taymi. She learned that many of these circular forts were built on high hills as long ago as 500AD. A high wooden fence kept intruders away from the crude huts and their precious treasures (not money or gold but animals). A stone fort was especially fancy and was called a *Caiseal*, a bit like a castle. Years after these forts had fallen into ruins people became afraid of them, believing they were Fairy Forts full of Druids magic. No-one would work in or around these areas for fear of offending the Fairies.

Taymi gawked over Sophia's shoulder and smirked at the next bit. 'Some people thought that the Leprechaun kept his gold hidden in the Fairy Fort.....Oh come on, that's just silly, these people were so gullible.'.

'Aren't *we* looking for gold in a Fairy Fort!' Sophia pointed out.

'That's different, that's completely different' sputtered Taymi.

There was endless farcical folklore about fairy forts. 'Says here you must not take a photograph of a fairy Fort.' Said Sophia, 'It's an affront to the fairies, if one appears in your photo, be prepared for them to take their revenge. Thorns in your bed and all that! Trouble is,' she continued, 'doesn't say here where to find these Fairy Forts.'

'You weren't listening to yourself then,' said Taymi, 'said exactly where to find them.......on a hill.'

Taymi had already scouted the history books for any reference to 'drui' and had turned up not a dickybird. She edged Sophia to the side consigning the fairy search til later. The second she punched in the searchword drui, all the references threw up the same result word. Of course, it was so obvious now.   *Druid.*

'Druid?' she blurted. 'Drui was an older Celtic version of the word Druid.' Taymi sat back, and fixed her face at an angle, thinking back. 'Was there a Druid in the Woods!' She wore an expression of discontent.

'Is that like a wizard from ancient times?' said Sophia but Taymi had already grabbed back up her history book. 'I just saw a section on Druids in here, I'm sure.' And she rifled backwards through chapters til the offending section yawned before her. Sure enough there was a section on Druids telling how before Christianity they were some of the most important people in the land, second only to Kings.

'Gosh, a Druid could spend up to twenty years gaining great wisdom, learning poems n'all.' She said.

'Twenty years of learning? That's ridiculous!' puffed Sophia, before realising; 'Oops, I guess that's what we'll have done by the time we're out of school!'

The Druids seemed to have huge influence; they arranged worshipping to the Gods including, (to Taymi and Sophia's disgust), performing animal sacrifices. The seemed to have magical powers too, reading predictions from the entrails of the deal animals (more disgust) and reading predictions from the sky or birds in flight. They organised holy days for Boann, Goddess of the river, Lug, a Great Warrior God and many others.

'This bit is interesting,' said Taymi, 'February had the Druid day *Imbolg* for a Goddess Brigid, but later on it was taken over by Christians for Saint Brigid….so that means St Brigids day was once a pagan day? That must have really peeved the Druids' she said.

Sophia regarded this pensively. 'I know that word.' She murmured. 'But from where?'

'What word?' said Taymi, 'Peeved or Pagan?'

'Imbolg.' Sophia had a habit of noticing new and interesting words. 'I saw it today.'

'Was it in..' began Taymi.

'The register, yes!' squealed Sophia and leaped off her chair to retrieve the register, clandestinely concealed in a cupboard.

'…this schoolbook?.' completed Taymi, letting the redundant history book flop back to the table.

Sure enough after leafing quickly, but carefully, through the pages of the register, about halfway in and amid some of the more mundane name entries, was written the same word. *Imbolg.* They stared at it in disbelief.

'Why did the Gatekeeper have this in his register?' said Sophia. 'Could the gatekeeper have been a Druid?'

'I don't think so,' said Taymi, 'his register talks about banishing the Druid, so he couldn't *be* him.

'How can we find out?' said Sophia.

'Maybe we can find out more…' said Taymi, '…in this schoolbook.' and blankly held up the useful again history book. There was no more mention of the druidic festival of Imbolg but there was certainly more about Druids. She read. 'Saint Patrick brought Christianity to the land and he converted many Kings. The Druids tried desperately to keep Patrick and his bishops away from the Kings but were unsuccessful.'

'Peeved again I'm sure.' Said Sophia.

'This bits important.' Said Taymi. "The Druids power was virtually destroyed by the arrival of Christianity. Apart from Druids, the Pagans generally did not resist Christianity as they felt that there was plenty of room for yet another God. The days of the Druid were numbered." Chapter complete, she closed her book mulling on the power and authority that the Druids had held in times past and what on earth these dark individuals had to do with the message in the register?

'I only ever thought of Druids going around casting evil spells.' Said Sophia. '....and that they went around wearing black hoodies of course.'

'With a white rope around their waist.' smirked Taymi.

'and long white hair too.' added Sophia.

'and a long white beard.' Taymi stroked her chin.

'and a craggy face' said Sophia with a nod and Taymi looked round to see Dad peeping through the pane and shrieked with fright and laughed, making Dad grump at being the object of their hilarity and he hurriedly left casting them a dark look.

'and he had a knobbly stick to chase off children' Sophia shouted.

'and he used it to curse everyone with' Taymi squealed. As soon as she had said it, both girls stopped dead and looked at each other.

'A *curse*' said Sophia.

'The curse on the tree,' said Taymi,' It could be a *Druids* curse.' She was thinking of the ancient Ogham and thinking too of something Sir Jack said. 'A Druids curse?' she let the words slip away, 'Or a *Devils* curse?'

A thump on the window and they jolted. Christian was staring in. 'Whats up.' He muffled through the glass. Taymi cranked open the window. 'Come in, we have stuff to tell you, and get the other guys too.'

Sophia and Taymi replayed their findings to the others; the stuff about Fairy Forts, that *Drui* actually meant *Druid*, the Druidic tradition of sacrifice, Imbolg appearing in the register, and their theory that the message on the tree was a curse put there by a Druid. It seemed like an astounding amount of information garnered quickly. And Sophia just remembered something too. 'People thought the Fairy Fort was *imbued* by Druids magic and they were afraid of it, I read it a while ago.' She pondered on this. 'Maybe they wanted people to think this so they would stay away. Away from hidden treasure.'

'That sounds more plausible.' Said Christian.

'What're we gonna do next?' Morgen was wide eyed and eager to take the next step.

'If I could get my hands on a map I might be able to try and identify the Forts location.' Christian said focusing tightly. And Morgen could see it now, finding the Fort, excavating the treasure and being photographed for the cover of 'National Treasure Magazine'... or was that a movie?

'What if...' said Mols hesitantly, 'there *is* real magic in the Fairy Fort, or a curse, or bad luck even?' not wanting to find thorns in her bed as discommoded Fairies are wont to do, or a druidic curse and not to forget the emergence of the shadowy man that Christian had seen now three times or even worse than all that... 'What if the beast protects the Fairy Fort?' She was still thinking of that most mysterious Panther.

Christian stayed quiet amid all the gabbling, he was looking again at the register, the words of the verse, and one word in particular which was staring out at him....Sacrifice. *What if there is a sacrifice to be made?* He thought. The girls had said animal sacrifice but could this have been extended to *human* sacrifice as the verse seemed to suggest? *Are we putting ourselves in danger?* That's another word which appeared in the verse; *Danger. Are we safe amid all this digging and discovering?* Quite suddenly he felt not safe, uneasy. The others were excited, buoyant even. He wasn't, he just had the feeling he had walked on someones grave, just like Dad had suggested. But nonetheless he felt he was well and truly on a quest, a mission. And that is a feeling he liked. He had no doubt, they were onto something here and he was going to take them all the way.

XI

CONSILIUM

(Advice)

'Do you think Saint Macartan ever walked this road?' It was Saturday morning and breakfast was somewhat more leisurely and with the arrival and departure of persons at such diverse times that it appeared as if breakfast was everlasting. Christian was testing Dad about his knowledge of Macartan, Dad was reading yesterdays newspaper.

'That's interesting, very interesting indeed.' Dad began without looking up and Christian wondered if his question or something else was. 'Yea.' said Dad and continued to read, leaving Christian in limbo again holding out for elaboration or some sign of intelligence and just about to lose his cool.

'There is,' Dad looked up in practiced pitch perfect time, 'a very good chance of that. He probably would have been to Rockwell.' Rockwell was well known to Christian; an adjoining townland within a mile of Westwoods, defined by a spattering of houses, a country school which Dad had attended up to age twelve and the river, the same river that they knew and loved. Oh and there was something else too Christian remembered about Rockwell, there was an ancient graveyard there, site of a hitherto ancient holy gathering place.

'Rockwell in actual fact, is the site of the first Christian settlement in the region did you know that?' Dad was in lecturing mode now. 'So chances are that Macartan may have visited Rockwell or even been part of establishing the settlement. It's possible too, that he might have made his way from there to Cathedral City, if so we would have been on his route.' Cathedral City was Armagh; the nearby City that St.Patrick made the Christian Capital of Ireland and which boasted two pointy Cathedrals, (hence Cathedral City) both called after Partick himself. In prior times it had been a Pagan Capital, Christian remembered Dad telling them this when they visited, more evidence, Christian now thought, of Christianitys overthrow of pagans and no doubt, Druids. And it made him think.

'What about Partick, would he have ever been around?'

'Patrick who?'

'The Saint.' Sighed Christian.

'Oh….Yes, good possibility that Patrick passed here.' Dad seemed intrigued by this concept. 'Tell you what,' he said, 'if you really want to walk in the footsteps of the ancients, we can go up to Rockwell later and explore the ancient graveyard. And when I say ancient, I mean its totally grown over and in ruins and hard to find, but…. theres something in the air there.' He stared off, 'That makes you feel that you can reach back through time…..' Christian watched him float into thought, his eyes far away and then abruptly blinkingly back. 'Lets do it.' said Dad and they were sold on it.

Since an inquisition had begun, Mols didn't let it go and piped up as Dad tried to raise his paper. 'Do you really think it was a beast that killed the deer in the Woods, do you think it could have been the Black Panther?'

'Despite what they say,' Dad sighed, 'I really don't think there is a Panther around here Mols, don't think a Panther could survive in this country, they're accustomed to warmer climates; here they would need special care like they would get at the zoo.' 'Tell you what,' he said, noting her mixture of relief and disappointment 'What say we take a drive to the zoo soon and then we can see a Black Panther *and* some deer up close. How about that?'

That, they agreed, sounded pretty good. Dad uncrumpled his newspaper delighted with himself.

'What's important about being age seven?' asked Lila to the sound of exasperated paper re-crunching but Mom was there to field this question. 'It's the most special age in the world Lila,' she said grabbing Lila in a hug, 'and you are it!'

'What's so special about seven.' huffed Morgen not recalling anything too special when *he* was it.

'Well,' said Mom thinking fast, 'there are seven colours in the rainbow and..' she thought again quickly, '..there are seven seas!'

'Seven days in a week.' Added Sophia.

'There are seven charkas and seven food groups' said Moms drawing on her knowledge of healthy living.

'There are seven continents.' was Taymi's contribution.

'There are seven elements.' said Christian harking back to his geographical interest.

'The seven ages of man.' Dad now interested again piped up thinking of Shakespeare, 'And seven deadly sins.' he said thinking now of himself.

'There are seven holy sacraments' said Mom and this prompted her to think of another one, 'Believe it or not, there are seven holes in your head.' All began in some morbid fashion to count the holes in their heads, yep there were seven alright, although Lila could only find five.

'There are seven types of catastrophes,' said Dad, '.......and seven wonders of the world.' he added.

'There are seven archangels.' said Mom

'Seven seconds!' Dad blurted out, determined to beat Mom at this *and* any other game. 'When the President looks your way, you have seven seconds to make your point.'

'Doesn't really count,' said Mom calmly, 'but there are seven virtues.'

'I know three of them,' said Sophia, 'Faith, Hope and Charity; They're virtues but also the names of the daughters of the Saint Sofia whom I'm named after.' She said smugly.

'Cheater.' Said Dad without giving any reason why on earth her contribution could be considered cheating in any respect. He struggled to think of another prominent seven. 'Seventh month' he chanced, 'July, the month we are in now.' and sat back smugly.

'Vague,' Said Mom 'but there *are* the seven fundamental years of youth.' She had trumped Dad much to his chagrin and he promptly joined Morgen's disgruntled ranks.

'Whats the fundamental years of youth?' enquired Mols. Mom explained; 'These are the years you form your beliefs and habits.' She said. 'You learn more in your first seven years than at any time in the future. When you are in your seventh year, as Lila is, it is a special age because you are becoming more aware of good and bad and deciding between them.'

'It's not working for Lila.' Said Morgen.

'But you are still at the point of believing in magic,' continued Mom, 'so a child's mind and spirit can believe in miracles as a practical reality. It's why children prepare and receive communion at this age. Because of this, a child is considered an infant up to age seven.' Lila sat proudly lapping up the attention and importance of her age. It did seem after all that seven was a very important number. Taymi noted this too and something else. It was the Childs spirit that Mom had referred to. *Spirit of the Child* had been written in the verse they had found in the register and not alone that but a reference to an infant too. These all added up to convince her that the child, the infant and the seventh age were all references to the little girl Oriel. But she had a disturbing realisation that they all added up to Lila too.

'Is a fairy fort a holy place? Sophia swung the conversation in yet another direction.

'No, I wouldn't think so,' said Dad, 'only ground which has been consecrated could be considered holy ground,' he continued 'like a church or graveyard.'

'Like Rockwell ancient graveyard.' asked Sophia,

'Exactly.' Said Dad

'What precisely does consecrated mean?' asked Sophia.

'It means blessed ground, probably blessed by a Bishop.' Said Dad

'or a Saint?' said Sophia.

'Precisely.' Said Dad.

'If a Saint blessed a fairy fort would it be holy ground?' said Sophia.

'You got me there,' said Dad to Sophia, 'yes it would.' And Sophia secretly ticked another box.

'Did you ever hear of a Golden Stone?' asked Mols now.

'I've heard of a golden egg from a golden goose,' said Dad. '...have *you* ever heard of a golden stone?' he came right back with.

'Well I saw a goose today.' Mols swiftly changed the subject.

'Where?' said Dad.

'It flew just over the garden, on its own, honking.' She advised, relieved that this seemed to have distracted Dad.

'On its own? Which direction?' he asked.

'Towards the woods.' she answered.

'That's odd.' said Dad, 'A lone goose and the direction it flew. Normally geese fly in formation and towards the West; I've never seen one fly East.' He considered this carefully. 'I'd take that as a sign.'

'A sign?' said Mols.

'A sign of things to come.' Said Dad; and immediately Taymi thought of the druidic predictions of the future from observed the flights of birds. Perhaps this was the type of unusual flight pattern they were observing.

'What kind of things?' she asked. Dad looked at her darkly. 'Perhaps a change is gonna come,' he said cryptically, then less cryptically, 'perhaps a change in the weather.'

After that the conversation drifted away and eventually everyone drifted away from the table leaving only Dad and Taymi sitting there, each of them stewed in their own thoughts. Taymi was trying to make sense of what they had learned today and was astounded with the significance of the number seven and wondered how this fitted into their investigation.

'Seven Fires of Hell!' Dad growled, making her jump. 'Dammit,' he lamented, 'why didn't I think of that before.'

The Seven Fires of Hell, he didn't think of it before but Taymi was thinking of it now.

XII

CIMETERIUM

(Cemetery)

THAT AFTERNOON, AS agreed, but with the exception of Mom and Lila who had other plans in town, they made their way to Rockwell. It was a pleasant amble, the hills were not too taxing and summer bloomed densely all around. The defining monument of Rockwell stoood staunchly on its raised pedestal; the schoolhouse. They stopped to admire it as it shone newly whitewashed in the stark sunlight, silently resting in its summer recess. Its windows a row of military sentinels and two chimneys, captains of the guards, commanding their posts at each gable. Once children brought coal to school to fire them up Dad had onetime told them; quickly clarifying that it was before his time!

'Saint Michaels.' Said Dad now. 'The Archangel. Learned all about him from the Master.' He said reminiscing, looking up at the old fashioned building. But they already knew about St.Michaels the school and St.Michael the Archangel, Dad had recounted these stories many times.

'Master Tom was a great historian. He taught us so much that wasn't on the cirruculum; about history, geography, science, nature, art, music; took us on field trips to the ancient graveyard too. Probably the best teacher I ever had.' He said wistfully. 'He's gone now.' He said, 'Rest his soul.'

Christian let this moment of poignancy sit before asking and then answered his own question.

'The school is very old isn't it.'

'It's not that old really.' Commented Dad as he walked on. Christian looked at the datestone set in the front wall of the school, it read 1933. *If that's not old*, thought Christian, *what is?* Taymi stood nearby looking around, scouting for the ancient graveyard which she knew from remembrance to be somewhere within viewing distance. 'Where exactly is the graveyard?' she called out to Dad.

'Where the sentry stares!' He barked back whilst marching on. She took a look back at the school and then followed its gaze down across the hillocky meadows. There was nothing to distinguish where the graveyard might be among the heathers and brambles and hedging and pastures. *Probably totally grown over by now.* She thought. Sophia was noticing something a lot closer that was quite unusual. In the field in front of the school a single tree stood alone right in the middle of acres of neat green grass. Why is there one tree there? She enquired. 'A fairy tree!' was Dads retort. 'You don't mess with a fairy tree!'

The route to the ancient graveyard took them offroad along a rough lane pitted with potholes and overhanging with hedgerows, into a field full of clumpy lumps, stepping stones across a river of rattling rapids and a wading through a pasture of stalky scutch. They were beginning to wonder how on earth Dad knew where to go or indeed if he did know. Eventually as they beat past a bushy hedgerow, out of the growth, a narrow gate revealed itself sitting among the greenery.

'This is it.' Announced Dad to an audience which was much underwhelmed. Except Morgen; He looked around, there were fields and hedges for as far as he could see, he was astonished that Dad could find this little gate hidden here. He had walked straight to it as if drawn by invisible force to a mysterious vortex. Taymi looked up too; sure enough St.Michaels stood in the distance looking directly down on them.

One of the slim wrought iron bars of the gate was missing; Morgen spotted it on the ground and grabbed it; 'We need to replace this,' he said in faux trepidation, 'so that we can gain entry into the sacred space.' He was re-enacting a scene where Indy Jones had found an ancient cemetery, just as they were doing and he loved the drama of it. Dad, shaking his head, slotted the bar back into its rightful place and then tried the gate, to Morgen's mock amazement it opened, slightly, before being tangled in briars. They squeezed through the small gap into a small overgrown plot of land surrounded by high hedges.

'Not much to see is there.' Christian called it as the others saw it.

'Oh, contraire my boy!' reprimanded Dad, 'Have a look over here, and mind your step, don't be walking on the dead.' He led them through thickets and tall grass and stopped at a large stone laid horizontally on the ground. It was a gravestone etched with feint weatherworn writing. Taymi leaned down and scraped away some of the lichen and moss that clung to it. She was barely able to distinguish any of the letters never mind the words.

'Most gravestones have collapsed,' said Dad behind her, 'so have many graves, so watch you don't land in one.' Taymi hastily moved back from resting on the stone. Morgen conjured up a vision of crashing down into a grave and awakening a zombie, mummy, corpse type skeleton.

They hoked around in the long grass searching for and finding burial markers for those long gone. One groundstone was subsided and cracked, a hole exposed an open dark crevice beneath. Morgen put his face close so that he could look into the tomb.

'Put your hand in.' Whispered Dad leaning in beside him. Morgen tentatively extended his hand and gradually put it into the hole in the stone.

'Aaaaghh' screamed Dad grabbed Morgens hand and struggling with it.

'AAAGGHH' screamed Morgen desperately trying to retrieve his hand from Dads grasp.

'Aaaaaaggghhhhhhhhh.' Shrieked Mols seeing the melee.

'Aaaaghhhh.' Shouted Sophia for some distance away reacting with fright.

'Aaaaaaagghghh.' Erupted Taymi and Christian in unison reacting to Sophias scream. Dad almost keeled over laughing at the domino effect.

Unearthing the old tombstones had given them a feeling of discovery and a sense of connection to generations past, they could feel the history at their feet. Morgen delivered an interesting question;

'Why was such an important place put here in the middle of nowhere?' which Dad fielded in an interesting way.

'Because its quiet now doesn't mean it always was.' He said, 'It's all about location, location, location.' This left Morgen more confused than before. After a time they began to make their way out of the hallowed ground pulling the old gate closed and sealing the ancient history behing it.

Picking his way over the stepping stones of the river, Dad decided to have a little more fun with Morgen.

'Watch this' he told Christian and then called out. 'Morgen do you think I would be able to pitch this stick over the waterfall from here?'

Looking around and not seeing any such waterfall nearby, Morgen shrugged; 'No.'

'Then watch this' said Dad and he easily tossed the stick into the flowing stream where it floated away.

'That's a crock.' said Morgen.

'Well,' said Dad 'I threw the stick into the river and this is the same river that flows right by our house, into the Woods and over the waterfall. So in your face Morgen, you owe me two euros!' Everyone whooped at Morgen who disputed the outcome vehemently.

'How do I owe you two euros?' he said 'I didn't even bet any money.'

'Pony up.' said Dad guffawing and skipping ahead.

They were tracing their trail back through the rutted field, Sophia and Taymi walking side by side when without warning, Taymi grabbed Sophia aggressively swinging her to the ground.

'What did you do that for?'

'You almost disappeared,' Taymi looked stricken, '…in there.' She pointed to the ground where Sophia had been about to step. Sophia did a double take, they were in the middle of a field yet she had been about to step onto something that was not grass, it was another type of growth, a mossy, clovery carpet, and there was something underneath, because it moved!. Sophia stood up, took a stone in her hand and tossed it gently onto the moss; the stone disappeared with an accompanying plop. The moss was growing on a swamp. By now the others had caught up on the situation.

'How deep is it?' said Sophia.

'Could be endless.' Said Dad. 'A bottomless pit. Could have swallowed you whole.' 'But don't worry I would have rescued you…. by sending in Morgen.' Sophia had no doubt that it would have swallowed her up; when she tossed the stone in, it had broken the surface in a large ripple, exposing the murky black water beneath, but as soon as the ripples subsided, the floating growth had converged, closing the tear as though nothing had ever disrupted it.

'Nature has a way of recreating itself.' Dad said staring blankly at the recarpeted abyss. Sophia considered what might have happened had she been tagging along behind the others. They would have assumed that she had disappeared into thin air. An involuntary shudder ran through her bones at the thought.

'Worst death ever…' Said Dad before they moved away, '… Drowning.'

As they wound their back home, they noted that they were following the same general route as the river. It ducked and weaved under the road and cut itself a valley when they had to overcome a hill. But it was never really out of sight. Christian had his eye on it but there was something else in view too, on the far side of the river, something that gave him the feeling that they were being watched.

They were halfway home and there high up in the distance, in a secluded drive amid a clamour of dark trees, a dark house looked coldly across the river as they passed. There was no way that he could say for certain that eyes were on them but it was there in feeling. He knew who owned this house and whose dank black car sat in sullen standby. It was the Dark One. Christian had never seen anyone come or go from this house. The only signs of life were that sometimes the car was there and sometimes not; and then the music. The house was secluded and windows dark, but at any hour, a deep thrub thrub of sound could become apparent, emanating from the thick stone and rippling out into the night. Christian had heard it before, and he could hear it now in his mind, repeating, repeating, real or imaginary, a subliminal pulse of darkness. This was the Dark Ones castle, his lair. Christian had no evidence to convict the Dark One of any crime or any malice, except his intuition. He turned away and quickened his step to catch up with the others.

As they neared Westwoods, road and river crossed swords again at old Brockrady Bridge. It swept through the stone arches under their feet and off into the woods. They spoke to Marc, a neighbour out tending his garden, his house stood guarding the bridge, the river flowing tightly behind it. They stood looking over the bridge and into the water and Dad claimed that he saw his stick flow past, gaining interest, he said, on the money owed by Morgen. From here the Westwooders knew the exact course of the river as it pitched through the woods and had followed it along its meander many times. When the river was low they could pick stepping stones all along it but if it were fast flowing they had to stick to the banks. Their first excursion had been a journey of discovery, the river twisting and turning and dipping. It had been raining and there were many mangly branches traipsing damp in the water. They'd discovered *the chicane* where water swirled and spat foam onto black rocks in a deep dark nook. They sat on a grassy bank watching the water churn relentlessly; some broken sunlight splintered through to this dark place and sent up a scattering of light fragments from the splashing water onto their faces like a reverse glitterball. It made Sophia tingle with the wonder of it all and they all knew they had found a special place known to no-one in the world but themselves.

A little further along they had found the *Fallen Bridge*. At first they were unsure *what* they had found but after careful examination they figured that the formed stones on either side of the river were the strikings of the stone arch of a bridge. The entire centre had collapsed or been washed away and destroyed. It seemed unusual, as there was no evidence of a road or path leading up to the Fallen Bridge from either side and so they sometimes called this the bridge to nowhere.

Many rivulets flowed into the river from both sides, sometimes just a trickle and at other times a much more strong flowing brook, all adding to the character and personality of the living changing and maturing river. Next stop on the river route was the waterfall itself, the crowning glory of the woods, always regal and resplendent, sometimes gentle, sometimes angry, sometimes quiet, sometimes noisy, always and ever moving, always and ever changing. The pool beneath the waterfall was deep and dark and surrounded by high walls of craggy black rocks. The water was cold and the sun could barely make it through the tall surrounds of trees. After the excitement of the fall the river flowed more serenely, widening in sweeping curves through the deep valley, past The Beach, the Rope Swing and The Dam before narrowing again as it approached the Shallow Crossing. From there it was not too far until it exited the woods and thereafter running on and on, like a child runs to its mother, on and on to the sea.

Today they wouldn't be following the river route. As they stood there on the bridge looking at the river disappear into the woods and then looking back up the valley to where the river had come from, Dad had another nugget of historical interest.

'If you look along the line of the valley and towards the top of the field on the left.' he directed using his hands. 'You'll see it tapers off into a point where it's totally grown over.' They tried to follow his guiding gestures. 'Among those bushes,' he told them, 'is another sacred spot. It's the location of a mass rock.' 'Masses were held there in penal times,' he went on to explain, 'when the Christian mass had been banished in Ireland. They used a natural rock as the altar hidden among the ditches and the valleys. It was a forbidden practice so they worshipped in secret. No grand cathedral there, eh, just a stone in the hedge in the dimming of the day.' Christian couldn't help but think how much like an occult worship it must have seemed. Secretive gatherings in hiding, cloak and dagger type stuff, no doubt their praying and chanting was low murmers not to draw attention to their practice. Women in shawls, men in overcoats, vestments, beads and candles, it sure seemed like a dark scene, funny how it could be perceived that way!

Dad had identifed the names of the various townlands they had passed. 'What are townlands?' Morgen had wanted to know. 'They're like parcels of land.' Dad explained. 'Some bigger, some smaller, maybe a square mile in size, maybe not, usually split on a river. We're standing on a split now.' He said pointing down the the bridge at his feet. 'This side, where your Grandparents live is called *Annaglough*. It translates in old Irish to *Achadh-na-gCloch* which means *Field-of-the-Stone*. I know that because guess what, I lived there!'

At the mention of a stone, Christian perked up a little. Could it be anything to do with a golden stone?

'And of course our house Westwoods sits in the townland of *Cordevlis*.' Dad completed his lesson.

'What does Cordevlis mean?' queried Sophia.

'You know I never checked it out, leave it with me and I will do some research on that.' He promised.

Christian was deep in thought; He thought of the stone and the rock; He viewed the lay of the land, the location of the mass rock, he pictured the position of the ancient cemetery beyond and over the hills. A concept was building which he put to Dad.

'If I were to draw a line from the ancient cemetery, through the mass rock and extend it by an equal distance, do you think there could be a third ancient site?' He was thinking of Macartans trinity and he felt that maybe somehow he had stumbled on it.

'That's a very good observation Christian.' Dad eyed the imaginary line that Christian was creating. 'It would almost certainly lead to a somewhere in the Woods.' This was exactly what Christian was thinking.

'Would you be able to help me get a map of the woods so I can draw it out.' Christian asked.

'Sure, leave it with me; I can get you a map alright.' Dad was accustomed to working with maps and drawings and delighted that his son was taking a similar interest.

Christian's heart beat strongly; could he have just pinpointed the location of the fairy fort, the holding of the ancient secret, the place of the Golden Stone? It was a very real possibility.

XIII

CALCULUS

(Stone)

THAT EVENING CHRISTIAN decided to dig deeper into the story Saint Macartan. He dug out what he could find of his school textbooks and found references to the Saint under history and religion. He cobbled together as many facts as he could; some he knew and a lot more besides he didnt. He reviewed his findings.

Macartan was originally a Pagan! What, this was a surprise, the great Christian, once a Pagan? Christian was bemused. Macartan was known as the *Strong Man* and it turned out he was also St.Brigids uncle, another surprise! Brigid had cropped up in Taymis research. A day in her honour, Imbolg had been stolen from the pagans by the Christians. Now it was St.Brigid day when schoolchildren learn how to make a Christian cross from long grass rushes.

St.Patrick made Macartan the first Bishop of Clogher and Macartan built himself a Cathedral there in Clogher village.

'Aha.' Christian spoke to himself. This presumably was the original St.Macartans Cathedral. There were three Macartans Cathedrals and now he knew the location of two of them. 'Two out of three ain't bad.' He wondered where this Clogher village was and if it was worth a visit.

Seemed Macartan was quite a powerful guy- he could even work miracles apparently! Seemed also that if he wanted to get a look at Macartan there were depictions in Monaghans Cathedral including an icon, a tapestry and a statue describing scenes from Macartan's life. *If this guy could work miracles*, thought Christian, *maybe he could work one now and guide us in our quest.*

'Fortis et Fidelis, old boy, Strong and Faithful.'

Just then Mols ambled into the room and sat down with Christian to see what he'd been getting up to.

Christian told her how he'd been hopeful that he might have found something about Macartan's hiding place or about buried treasure however he was out of luck on both counts.

'I wanna check out this Golden Stone.' She said, 'Maybe I'll have better luck.' She buzzed up the pc and punched the words into search getting over thirty six million hits. 'Which one?' she sighed, skipping through umpteen pages and finding interesting stuff but nothing which looked a likely candidate for buried treasure in a woodland fort; she soldiered on but none of these links tied with what they needed.

'Let me try.' Said Christian, 'Might be something more on Macartan here.' There was a lot more on Macartan there and one account in particular looked very promising. 'We could be on to something here.' Said Christian. He read that St.Patrick had given Macartan a precious box containing ancient gospels of immense value and also contained a priceless relic. The box was cased in silver and gold,decorated all around with images of saints and in the centre; Christ on the cross.

'Could this be the Golden Stone?' asked Mols.

'It does seem very valuable,' said Christian reading on, '...but its not the stone, this is called the *Silver Shrine* sometimes called the *Silver Church* and its now in the National Museum, so you can go see it.'

'I wonder what the priceles relic is.' Mols commented. She was unusually familiar with relics and if there was a relic in this Silver Shrine or whatever it was called, it could have a very strong power; maybe one they could use in their favour.

Two years ago Mols had fallen quite sick with an infection that wasn't healing and it looked like she was heading for an operation. Granny's sister, Auntie Mae, visited Mols with something that she said would help; It was a relic of Saint Padre Pio, and Auntie Mae explained;

'A relic is something touched by a Saint, so it has a special power. But you must believe, you must have faith, for it to have effect.' This item was a fingerless glove; it had an obvious stain in its palm Auntie Mae explained further, 'He suffered from Stigmata – the same wounds that Christ had on his hands and feet.'

'Then how did Pio get them?' asked Mols.

'They just appeared.' Said Auntie Mae.

They were astonished by this macabre information and examined the glove more closely; the stain in the palm was from the blood that had flowed from the hand of Pio in the same way that it had flowed from the hand of Christ. It was a surreal experience.

Auntie Mae told them more about the stigmata saint, how as a child he had visions of a Guardian Angel. 'He thought this was normal for all children, that everyone could see their Angel.' She chuckled at this and Lila frowed at her. 'Later in his life he had darker visions.'

'What like?' said Morgen.

Auntie Mae seemed a little reluctant to go into this area but she acquiesced. 'Some of his visions were very dark.' She said, '…I mean, well, he said that sometimes a vision of an Angel could be a trick by the Devil, it was the Devils deceit.' She went on to tell them about how Pio had cured many people over his lifetime. 'He died a long time ago, on the 23rd of the month, I remember the exact day.' she said. 'He was already presumed a Saint then. But it was strange, it was very strange.'

Morgen craned to hear what was so strange and Auntie Mae obliged. 'Within minutes of his death,' she said, 'just straightaway after he died….' Morgen clung to his breath, '….the stigmata on his hands, the open wounds that had caused him so much suffering his whole life….' Morgen held on to his breath listening, '…had completely healed, then and there, no wounds.' She completed. Morgen gasped simultaneously exasperated and amazed.

'It was a miracle.' Said Auntie Mae.

The date of the 23rd struck a note with Christian, the date Pio died was the day he lived, that he was given life, it was his birth date. He thought of the 23 enigma, the theory that most events are connected in some way to that number. But that was another day's work. Auntie Mae had really intrigued them with the story of Pio's life…and death. But she wasn't finished yet; there was more to the story of this amazing man, even after death.

'Recently his body was exhumed.' she told them.

'Bought up from the grave.' Christian whispered to Morgen..

'…and it had remained in good condition, in fact it was said that his hands looked like they had received a manicure. That's how perfect they were.' Auntie Mae told them. 'And that's from being buried over forty years ago!'

Mols believed in the power of relics. She believed that it was the power of Pio's glove that chased away her infection and saved her from a complex operation. A rattle at the door jolted her back into the moment.

'Let me know when you're finished guys, I need the pc.' Dad had his head stuck around the door.

'Sure Dad.' It was Wimbledon season and Dad went back to watching some tennis re-runs on TV.

Christian had moved along with his research. He had found a story telling how Patrick and Macartan were prevented from entering the kingdom of Oriel. The King had sent his young son to warn them off however after meeting the two men, the Prince instead asked to be baptised. He then took Patrick and Macartan to meet the King who drew his sword to Patrick but was stopped by Macartan. The King allowed the missionaries to continue and eventually befriended them. In later years Macartan became Bishop of the same area.

'So that means,' surmised Christian, 'that the kingdom of Oriel became the Dioscese of Clogher?'

Mols was distracted by something else, she was smirking. 'See this,' she said, 'When he met Macartan, the little Prince gave him an apple as a peace offering. But look, it was the apple his Mom had given him for the journey.' Mols thought this little anecdote was hilarious.

Dad popped his head past the door. 'Are you guys nearly finished yet?'

'Sorry Dad, we're still in the middle of something'

'You *cannot* be serious.' Dad snorted, in a strange mid-atlantic accent and stomped off. The two looked at each other and shook their heads.

Suddenly Mols gave a startled outburst. 'There! There!' she sputtered, pointing '....The Golden Stone.'

Christian swung to the screen, the very next paragraph was titled, *The Golden Stone!* He read quickly, 'The Golden Stone is a sacred Pagan ceremonial stone which was once covered in traces of gold.'

His mouth gaped open as he sped read the remainder to discover that the stone was given to Macartan by an old King after Macartan has persuaded him to become Christian instead of Pagan. The Golden Stone name came from the words *Cloch* (Stone) and *Oir* (Gold) = *Cloch-Oir* which eventually became *Clogher* the name of the Diocese.'

'I can't believe it!' gasped Christian, to the fact that they had found information on the Golden Stone and moreso what that information told them.

'All of this time we were looking for the Golden Stone and we are living in this whole vast area named after it. Why hasn't this been mentioned? Is this some kind of a conspiracy? Does anyone else know this?' he raved energetically.

'Well Dad didn't!' said Mols, 'He said that he hadn't heard of a Golden Stone.'

'He never actually said if he had or hadn't.' Corrected Christian and Mols tried to recall what Dad had actually said. But it was clear; the name of this Diocese came from this ancient and precious stone. But this fact was mysteriously concealed from the thousands of people who lived here. A coincidence? No such thing he thought, yet Christian knew from his history lessons that often olden names became buried after years, centuries even, eventually becoming known only to historians.

'It's hard to believe that this has been staring us in the face the whole time.' He said. 'Our whole lives!'

'This is the same King.' said Mols, 'that we have been reading about, the one with the little Prince. He's the one who gave Macartan the Golden Stone.'

'The Golden Stone exists!' Christian whispered, harking back to the words of the verse. Now he knew what the Golden Stone was and that it did exist. But there was something more to discover as Christian read on;

'The remnants of the stone are still contained in the old Cathedral in the village of Clogher however the gold and silver adornments from the stone are missing and with them, the power and wealth of the stone.' 'The secret to great wealth and power.' whispered Christian. 'The mystery that's always surrounded the Woods, it's the Golden Stone!'

'But the stone is in Clogher Cathedral.' Said Mols.

'But not the gold,' said Christian, 'it says here; *the missing gold is said to have been cast into a smaller Golden Stone that carries on its power. Its whereabouts are unknown.* But Mols I think I know where it is.'

'I can see where the wealth comes from' said Mols, 'but how does it have great power?'

'I guess wealth is power' said Christian shrugging, 'but look, this was a sacred pagan artefact. It must have held great power for the pagans. Until they gave it away to the Christians.' A face was squashed up against the glazing of the door looking in. It was Dad looking forlornly towards the computer. He was wearing a headband.

'Alright we're finished.' called Christian, to which Dad with his face still squashed against the glass smiled distortedly.

'Tell the guys to meet me in my room and we'll tell them.' Christian urged Mols and within a minute the westwooders convened in Christian's room for the urgent update. Christian and Mols related to them what they had found out in relation to Macartan and then revealed the crowning glory, the finding of The Golden Stone, in cyberspace at least. They spent a long time discussing all of these findings and trying to figure out what direction to take next to try and pinpoint the treasure spot. It felt exciting and historical to be on the trail of an ancient artefact.

'We know what the Golden Stone is; now we've just got to find it.' Christian told them, 'Just think we could soon be holding in our hands the key to wealth and power.'

XIV

BASILICA

(Cathedral)

It was Sunday morning and time for mass. The family prepared and made their way to the towering spectacle of St.Macartans Cathedral. They entered through the right transcept and in the entrance porch Christian took note of two statues, one entitled St.Brigetta, which he recognised as St. Bridget, and one entitled St.Patricius, which was clearly St.Patrick, the patron saint looking particularly stately as he squashed the neck of a snake with his foot. That is if snakes have necks.

Today, fittingly, mass was to be celebrated by the current Bishop of Clogher, Macartans successor. As he swept up the altar steps, Mom reminded Christian 'He baptised you.'

Christian was already aware of the story, sure wasn't he there! Of course he couldn't remember it first hand but had been told it many times. Because he was born near Easter, in a custom of the Easter ceremonies, if a child was due to be baptised they were invited to receive the sacrament at the Easter Vigil Mass, a night-time ceremony on Holy Saturday, the eve of Easter Sunday and a prestigious date to make your debut. And so it was that Christian was the chosen one to receive this honour on this memorable occasion. The entire Cathedral had been plunged into darkness for the outset of the ceremony and then from the flame of the mighty entrance fire little flames were lit on everyones candles. A shimmering, flickering light fanned throughout the congregation, Christianity spreading throughout the world, faces lit up and jumping with shadows, a warm glow to welcome the new dawn, new life and resurrection.

Baby Christian wrapped in infant swaddlings was hushed towards the magnificent stone baptism font and held over the water in front of a packed and attentive church. The Bishops voice boomed throughout the magnificent Cathedral as he christened the tiny child;

'I baptism you; *Christian-* In the name of the Father and the Son and the Holy Spirit'.

The water trickled a tiny waterfall over Christians head and tinkled back into the font. A no more appropriate name could have been chosen for the newborn child. It was a special moment and Christian had been honoured in a special way.

Christian had always felt special; he carried a strong name and a caring nature. He made friends easily and generally walked with ease through life, except when antagonised by mischievous Morgen. Christian looked over at Morgen and received a devious look in reply.

'Shoulda called you Damien.' Dad sometimes said to Morgen, but they didn't know why.

Christian also knew he was lucky to be here at all. At birth Christian didn't cry like newborns are supposed to, it was a bad sign, he was rushed from the delivery room to ER for emergency breathing assistance. He pulled through. The birth cord had been wrapped around his neck three times, like the snake that Patrick had been keeping down. Life giver, nearly life taker. That was what had made his baptism here even more special, the fact that it, that he, might never have happened. No one noticed Moms tear roll into the font with the baptism water.

As mass ended Christian asked if they could stay to have a look around at the references to St. Macartan and so while Mom and Dad chatted to friends, he and the others wandered off to see what they could see.

Christian found the icon straightaway tucked neatly in an alcove. It was a recent artwork commissioned to commemorate 1500 years since Macartans reign. Macartan stared down from the painting looking reverent and holding up his right hand in blessing. He was surrounded entirely in gold. Christian wished it were possible to just ask Macartan about the golden stone and its power. Written above Macartan were the familiar words and motto of the saint; *Fortis et Fidelis*. 'I am strong, I am faithful,' whispered Christian, 'and I will find this treasure.'

Below the main image of Macartan were several mini depictions capturing the life of Macartan. Christian examined them and instantly recognised the scene of Macartan carrying Patrick on his back, meeting the little Prince and the King at a river. He chuckled to see the little Prince with the apple but there was no sign of the Golden Stone in this image.

In another depiction Macartan was being ordained by Patrick and in the background stood Bridget and another Saint, Tiernach. Conveniently their names were written above their heads. In the image Tiernach held something close and Christian leaned in closely to see if it might be the precious stone. It wasn't the stone but with surprise he thought he recognised what it might be. It was a type of box, in the shape of something like a little house; *It must be*, he thought, *surely it is, the Silver Shrine!* Christian has walked past this alcove with its obscure painting hundreds of times completely oblivious to the treasures and history that were being revealed by it. It must have looked an odd sight to any onlookers, this young guy studiously observing a religious icon like a professor of ancient history. But Christian was seeing something else, a treasure trail, great power and wealth, hidden somewhere but with clues to its location scattered all around. *Dig deeper*, he thought, *if you look carefully*, he repeated the words of Sir Jack, *you will find it*.

There was one more depiction. Here Macartan was receiving a message from the heavens directing him towards a faraway village.

Clogher, thought Christian. He examined the image closely but there was no other clue apparent. *Look carefully!* He urged himself, poring over it again, and then he saw it. As the message directed Macartan to Clogher, so it directed Christian to go there too. Although its gold was gone, the stone remained there. The ancient stone that once held the power of the pagans resting now in the ancient Cathedral of Clogher where Macartan had put it to rest.

Yes, thought Christian, *follow the clues.*

Christian stood back from the icon and looked around for the others. The Cathedral was a masterpiece of architecture and construction taking more than thirty labourious years to build with stones from local quarries. Internally it was striking with dramatic stone carvings, a resplendent pipe organ which dominated the rear wall and a magnificent hammerbeam ceiling soaring high. It was common during mass to see Dad with his face gazing upwards, either in heavenly prayer or more likely in awe of the design and workmanship that went into that ceiling. The altar and ambo were much more modern modest affair, hewn in curves from strong smooth stone. Behind the santuary hung a series of colourful abstract tapestries being admired by Sophia and Mols.

Meanwhile, Taymi was taking a tour of stained glass windows. She marvelled at their intricacy and colours, and wandered around with Morgen examining the depictions. Intermittent snatches of sun cast colourful hues into the building and on their faces. Morgen, two steps ahead as usual, stopped at an image he didn't expect to see in a Cathedral.

'This guy has a flaming sword.' He said.

'Don't swear!' hushed Taymi.

'No, he has a *flaming* sword.' Insisted Morgen, pointing at a powerful man wielding a lethal weapon of fire. Taymi looked up.

'My God.' She exclaimed, 'I know who it is!'

'You do?'

'Yes, and so should you.' She said, 'It's Saint Michael....Saint Michael the Archangel.'

'How did you know?' said Morgen.

'It says on the inscription.' Pointed Taymi making Morgen feel silly, 'Besides,' she said, 'he's got wings.'

Morgen was a little embarrassed about not recognising St.Michael. Dad had told them all about the Archangel whose name adorned the schoolhouse. Not alone that but when they went on a camping trip to France, Dad had insisted on taking them to medieval *Mont San Michel*, an island named after the saint. Initially Morgen hadn't wanted to go visit some boring historic town, even if it was on an island, wanting instead to stay near the pool and all the fun stuff, but Dad had insisted they all go. 'You might learn something important!' he had said.

Morgan could hardly forget the moment they arrived there. The island rose out of the sea like a magnificent empire, its cascading battlements tumbled steeply into the waters and an abbey cathedral rose out of the pinnacle in pointed defiance. The island sat a half mile into the sea only accessible when the tide was out. You could park on the sandbank but you better be gone when the sea comes back, they were warned because *the tides change as swiftly as a galloping horse.* The entire island was a medieval paradise with ancient streets and cobbly buildings all crowded around the narrow, winding, rickety thoroughfares which crept their way to the peak. It dripped with the smell of history, and clanky amour, and fortifications, and battles, and royalty, and prisoners, and pilgrims, and prayers, and massacres, and tradgedies and victories and....crepes.

At the tip top of the steep island was the Cathedral of St.Michael the Archangel. The island was named for him because St.Michael appeared to the local bishop and ordered a church to be built on the rocky islet. When the bishop at first disobeyed, St.Michael burnt a hole in his skull using his finger. Morgen was starting to realise that Michael was something of a pyromaniac.

Morgen remembered making it all the way to the top of the island, entering the cavernous doors of the Cathedral and seeing a huge stone statue of St.Michael slaying a demonic beast by slicing through its throat with a lance as it writhed below him in the throes of death. Morgen liked this Angel, he was cool. And he wore his hair long, just like Morgen.

The spire of the Cathedral at the top of Mont San Michel was dominated by a dazzling gold statue of Michael in full flight brandishing his golden sword, armed and ready to protect the island and its inhabitants from the scourges of evil. Michael *–Demon Slayer.*

The journey down from the pinnacle had been equally memorable as they squeezed their way down a steep passage which narrowed and narrowed until Dad had to walk sideways to fit and he was sure relieved when he popped out the end grateful he still had his shirt on.

Morgen *had* learned something important on that trip; history can actually be fun. He thought back to their return from the island; their campsite was in the country demesne of an historic chateau of royal connection. It had tonnes of pools and slides and lovely food...

'Ah Crepes!' He reflected wistfully now making Taymi stare at him askance.

'I mean…. there are Angel's everywhere.' Said Morgen. And he was right, there were tiny angels in the corners of the stained glass windows, angels carved in stone on the choir balcony pillars, angels everywhere, watching, spying, protecting. But there were others looking too, carved stone heads of men with beards and women with long faces, staring straight ahead or gazing up at an angle. Taymi reckoned these were people of the parish who had gone before, consigned now to stare in stone for eternity supporting some roof strut or other on their head. But not all of the images were strangers.

'That's Tiernach, Bridget, and here's Patrick.' Said Taymi, pointing at the next set of stained glass.

'Read the inscriptions did you!' Said Morgen.

The image of Patrick was particularly colourful, dressed in flowing garments, a snake at his feet and a shamrock in his hand.

'He used the shamrock to tell how there could be three people in one God,' said Taymi, 'just as there are three leafs on one stem. It's called the Trinity.' For a second the mention of the word trinity rang a tiny bell in her head, but she couldn't figure out why.

Morgen was looking at something unusual that Patrick was holding in the crook of his arm.

'Is that …….a tiny church?' Said Morgen.

Taymi strained her eyes to see. 'So it is.' She exclaimed, 'It's a tiny Silver Church, he's holding *the Silver Shrine* that Christian has been telling us about.' It did indeed appear to be the precious relic box that Patrick in time had given Macartan.

They saw Dad at the other side of the chapel intently viewing another stained glass scene and Morgen toddled over to him.

'Gee why is that old guy trying to kill that boy?' said Morgen referring to the picture Dad was so absorbed into. He certainly didn't think this was a very Christian scene although he was kinda sorry now he hadn't paid more attention to these glazed storyboards before; they had a lot going on. In the picture the bearded 'old guy' was about to plunge a weapon into a young man who knelt in prayer.

'This is the story of Abraham,' said Dad quietly, 'he was asked by God to sacrifice his only son Isaac.'

'Why?' asked Morgen incredulous just as Christian sidled up behind them.

'It was a test of loyalty,' said Dad, 'to see if Abraham would obey God. So Abraham was carrying out the order in this picture here, but at the last minute God sent an Angel to call him to stop. That's the angel in the background there.'

'What if Abraham didn't hear the Angel?' said Morgen.

'He did hear him, he had very good hearing.'

'What if there was a thunder roll and Abraham didn't hear him.'

'It was a sunny day, see, there were no thunderstorms.'

'What if a dog barked?'

'There were no dogs around or no thunderstorms, just two guys and an Angel in the desert.' Said Dad, well used to debating at this level with Morgen.

'I just think God took a bit of a risk is all.' Muttered Morgen as he wandered away.

'I don't disagree with you there.' Said Dad thoughtfully, although Morgen was too far away to hear.

'That's the Lamb of God,' said Dad seemingly to himself or did he know that Christian was there just behind his shoulder. The lamb appeared in the rear of the picture. 'It was sent to replace Issac.' Said Dad, 'It's known as the perfect sacrifice.'

'Why sacrifice?' asked Christian quietly thinking of the word that had cropped up in the verse.

'Before Christianity,' Dad said, 'it was thought to be the best form of worship; to offer a sacrifice to God. A human sacrifice would have been the utmost, so this sacrifice of his only son would have been the greatest sacrifice that Abraham could make, to God..... and to himself.'

Christian looked at the disturbing image of father and son.

'What would *you* have done?' he asked Dad.

Dad didn't reply for a moment, but then he spoke lowly. 'What's that God? You want me to conduct a sacrifice? But who? Not Christian, surely.'

Christian shook his head, 'Stop messing Dad.'

'Not for thirty pieces of silver God, I won't do it…. Alright thirty euro then, deal.'

Why does Dad make a joke about everything. Thought Christian. They both stood there silently looking at the window.

'I wouldn't have done it Christian.' Dad said quietly. Christian looked at him but Dad held his eye on the image.

'Then you would have suffered the wrath of God if you didn't make the sacrifice.' Christian said.

'Nothing new there then.' More silence.

'I would have made the sacrifice alright; it just wouldn't have been you.' Dad said eventually. Christian realised that Dad was saying he would sacrifice himself before his son.

'It would be the ultimate sacrifice.' Dad said looking at Christian now. He turned to look across at a large bronze casting of Christ nailed to the cross, being crucified in front of the people.

'The ultimate sacrifice,' he said, 'is to give up your own life to save others.'

Christian looked at the gruesome crucifixion, *How could anyone even think of doing that?* He thought. *Handing over your life, don't they know that would be the end, the ultimate end?* He couldn't understand it, nonetheless he was moved by what Dad had said. He was conscious of the minute weight of the small crucifix around his neck.

'Thanks Dad.'

'Besides,' said Dad, 'you being alive is a miracle. I would hardly do anything to compromise it.'

'How do you mean?' asked Christian.

'When you were born you didn't breathe at first, the cord was around your neck. I was with you when you were rushed to the resuscitation facility.' Dad paused, he was looking up at the stained glass again.

'Your Grandmother had a younger brother, my uncle,....... his name was John. When he was born he couldn't breathe, just like you, but for too long. The lack of oxygen caused him permanent brain damage. He was incapacitated; but he was a beautiful young boy. He wasn't even your age when God sent the angels to take him.....It was Christmas morning.' Christian could see that this was an emotional thing for Dad.

'Is that why your second name is John?' asked Christian.

'Yes,' said Dad, '...Even though he died before I was born, I often think about him,.....moreso now.' Dad looked again at Christian and then back at the window design, to disguise the fact that his eyes were moist. 'The difference is Christian.' he said, 'you breathed; you lived.'

All these messages fed into Christians mind. He breathed, he lived. There was a purpose to him, a reason he lived; and what he could not do, could not contemplate was the thought that anyone could throw it all away, could sacrifice themselves, considering the vast and complex sciences that brought them to breathe, brought them to life. He excused himself to allow Dad, who was lost in the moment to be alone with his thoughts. He wandered towards the Cathedrals left transept and over to the baptism font, a huge curved stone from which was hewn a deep circular dish cupping the holy water.

He dipped his finger in, making ripples emanate like a message spreading out across the world. He thought of the night 14 years ago when he as an infant had the sacred water trickle over his head in baptism at this exact spot. Christian looked back towards the stained glass image of Abraham and Isaac, Dad was still there. There was another window of stained glass there, the baptism in the river Jordan, John the Baptist baptising Christ. Back then baptism meant complete submergence in water and the picture showed Christ emerging from the deep water into new life. Ironically Christian thought, his own baptism had been carried out with more pomp and ceremony than that of the first Christian; until he remembered that at Christ's baptism, the Heavens opened and a great voice spoke; A little more spectacular than the sound system at St.Macs.

Christian scooped some water in his hand and let it trickle back into the pool. The splishing sound it made reminded him of the river and waterfall. He noticed something at the bottom of the dish, a glint, light reflecting off a small object in the shimmering water, *Gold?...* it was a coin. Christian smiled at seeing a coin in the baptism font. *Someone must have thought this was a wishing well.* He thought and holding back his cuff, he reached in and extracted the coin.

It was a one euro coin, with its golden rim and silver inner circle. Christian flipped it over, as he liked to do, to look on the rear for the insignia of the country of origin. This coin didn't have the traditional Irish harp but another image, instantly recognisable, and one that sent a jolt through Christian the moment he saw it.

It was Leonardo DeVinci's Vetruvian Man. The image was well known by Christian, it was well known across the world. It had been presented to him at school in technical graphics 101 in a lesson on proportionality. The image of a man stood inside a circle *and* a square and all three made a perfect connection, touching together at key points. Teacher had told them that it had been described as *The Design of Perfection,* designed by DeVinci to represent the workings of the World and the centrality of the Universe....obviously.

Merging seamlessly within this one powerful image were references to Science, Mankind, Geometry, Anatomy, Architecture, Proportionality, Art, Physicality, Symmetry, Universality, Infinity and Harmony.

The first time he had seen it, Christian had thought that the diagram of the man was Christ during the crucifixion but he had learned that it was not the image of one man but of every man. Yet this same thought crossed his mind now again and he looked back at the bronze crucifixion, the ultimate sacrifice, seeing the similarity in the Vetruvian Mans outstretched arms, slightly raised, and those of the man on the cross. But the jolt that ran through him came not from this comparison but from the fleeting reminder he got of his spectre, who he believed to be the gatekeeper, who had appeared to him three times, it was an almost identical pose.

Christian had seen Da Vinci's man many times in books, magazines, movies; even in *the Simpsons.*

Perhaps it's a sign. He thought. He knew the coin was Italian, the home of Leonardo, and he decided to keep it for good luck, popping it into his pocket. *It might come in useful someday.* Perhaps thinking about being shortchanged sometime, or needing a lucky coin for some reason; although he could have had no idea at that time how useful it would become in the not too distant future. Then a thought occurred to him; *To raise the Fee*, the words from the verse, perhaps this was in some way connected, a payment of some sort. Although he could not quite figure it our, he felt that he had somehow been given a clue.

Christian left the font and wandered into the stone cloisters which led towards the sacristy, taking note perhaps for the first time of the statues and images which adorned the route. There were still some people around sharing conversation and laughing aloud. He stopped at an austere stone plaque cast into the wall and carved with a long list of names, a list which was clearly incomplete. He looked at the last name in the list. It was the Bishop. Therefore, this must be the list of all the Bishops going right back! His eyes raced back to the top left corner of the plaque, to the name on the top of the list,…. it wasn't Macartan! Christian was disappointed but he noticed that the list began at 1135 AD well after Macartan had been and gone. Morgen sauntered up beside Christian.

'Whatcha looking at?' Morgen enquired in a drawl.

'These are all the Bishops of Clogher.' Said Christian. 'Well, not *all* of them.' As he began to scan through the list, he had a feeling like a cold breeze, a presence enter his aura.

'Good morning gentlemen.' A distinctive voice made them swing round. It was a voice they knew and he stood there now smiling down on them benevelontly. It was the man who now carried the title that Partick had given to Macartan. It was the Bishop of Clogher.

'Good morning.' replied Christian.

'Hey.' said Morgen.

'It's nice to see young men like you taking such an interest in the history of the church.' said the Bishop. Morgen was about to correct him but the Bishop continued speaking.

'What are your names?'

'Christian; and this is Morgen.'

'Christian...a strong name....I think I've met you before' The Bishop studied him up.

'You baptised me.' said Christian.

'I see.....and I confirmed you.' Said the Bishop. It was true; when he was twelve, Christian had received the sacrament of confirmation, the drawing down of the Holy Spirit, from the Bishop, together with all twelve year olds from the dioscese. Considering this, Christian was impressed that the Bishop remembered confirming him in particular out of hundreds of kids. Then he realised his folly; if the Bishop confirmed *all* boys and girls then of course he *must* have confirmed Christian too. It was a smooth move.

'Christian … Gilla-Chroist.' said the Bishop. It was the Irish translation of Christian's name, one he was well familiar with. The Bishop walked past him to the stone plaque and pointed up to a name near the very start of the list; *Gilla-Chroist*. Christian gaped at the name, *his* name, in the historical list.

'The name of this Bishop was Christianus.' said the Bishop, 'An interesting guy, he was Primus Abbas of Ireland, perhaps you are related.' He smiled a broad smile and then turned and went about his business, exchanging polite words with those he met along the way. Christian was still in shock, could he be related to a former Gilla Chroist. He talked himself through it.

'Could that possibly be? No wait, it couldn't. Could it?'

'This is too weird' said Morgen and he sauntered off again to let Christian figure it out himself.

Mols met Dad, with a question. She had seen something disturbing and very out of place in such a venerable building.

'Why is there a *beast* in that carving up there?' She asked, pointing at a small carved stone projecting out of the wall high up above the altar. 'And there.' She pointed to a similar stone directly opposite.

Dad studied it. 'That's not a beast.' He said. 'It's a Fluer-de-lis.'

'Say again?'

'A Fluer-de-lis, a decoration, very traditional in architecture, a swirling pattern, represents French monarchs.' Dad squinted to see as best he could, 'In fact it's two of them back to back; but they do make a strange shape put together that way.' Mols noticed that there were other such stones sticking out of the wall carrying roof timbers. These two strange stones however did not carry anything at all.

'They look like a Panther.' Said Mols, convinced no matter how Dad explained it, that she was looking at the face of a beast the same as the one supposedly on the prowl nearby. As they walked away from it Dad looked back over his shoulder with a perturbed expression. He didn't say out loud, but secretly he agreed with Mols, these two stones looking directly down over the altar, *did* look like panthers.

Mom always maintained that the family instinctively knew when it was time to get together again and insisted on this again as they all made their way out of the Cathedral having conveniently met in the centre aisle. Dad used the opportunity for a quick architecture lesson.

'Medieval French Neo-Gothic in style.' He went on, 'Plan is in the form of a Latin cross. Designed with seven bays, theres that number again, but only five were actually built. Five hundred horses and carts delivered building materials.' He turned around as they exited and pointed up at the spire. 'The most difficult bit to construct.' They looked up at the great spire rising dizzyingly skywards. 'And the scene....' Dad spoke more deliberately and darkly now, '....of a terrible tradgedy.'

'What tradgedy?'

Dad continued looking up to the very top of the spire, ignoring Morgens question, *was he admiring the stonework or holding back on telling them about the tradgedy?*

'What *tradgedy?*'

'When the final stone was being placed on top,' Dad began slowly, 'the stonemason putting it in place suffered, what will I call it.... *delusions*. They say it was due to the extreme height. They said he was seeing things, a bout of madness. So they don't know if he did it on purpose or not.'

'Did *what* on purpose...or not?' pushed Morgen a little more tentatively.

'He fell to his untimely death.'

They were horrified to hear of the stonemason's shocking death and looked up agast at the great height to the top of the spire. Christian picked up on Dad suggesting that the death might have been on purpose, like he had thrown himself from the spire to certain death. *Why?* he thought, *Why would someone do that?* And why he thought did people say *his untimely death*, was there any such thing as a *timely* death?

Sophia fought the image of the mans body hurtling downwards and felt sickened to think that if he had fallen to the ground and not on the roof that he would have landed exactly where they were standing now. She took a step back.

Taymi was shocked. She could never have thought that in the process of building this magnificent house of God, this home of peace and tranquility and spirituality, that death would also factor in the equation. It seemed so wrong.

Mols was thrown back to the disturbing beastlike carving inside. Was it a delusion? Was she seeing things? As perhaps this stonemason had done.... or did he see something real?

Lila wondered where the angels were in this moment of tradgedy. Why did'nt they do something?

And Morgen, speechless for once, was thinking something similar. If the spire had been completed with St.Michael at the top like Mont San Michel, surely he would have been there to save this mans soul.

'It was one of countless delays to the building.' Said Dad. 'Constructing the spire was fraught with difficulties and held it up for months. It almost seemed like there was a curse preventing its completion.' The mention of another curse gripped Taymi.

'See the lightening conductor at the very top.' Said Dad, 'Because of its height, the spire is prone to lightening strikes. The conductor takes the lightening and sends it below the ground.' He pointed out the conductor cable pinned neatly to the stone. 'Just like it says in the bible,' he said, 'Satan was thrown from heaven like lightening.' *Spooky analogy.* thought Christian. 'You see the spire is also a Bell Tower,' Dad went on, 'and because we're on top of a hill the bell toll can be heard up to ten miles away. If the wind is in the right direction you can hear it at Westwoods. Does that ring a bell?' He quipped, ruffling Morgens hair. But no one laughed.

'There's just one more thing I want to see.' said Christian, and he led them towards the front of the building and down impressive sets of stone steps which flowed onto an expansive stone plaza which rolled all the way to magnificent gates and rails. Standing over the plaza, overseeing, with his right hand raised was St. Macartan, his statue, the object of Christian's interest. It was a modern statue representing Macartan as a strong and imposing man. But Macartan was not alone in statue. Beside him was a young man, holding an apple in offering, the apple that him Mom had given him.

'Hey it's the Little Prince.' Said Mols. 'Hasn't he eaten that yet!' she said bemused.

'Cool lance bro.' Morgen said to Macartan. 'Gotta get me one of them.'

'It's called a crozier.' Said Mom.

'I like to call it a lance.' Said Morgen.

Mols spotted something in the insignia on the carved vestments that Macartan wore and did a double take. She could hardly believe her eyes, one of the images clearly depicted, she was sure of it, what appeared to her, it could only be…..a *Buzzard?* Perhaps it was an Eagle, either way they were both from the same family. She looked up at Macartans face; *what was the connection with the Buzzard?* There were other animals depicted on the vestments too, what appeared to be a lion, and a bull and the image of a man. But her interest lay in the carving of the bird, and whats more its head was surrounded by a circle, a *halo.* Symbols in religion always seemed to have deep meaning and she wondered what the connection was here.

'Something interesting Mols.' Said Dad.

'Just looking.' Said Mols.

'Maybe that's the golden goose you were looking for.' Said Dad.

'Sure.' Said Mols.

'I want to show you something.' Said Dad suddenly, 'Follow me.' And he led them away from Macartans statue and across the paved plaza, the sun now throwing fresh sharp shadows behind them. 'If you think,' said Dad, 'that the death of one man was a tradgedy, then brace yourselves for what I am about to reveal to you.' They exchanged anxious glances as they followed him towards a small stone house beside the entrance; a gatehouse. Dad turned and stretched out his arm, leaning against the corner of the little house and bringing them to a halt. 'This Cathedral was begun more than a hundred and fifty years ago.' He began. 'But just fourteen years before the first stone was laid, something happened here that should never be forgotten.'

They were certainly bracing themselves now, for this sounded ominous. Taymi for her life couldn't possibly think what it was that could be as devastating as Dad was leading them to believe. Although she took note of one thing, the recurrence of seven syndrome, in the fourteen years that Dad had mentioned.

'What I am going to show you, you may not be able to comprehend.' He said, 'Evidence of the greatest atrocity to ever occur in this dioscese. And it didn't stop there, it swept the entire country. Families, whole families, like ours just.....' He trailed off the end of his sentence. He just stood there, then dropped his arm and stood back a step, turning to reveal what he had been concealing.....writing; writing on the wall.

Christian stepped forward and then they all gathered around to read what was written there. Sophia gasped and the others were sombre in silence.

'The Great Hunger.' Said Dad quietly.

They could not believe the magnitude of it. They knew about the famine from history lessons but to see the numbers of deaths and emigrants here in their own dioscese in just three years was numbing. It was like a slaying of the population where every man, woman and child ran a huge risk of dying of starvation. Dad was right, it was incomprehendible.

Christian read the words in the cut stone aloud;

> *At the time of the Great Famine 1845-1848, 100,000 people from the Diocese of Clogher, a quarter of the population, are known to have died or emigrated. This tablet is erected to their memory.*

The number was staggering. One hundred thousand people, a quarter of all the population of Clogher, left or died during those short three years. They were crucified by a horrible evil. Cut down in their thousands. He knew the weakest were the first to go, many of them children. And he knew why *died and emigrated* were more or less considered to be as bad as each other. It was because many of those emigrating never made it. They died on the ships that were taking them away from the plague. These wretched vessels became known as coffin ships. And for those who did survive the ships, many never saw home again and many were never heard from again. To their relatives, they were as good as dead.

Yet these people were so resilient. Thought Christian. *They got up and soon began to build a new life.* He looked back up at the magnificence of Macartans Cathedral. *And then they built this,* he thought, amazed that the poor and devasted people could create a structure so incredible that no building of today could even come close *They built it,* he thought to himself, *to banish all evil away.*

They were already at the gate and it was time to go. And they all had something to think about. Morgens admiration for the golden boy Michael. Sophia's horror at the plummet of the stonemason. Taymi struck into silence by the dizzying numbers afflicted by the horrendous hunger plague. Mols seeing beasts and haloed birds carved into stone. Lila, like Morgen, had observed how many angels there were and how there was not one inch of the Cathedral that didn't have a cherub or archangel watch over it in a ring of protection. Christian had hoped to perhaps discover something more of the Golden Stone, perhaps even the whereabouts of its gold, but alas, that was still very much hidden. No matter, he certainly had much more fodder on his mind, not least, how his name was carved into the stone of the Cathedral.

'Is it possible that I could be related to Gilla Chroist?' he asked after explaining about the name in the cloisters and the Bishops comment about it.

'It's possible.' Said Mom, 'You could be connected to him in some way, perhaps he is an ancestor.'

'The Bishop said something about Christianus being Primus Abbas of Ireland, what does that mean?'

'That was the Primary Abbot.' said Dad, 'He would have been a very powerful man, probably equal to a King. And he had the distinction of being the number one Christian.' Dad laughed then. 'Seems you're not the number one Christian after all....Christian.'

Christian considered his own name, it was a strong one with deep meaning and a heavy history. *Follower of Christ, Believer in Christ*, he also knew that Ten Monarchs of Denmark had carried this name. It was the name of the king of kings. *I hope I can live up to the reputation.* he wished.

'Speaking of Ancestors,' said Dad, 'How about we go say hello to Katie James.'

'But isn't.....' began Morgen.

'I mean at the cemetery,' said Dad, 'it's always good to call upon your ancestors once in a while.' Dad often spoke like this, like the dead were still part of the living, and often joked about his own death as thought it was just around the corner and no big deal. They pulled into cemetery road and parked between three graveyards of various age which formed one large cemetery…a trinity. There were relations in all three sections.

'That's the one I'm going to eventually.' Joked Dad pointing to the newest cemetery. 'It's the best.'

They entered into the central cemetery passing a statued depiction of Calvary, the scene of the crucifixion, the ultimate sacrifice. Christian looked at it in a new light now and he touched on the coin in his pocket which reminded him of it. Dad led them to the grave of his Grandfather Joe and Grandmother Katie James and stood chattering, telling them about their great-grandparents and telling their great-grandparents about them.

Morgen had heard most of these stories before and quickly his impatience got the better of him. His reverence was on the wane and he began to wander. He cast an eye over the rows and rows of headstones. Some of them were kept clean and neat, some were crumbling and mossy. Some were ostentatious and expensive, cut from marble, some were simple, a cross cut from timber. He looked across at the old cemetery. Its graves were mostly grown over; the gravestones slumped of old age, pretty soon it would look more like the ancient graveyard of Rockwell. The people who had tended those graves were most likely in the middle section graves themselves now, and the people who tended these would soon end up in the new section, just as Dad had predicted for himself.

Morgen swung back into the moment and swung back round to see where the others were and stopped dead! He was staring straight at a ghost, he stood there frozen rigid, his mouth hung open and his eyes in a fixated stare.

Nearby Mom instinctively looked up, 'Are you Ok Morgen?' She called out to him. But he wasn't.

Taymi rushed to him, 'What is it?' she urged. Morgen raised his finger and pointed at a gravestone.

It read *Henry James –Castle Hanes– Died 1935.*

XV

PRIORES

(Ancestors)

MORGEN WAS SHOCKED at reading Grandas name on a tombstone and so were the others when they saw it.

'Don't worry.' Said Dad hurriedly. 'Granda hasn't risen from the dead; but this is a relation of his. If we call to see Granda on our way home, you will see that he is very much alive, and he can tell you about *this* Henry James.' That seemed to ease Morgens concern somewhat.

'But before we go,' added Dad, 'if you're not to freaked by that, there is another name written over here you might recognise.' He led them to the oldest graveyard where stones stuck out in slants.

'As you know,' Dad continued, 'Lila here is named after a relative. The first Lila James was a great matriarch of the family and she once owned the lands at Westwoods.'

'What's a Matri...arc.' Said Lila.

'It means a strong, independent lady,...like you.' Said Mom.

'She was my father's aunt, which would make her my Great Aunt and your Great, Great Aunt.' Dad puffed, slightly out of breath, as he led them up the headstoned incline and drew alongside an imposing grey plaque. The name read *Lila James*. It was disconcerting looking at Lila looking at her own name written here.

'She was a great teacher.' Said Dad putting his arm around Lila's shoulder. 'Perhaps one day you will too.

Granda laughed when he heard about Morgens fright.

'Did you think I crawled out of the tomb Morgen?' he asked.

'I was starting to think you might be a zombie.' Morgen replied and Granda laughed more heartily.

'The Henry James you saw was my Uncle,' Granda explained, 'he was a fine man and I was named after him. But unfortunately I never got to meet him, as he died an untimely death shortly before I was born.'

'What happened to him?' Sophia asked.

'He was foresting,' said Granda, 'in the woods. He was killed by a falling tree, it was an accident. His life was over too early, a young man, he had more to give.'

Taymi felt sad for this fine young man, his life cut short deep in the woods, the woods where they thought that no harm could come to them. Now she realised why Granny had harped on about the dangers in there. Christian wanted to join the dots.

'Was Owen related to Great Aunt Lila?' he asked.

'Yes.' said Granda considerably pleased to see the grandchildren taking an interest in the family orchard as he called it, 'Her brother, and they were siblings to my mother Katie. All of them were born and raised right here in this old house.'

'Who lived here before your Moms family.' asked Sophia becoming interested in just how old this house was. Granda thought about it, Morgen thought he could hear rocks rumbling inside Grandas head.

'My Mothers father was Owen James, and his Grandfather had originally lived in this house. That would make it your Great, Great,... Great,.... Great Grandfather. That's as far back as I know but the family extends further back than that.'

'What was his name?' said Sophia, 'The great, great, great..... great guy.'

'He went by the name of Treanoir,' Said Granda, 'But he was known as The Strong Man.'

Christian's ears pricked up at this last piece of information. *The Strong Man,….. The Trean Fhear!* It was the name that Macartan had earned.

'Beyond that.' Granda concluded. 'I can't tell you anything more.' He used his stick to tease Morgen by poking him.

'New stick Granda?' asked Morgen noticing the slender, sleek and strong implement that Granda held. He had been thinking of getting one like it since seeing Archangel Michaels lance. Grandas stick narrowed towards a point in the same way.

'You like?' said Granda, 'Then you can have.' He lifted the stick/lance horizontally with both hands gripping the middle and presented it to Morgen. 'Use it wisely.' He said. Morgen was delighted with his new piece of equipment.

'Its from a Rowan tree.' Said Granda, 'It's perfect for the job.' Morgen examined it more closely, *Yes* he thought, *It is perfect for the job…whatever the job might be!*

At home Christian rushed to a website of historical names, quickly typing in *Treanoir* using the spelling he got from Granda. The search threw up variations of the name as it morphed over the decades. But he was right, the name was anglo derived from the old Irish Treinfheir which came from the words *Trean-Fhear.* And its meaning; *Strong-Man, Champion, Very Brave, Valiant.*

'The name honours the patron Macartan.' Read Christian and sat back. His ancestors had carried on the name of Strong Man! It explained why great, great, great, great grandfather got his nickname.

Strong Man. He thought, wondering if the honour of this name still extended down the line. To Granda, to Dad, to him? He looked at the name Macartan. Though it had produced the name Strong Man, it had a meaning entirely of its own. *Son of the Rowan Tree.*

'Rowan Tree?' This was the name of the tree that Granda got his stick from, now Morgens lance. Christian flicked up a page on the Rowan Tree. The tree was assumed to have magical powers expecially affording protection against malevolent beings and was commonly found in the ruins of ancient settlements. Morgen entered the room then and Christian read the remainder aloud.

'Rowan trees were planted in churchyards to send away evil spirits but also to keep the dead from leaving their graves.'

Morgen halted in his tracks. 'Zombies!'

'Listen to this,' said Christian, 'Some believed that to protect your soul from the Devil you had to touch a witch with a branch from a Rowan tree. Then, if the Devil came demanding a soul, the witch would be taken instead.'

'I'm glad I got myself one of them.' Morgen commented.

'Here's more,' Christian read, 'A cross carved from Rowan was sometimes placed above a child's cradle to protect it from bewitchment or from being stolen by faeries. The Rowan has the ability to increase psychic connections with the spirit realms.'

'Cool.' Said Morgen. But Christian didn't hear him, he was thinking of the small carved cross that he carried, he was thinking of his contact with the spirit gatekeeper, a physic connection to the spirit realm?

'Its special significance in mythology,' he went on 'ranks with the Oak and Yew Trees.' Christian hovered on the Oak Tree, the image which adorned the plaque on their house, the symbol of Westwoods. Dad had told them that it symbolised the entryway into another world. He clicked on it.

'The Ancient Celts had an affinity for the Oak Tree....its signifies Strength and Wisdom. But the Celtic word for Oak is Duir, which is believed to be the origin of the word *Druid*.' This stopped Christian in his tracks.

'Druid, did you say?' enquired Morgen.

'Yea,' said Christian softly, 'Druid.' Then turning to Morgen. 'Why do we have a Druid symbol on the front of our house?'

Morgen was blank except to say. 'I'm definitely going to need that stick.'

'The Yew,' said Christian, 'was another tree associated with the Druids,' he read, 'sometimes known as the Tree of Death due to its association with cemeteries.'

'Keep away from Oak and Yew, stick with Rowan.' Commented Morgen, but Christian was'nt listening, he was poring over more tree mythology and he didn't like what he was reading.

'Sacred tree groves were used for performing ritual sacrifices. Druids oversaw the rituals offered to the Goddess Nemetona who was worshipped in Gaul, German and Celtic lands. The Goddess is believed to continuously visit these sacred sites summoned there by Neo-Pagans.'

'Whats Neo-Pagans?'

'As far as I can see.' Said Christian, 'They are modern pagans.'

He thought of the sacred site they were seeking, and the groves of trees in the woods, and the mention of the word Druid and sacrifice, the opening to another world, ancient settlements, the spirit of the gatekeeper, the physic connections to the spirit realm. All these words whispered in his mind. He shook them away, there was something else he wanted to check.

'Christianus.' Said Christian tapping quickly but realising nearly as quickly that it would be a struggle to get much information about the former Bishop and Primus Abbot.

'He was the head of the Primary Abbey in Ireland which made him Primus Abbas or Chief Abbot....Mom was right.' Said Christian, talking to himself as Morgen had ceased listening.

'The Abbey is in the historic town of Clones making the town one of the most important of its time.'

'Clones town?' Morgen heard this, 'that's not far from here.'

'Bout 20 miles west.' Christian told him. 'But guess who put the abbey there?' he asked but continued without waiting for Morgen to think about it, 'Tiernach, the guy who succeeded Macartan. Remember him from the icon in the Cathedral? Carrying the Silver Shrine?' But Morgen didn't.

'Anyway the Abbey and the town were destroyed by fire in a ferocious war but were rebuilt later. The tiny ancient abbey still exists as an historic ruin.' Christian scrolled through more paragraphs but there was no more information on Christianus.

'Destroyed by Fire.' Said Christian thinking of the castles similar fate. 'But rebuilt.' The abbey had been given new life but unfortunately the castle had not. 'I was kinda hoping Christianus could have given us some kind of a clue to do with the Golden Stone.' Said Christian shutting down the web.

'Not today brother.' Said Morgen. 'Not today.'

XVI

FERA

(Animals)

Mᴏʟs ꜱᴛᴏᴏᴅ ꜱʟɪɢʜᴛʟʏ crouched but perfectly still. She was watching and listening. She couldn't see it but she knew that an animal was very, *very* close. She slowly turned her head and saw it; coming through the long grass *straight towards her*. Her heart pounded. Her eyes locked contact. It stared directly at her from just a few metres away and fully materialised through the grass. It moved towards her to within *one* metre. She could'nt believe what she was seeing, it was so huge it could devour her in seconds. She was staring straight into the face of a monstrous Black Panther.

Mols froze; her jaw dropped slowly open; she could hear herself exhale in slow motion. She looked straight into its deep green killer eyes; she could see its whiskers vibrating with its hot breath. She could have reached out to touch its rich black silky fur that moved like an oil slick flowing through the jungle. The panther began to open its mouth revealing a bone crunching set of sharp teeth in a deadly snarl.

'This is it!' Thought Mols as the beast opened its mouth gapingly wide.....in a huge yawn.

'Its amazing.' said Mols staring dumbstruck into its stretched mouth and examining the big cat's teeth. She had her hands pressed up against the glass of the zoo enclosure. This is what she had been waiting for, to see the big cat at the zoo. All the talk recently of the

Black Panther had made her keen to see one up close and she had reminded Dad regularly of his promise to visit the zoo.

'Did I say that?' Dad tried his old memory lapse trick, but he was true to his word and had taken her *and* everyone to the city for the day. In anticipation of the zoo visit, Mols had conducted a study of the Panther, *her* prey on this occasion, eagerly called out salient facts, to her able but unwilling assistant Lila.

'The Panther is actually of the Jaguar family, are you listening Lila.' Mols advised. 'They live in tropical rainforests and grasslands of the Americas. A Jaguar which is born completely black is called a Black Panther' Lila thought this made perfect sense; after all, it would hardly have been called a White Panther.

'They will climb a tree and wait in it for prey.' Mols read and she pictured the Black Panther resting lazily on a strong branch in the woods waiting patiently for prey to come along. Perhaps that prey would be a child, perhaps even a young girl like herself….or younger, like Lila!

'The Panther enjoys the presence of water and swimming. That's odd,' she said,' for a cat!' It made her think of the river running its course through the woods and the dark pool at the base of the waterfall, a pool perfect for a feline swim in the shadows.

'It has a hugely powerful bite and an unusual killing technique…..' the remainder of this sentence gave her such a horrific graphic image she read it quieter so Lila couldn't hear. '. …. *by biting through the skull to the brain.*'

'What?' said Lila.

'Oh, It can also…' said Mols, racing ahead to the next sentence, but realising too late that it too was particularly grusome, '…kill efficiently by giving a suffocating neck bite.' she groaned. Lila gave her a look of disgust.

'The Panthers roar,' said Mols, moving on, 'can sound like a repetitive cough but they also make mews and grunts.' *Strange.* thought Mols, *the Panther* mews *just like the buzzard.*

'It will eat large and small species but prefers large prey such as…..' There was a whole host of preferred Panther prey listed including a wide variety of exotic species large and small, but Mols was straightaway attracted to only one type of prey, the one which seemed most close to home and that is the one she read out, '....Deer!'

Was it a conincidence that the deer had disappeared from the woods during the same time as a beast fitting the description of a Black Panther, who incidently prefers deer for dinner, was roaming the same jurisdiction? Or did they just wander off into the sunset? She thought not!

As she had been talking, Lila had quietly left the room whilst seconds later someone else quietly entered the room.

'A Panther will walk slowly and silently,' she went on as the intruder emulated the panthers movements, 'down forest paths, listening and stalking its prey before ambushing it with a quick pounce.' Someone had moved directly behind her, paws raised ready to pounce.

'Morgen?' said Mols, sending him stock still until she spun around to face him.

'How?' Morgen asked amused and amazed.

'I've been honing my sixth sense.' She said smugly. 'It can be learned you know. Much to do with movement of air, vibrations, sound, smell..... And boy do you!'

Hey!' said Morgen. 'Everyone smells, it's why we got noses. But I want to hear about the Panther.'

'It can leap into water for its attack,' she continued, 'and its so strong it can haul a heifer up a tree out of the water before devouring it.'

'*Wow*!' said Morgen thrilled with this gruesome morsel. 'Whats a heifer?'

'A young cow.' She said.

'Oh boy.' He said. 'Tell me more.'

'Black Panthers were famous in Native American folklore where they, together with the Owl, were known as the symbol of.....' Mols stopped but Morgen finished it.

'Death!' he said.

Now in the Zoo, Mols was locking stares with the Beast of Death, the carnivore, the *Panthera-Onca,* to give it its official name, the third largest feline after the Tiger and the Lion and a solitary predator. She also found out that the Black Panther was often known as the *Phantom Panther* because it had been smuggled into parts of the world where it was not meant to inhabit and had disappeared into the wilderness there, only occasionally making an appearance. This could explain how there could possibly be one at large here in the northern hemisphere, thousands of miles from its natural habitat; it could explain how a black beast was known to raise its head occasionally and make its presence known and how it could devour an animal as large as itself and still have room for a lesser morsel.

Tales of mystical folklore grew around Phantom Panthers expecially the belief that they had the power to appear and disappear with the ability to shape-shift; to reform itself into the shape of another beast or being. It was considered a symbol of darkness, death and rebirth, a symbol of the feminine and power of the night. The Black Panther played on a human's primitive fear of the dark and of death, fear of their powers and mysticism; fear of the unknown and of the spirit world.

'Did anyone ever get killed by a Panther?' Morgen had asked that day at home. Mols scanned through more paragraphs.

'Says here that they *can* attack humans.' She had been hoping to read the opposite, 'particularly if the Panther is cornered, or even if the person is running away.' (she considered herself in the latter not the former category) 'But it *is* possible to ward off an attack of a Panther' she was heartened to learn, 'by threatening the animal! …..either by intense eye contact, shouting, fighting back with sticks or rocks or appearing larger and more menacing.'

'Oh good….' Said Morgen; picturing himself with his Rowan stick, looking menacing and whopping that Panther's ass good. '…I think we could survive against a Panther.'

'Em...Not to sure about that,' said Mols weakly, and she read the next bit, which got stuck a little in her throat and made Morgen rethink his whopping move.

'At greatest risk of a Panther attack and the least likely to survive are....children.'

Mols watched the Beast pacing up and down numerous times behind the glass of its enclosure, flexing its muscular frame and she studied it resting in the sun, its black glossy coat absorbing the deep warmth of the summer sun. She stayed studying the Black Panther for as long as she could until everyone else in the family eventually dragged her away to see another peculiar kind of cat...the Meerkat. Yet she remained mesmerised by this creature, the creature of the dark, the creature of death, the creature that according to local legend, roamed wild in the drumlins where she lived, where there was no enclosure fence, no protective glass and no knowing if and where and when it would choose to reveal itself again.

XVII

PRAETERITUS

(Past)

THERE WAS MORE than one purpose to today's trip, they had planned to strike to the very heart of the city where a scattering of stately and austere buildings converged and where Christian had told them they could witness a great treasure of particular importance to their project. Mom insisted that he meant a sojourn to her favourite coffee shop for a creamy latte but she was willing to wait til later to receive her little treasure.

Christian had explained to his parents all about his findings in relation to St.Macartan, well most of it anyway and had asked if they could visit the National Museum, to look at the historical artefact, *The Silver Shrine* which had been given to Macartan from Patrick.

The National Museum building was an architectural landmark. 'Palladian Style.' said Dad. It boasted a colonnaded entrance looking over the courtyard of government buildings and when they entereded they stood under a huge domed rotunda of twenty metres height.

'The dome is modelled on the famous Pantheon in Rome.' Dad gestured after stealing a look at the information leaflet. The rotunda floor was decorated with a mosaic design of classical mythology in the centre of which was the wheel of the zodiac, aka; the circle of animals. The central court was surrounded by an elaborate circle of columns decorated at their bases with gatherings of cherubs.

'Baby Angels....or Fairies?' Lila queried.

'They could be either.' said Mom.

Dad was still looking up, as ever, at the complex roof structure sitting atop the columns.

'See that detail.' He said, lost in wonder. 'See that workmanship.'

'See that step.' Snickered Morgen as Dad stumbled from not watching where he was walking.

Mom read from a display board.

'The museum contains one of the finest collections of gold artefacts in all of Europe with examples of ecclesiastical medieval objects.'

'Whats ecclesiat, ecclesiast, whats that now?' Morgen struggled.

'Bless you.' Said Taymi.

'Ecclesiastical' pronounced Mom, '.... belonging to Christianity.' She explained.

'And we are here to see one of them.' Said Christian.

'Looks like we can see a lot more besides.' stressed Taymi. She pointed to a list of exhibitions that were currently showing; *The Treasure Collection, The Viking Collection, Ancient Egypt, Ancient Rome* and an interesting section titled with a word they were starting to become a little too familiar with......*Sacrifice!* Despite the macabre title she thought it was definitely one they should visit before leaving the building. But first, they made their way to the Treasure Collection which proclaimed to house precious metalwork from Pagan to Christian times.

There was a cool ethereal mood in the exhibition rooms; the atmosphere was calm, laced with reflective Celtic panpipes, a sharp contrast to the bustling noise of the city and the loud echoes of the entrance rotunda. They viewed ancient items aplenty, including a golden neck decorations, early necklaces, which were made of real gold but still didn't quite have the bling factor that the girls would have desired. An ornate silver brooch of delicate detail appealed to Mom; she declared to Dad that it, or *something similar*, might look pretty good on her; He slunk away quickly.

The boys on the other hand were intrigued by altogether different paraphernalia; some early boat models and a huge bronze trumpet;

but that was before they discovered a hoard of silver bullion and coins, a true treasure trove of tremendous value.

Central to the exhibition was a series of Christian artefacts; a belt studded with precious metals, incredibly ornamented which had been discovered by a farmer cutting his turf out of a boggy bank.

'I didn't know they had wrestling tournaments back then.' Said Morgen, figuring that the belt could have passed for the WWF title trophy.

Another precious item was a chalice of silver, bronze and gold, embossed with precious stones and enamels and described as *a work of precise technical proficiency.*

'Hey!' Sophie exclaimed, 'This chalice was found by someone digging in a Fort!' It was what they hoped to do, find a fort, find the treasure in it, and avoid if possible the wrath of the Fairies in the process, so she kept reading. The chalice had been used in secret masses held at the Fort in penal times just as Dad had been telling them about; for this the Fort been consecrated as a holy place. The treasure was dropped or buried in a hurry to avoid capture. Sophie thought this could explain why Macartan may have hidden the Golden Stone in the Fort? Was he avoiding being captured? Or was he avoiding the Stone being captured? Sophia played out the questions in her head. Christian whispered to her.

'You thinking what I'm thinking?' he said.

'Yea.' Said Sophia, glad someone else was on the same wavelength without having to spell it all out.

'I'm starving too.' said Christian. 'Absolutely *starving!*'

Sophia gave him a dig in the ribs with her elbow.

'Havn't you been taking notes?' she said and pointed out the information she had been reading. Christian quickly caught up and read out the last sentence.

'*The chalice was found with other artefacts buried in the same Fort.* Do you think there could be more that one treasure in the Fort?' he said.

'Only one way to find out.' Said Sophia, 'Find that Fort!'

Taymi had moved along to another elaborate item.

'Hey Guys.' she called out, 'This is the bell that Patrick used to cast the snakes out of Ireland.'

It was a well known story that there were no snakes in the entire land; Patrick had banished the serpents as the *demons of Satan*. The only snakes in the country now were imported or in the Zoo, those they had been recoiling from this very morning. Taymi thought the story behind this bell was comical; Patrick failed in banishing the venomous snakes and hostile birds that plagued him with his crozier alone, so he prayed for divine assistance which came....in the form of a shiny bell. The bell worked on the birds but not the snakes, so instead he threw the bell at them! And that seemed to work!

'A flamethrower would have done it easier.' Said Morgen shaking his head at the thought of Patrick throwing the bell after a bunch of snakes and chasing them over the hills and far away.

The bell had got the nickname *The Black Bell* because it has lost its lustre being thrown about but also because it was used to the banish the *black snakes* that were under the command of the Druids. This rekindled Taymi's suspicion of a Druidic involvement in the curse.

'The Devils henceman.' Read Taymi, 'That's what Patrick called the snakes, because of what they did in the Garden of Eden.'

'That's right' said Christian, 'it was the *snake* who tempted Eve to eat the apple from the Tree of Life.'

'She may as well eat it,' chirped in Morgen, 'the little prince doesn't seem to want it.' They laughed again at Morgen's deadpan reinterpretation of history, their mirth splintering the quiet calm of the museum exhibition space. Taymi was pretty certain now, having read this, that Patrick and no doubt his sidekick Macartan had made themselves arch enemies of the Druids back in the day.

There were a selection of Bishop's croziers on view, one which was decorated with animal motifs and colourful beading, it had been found hidden in a blocked up doorway in a Castle for years. Taymi read the detail.

'The crozier is the symbol of the shepherds crook and usually always held in the left hand…..Left hand is the best hand.' She said smugly since she herself was a left hander, the only one in the family. '….This allowed the right hand to conduct the blessings.'

'Ha Ha,' said Christian. 'Right hand is the …..better one!'

'The Bishop always holds the crozier with the curve pointing out and away from him.' Taymi thought back to the statue of Macartan and indeed he did hold the crozier in his left, pointed out and with his right hand raised.

'It is considered both a staff for leading the faithful and a rod for punishing the recalcitrant.'

'What's that mean?' she asked of the last word.

'Those who resist authority,' said Dad, 'like you guys.'

'Reminds me of the one I've got.' said Morgen.

They maneuvered their way along towards the treasure they had come here to seek; The Silver Shrine.

Christian felt a great sense of anticipation; this was a treasure that had been gifted from Patrick to Macartan and was of considerable significance, demonstrated by the number of depictions it appeared in.

They came to the glass case that houses the important artefact. The Westwooders gathered around to inspect it closely. It was an elaborate metal box with the most intricate arrangement of figures and decorations fashioned into precious metal. There were depictions of scrolls, men on horses, Celtic designs, winged beasts and Angels. On the top was a large figure of the image of Christ on the Cross, above which was a small square crystal stone. Along the sides were images of various saints and more decorations and more precious stones. It certainly was impressive and Christian thought of how important and precious it must have been back more that fifteen hundred years ago. No wonder Patrick needed his security, aka Macartan, with him at all times and how generous of Patrick to give it to Macartan as a gift.

There were information labels pinned to the display and Christian passed on their information.

'The Saints include Brigid and Patrick. Some of the Apostles are also included,' he said 'and the Archangel Michael too.' Morgen was delighted to hear his old friend was featured and craned to see. Archangel Michael didn't disappoint, bearing his shield and driving what appeared to be a lance, through the throat of a Demon. Morgen happily pictured himself impaling a demonic beast on the Rowen lance he had received from Granda.

Lila was less impressed, this was not the type of Angel she preferred, thinking more of little fat faced cherubs. Sophia too preferred the notion of angels as graceful celestial beings like those pictured in the daily calendar.

Christian went on to tell them that the shrine was not always as decorative, over the years it had been encased and decorated further. But there was news about what was inside the box.

'The documents contained in the original wooden box are thought to be among the oldest versions of the sacred word of the holy gospels that exist.' He told them.

'Precious cargo.' commended Dad.

'But listen to this.' said Christian, 'The crystal conceals a small compartment which once contained a priceless treasure.' He looked back at the Silver Shrine to observed the square crystal prominemtly placed The crystal was quite small, therefore the compartment beneath it must have been similarly so.

In that small place? he wondered, *What kind of a priceless treasure could fit in there?* He had his finger on the next sentence.

'The treasure which it contained was a relic of the most precious kind......' He read what it was before he announced it. He understood now that it this priceless treasure was not silver or gold, not even an important document, it was much more priceless than any of these. So much so, he could hardly believe it. He looked up again in wonder at the little crystal stone that had concealed the priceless and *precious* treasure. He was so disappointed that it was no longer there but still impressed that it once was right here in this shrine.

'Well, what is it?' Taymi almost barked at him, snapping him to.

'It was a relic.' He said.

'That's no big deal.' scowled Taymi, 'we've seen relics before.'

'Not like this.' Said Christian, 'This wasn't just any relic, it was *the* relic.' Taymi just looked, trying to figure him out.

'It was a fragment...an actual little piece.... of the True Cross.' He told them. The importance of this relic began to slowly dawn on Taymi.

'Incredible' gasped Dad, 'A piece of the One True Cross!' and he leaned in closer to look at the little compartment as though the fragment was still there and he could see it.

'Is that the Cross that Jesus was.....you know.' Mols didn't want to spell it out.

'Yes.' confirmed Mom, 'The cross of Jesus' crucifixion.'

Christian couldn't believe that there had been a piece of the cross of Jesus here in this shrine. No wonder the shrine was considered so precious, no wonder Tiernach was holding it so tightly in the depiction in the golden icon; No wonder Patrick held it in his arm in his stained glass portrait; No wonder it had been recased and decorated with precious metals and jewelry; No wonder Patrick had given it to his right hand man, his security, his strong man. And what a gift to have given. But the obvious question stood out. What had happened to this oh so precious relic? Where was it now? Had Macartan lost it on his watch? Had he misplaced it or was it stolen?

Christian recalled images of the crucifixion, the bronze version in the Cathedral, Calvary in the graveyard, the ultimate sacrifice. He remembered the small crucifix that he kept in his own pocket. A piece of the actual cross had been handed to Macartan about 500 years after the crucifixion, but now, 1500 years later, it was missing presumed lost.

'The wood of the One True Cross is said to posess special powers.' Said Mom, breaking into Christians thoughts.

'Powers? Said Morgen, 'What kind of powers?'

'Healing powers mostly.' said Mom tousling Morgen's hair and noticing that he might have been anticipating other more incredible powers. 'And probably the power to destroy demons.' She added.

'Actually,' said Dad, 'the wood of the One True Cross is said to have come from the Garden of Eden.'

'We were just talking about the Garden of Eden.' Said Christian harking back to the story of Patrick, snakes, Adam and Eve.

'This story also involves the Archangel Michael.' Dad said. 'The story was kept alive over the centuries in a book called the Golden Legend. It told how the Wood of the True Cross came from a seed from the Tree of Life. When Adam was dying, he sent a message to Archangel Michael asking for a seed from the tree. The seed was placed in Adams mouth as he died. As Adam was buried, so was the seed and in time a tree grew from his mouth.'

'Another tree of life?' asked Morgen.

'Quiet you.' Said Dad, 'Patience is one of the seven virtues you know.' He glanced at Mom recognising that he had used one of the sevens references that *she* had come up with. He went on.

'Centuries later the tree was cut down by the Queen of Sheba and used to build a bridge to help her on her journey to see King Solomon. But when she saw the bridge she realised its significance and kneeled down to pray. She told Solomon about the bridge but he feared it and had it buried.'

'But how did…' began Morgen.

'Zip.' Said Dad. 'The wood was unearthed many centuries later and became used to build the cross of the crucifixion.'

Taymi was amazed at this link between old testament and new, BC and AD.

'After the crucifixion,' said Dad, 'it was buried for another 300 years before being somehow found again.'

'But,' said Morgen, 'where do apes becoming men fit into all this?'

Dad sighed a longer than usual sigh. 'We'll talk about that later.' he said.

'Where could this piece of the True Cross have gone to?' Christian asked.

'Perhaps stolen, perhaps lost.' Said Dad, 'People back then seemed to lose a lot of things. But I don't know how you would find a small wooden fragment if it were lost. It would be like trying to find your school tie in your room.' He was teasing Christian's serial untidiness.

'Maybe it was hidden somewhere else.' Suggested Taymi.

'What Christian's tie?'

'No. The *wood* fragment. Maybe it is hidden with some other treasure or artefacts.' She said, hoping that Christian would latch on to her meaning.

'Its possible.' said Dad returning to inspect the Silver Shrine more closely.

'Do you think it could be hidden with the Golden Stone?' Christian murmured to Taymi.

'Well we know for sure that Macartan had the Silver Shrine once and there was a wood fragment in it once. We think Macartan hid the Golden Stone in our Woods, so who knows, maybe he buried the wood with the stone for safekeeping.'

Christian had to admit there was a certain logic to it, after all it appeared that most precious items of those times had fallen in to wrong hands or had been dug up centuries later. But then again why would you bury a holy icon and an unholy one in the same place? Their investigation seemed to get deeper and deeper he thought. Was there anything in the register to suggest that there might be a fragment of the True Cross in the hiding place? He realised that they were referring here to the Greatest Story ever told, linked back to the beginning of mankind, not withstanding the apes of course. The enormity of the scale of connections swamped him. Where was this trail taking them and why? There were so many questions, questions he could not answer.

'Do you want to come and get a sandwich?' Dad asked him.

'Yes! For sure.' This was one question he could answer!

XVIII

UNIVERSITAS

(University)

Having broken for food they reconvened for some more archaeological studies; but where to start? Morgen wanted to see the Ancient Egyptian show and Taymi wanted to see the Sacrifice exhibition. After a quick negotiation it was decided that Morgen would be placated first, given that he had the least patience although that too was negotiatable.

Morgen was fascinated, as were all, with the remnants of foregone Egypt, especially a sarcophagus which housed an actual corpse; a mummy. He discovered how jars containing the dried body organs of the mummy, were placed in the tomb and a Book of the Dead containing scrolls was also buried there. These scrolls contained spells which the dead person may need in the afterlife.

There were texts inscripted on the sides of an ancient sarcophagus too; recently experts had finally deciphered some of these messages from Egyptian tombs as far back as centuries 25 to 30 BC. They were discovered to be spells to ward off snakes in the afterlife. After centuries of deciphering the complex texts, they were eventually translated to into a startlingly simple set of words; *Keep away from my House.* Morgen read how a mummy was wrapped in linen and for protection had an Amulet placed on its chest.

'What is an Amulet?' he asked Taymi.

'It's a medal or some kind of a symbol, it can protect you from evil, you wear it like a medallion or it can be a tattoo too.' She told him.

'A tattoo too?'

'Don't even go there!'

Morgen learned how bodily organs were extracted from the mummy at burial time.

'Guess how they get his brain out?' he challenged Sophia.

'Brain surgery I expect?'

'No need for that, they pick it out through his nose with a long hook!' He grinned at this, taking great delight in seeing her look of utter disgust.

Taymi's interest in the Sacrifice Exhibition revolved around the word Sacrifice, the same word which had appeared in the Gatekeepers verse. She was interested to see what this exhibition had to say about it. but she hadn't thought about it enough to deduce that the sacrifice referred to here was that of *Human Sacrifice*.

Now she had read the display poster in more detail and wasn't so sure if she wanted to see it after all. This was getting a little deep and it was described as graphic. Nonetheless she did eventually decide to proceed into the room, albeit with some trepidation.

The Sacrifice Exhibition continued along the similar themes of disembowelment and body preservation to that of the Ancient Egyptian section. The most gruesome part of the display were some mummified bodies which had been found in ancient bogs and had been preserved over the ages by ground conditions which kept them intact. The bog bodies were the central focus of the macabre exhibition which also included a selection of medieval accoutrements. Apart from Mom and Lila who politely declined, the others meandered along a short spiral corridor which surrounded a secluded circular enclosure. There in a glass case were the leathery remains of the body of a man, wasted away, his arm crucked perhaps to protect himself. To Taymi, it was grotesque. To Morgen, it was awesome.

Taymi examined the leathery hand, her face disclosing her disgust. Sophia and Mols spent just a minute looking around, then decided it really was too gory for them and left to find Mom and Lila. Taymi, Dad, Christian and Morgen stayed put to see what they might glean from this ancient gentleman who once lived, who once breathed and once died.

Dad seemed quite at home in the company of the decayed cadavers, the ancient men whose corpses were mutilated and killed probably at the crowning of a new King. The mutilation was quite obvious, one of the bodies was minus a head. The bodies were discovered at the edges of the Kingdom, a ritualistic marking of ownership. 'What a way to mark your turf.' Dad said before reading aloud, 'The sacrifice of a human would have been suggested by the Druid as the most extreme Pagan tradition used at special festival ceremonies…Way to celebrate dude! Or should I say drude!'

A Druid. Taymi thought, *A Druid was behind the sacrifice of these bodies.* She thought of the words from the diary, *Now I fear my sacrifice.* Perhaps the Gatekeeper knew the Druid was capable of Human Sacrifice, was this the sacrifice he had meant? What had become of him? Had he become the Human Sacrifice? Her ruminations were interrupted by Dad.

'Poor soul….wrong place, wrong time, wrong era, wrong everything.' Dad said. The others looked on too at the poor unfortunate who had met his death most likely at the hands of a Druid. What had been his last minutes, how had he ended up as a sacrifice and what were his last thoughts as he fought through the agony of dying and death. They looked upon him closely, his body preserved and tanned by the cold acidic bog water. But the acid that preserved his skin had eroded his bones, leaving his remains sunken, flattened, like a heap of dirty old clothes laid out in the shape of a man. An inhuman end to a life.

They moved on, out of the enclosure but into the next one. Another bog body, another sacrifice, another man wasted and twisted into a sunken pile. A life lived, a life lost. This one was even more gruesome, the lower half of the body was totally severed. This body may have actually been a King, perhaps sacrificed to a pagan Godess. He was killed by an axe to the head and then cut in two. Seems they had to kill him in *several* ways to satisfy the Godess; Why? Because she herself took several different forms. It was all very strange.

Taymi thought how this King had been slain probably at the behest of the Druid, his own right hand man. It was a betrayal of the worst kind, not the kind of loyalty here that Macartan had shown Patrick. She turned away from the disembodied and disembowelled torso.

'Do you think,' She murmured to Christian, 'the Gatekeeper became a human sacrifice? He mentioned it in the verse?' He looked at her, unable to answer, he had been thinking about the same thing. The Gatekeeper had disappeared, and had left a note, and now Christian was convinced that the figure who had appeared to him was the Gatekeeper in spirit. But he hadn't considered that the Gatekeeper could have suffered such a gruesome death, a ritual killing, a murder! Morgen for once was unusually subdued, troubled thinking of how these two had met such a bitter and unfair end.

'I think it might be time to go?' said Dad, noting the downturn in atmosphere; and they felt it was time to leave not just this exhibition, but the entire building, time to leave the ancient and the dead behind.

◆◆◆◆◆

Stepping back onto the busy sidewalk was a breath of fresh air despite plumes of bus fumes that initially greeted them. While the atmosphere in the museum was clean, it was the feeling of time and decay that had made them feel quite stifled and they were glad to feel the cool breeze cross their faces like the breath of life itself. They whittled their way through a myriad of side streets to Mom's favourite emporium, Joe's Coffee House; a tiny cafe but with the best coffee in the kingdom, according to her. Everyone refuelled with something refreshing; hot chocolate, cappuccinos, pastries and ice cream. Outside were street noises, pushing, shoving, movement, traffic; inside was sanctuary. Dad was deep in thought and deep in pastry, Taymi could tell he was working something through in his mind.

'Would anyone like to see one more ancient treasure?' Dad proffered as they hit the footpath once again.

'Depends what is it?' Taymi answered.

'Oh nothing much,' he deadpanned, '...just the greatest treasure ever discovered in the history of the state and one of the greatest in Europe.'

'You mean greater than the Silver Shrine?' asked Morgen.

'Yes. And more widely known.' Said Dad as they rounded the corner onto the grandeur of tree lined Dame Street.

'It must be a pile of gold then.' Said Morgen assuming it must out-trump the silver bullion they saw earlier.

'Nope,' said Dad. 'Not like that at all, in actual fact it's a book.'

'A book is the greatest treasure?'

'Yep, ever hear of the famous Book of Kells.'

Except for Lila, they were all familiar with this great book, an ornately decorated and treasured manuscript hundreds of years old. It contained extravagant illustrations and ornamentations of Christian scriptures. It was included in school curriculums at all levels. It fit right within the type of research they were doing. They all agreed that it would be worth a visit.

'So where is it? Asked Morgen. 'I don't think my feet can make it.'

'Don't worry old boy,' smiled Dad, 'its right there!' He stopped and pointed directly ahead of them. The remainder of the street split in two directions around an imposing stately building, a full stop for the street. It had a most impressive façade with a strong wrought iron railing surround and it was teeming with hundreds of *students*.

'It's kept here,' said Dad, 'in one of the worlds most renowned universities...' he paused for effect the way one would when revealing a special guest or the winner of the best actor oscar, and then he announced it, and it was a name they were already familiar with in other ways,

'....Trinity!'

Trinity College University was over 400 years old, one of the seven most ancient universities in the world, the name reminded Christian of Macartans Trinity, the reference in the Gatkeepers verse, the number reminded Taymi of the importance of the number seven. The college library contained over four and a half million printed volumes and many precious manuscripts. They battled through the hordes of students, pedestrians and tourists, past the iron rails and through a set of pinned back heavy wood doors. The sound of traffic and pedestrians melted away behind them in the cool of the great entrance and they walked on through to be greeted by an expansive courtyard and lawns that formed the main square. There was a buzz of energy, youth, learning and excitement in the college air. They negotiated their way to the library building, secured tickets, looked at the preambles and eventually entered into the darkened room where the Book of Kells, the great scholarly treasure, was displayed.

'Master Tom told me my homework copy reminded him of the Book of Kells,' Dad whispered as they approached.

'Must have been very precise and neat.' Said Christian.

'Er, no, it was because of all the little scribbles around the edges.' Dad admitted.

The book was laid out in a glass viewing case in the centre of the room and was surrounded by a cluster of visitors. There were individual pages from the book in other displays and magnified extracts of pages showing detail and decorations which would have been extremely difficult to see with the naked eye. They each squeezed in to get a close look at a page of the book and were truly astonished at the level of intricate detail that informed its pages. Morgen examined one magnified page which had been scaled up to poster size. The detail was amazingly intricate, even at this scale. How they did it in real size he couldn't imagine. A little typed note told him more about the extract;

This page is one of the most famous from the Book of Kells containing such depictions as cats feeding kittens, butterflies and Angels. It is known as the Chi Rho page.

Morgen studied the magnified page and was able to identify the tiny detail of the cats, kittens, butterflies and Angels referred to. He thought how the monk who painted this must have had the tinyiest paintbrush imaginable. He realised that all of these details were contained in one big symbol the size of the entire page. The symbol was the Chi Rho itself which looked like an 'X' and a 'P' put together; ☧.

Morgen read that this was a very powerful Christian symbol and his eyes widened in amazement.

'Christian, come here!' He flagged to his brother frantically and Christian made his way over.

'Read this.' Morgen pointed to the bottom of the note.

The words Chi Rho combined can be translated into the single word 'Chreston', which means 'Good'.

'That's your name, Christian – its *Chreston.*' Said Morgen. 'It means Good.'

Christian nodded, marvelling at the connection.

'It means Good.' said Morgen ambling away, '...not Great!'

Christian saw that there was a further note. *Though not technically a cross the Chi Rho signifies the crucifixion.*

'Sacrifice.' Murmured Christian, 'The ultimate sacrifice.'

Across the room Mols was examining another magnified page. She was attracted to it because it had four images that she recognised, a man, a lion, a bull and the bird that she reckoned resembled the Buzzard. She had seen these before; they were the same images as those on the carved statue of Macartan.

She read the inscription, it informed her that the actual four were a Man and a Lion joined by an *Ox* and an *Eagle*. They represented the evangelists Matthew, Mark, Luke and John, the writers of the Christian Gospels which in turn made up the Book of Kells.

She looked carefully at the Eagle and was sure it was more like the Buzzard, perhaps it was a relative, and she thought of the Buzzard which circled endlessly over her house. Sometimes it just stayed in one place, suspended high in the air, flickering on the updraft like a guttering candle. The bird represented John. The Book of Kells contained the writings of these four Saints, but there was a noticable exclusion, the latter parts of the writings of John had been stolen and were missing. They were taken together with the books precious bejewelled cover. But it wasn't a recent crime; it had happened over a thousand years ago.

Why the Bird? Why John? She thought and at the same time she determined to try and find out.

They discovered that at the time the Book of Kells was created, Ireland was known as the land of saints and scholars leading the rest of Europe in writing and fine art. Indeed Taymi had noticed signs indicating another precious manuscript being kept in the hallowed Trinity library, it was called The Book of Armagh and included a section called *Liber Angueli - The Book of Angels.*

'Can we have a look at it?' She asked and they made their way to go see.

This book was rather more low key, compared to the ornate pomp and ceremony of the Book of Kells. It was monocolour with little decoration but hailed from the 9th century with texts telling the story of Patrick. Taymi picked up a rather interesting snippet from it.

'Says here that Patrick was given the rights to rule by an Angel.'

'So that means a Saint can talk directly to an Angel?' said Morgen.

'Well if anyone's going to, it would probably be a Saint.' Said Dad.

'Can I talk to an Angel?' asked Lila.

'Of course you can.' answered Dad. 'And you can talk to a Devil.'

'Can we go now?' asked Lila.

'Yes,' said Dad, 'I think its time.'

The journey home took a couple of hours. As the large car sped along the smooth highway, Lila slept, while the others looked out the windows, reflections of their own faces and of the day they had.

'We're almost home.' Dad called out eventually. He always said this at exactly the same point in the journey, when the recognisable square spire of Clonragget Church came into view. Sophia looked out at the familiar spire; nearby was the historic site of a great battle where a famous celtic general O'Neill had defeated the invading army. The green pastures she looked out on once ran red with the blood of young men throwing themselves into battle. *They threw their lives away.* She thought. *Sacrificed, for nothing.*

She turned and looked at the road ahead, two miles from home and the highway descended gradually all the way down towards the Woods, their Woods, which loomed in the distance.

'Why are there such dark clouds over the Woods?' she asked aloud.

'It's a sign,' said Dad 'The Woods sit in a depression, a dip in the landscape, and they create their own micro-climate. So you will often see clouds hanging over them when there are fewer clouds elsewhere.'

He looked in the mirror and observed Sophia's pensive expression.

'But whats it a sign off?' she asked.

'There's going to be a turn in the weather.' He predicted.

And he was right.

XIX

LIBER

(Books)

BY NEXT DAY rain had fallen just as Dad had suggested, but the weather was still warm. The Westwooders were spending the afternoon in the local town library, a place they frequented regularly and where they felt as much at home as home itself.

Christian was tracking the Golden Stone, wanting to learn more about its supposed wealth and power. Eventually he found something about it in a diocesean history book and called to Taymi to tell her what he had found. He thought she would be very interested indeed.

'It was a sacred ceremonial stone to the *Druids*.' He told her, not too loudly so as not to earn a shush. Taymi balked at the word Druid, she already had two books in her hands about Druids which she was just about to delve into.

'Macartan converted the owner of the stone, a King, to Chrisitanity and the King in return gave the sacred stone to the Saint.... We already knew that bit.' he confirmed. 'Later when Macartan died he was succeeded as Bishop by the Kings Grandson. The stone minus its gold is still preserved near where the Saint is buried at Clogher village and it is still possible to see the joints which housed the gold.'

'So Macartan is buried at Clogher, near his Cathedral …and near the original stone.' Said Taymi.

Christian nodded, his head still stuck in the book reading to himself about the stone which was also known by the ancient name

Cermand Cestach or in German as *Kermand Kelstach. That's strange,* he thought, *that it had a German name. Anyway,..* 'The stone was worshipped as an Oracle and spoke with voice of the Devil.' He read.

'The voice of the Devil.' He repeated in a whisper, he was beginning to not like this stone at all knowing that the Devil was the greatest evil that ever existed. 1. 'Is that what the stones power is?..... the voice of a Devil? And what exactly is an Oracle?' Christian looked up at his sister.

'I know what an Oracle is;' she said, 'A prediction of the future. It can come from a person...or even a Devil like you say, or from an object, like a stone. In this case,' she continued, 'it seems to be from both, a Devil and a stone!'

'Right,' he said with his head back in the book, 'The Oracle voice didn't come out of the stone but *through* the Druid.'

'Typical.' interrupted Taymi; she really was not a fan of Druids and their dark ways.

'The Golden Stone was modelled on the Oracle of Delphi... the greatest Oracle in the World; its in Greece.' Christian completed the passage. 'We need,' he said as he closed and set down the book, 'to can go and see it.'

'Greece?'

'No, the Golden Stone, Dimwit.' He had already decided that he would be following the trail to Clogher and now he was even more certain that he needed to come face to face with the original devilstone.

'Yes, we should do that.' Agreed Taymi.

'But I'm convinced that the gold from the stone is buried in the Woods, thats where the wealth and power is.' Christian said.

'I believe in the Golden Stone,' replied Taymi, 'and you may be right about the gold being in the Woods, but I really don't believe in the voice of the Devil....that's just too far fetched for me.' Taymi flicked open one of her own books that she held and picked through the chapter on Druids, reading the salient sections.

'Druids were big in Gaul and Celtic culture but were crushed by Christianity. They were priests, teachers, judges and poets but had many beliefs including the power of human sacrifice.

'See, I told you,' she ranted at Christian, 'Druids are evil.'

She read that they had other strange beliefs; that souls can migrate from body to body, human to animal, whether dead or alive (*Metempsychosis*) and that souls and spirits can exist not only in human and animals but also in nature, a river, thunder or even a rock! (*Animism*).

'Or perhaps a Stone.' Taymi added, thinking of the Devil inhabiting the Gold of the Stone. She turned back to her chapter;

'Druidic practices are kept alive by Neo-Druidism.....What? There are modern Druids.' She was aghast. She had known there were neo-pagans but thought that Druids had been well and truly got shot of. Now she was finding out that there were new ones around. Taymi pressed on with her research reading that Druids believed that their soul passes along from one body to another after they die and that they often gave advice with Yew wands inscribed with *Ogham*!)

'I knew it! I knew it!' Taymi almost leapt up from her seat squealing. 'I *told* you the Ogham was the Druids curse. This is the proof.' She flapped her book at him.

'Yea, but settle down,' he implored, 'you're drawing attention to us.' He nodded towards the librarian who was indeed raising an eyebrow in protest.

'Sorry!' mouthed Taymi apologetically.

Taymi became engrossed again in the chapter on Druids. 'To prevent the progress of Christianity the Druids raised clouds and mists called a *Magic Fog* or a *Fe-Flada* that could make a person or a place invisible. They did this by casting spells or incantations.'

'Something like this could have been used to conceal the location of the Gold.' she pondered.

'But Macartan hid that.' Christian pointed out and she realised he was right. Taymi continued,

'Many thought that Fairy Palaces, or *Shee's*, had a Fe-Flada around them to disguise it from the view of mortals!......*The Fairy Fort!*' She almost shouted.

'Shhhhh' came the response from several directions.

'Sorry!' whispered Taymi sheepishly. 'The *Fort*, the location of the Stone…if it was concealed by a Magic Fog, then mortals like us wouldn't be able to find it.

'You could find it,' considered Christian, 'By just looking for the Fog!' But he was just being flippant and Taymi returned to the book ignoring him.

'Druids drew auguries or predictions from the clouds, dreams and from bird voices.' She read.

Christians thought of how he had predicted, or *drawn auguries*, from various cloud formations. His interpretations he now recalled, all seemed to infer some sort of impending catastrophe. He thought too of the voices of the birds in the Woods, the multitude of squeaks, chirrups and hoots. He thought also about the shadow visitor, a vision, or a reality as he believed, or was it a dream to be interpreted?

Taymi was ploughing on; 'Ceasar said the Druids were the guardians *The God of the Underworld* or *Hades*.' She looked up at Christian. 'AKA, The Devil' but he already knew that.

'Druids carried out their incantations in caves and woods,' she paused at the mention of woods, but kept reading, 'Certain wood groves are sacred to Druids. Listen to this.' She exclaimed. 'Many historic figures were thought to be Druids such as *Winston Churchill….* thats bizarre.' She recalled Churchill's connection to Sir. Jack and his baptism gown in Castle Leslie.

'How could he have been baptised and then become a Druid?' she said, but did not really expect Christian to have an answer to this so she carried on relentlessly.

'A Druid could use a *Mantle*, an animal hide which he wore allowing him to take the characteristics and shape and instincts of the animal.' She had reached the end of the passage and vigorously panned through further pages, there was nothing further regarding Druids. She turned to Christian.

'I don't know whether to believe all this or not.' She sighed. 'It seems like it could be true, but it seems unreal. Maybe we are trying to read too much into it…theres a word for doing that.'

'I believe it.' Said Christian. 'I believe there is a Fort and that theres a Gold hidden there…..and I believe we will find it.'

Taymi looked around, everyone else seemed to be going about their everyday business without a care and yet here they were facing down a trail of supernatural forces and ancient artefacts. Christian noticed.

'We'll just put together all our findings and see where it takes us.' Christian reassured her.

Meanwhile Sophia and Mols were undertaking their own project research. Sophia was keen to pursue more on Fairy Forts but was becoming increasingly interested in Fairies themselves. She and Mols had searched out some authoritative books on the subject and were trading passages.

'In ancient times they were regarded as Gods and Goddesses who had come from the sky.' Quoted Sophia. 'and they lived in a fairy mound called a *Sidhe* or a *Shee*. Fairies were often worshipped as Gods but their power dwindled with the coming of Christianity when they came to be considered evil.'

'I always thought of Fairies as good not evil.' Said Mols

'Me too.' Said Sophia before continuing; '….They were often considered Animistic and were thought to have been related to the stars at night.'

'What does that word mean?' Mols asked.

'I don't know, we would need a dictionary.' sighed Sophia. 'But listen; Sometimes if a family noticed that a child had a change in habit but no change in appearance it was considered a *Changeling*, which was a child swapped by the Fairies for the human child. The stolen human child was often used by the Fairies as a tithe to hell instead of their own Fairy child……I'm not too sure what a tithe is but it sounds like Fairies really are more evil than good.' Sophia summed up.

'I've found something interesting here.' said Mols with her finger on a passage in her own book.

'Fairies are sometimes considered as Fallen Angels.' she read. 'When there was a revolt in heaven, God closed the gates and those on the inside remained Angels, those in hell became Demons and those in between became Fallen Angels.'

'Maybe we should be researching Angels.' Said Sophia and Mols nodded as she continued.

'Because Fairies were Fallen Angels, they became known as subjects of the Devil and obliged to pay a tithe to hell, usually paid by the Fairy Queen every seventh year!...that's what a tithe is, a payment, and that's why the had to pay it!' Mols voice grew louder with her excitement of discovery.

'Shhhh'

'Ooopps' Mols was ashen faced.

Lila arrived beside the girls. 'I've got a loose tooth.' She said.

'You've just lost one.' Said Sophia examining Lila's mouth and sure enough another one was about to fall out. 'But don't worry, when the Tooth Fairy comes, you will be rich!' This earned a toothy grin.

Morgen was wandering around the library uncertain what book to choose, so he decided to ask Dad. Bad idea.

'I'll name a book for you but I dare you to ask for it.' said his Father. 'Its *Hawking – A Brief History of Time.*' he instructed, 'But I warn you it's a really complex book all about how the universe was created, black holes, the lot. Stephen Hawking is an award winning physicist.'

'I know who he is,' said Morgen, 'I saw him on the Simpsons.'

Morgen walked over to the desk to request the Hawking book. The librarian was ever so obliging and somewhat taken aback at the reading material of a young boy who must certainly be a child genius.

A small book with a colourful cover had caught Lila's attention. It was a book about St.Patrick and she brought it to Christian knowing he had been researching the Saint. Christian flicked through the book which had a series of quotations transcribed from the Patricks own written diaries. The book was so small however, only one quote fitted on each page.

'Thanks Lila, this is very interesting.' He said and flapped through several more pages as she skipped away. Suddenly he stopped. One particular quotation caught his eye. He read it again, then folded the corner of the page back to reference it. What a conincidence that Lila had brought this little book to his attention.

Mols and Sophia were taking turns reading snippets to each other about angels.

'Earth bound angels are sent by God to protect humans.' Read Sophia. 'That would make them different to Fallen Angels then.' She concluded before Mols took her turn.

'Angels are messengers which have been sent to do a task. Most of them are given a human shape and may have been former humans or Saints. In scriptures angels stood in the way of evil and danger.'

Sophia found something on Guardian Angels.

'Many people believe that they are guided by a Guardian Angel and protected from harm. A white feather is a symbol that your Guardian Angel is protecting you. It says here that angels are spiritual beings who battle other spiritual beings on behalf of humans.'

'Some people can actually see and talk to Angels.' Said Mols, 'If you ask, an Angel will help and guide you.'

'I prefer angels to Fairies.' said Sophia, 'You could never trust a Fairy.'

Mom was ushering them to wrap up their reading and check through books they wanted to take home. Taymi and Christian took further reading on Pagans, Druids, and history. Sophia and Mols took a selection on Angels and Animals. Morgen borrowed *A Brief History of Time by Stephen Hawking* the masterpiece from the award winning theoretical physicist.

Lila had just borrowed a book about the Tooth Fairy when it happened. 'My tooth just fell out!' She smiled a toothless smile.

Christian never heard her little piece of news, there was something on his mind, it was a quotation in the little book of Patrick that Lila had given him and he recanted it in his mind.

The Mist will be dispersed by the Wind, as will the Demons perish with the coming of Good.

He thought of how it might have meant that if there was a Magic Fog, it will be dispersed with the coming of Good…. Good as in the name Chreston….. AKA himself.

XX

QUAERO

(Search)

'SOMETHING FOR YOU.' Said Dad to Christian giving him a large new envelope.

'…and something for you.' He said to Taymi giving her a large slightly crumpled envelope. Dad had been in town all morning on business and had just returned home. Both Christian and Taymi were surprised as they hadn't been expecting anything.

Christian opened his envelope first, there were two documents in it; Maps! He looked at the first one closely and recognised the shape of the Woods. The second map was a scaled up version of the same area.

'Thanks!' he said, glad that he could now begin his experimental deduction of the Fort location. 'Hey, I can see our house!' He exclaimed as he scrutinised the enlarged map.

Taymi opened the envelope she had received. It was a selection of well worn prints and copies from old documents and newspapers.

'It's all about the Castle.' Said Dad. As she flicked through it she noticed newspaper dates from over 90 years ago and information about the family who had lived in the Castle back then.

'Where did you get all this?' Taymi enquired.

'I have my sources.' Said Dad elusively.

'Lila got some money from the Tooth Fairy.' Mom told them.

'See what I got.' Lila showed Dad a selection of coins that the Fairy had left her.

'Silver and Gold.' Said Dad.

Lila had developed a hoarse throat overnight and with two teeth missing she had also acquired a lisp. Her voice was raspy and lispy.

'It's not Lila.' Said Mols, 'It's a changeling. The Fairies came last night and exchanged Lila for this other child and left some money. Her voice is not the same and she looks different.'

Lila was insulted, she bared her teeth at Mols with the gap showing.

'See!' Said Mols.

Christian went to the project room to begin his mapping work. He taped the map to his drawing board and then overlaid it with tracing paper and overdrew the shape of the Woods and key markers. He studied the map closely to locate Rockwell Ancient Cemetery and the Mass Rock. He found the Cemetery, a small square field and he marked its position.

The Mass Rock was not so easily identifiable. Christian followed the trace of river and valley locating the field where the rock was located. He marked its position using his best judgement. He drew a line joining the two sacred sites and then extended it by exactly the same amount creating a third point.

He had identified a position in the North section of the Woods, close to woodland edge. It was an area that they hadn't spent much time in because it wasn't as spectacular as other parts of the Woods and was quite close to the extremity. He felt confident that this was the place.

'I name this point *Northwood*.' He quietly declared drawing an X at the chosen location. He detached his tracing, folded it up and set about planning an expedition.

Christian assembled his troops in the early afternoon and briefed them on his mapping exercise.

'I intend to lead you to the place where I think the Fort is located.'
He told them in clipped military tone and they eagerly assembled
some exploratory tools and trooped off in high spirits.

They headed through the West Wood Gate and into the trees
towards Northwood. There was no immediate sign of a Fort although
the ground was uneven with mounds and depressions but with no
obviously defined arrangement.

'Lets just look around here and see if you can turn up something.'
Christian directed.

They explored the ground closely, poking and digging in several
locations, although the clay was stubborn and there was no hard
evidence of anything historic or remotely fortlike. Taymi was more
inclined towards taking photo images. Christian was sweating from
having dug aggressively; when he looked around he observed Taymi
paying great attention in photographing a bluebell. Lila was watching
her. Sophia and Mols were poking amongst branches lackadaisically.

'Oh that's just great, I'm killing myself here and you are just
flouncing around doing nothing.' He accused Taymi.

'I'm photographing.' She said non-plussed. Her flippant answer
irritated Christian and when she raised the camera and shot him, he
blew a fuse chasing after her with a branch.

By now everyone was fed up, they had been searching for over
two hours and there were no indications of anything that resembled
a Fort or anything even interesting. Most fed up was Christian who
felt that this was almost certainly *not* the location he had hoped for
and was wondering if the Fort may ever be found, or if there even was
a Fort despite all the hints and clues and rumours. Perhaps people
had meant that the Castle was the Fort. Perhaps it was all a mistake,
they were barking up the wrong tree; it was all in his imagination.
He felt deflated and suggested that they all go home. They were glad
to follow this instruction so they packed up and moved out.

It was quite a bit later when Taymi reviewed her photos; she felt
that she had taken a nice selection of compositions and studied them
closely. Perhaps a career in photography would be an option. She

stopped at the last one, it was the photo she had taken of Christian which had set him off. It was a slightly blurred image, but behind Christian she could see something else, among the leaves, among the branches, was it ....a person?

Lila was nearby, so she asked her. 'Can you see something there ...in the background?'

'Yes,' said Lila, 'It's Mom.'

Taymi had been a bit freaked out when Lila said she recognised Mom in the photo. It couldn't possibly have been Mom, who was nowhere near at the time. It was a trick of the light she told herself, a blur, Lila wouldn't have noticed anything unless Taymi had pointed it out. Looking at it afterwards there was nothing to see at all, it was like making shapes out of clouds, the use of a good imagination.

Now Taymi had diverted her attention to examining the contents of the envelope she had received from Dad. As she flicked through the pages of information, her attention was drawn to a small section on the history of Castle-Hanes. She burst into the other room startling the rest of the family.

'Guess what.' She squeaked clutching a page.

'What.' Said Christian.

'Castle-Hanes doesn't mean Hanes Castle as we thought, it means something more interesting.' She piped.

'Go on.' Said Dad suddenly interested.

'It says here that the old Irish for Castle-Hanes is *Caisléan an tShiáin.*' She advised. 'A Caislean or a Caiseal is a...'

'Fort!' interjected Sophia thinking quickly back to having read this before.

'The total translation means *Fort of the Fairies.*' Said Taymi excitedly, '....so that's evidence that there *is* a Fort and the area of Castle-Hanes is named after it.'

'Excellent work.' Said Mom, 'I knew this project would keep you guys busy.'

You bet! Thought Christian, this new information washing away today's doubts and giving him new heart. *And I predict we're about to get busier!*

'That reminds me.' said Dad, 'I forgot, I should have told you this sooner.' They tuned in to hear what Dad had to say.

'This morning when I was in the mapping office, I found out the translation for the townland of Cordevlis which you had asked me for.'

'Go on.' Said Christian.

'Well my findings are quite interesting really.' He declared. 'The word Cordevlis can be broken into sections, *Cor-a-Dubh-lis*,' Dad explained, '*Cor* means a hill, *Dubh* is the Irish word for black, *Lis* is also a name for a circular earth mound.' He explained. 'Combined they translate to Hill-of the-Black-Fort.'

'More evidence of the Fort.' Said Taymi, 'But why would it be called the Black fort.' She was not entirely sure if she wanted the real answer to her question.

'I'll tell you why.' Dad enticed. 'There is another meaning for Cordevlis…and it's quite obvious really if you think about it. The clue is in the name.' He said the name slowly and broken. 'Cor-Devlis'

Morgen had a sudden moment of enlightenment.

'Does it mean Cor-*Devils*?' he asked. Dad laughed.

'Yes it does Morgen, well done.'

Morgen beamed with delight but Christian felt a slight pang of fear. Dad continued.

'It means the Cor of Devils or the Devils Cor.'

His words sent a chill around the room.

'It turns out we live at the Devils Hill.'

XXI

OPTIMUS

(Aristocrats)

TAYMI RETURNED TO her package of information and was poring through the contents in more detail putting all thoughts of the Devils Hill behind her. She studied the Lucas family tree. The earliest recorded member of the family to live in Castle-Hanes was Francis Lucas whose will was validated on 8th December 1657. She had seen that date before. Taymi was amused with the spelling of words which as they had previously discovered replaced some of the 's' with an 'f'.

He fealed his will with the coat of arms of Lucas, gules, a fefs between fix annulets.

She reckoned this translated to;

> *He sealed his will with the coat of arms of Lucas, gules, a fess between six annulets.*

There was a picture of the coat of arms which had been used to seal the will and which was the family emblem. It was principally a shield with a horizontal band across the middle with three rings above and three rings below it. She examined the Lucas family tree and tried to make sense of it.

The Castle had passed down the line from Francis Lucas to his son, also Francis, to his son Francis again; then to his son, Edward, then Thomas, then his son Edward....*This is very confusing.* She thought.

Then there was his son Charles and his son Edward, then Fitzherbert, then Edward again and then Edward..... *Dammit, couldn't they have thought of Bernard or something.* She moaned.

But it was this Edward who was the last owner of the Castle. He had three children, John born 1902, Geraldine born 1903 and Oriel born 1913...... seven years before the fire.

Taymi looked at the name Oriel, the little girl who was driven out of her home by the fire, the fire that it appeared was intended for her. The little girl that Sir. Jack had played with at Castle Leslie, the last inhabitant of the Castle in the Woods, the House of Oriel. The infant of the seventh age. What was the significance?

She picked up a newspaper article, it was an extract from local paper *The Standard* dated Feb 21 1920. She recognised the local paper since it was still in circulation. *Wow, I didn't know the newspaper was so old.* She thought.

'Castle-Hanes House Destroyed.' She read through mumbling any interesting facts aloud.

'The news reached town......the residence was on fire.......many people came to witness it.....It was first noticed by a servant girl who was awakened by a commotion....'

That's what the verse said, Taymi told herself, *he alerted the house to warn them.*

'The Lady of the house and her young daughter escaped.....That's Oriel,' Taymi felt like she knew the little girl. '...as did the eight maid servants. The men of the estate arrived quickly......'

was the gatekeeper among them? she wondered,

'......but they were unable to contain the flames. They tried to save the valuables and most of the silverware..... many valuable books and paintings were lost...most especially a precious early edition of the *Nuremberg Chronicles*.....'

She thought she had heard of this book before, but did not know what it contained.

'...young John heir to the estate, is presently serving on the battleship *Revenge*....scavengers continued to come for days pursuing the rumour that the Ladys diamonds were lost in the fire....creating a treasure hunt frenzy....'

Looking for diamonds, thought Taymi, *but the real precious treasure seems to have been this book.*

Taymi perused through other pieces of information. There was a picture of the house taken immediately after the fire, most of the walls were still standing then, many had since whittled away like falling soldiers. But there was another picture, a glossy photograph of the Castle at its most brilliant. Beautiful white walls, projecting windows and sweeping landscaped grounds.

She thought of the Castle as a busy place with maidservants and regular comings and goings. The register had revealed dates and names of those who passed the Westwood gate, there were some recognisable surnames such as that of *Leslie*, most likely one of Sir Jack's relatives and in another place the name *Lemass*.

Lemass was a name she had seen in her history book, a noted politician, could this have been the same person? There were numbers opposite his and several other names. She looked at the numbers opposite Lemass, 13 and 27; *what was their significance?* Another name she had seen in the register was a single name, a name she liked, Anastasia. She thought that this might have been a friend of the young girl Oriel, perhaps visiting for the day.

She read how the private Castle grounds were called a Demesne but all the other lands were rented to locals with payment each quarter year; most of this money went to the King and was recorded in his Book of Judgement. *The King of the Woods* thought Taymi.

The newspaper stated that there were 52 rooms in the Castle and that one of those rooms was haunted.

'I don't doubt it.' Taymi told herself with a shiver. The Castle was built in the 1800's on top of an older Castle so when it burned down it had lasted less then 100 years. The article also mentioned the nearby waterfall and the giant tree which can be seen from all around, the King of the Woods.

'On our to-do list.' She reminded herself of their intention to find the great tree that had thus far eluded them. She read the conclusion of the extract;

'Even decades after the burning of the Castle, treasure hunters still pick through the ruins in hope that they might find the supposed lost treasure but to date nothing has ever been found.' *No wonder,* she thought, *they were looking for the wrong treasure, and anyway a book is not likely to survive such a great fire.*

Taymi returned to the picture of the coat of arms of Lucas; *gules, a fess between six annulets.* In some way it was familiar to her but she couldn't quite place it. A description said that annulets were interlinked rings, the mark of Bishops of Royalty. A fess was a simple band across the middle, so what was gules then? Gules, she read in Heraldry meant scarlet or the colour of blood, or even blood itself. The word came from mixing the old French word goules and Latin word gula and meant *Throat;* but strangely it was thought that it was the throat referred to was that of a beast, a carnivous heraldic beast!

Gules is the most honourable heraldic colour, signifying valour, justice, and veneration. She read.

'What is Heraldic exactly?' she checked; *Heraldic; Sign of what will happen / Official Messenger.*

'A sign of what will happen.' She repeated. 'A prophesy?'

Taymi checked the time display in the corner of the screen. It was just gone nine o'clock. She stood up and walked into the other room where Dad was working.

'What time is it?' she asked him. He looked at his watch.

'It's nine o'clock.' He eyes her suspiciously. 'There are clocks all over the house you know.' He said.

'I just meant for you to know how late it is to be working.'

'Thank You? I will be finished in just a moment.' He replied.

Taymi left to go and switch off the computer, Dad had confirmed to her exactly what she thought.

When he had looked at his watch she had got a clear view of the ring on the little finger of his left hand. It was a silver ring but with an image that was now very familiar; a gold band across on which sat three interlinked gold rings…. *a fess and three annulets.*

She had been reminded of something else too; Dad also wore another ring, a Russian wedding ring, three more interlinked rings of white, rose and yellow gold combined as one. She quickly looked it up.

The Russian wedding ring symbolizes strength spirit and love and the Holy Trinity. Traditionally worn on the right hand in accordance with tradition.

Another symbol, another sign. She had noted however that Dad was wearing his on the left hand.

She began putting the pages back into the envelope but stopped when she noticed something. It was a small piece of folded paper at the bottom of the envelope which she hadn't noticed before. She took it out and unfolded it. It was a note in handwritten script which had the appearance of having been written to Dad. She read through it and gasped aloud when she got to the end. Her face paled, this could not be true, or if it was then something else was a lie. It read;

> *This is all the information I have on Castle-Hanes house; I hope it is useful to you.*
>
> *Best of luck with your research.*
>
> *If you have any difficulty with it please don't hesitate to contact me.*
>
> *Yours,*
> *Master Tom.*

Dad had said that Master Tom had passed away, hadn't he? Now here was a note to Dad from the Master, telling him to contact him. Why would Dad have said that? There a number of things building that she wanted to straighten out with Dad and she was beginning to become a little concerned as to where they might lead.

XXII

ADVOCO

(Advisor)

THE LARGE FIELD behind Westwoods had been mown of its crop and looked freshly clean shaven. It provided an immediate attraction for all kinds of animal opportunists by exposing the little field creatures who had previously hidden in the long grass.

For Mols it was like a blank canvas onto which all the beautiful woodland animals would stray; an amazing opportunity to see them up close. Several pheasants wandered elegantly around inspecting the terrain. The Buzzards swept across the field repeatedly and on several occasions landed and walked, actually *walked* around the plain having a peck at whatever took their fancy. *Two* Foxes arrived, and spent an afternoon mooching around the field.

'Hello Fox,' said Mols, 'I see you have found a mate.' She was delighted to see that he had company. Varieties of birds flew down, often straying very close to the Foxes, on one occasion she saw a raven playing a game of catch-me-if-you-can with the Fox.

'Cheeky rascal.' Mols said. 'You better beware Raven; Fox might look mild, but he is the most devious and the most cunning of them all.'

Mols didn't like the Raven, she thought that it was ugly and dirty and often saw it feast on road kill or foraging in bins. It often flew in flocks which she thought were morbid and she didn't like the variety of noises they made which sounded like they were chattering.

She knew too that *they* didn't like her friend the Buzzard. She had witnessed a bunch of Ravens attacking the Buzzard and chasing it away. Although the Buzzard was bigger by far, the flock of Ravens were too strong for it. But she had also seen a *single* Raven attacking the Buzzard. It had flown above the Buzzard and dive bombed from above pecking the Buzzard on the back of his head repeatedly. The Buzzard was so large; it couldn't manoeuvre as swiftly and by keeping above, the Raven kept himself safe.

'What has the Raven got against the Buzzard?' Mols asked Dad about it.

'I really don't know enough about wildlife Mols, but I know someone who everything.' Said Dad. He told Mols about Mr. Kelly, a retired wildlife ranger he knew who had an immense knowledge of animals and apparently kept quite a collection of them. He lived close to Clonraggett.

'We can go see him if you want; and ask any questions you have of a true expert. I know Dan a long time and he will be only too glad to see us.' he promised.

'What type of animals does he keep?' She asked.

Dad blew out a strained breath. 'Some you will like,' he said, 'but others.....may not be to your liking at all.'

Mols pressed Dad insistently on what exactly he meant by this but he wouldn't go into any more detail.

'Lets just go see.' Was all he would say.

The idea of visiting a wildlife ranger, albeit retired, generated quite some interest in Westwoods, to the extent that everyone else wanted to go, especially if there was something unusual to be revealed. They took the short drive to Clonragget, past the square spired church, in winding roads buffered by whins. Christian noted that the route ascended all the time and at gaps in the ditches they saw with a sharp intake of breath how high they had risen and the steep drops they would tumble if the car veered of the road for any reason. Mr.Kellys house was nestled into the high hillside, sheltered from the buffering breezes.

Mr.Kelly was already walking through the yard. He approached smiling, his face told how he had spent his entire life outdoors in the elements, amid nature and wildlife; it was strong and coarse with a rosy colour from a life of exposure to the wind.

'Hullo, Hullo.' He hollered. 'Good to see you Leon, good to see you all.' He grasped Dads hand and squeezed hard. Dad smiled and winced at the same time. 'Hello Dan.'

'Come on and have a look at the collection.' Mr.Kelly abruptly waved them to follow and they followed. He was straight to the point, no time for smalltalk. 'Who was it that was enquiring about the Buzzard?' He asked having been tipped off by phone that they were planning to visit.

Mols put up her hand. Mr.Kelly stopped and leaned towards her.

'Well then you will be very interested in what I am about to show you.' He whipped round again and marched off with the others in tow. He led them past his house and into a leafy garden. There was a wire fenced enclosure sectioning off one end of the space and he walked up to it.

'Say hello to Mr.Buzzard.' said Mr.Kelly in a more toned down voice, and there just inside the enclosure was a fully grown Buzzard.

Mols went right up to the wire to get a closer look. This was as close as she had even been to the magnificent bird. Behind, there were other birds in the expansive enclosure including Doves and Ducks but the Buzzard was by far the most impressive.

'Bueto, Bueto.' Said Mr.Kelly gesturing, 'That's its actual name. It's connected to the Eagle family and they have many similarities. There are some types of birds which are actually known as Buzzard-Eagles.'

Mols studied its hooded beak and stern look; it had what she considered a noble appearance.

'The Buzzard, and the Eagle, have a wingspan of up to a metre and a half.' he went on, 'They have the capacity to catch the wind and soar upwards to incredible heights.' They were impressed with the shear muscular size of the bird.

'When soaring they hold their wings in a shallow V shape, like this.' Mr.Kelly held out his arms spreadeagle and slightly raised. When he did this Christian immediately identified the posture, it straightaway reminded him of something...*three* things; Vetruvian Man, The Crucifixion and the raised arms of the Spirit that had visited him in his room....the Gatekeeper.

'That is why they are often mentioned in the Bible,' Mr.Kelly told them, 'as a symbol of the Resurrection. Not alone that, but they are considered a biblical messenger.' He said.

Mols *knew* the Buzzard had to have been on the side of good not evil, she had always felt its presence to be uplifting.

'In fact,' Mr.Kelly continued with his lesson, 'It can sometimes have a ring of white feathers around its neck called a halo. Because of this it is associated with a Saint....'

'Saint John.' Said Mols.

'That's right.' Said Mr.Kelly mighily impressed. 'Saint John, the messenger.' He studied her closely, the way she studied the little animals that intrigued her.

'Why does the Raven attack the Buzzard?' Mols asked him by way of a distraction.

'Possession.' He said, 'Mr. Raven is saying to Mr.Buzzard, *This is my place, I don't want you here.* He and his friends can gang up on the Buzzard and chase it away. He who has possession has the power.'

'I saw a flock of Ravens chasing the Buzzard.' said Mols.

'Actually, there are several terms for a group of Ravens,' One is an *Unkindness*.' Said Mr.Kelly. 'another is a *Conspiracy* and the other is a name also used for crows....a *Murder!*'

Christian thought back to his theory of a conspiracy to hide the Golden Stone, but the mention of murder cast a very dark shadow.

'You see the Raven is not a very nice fellow,' said Mr.Kelly frowning his words, 'it is considered a bird of ill omen. They say that Ravens are the ghosts of murdered people, and sometimes it is said that they are the *Souls of the Damned.*' He emphasised the last phrase by way of a threatening growl.

'Either way they are not very nice.' He then said chirpily. 'They are tricksters and can get other animals to do work for them, like...... opening up a carcass making it easier for the Raven to get his pickings.'

'How do they get another animal to do that?' asked Mols somewhat amazed.

'They can imitate other animal calls, in fact they have quite a repertoire of vocal skills.'

Mols thought about all the chattering and clicking that she had heard the Ravens make, like they were plotting amongst themselves, making arrangements for some conspiracy or unkindness, or worse still planning something more devious that they were associated with in name, a murder. She was astounded at the dark behaviours of the Ravens but pleased with how she had instinctively known they were a bad lot.

'That's all I can tell you about the Raven.' Said Mr.Kelly, having said more than enough already.

'Oh,' he concluded, '....they are thieves as well.'

Mr.Kelly had limitless knowledge of the animal worlds and he spoke at length about other birds he had nursed back to health and woodland animals he had rescued from peril. He intended to build an entire wildlife centre here on this high hill where through the hedge they had glimpses of his birds eye view over the woods in the distance.

'Come along here and I will show you something else, something amazing.' He promised and led them towards another part of the garden. As they walked a widesweeping panorama opened up before them.

'This is the best view in the land, you can see four seperate counties from here.' He told them. It was indeed splendid and Mr.Kelly pointed out each of the neighbouring counties. He pointed out the direction of Armagh, the Cathedral City, 'and if you have good sight, you can just about see the spire of St.Macartans above and beyond the woods.' He pointed, and they could see it as a tiny spec in the distance, a little spike sticking into the sky.

'There's the famous woodlands my friends, your house is on the other side. Look there, can you see one tree projects higher than the others?' and they could.

'That's the King of the Woods.' He informed them. 'It's easy to see from here but it's impossible to find when you are among the trees. The Buzzards, finds the tallest tree in the Woods to nest, so we're probably looking at the nesting place right there, but I've had damn'd bad luck trying to find it.'

Mol's looked across the valley at the King of the Woods; did it hold the treasure that *she* was looking for, The nesting place of the Buzzards?

'And over here is Clonraggett,' Mr.Kelly pointed and they could see the square spire in the not too far distance. 'The church is about a hundred years old but an even older church previously existed there.' He told them. 'Just a mile beyond is the site of the Battle of Clonraggett. That's where the great O'Neill took on the might of the British army and defeated them.' He seemed proud of the achievement but then spoke in more hushed tones. 'Many lives were lost on the battlefield.... hundreds died.'

'Were you there?' asked Lila quietly and Mr.Kelly looked at her despairingly.

'That was more than four hundred years ago!' He said aggrieved.

Looking again in the direction of the battle, he said. 'It was a massacare. The rebels ambushed the army and came at them from all angles. The army were unprepared and didn't have enough ammunition.' There was a conspicuously long silence, Mr.Kelly's concentration remained in his story and his gaze remained on the distant hills. Everyone else looked at each other.

'That's all I can tell you about the Battle of Clonragget.' Said Mr.Kelly snapping back to the moment.

'We didn't even ask about the Battle of Clonragget.' Whispered Sophia.

'Perhaps,' said Mr.Kelly, 'some of those Ravens are the souls of those murdered soldiers.' Mols felt a shiver go down her spine at the thought.

'There was another great O'Neill from Clonragget,' Mr Kelly continued, 'He fought in the American civil war and led an invasion of Canada. Unsuccessful unfortunately.'

Christian thought Mr Kelly had a good grasp of history.

'Two great soldiers.' Said Mr Kelly.

War-mongers. Thought Christian.

'Have you ever heard of a goose flying alone Dan?' asked Dad.

'...Yessss.' Said Mr.Kelly slowly and he looked at Dad with a frown that was as heavy as creeping lead.

'Geese always fly in a family, they will only fly alone if one had lost its mate and it's in mourning. It's unusual, but if you see a single goose in flight you should look the other way, it's a symbol of grief.' The frown raised slightly like he expected Dad to know more about this, but then he continued himself,

'It means that someone is going to die.'

Everyone stopped.

'But of course,' Mr.Kelly said now, more happily and frown free, 'all that is just superstition.'

But the words lodged in Christians mind; *Someone is going to die;* these words he had heard before, the night he received the visitation these were the words that brought him to conciousness, from dream to reality and now here they were spoken again in the cold light of day. A coincidence? Superstition? This he did not know, but what he did know that was since they began this project, this quest, he had been haunted by many words and many messages.

Mr.Kelly led them back past the house and across the yard and they followed tentatively, unsure how to respond to his deathly prediction.

'C'mon,' he said, 'I want you to see my *other* collection.' Mols suddenly got a nervy feeling, remembering Dads suggestion that she might not like some parts of the collection.

They entered into a large outbuilding which was seemingly undergoing some renovations. The light from the open door threw itself onto the floor but otherwise it was dark.

'Let me just get the lights.' Said Mr.Kelly as he walked ahead of them and disappeared into the dark.

They stood waiting for a long moment before a series of hesitant bulbs began blinking to life revealing a sight that caused them a collective sharp intake of breath.

There were dozens and dozens of animals staring back at them, all standing stock still, fixed in position, suspended from movement, suspended from life.

'They were once alive.' Mr.Kelly said, 'Some died in accidents, some of natural causes, some I tried to save but they didn't make it. Others did make it; I reintroduced them into the wild. 'But these fellows here are going to stay with me.'

There was a startling array of animals and bird of all shapes and sizes, all mounted and reproduced in a pose they would have adopted in life. Mr.Kelly had them taxidermied, preserved in a permanemt posture. There were squirrels, a badger, wrens, pheasants, mice, stoats, all varieties of birds and woodland critters who had their day and then succumbed to lifes cruelties.

They stayed a little while to examing the dead zoo in more detail but Dad was right about Mols not liking it, she preferred her animals real, alive and well.

After Mr.Kelly had shut down the lights and consigned his collection back to their dark habitat, they were ready to take their leave. Dad thanked Mr.Kelly for his time and they shook hands warmly. As they loaded back into the car, Mr.Kelly noticed Morgens metal detector.

'Oh, you'll be looking for the Gold then.' He said.

Christian's jaw dropped, how did Mr.Kelly know about their search for the Golden artefact?

'There's always been talk about gold buried in these hills,' continued Mr.Kelly, 'now it seems a mining company figures there could be a five hundred million euro fortune in them.' He turned to Dad,

'Have you had someone around testing your soil for gold yet?'

'No, I haven't seen anyone.'

'Don't worry, they'll be around sooner or later.' Said Mr.Kelly. He smiled at Morgen.

'So if I were you I would keep looking and you might get there first.'

Christian was relieved that Mr.Kelly hadn't mentioned the Golden Stone but he was enticed by the story of the fortune of gold hidden in the ground, especially the amount of money it might exact.

Perhaps we will get to the gold first… Christian thought regarding their quest to find the stone, *and we could be very, very rich.*

'I'll tell you something else.' Mr.Kelly leaned in close, 'If you're looking for a real treasure, I know you where to find it……at the Castle. I've *been* there, among the ruins of the walls, I've *seen* it….. *The Golden Oriole.*

Morgen's eyes were wide open. *Mr.Kelly knew where the treasure was? A Golden Oriel?*

'Oriolus Oriolus,' went Mr.Kelly, 'It's one of the most intelligent birds in Europe and quite rare around here, golden in colour, it's a beauty, it comes to Europe in the summer.'

Morgen was disappointed.

'If you are down at the Castle, you can look out for it.'

I might just do that. Thought Morgen. Mr.Kelly had just given him an idea.

XXIII

FRAGMEN

(Ruins)

MORGEN HAD HATCHED a plan; he told Christian but kept it quiet from the others. He planned to get into the Castle. It was forbidden to enter the exclusion zone surrounding the Castle but without doing so how were they to get a look at the dungeons and the potential buried treasure. Mr.Kelly had been among the ruins so why should'nt he? When he called out, 'We're off to the Woods.' It aroused no suspicion.

They made their way to the Castle.

'Alright we're going in.' Morgen instructed when they reached the perimeter fence, and he squeezed himself through a hole in the wire.

'Have to be careful,' Christian warned, 'we don't want the remains of the walls falling on top of us.' He knew full well that Morgen was most likely to cause suchlike to happen. He could see it now, trying to explain why walls that had withstood a raging fire and remained for ninety years thereafter, were suddenly in a pile on the ground... with Morgen on top of them... or on the bottom.

They pushed themselves through the long-grass and thistles. Suddenly Morgen yelled out in fright. A huge dragonfly had risen up from the grass directly in line with his eye and hovered there momentarily before zipping away. His heart thumped with shock, he had never seen a dragonfly as large as this before. Where was Mr.Kelly now when he needed him to organise a bit of stuffing.

They stood close by the remaining full height walls; they still retained their decorative cornices and moulding and staggered in and out in bays.

'Look, a lightening conductor is still on the top of that one.' Christian pointed out. One timber window casement was still in place, hanging together precariously. Morgen thought about the faces that might have looked out that window in previous times. Perhaps Oriel had gazed out on the once beautiful gardens or watched horses and traps arrive up the avenue. As he turned away he noticed something flicker at the window and looked quickly back. *Was it a lock of blonde hair that had flicked on the other side?* He watched carefully; *There it was again;*

'Look!' He called to Christian, but Christian had just seen it too. They both stared. A distinctive yellow bird flitted up behind the frame and then disappeared again. *That's what it was.* Several more appeared in and around pockets in the Castle walls.

'The Golden Oriole.' Said Morgen. Its colour was certainly striking and he could hear them singing, they made a song that sounded like *'or-iii-ole'* and he could understand how Mr. Kelly was impressed with this little treasure. But it was not quite the same as real gold.

Behind these walls was a hollow mostly filled with a huge mound of grown over rubble. Years of shrubbery and trees struck out from where the main house had fallen in upon itself; burned at the stake so many years ago.

'Let's get a little closer.' Said Christian leading the way. They stepped down into the hollow which was considerably lower than the surrounding ground.

'This must have been the basement.' Christian surmised.

They found themselves walking on the collapsed remains of the Castle. As they clambered over it they could hear bricks and stone rattling beneath their feet. Now they were standing inside the remaining Castle walls and Morgen looked up its full three storey height to the top. From the inside they could see that the wall was more precarious than it looked from the outside, bricks were clinging together loosely, each supporting the other like a bunch of boozy sailors. It looked like it could crumble at any time.

'Someday we will come here and it will have fallen down.' Morgen said.

'Lets hope that someday is not *to*-day!' urged Christian noting that the tradjectory of falling wall could easily reach where they were standing.

Morgen noticed something at the base of the wall, lower than the proper ground level.

'Look there,' he pointed to Christian, 'it's a dungeon!' Sure enough at the foot of the outer walls there appeared to be a narrow arched passage, narrower than the thickness of the hefty basement wall. Where the walls had crumbled the passage could be clearly seen. But it was tiny and looked like it could only accommodate a child. Christian pursued the course of its direction by eye.

'If it follows the outside wall of the Castle then it must come right along........here!' He turned and pointed behind them. Through the scrub he could see a tiny bit of an arch peeking through. He picked his way over and pulled the greenery back, exposing the top of the arch of the passageway, but only the top. The remainder of the arch had been backfilled with stones and debris, perhaps from the collapse of the Castle, perhaps as a council safety measure to prevent young Turks, such as they, climbing inside the dangerous structure. They peeked in to what they could see of the passage, it continued further but any possibility of getting into it was foiled by its backfilling. Then Morgen spotted something else.

'There.' He whispered. Christian looked, he could only see more green growth where Morgen pointed.

'Can you see what I see?' Morgen insisted.

Christian looked more closely, between the brambles and grasses he could see darkness behind. The growth was concealing a dark opening. They went towards it. It appeared to be an entrance opening of about Morgen's height. There was a second similar sized opening just beside it.

Christian drew back the growth like a curtain; it revealed a rounded arched opening leading into a dark space, a dungeon.

'Wow. Are you going in there?' Morgen asked.

'Are you?' said Christian.

'I asked you first.'

Neither moved.

The daylight illuminated the space to a small degree. It appeared to be a room and not a passage.

'This must be a stable.' Christian said. 'You hold back these and I will go look.'

Christian stepped into the dark, his shape obscuring the incoming daylight. He moved into the room and let his eyes grow accustomed to the dark. There was rubble on the floor, but otherwise this part of the building was in pretty good nick. There appeared to be scrawls on the walls, people's names, old graffiti.

He noticed something else; the remains of burnt sticks, and a blackened area on the floor. Someone had lit a fire in here, *Silly thing to do,* he thought. There was no other entrance or exit from the 'dungeon', so he turned to leave.

'Wait,' he said urgently, 'there's something in here.' Morgen stiffened.

'I think, I think….its a dead body ….!' Morgen froze.

'Haaaaaah!' Christian leaped out at Morgen with a wide grin on his face. Morgen gave him an angry box. 'You didn't even frighten me.'

'Oh no? Why have you suddenly gone white then?'

They examined the second opening nearby, this one was partially blocked with rubble which flowed into the dungeon, it would be difficult to get into and even more difficult to get out of in a hurry. They decided not to attempt to go in this one.

Nearby they discovered an arch carved into an overgrown wall, this appeared to be the courtyard entrance gate, the main door into the Castle buildings. Christian examined the arch; where the masonry peeped out beneath the greenery it was something to behold, the plasterwork was still smooth and embellished with precise decorative plaster lines. They picked their way through the thorny undergrowth to the other side of the big house, again they found themselves bobbling on loose bricks underneath and decided to have a little dig.

'Pull back that moss and we can get to the bricks.'

'Imagine if we discover some treasure exactly here.'

'Yea,… at the *exact* spot where everyone else forgot to look.' They picked through some bricks and stones, unearthing a variety of bugs and insects until Morgen suddenly stopped and held out his hand.

'Listen.' He said.

They heard a man's voice. It was close to the Castle, within the enclosure. Christian anticipated trouble, they were not supposed to be in here, it was unsafe and, he was sure, illegal. 'Hide.' He whispered.

They ducked down where they were, concealed by the mounds of rubble, grass and bushes. They could no longer hear the voice but they dared not move. So they waited.

Christian broke the silence after a time. 'I think we should try to go now.' He whispered.

Then they heard it! It was………chanting. A slow hollow mumbling, repeating, almost like singing.

'Is is a radio?' Morgen detected that the sound had an echo effect, a resonance.

Christian peeped up. 'It's coming from the dungeon!' he whispered hoarsely. Someone, a man, was in the dungeon chanting in a low monotone voice. They could not hear the words.

'Let's get out of here.' Christian motioned Morgen to follow and they picked through the difficult terrain as quietly as they could steering as far away as the dungeon and the disturbing chanting as possible. As they clambered out of the pit of the Castle, Morgen heard the voice grow in strength, he could hear the words, and they frightened him.

They frightened Christian too as he scrambled out through the hole in the fence even after he could no longer hear them. They frightened him all the way home and he thought of them for much longer.

The words repeated in his head just as they had repeated in the dungeon, getting louder and louder.

'Sacrifice…. of Blood, Sacrifice…..of Blood.'

XXIV

ODONATA

(Dragonfly)

'It's COULD HAVE been a Druid!....I'm telling you.' Christian was insisting that this was the only real explanation for the mysterious chanting. He and Morgen were telling the tale to the rest of the guys back in the project room.

'Calling for a *Sacrifice*, calling for *Blood*. Who else would want that? A Neo-Druid, I've been reading about them, they want to continue the pagan traditions.'

It was a frightening thought. Someone was indulging in dangerous and disturbing behaviour; it may be someone from around.

'We have to keep away from the Castle, you two shouldn't have been there in the first place. Then we wouldn't have known about all this.' Said Taymi.

'Better that we do know.' Said Christian.

Mols and Sophia would rather have not known.

'But who could that be using the Castle?' said Sophia.

'Don't know, but I can think of one or two people.' Said Christian, there were several people who admitted to having visited the Castle ruins and he had suspicions about others too. Sir Jack told them he visited occasionally and intended to go back there, Mr.Kelly too said that he had been within the ruins of the Castle, the Dark One was an obvious suspect, or perhaps it was none of these.

'Theres absolutely no point in guessing.' Said Taymi dismissively, 'let's just keep out of harms way for now. Is that understood?' She was looking at the boys, not the girls. Morgen was pensive, reflecting on their interrupted exploration and he had something else on his mind to ask too.

'What do you know about Dragonflies Mols.' He said, 'I saw a huge one in the Woods, do they sting?'

'Not sure, but I will find out.' She promised and set about immediately on the case of the dragonfly investigation along with Sophia who signalled her offer to help. They jabbered at the computer as the others considered the meaning of the chanting, and who may have been behind it.

'I hope you did'nt bring my camera down there without asking me.' Taymi said to Christian.

'No.' said Christian.

'Did you?'

'I said NO!'

'Better not have.'

'It could have been a Neo- Druid.' Said Christian quietly, 'We know there are Neo-Druids, who's to say there isn't one right here. Who's to say that wasn't him today?' It was a plausible thought. Taymi couldn't decide if a modern Neo-Druid would have all the powers of an ancient Druid.

'Why would there be a Neo-Druid here?'

'To workship the Golden Stone at the Hill of the Devil. Isn't that enough reason?'

'But how would he know about it? Nobody knows about it.'

'We do. Anyone who knew a little bit of history probably does.'

'Well now we know theres someone creeping around the woods acting like a ….Druid, we will have to be more careful. Although we have no proof whatever that it is a Druid.'

'Well whoever it is they're obviously performing some kind of spell or black magic.' Said Christian,

'So I say that's what we call him….beware the Black Magic. And I say,' he continued, 'if we are to stay safe, we should try to find out exactly who this Black Magic is.'

Mols interrupted on behalf of herself and Sophia.

'We will be back in a minute to make our report.' They left the room but came back shortly with some information written down. Mols was also holding something behind her back.

'Dragonflies are predators, they have six legs but they can't walk.' Mols started.

'Friend of the snake then.' Morgen commented.

'Their larvae are called nymphs and they can give a painful bite causing an infection.' Said Sophia.

'Friend of the snake then.' Morgen again.

'They can be larvae for up to five years before turning into an adult Dragonfly,' said Mols, 'which lives for….have a guess.'

'Ten years?' Said Christian.

'Fifty years?' Said Morgen.

'Seven years?' Tried Taymi.

'Seven months…' Said Mols leaving them astounded. '…and they are linked to evil.'

'Friend of the snake then.' Morgen again.

'In Romania they are known as the Devils horse,' Sophia continued, 'in Malta they are called Hells Mare, in Sweden it's said that the Devil used Dragonflies to weigh peoples souls.'

'The Devil.' Said Taymi, *the Devils Stone, the Devils Hill, the Devil, the Devil, the Devil…..*

Mols took over again, 'In England they are known as the Devils needle, in Norway they are supposed to poke your eye out….'

'Wow, you are lucky you didn't get your eye poked out Morgen.' Said Christian, 'It's all fun and games til someone loses an eye.' Morgen was familiar with this saying, it was on one of his tee-shirts.

'Not today brother,' he said, 'I'll see that Dragonfly in eight months.'

'….and in Wales,' Mols continued, 'they are known as ……' she directed the next part at Morgen, '…. As the snakes assistant!'

'Hah!' said Morgen

'Why does every evil guy have to have an assistant?' Christian said.

'Like who?' Taymi asked.

'Em…….Mini-Me.' It was the only one that Christian could think of on the spot.

'In South America,' said Sophia pressing on, 'the Dragonfly is known as the Devils Little Horse,' Lila looked at the toy she was holding in her hand, *My Little Pony*, 'and in the U.S. dragonflies are said to help injured snakes by *stitching* them back together.' This was a rather gruesome and unpleasant revelation that caused Morgen to turn up his nose.

'Soooo they are not very nice then.' Said Taymi sardonically.

'Actually,' said Mols, 'in Native America they are the symbol of pure water. In some parts of the world they are eaten.'

'Yesss!' said Morgen.

'In Vietnam people predict the weather by looking at the Dragonfly and in some places if it lands on you it means seven years good luck, especially in Japan where the dragonfly is a hero.' Said Sophia.

'What to believe?' Taymi sighed.

'*And* the Dragonfly is used a lot in jewellery,' said Mols, '….see exhibit A.' From behind her back she produced a small decorative ring box made of ornate metalwork. On top of its demountable lid was a decorative Dragonfly. The insect was fashioned from metal set into with blue stones creating its wings and body. They all recognised it; it was a gift that Dad had given to Mom some years ago. Lila loved it, Morgen was less impressed.

'Get that evil thing away from me.' He commanded.

'No wonder that Dragonfly was hovering around the Castle,' Christian said, 'The Dragonfly and the Druid, both the Devils assistants.'

The Dragonfly, the Oak Tree, the 3 annulets; these symbols all seemed very close to home Taymi thought….much too close indeed.

XXV

CONSCIENTIA

(Knowledge)

'FIND OUT ANYTHING interesting from your book?' Dad had noticed Morgen on several occasions having a quick peep at *A Brief History of Time*. In truth Morgen was mostly taking note of the diagrams as the text was too complex and convoluted for a ten year old.

'There are wormholes.'

'Really? How do they work.'

'It's a bit like a black hole except that you can come back out again, in a different place in space.'

'Cool.'

'And in space, time is curved.'

'Time is curved?'

'Yea'

'Ok'

'And there is something called Antimatter.'

'Do tell.'

'Everything is matter, antimatter is its opposite, for everything matter there is antimatter, if you put them together they will cancel each other out or explode.'

'Oh!....is there an antimatter me?'

'Probably'

'So I better not meet antimatter me?'

'Better not.'

'I see.' Said Dad, 'Might be too late for that.'

Taymi marched into the project room and thumped Christian on the arm. It was completely out of the blue.

'You lied to me.' She said.

'What? When?' He knew that he may have fibbed to her about a few things but he wasn't going to admit anything.

'You took my camera to the Castle.' She accused him.

'No, I didn't.'

'You did.'

Christian shook his head incredulously, 'You are completely wrong.' He stressed.

'Then explain this.' She barged past him to the computer. On the screen she pulled up photographic images of the Castle. Close ups. She flicked through them; they were all of the things that he and Morgen had seen when they had gone down there, the remaining walls, the detail, the dungeons, the arch.

'I didn't take these.' Christian thought he was going mad.

'Oh come on.' She said, 'These are all the things you told me about, you can't get out of this.'

'I know....but I didn't take these.' His sincerity was such that Taymi knew he was telling the truth.

'Did Morgen?'

'No.'

'Then who did?'

In the stillness of the seconds that followed, they both arrived at the same conclusion at the same time. The only other real potential candidate for having taken the photos was ....

'Dad?'

'Where did you find these?' asked Christian.

'I was looking through my camera pictures and I noticed that some were downloaded. These were kept in a separate folder... concealed, I just spotted them by accident.' There was a thought that each of them was having but neither wanted to say first.

'Do you think...' started Taymi.

'....that Dad could have been the voice in the dungeon.' Finished Christian. She nodded, it was possible and with this evidence that Dad had definitely been at the Castle, it was also very probable.

They looked at each other, this was very worrying, frightening, could there possibly be a more rational explanation for all this, they hoped so but somehow they didn't believe that there was. They stared at each other contemplating the consequences of this conundrum. Could it possibly be?

'Is Dad the Black Magic?' said Christian. His words hung in the air a long moment, Taymi didn't dissuade him, by saying nothing she was in agreement. They decided not to mention a word of this to the others.

XXVI

TEMPESTAS

(Storm)

'It's GONNA BLOW.' Dad was referring to the sky. It had darkened and he was predicting that a storm was brewing. The weather had been unbearably humid, clammy and damp. It was about seven o'clock in the evening when they heard the first rumblings and the sky was so dark that it already felt like night.

BANG! Suddenly there was a loud clap preceded by an instantaneous flash which lit up all the windows.

'Lets go see.' Said Dad, leaping up from his chair and heading for the front door. Sophia came along to observe, she was not fond of thunderstorms but there was something on her mind which she wanted to pursue. Dad threw open the front door and stood on the porch steps avoiding most of the rain but catching the wind on his shirt. Another flash, another crack and the sky electrified with a double burst of light creating an eerie pattern in the clouds.

'WhoooHooo.' Shouted Dad, 'Did you see that.' He was pointing, 'Just there! That was a cloud surfer, lightening jumping between clouds.'

The Westwooders stood behind Dad looking upwards. Mom reassured Lila that it was 'Just God moving his furniture around.' Dad was becoming more animated now, another dramatic flash, crash and rattle made him whoop again.

'Yea! Bring it on! Do your worst!'

Sophia noticed now that the rain was becoming heavier and starting to get Dad wet. A double whammy of lightening and thunderous rolling made them all jump except Dad who was now getting so carried away that he stood with his arms raised echoing the thunders roar with his own. He had taken on a manic presence and appeared as though he was conducting the storm.

'We're going back in.' Mols said to Sophie. Mols had seen this performance before and wasn't at all surprised. Sophia on the other hand was making observations.

–Dad had always been able to predict the onset of a storm.

–The force of the storm made him act in a bewildering way.

–He always watched the storm from the front steps as it always appeared to occur over the woods and not in any other direction.

Dad watched them all troop back indoors, but he didn't notice Sophia coming back out. She watched him now, rain streaking down his face, staring at the sky. She could hear him speaking to himself in low tones and strained to listen to what he was saying.

'I see the sky ripped open, the rain pouring through a gaping wound, pelting the women and children, pelting the women and children, who run...., who run...., into the arms ....'

Sophia looked up; Dad had become aware of her presence and was staring at her.

'I'm going in now.' Sophia said sheepishly and beat a hasty retreat back inside the house.

She felt disturbed by Dads behaviour, not alone tonight, but in recent times. There were certain things he had done, that he had said which she had taken note of, that worried her, and tonight she had just made up her mind about something. She decided there and then that she was going to reveal her findings to the others.

'I think I know who the Black Magic is,' Sophia started, 'it might be...it think it could be ....Dad!' she laid it straight on the line. Taymi looked at Christian.

Sophia had called everyone to the project room for what she had promised to be clue that could reveal the identity of the Black Magic. Mols spoke up.

'That's silly, how could it be Dad. That's bananas.'

'Listen to me.' Sophia insisted and she began by outlining her observations in regard to the storm.

'But Dad always does that.' Said Morgen, 'every single storm.'

'Ok, explain this then.' Sophia referred to her notebook into which she has catalogued other unusual events. I was watching Dad mowing the lawn two days ago. I thought it was interesting how the ride-on seems to suck up all the wildflowers just like a hoover.'

'Get on with it.' Said Christian, aware of Sophia's propensity for elongating a story.

'He began driving erratically, I could see him swerving and shaking his head violently, and he was shouting, even over the noise of the mower I could hear him.....' she referred to her notebook.

"I saved your life,' he said, *'I should have let you die. Damn you to Hell."* They were all quite startled to hear of this strange behaviour and dark words from their own father and Sophia felt they were beginning to come around to her thinking on the matter. She continued, 'One night when I went to get a drink of water, through the window I noticed someone standing in the middle of the garden. It was Dad. He was standing there, looking up at the moon; he was waving his hand in a circular motion. I could see something going around in circles above his head, as far as I could see in the dark, it looked like a Bat.'

'A baseball bat?' asked Morgen hopefully.

'A winged bat.' Confirmed Sophia. This evidence moved the Westwooders considerably in the direction of Sophia's theory although Taymi and Christian were already convinced before she began. Mols sat with her mouth open, shocked at what had been going on in her own garden.

'And there's the incantations.' Revealed Sophia. 'On numerous occasions I witnessed Dad chanting, or muttering and I wrote some of these down.' She referred again to the notebook.

'When Lila had her cough, Mom asked Dad to fetch the cough bottle. As he pressed it down and twisted it open I heard him say, *'Sleight of hand and twist of fate, on a bed of nails she makes me wait.'*"

'Another time when Christian asked Dad to pass his jacket over because it was getting windy, Dad muttered this, *'From Father to Son, the blood runs cold, see faces frozen still, against the wind.'*"

'I remember that,' said Christian, 'I thought he was speaking to me but he denied he said anything.'

'And finally,' Sophia had kept an even more shocking story until last, her coup de grace.

'Three days ago I was awoken one morning by a tapping sound.' She began, 'It was very early, about 5am, I thought it might be those birds which seem to be nesting under the gutter........' she hastened along under Christians impatient look, 'Someone was tapping at the front door. Dad came out to the landing and whispered down from the window, *What is it?* he said. They were whispering, then Dad went downstairs and I could hear more whispering.' Sophia had a slight quaver in her voice recounting this, perhaps from a small sense of betrayal on having spied on her Dad, or perhaps from what that spying revealed to her.

'I saw a young man dressed in black, walking out the avenue. For a second he looked back and I saw his face was all scratched, *bleeding*. I never saw this guy before. I could hear Dad talking low downstairs and after a while he came back upstairs to bed. Nobody else left the house and none of this was ever mentioned.' Sophia closed her notebook and looked at the others, but no one spoke.

'I rest my case.' She said quietly.

Mols, initial sceptical, was by now taken aback with the list of antics attributed to Dad. Whilst she could have barely believed it, she didn't doubt that Sophia was telling the truth.

'I have something to tell.' It was Taymi's turn to speak. She opened up about the photos of the Castle, the message from Master Tom and the mystery of the three rings althought she didn't know quite how these fit into the equation. But overall they had created a daming indictment of Dad.

Faced with such evidence Taymi asked, 'What will we do?'

Christian, who had been biding his time, now spoke clearly. 'There is only one thing we can do; we will have to confront Dad.'

'How on earth are we going to do that?' asked Taymi.

'We will do it today, at supper, when Mom is there.' He said, assuming the position of the eldest male in the family now that Dad had been discovered to be untrustworthy.

To Christian it felt like the last supper. They were going to confront their father about a list of suspicions and deceit. Most disturbingly they were going to accuse him of behaviour akin to that used by black magic cults and that they had found him out to be what they considerad a *Neo-Druid*.

At table everyone was unusually quiet and eagle eye glances were exchanged, if a storm was coming, this was the calm. At the appropriate moment Christian spoke.

'Dad, there is something we would like to talk to you about.' Both Mom and Dad had been noticing the subdued mood but now looked taken aback at this clearly planned announcement.

'Mom, its OK,' said Christian, 'we will explain as we go along.' He steadied his breath. 'Dad, we've noticed some strange behaviour from you recently and we want to ask you about it.' Dad looked at Mom and shrugged in seeming innocence, he sat back in his chair to give this approach its due attention.

'Sophia would you please read.' Christian asked and Sophia recounted her observations of Dad during the storm, she told of how he had been calling down a curse, damning someone to hell, and how she had seen him in the dark cover of night attractings bats to him. And then she told of his clandestine encounter one early morning with the strange blooded caller.

Mom looked stunned at these revelations, Dad just sat with his mouth open and his hands on the table.

'Also,' said Christian, 'we know that you have been chanting mysterious and strange enchantments sometimes directed at us and in one case at Mom.

Dad, and Mom, looked horrified

'and I quote...' said Christian plucking the sinister words from Sophia's notebook and reading them aloud. Christian closed the notebook and looked at Dad before turning his attention to his sister.

'Taymi.' He invited. Taymi cleared her throat before taking up the baton.

'You wear jewelry that has symbolic meaning, you gave a gift of a dragonfly, the Devils horse, to Mom, and you have been in contact with Master Tom, who you said had passed on.'

Christian took over again, his duty; to deliver the final devastating piece of evidence.

'We believe you were at the Castle; You took photographs there; You were chanting in the dungeon that you told us about; and you have been there previously and lit fires.'

Christian had no idea what the outcome of all this would be in the long term but he had no doubt they were taking the correct course of action, face the truth, live with the consequences. Strong and Faithful- Fortis et Fidelis.

'You are the person we've been calling the Black Magic.' He said.

Dads face had gone from pale to red to pale again. Christian felt nervous but in control, *He's going to admit it.* He thought.

'Are you a Druid?' Christian asked straight out.

Dad stood up from the table, he covered his mouth so only his eyes could be seen. His eyes welled up with water; he shook his head from side to side. He removed his hand and his bottom lip was trembling.

Christian wasn't sure what reaction he had wanted, but this wasn't it.

'I'm sorry,' said Dad barely able to speak, 'I'm sorry.'

And what he did next shocked them even more. He erupted into a violent hysterical fit.

A violent hysterical fit …..of *laughter.*

Dad laughed and laughed with tears coming out of his eyes, gripping his belly, almost doubled over.

He tried to speak but was unable to compose himself. He shook his head from side to side with the incredulity of it all and then erupted into another fit of loud laughter. Now he made no effort to contain himself.

The Westwooders were looking at each other and starting to feel perhaps they had made a rather large mistake. Mom was clearly bemused and interested to know what was really going on behind all this. Lila and Morgen had gotten over their initial anxiety and now were laughing along with Dad. He had gone into a world of his own and shook his head at them through teary eyes.

Christian felt mightily guilty, *Where did it all go wrong?* He was still as anxious to hear some sort of an explanation for this because he simply believed there wasn't one that was in any way plausible.

Eventually Dad had calmed down enough to be able to sit down again and communicate.

'A Druid?' he stuttered, 'What on earth are you guys thinking of? What the…..?'

'OK,' He tried again, 'I think I can have a go at clearing some of these things up.' He said. 'The easiest way to explain some of this is….well, not sure why I really have to explain myself….but in the interest of clarity…..did you say Black Magic there? Oh boy.' He sat back then and took a deep breath.

'I love nature, you know that, and that's why I love to go outside to see the storm, listen to its roar and roar back at it. Thunder and lightening is such a powerful thing, kenetic, energetic. Its nature at its most vibrant, most exciting. I like to experience it in a real way.' He explained. 'No more than that.' He smiled.

'At night, often before I go to bed, I like to take an outside walk to take in the night air, and if the moon is out I gaze at it, sometimes it can be beautiful you know. I can tell you there could be millions looking at that same moon at that same time as me.'

'But what about the bat?' asked Morgen.

'Yes, I have to wave away that pesky bat in case it tries to land in my hair.' Chuckled Dad. 'Every time I walk out there, he flits and flies around me like a maniac.'

'What about the incantations?' said Sophia.

'That's the best one of all.' Said Dad, 'those words that you quoted me are not incantations, or spells or whatever you think, they're song lyrics. My favourite record of all time, U2's Joshua Tree. I know the words by heart and often sing them or hum them. Sometimes the lyrics seem to fit with a situation and I will sing them to myself. They are strong lyrics, I'll admit that.'

It all seemed rather plausible and easily explained away.

'What about mowing the lawn?' Christian asked, not yet entirely convinced.

'I can't figure that one out myself.' Said Dad, '….Wait, I think I *do* know what happened there.' Dad snickered to himself and shook his head again.

'I was mowing the lawn and up ahead I could see a big fat bee sitting on a wildflower. I shouted at him to 'Get Away' but he didn't move so I swerved so as not to mow him up.' Dad pleaded a look at Lila. 'I wouldn't hurt a bee you know. Well because I drove so close to that bee, he flew up and tried to sting me. That might explain those words I used…... Sorry if they were a bit aggressive.'

They were beginning to feel sorry that they had questioned Dad in such a forthright way. The whole thing was a sorry mess and they felt that they had let him down; they should have known that there would be reasonable explanations for these unusual events. After all Dad was an unusual guy.

'What about the young man who came here early one morning?' Taymi knew there might be a reasonable explanation but wondered what it was.

'I'll answer that.' Said Mom and Dad's gesture said *The floor is yours*. They hadn't anticipated Mom coming to the resuce on any of the issues let alone this.

'A young man knocked on our door; he said he was lost and wanted help. Dad went down to speak to him. It seems that a bunch of young guys thought it would be a good idea to camp out in the Woods and have an all night party. This one guy had been visiting from Armagh. It appears they were drinking and at some point the others in the group seemed to gang up on this guy and chased him out of the woods. Dad ordered him a taxi which collected him at the end of our avenue and Dad then called the garda station to let them know about the incident.'

'But his face was all cut.' said Sophia.

'He ran through a lot of brambles to get here.' Said Dad 'We didn't tell you guys about it because there was no need for you to know. It was a one off incident, it hasn't happened before and hopefully won't again.'

'What did the guards say?' asked Christian.

'They told me that they went into the Woods and dispersed the group and calmed down the situation. Some of the boys were maniacal and suffering hallucinations. Seems they might have taken some curious substances. The young guy who came here told me that the others had become like vicious demons; they chased him away because he was from the Cathedral City.'

Christian glanced at Taymi at the mention of Demons in the Woods. He was reminded too by the mention of hallucinations, of the delusions that caused the death of the stonemason. Was it substances that drove them maniacal, or was it something else?

'Not everyone who frequents the Woods is there to enjoy the walking routes.' Said Mom turning her attention to Dad, 'So can you please explain about whether or not you were inside the Castle?' She folded her arms tightly.

'Alright,' he sighed resignedly and held his hands up, 'I admit it!' This was the first acknowledgement from Dad that he had done anything wrong and they awaited his explanation.

'After us talking about the Castle recently, I went down to see it and I couldn't resist going in past the fence to get a closer look at the building just like the old times. I shouldn't have done it, I know. I took photos but I downloaded them off the camera to disguise that I have been in there. Mom knew that I had gone to see it but I didn't say that I had gone inside the fence.' Mom nodded in the affirmative firstly and then in the negative latterly. Dad knew he was in the doghouse.

Christian was awaiting his admission on the chanting. Dad saw that he was still waiting.

'I peeped into the dungeons and took a photo ....but I didn't go in there and I wasn't chanting in there.' He looked at Christian, 'Which leads me to two conclusions. Firstly there must be someone else doing this chanting you are talking about and secondly, if you heard this, then you yourself must have been inside the safety fence.' The tables were turned, Christian was caught out. He nodded his admission.

'You know you are not to go in there.' Said Dad, '...BUT...' he hastily continued before anyone could their finger, '...since I broke the rule then I can hardly punish you. Let's just agree that none of us will breach the fence again and we'll leave it at that.' They both felt that they had come out of this one lightly, but most relieved was Morgen whose name didn't enter into the equation, thankfully for him.

'So then, what's this about a Druid?' said Dad laughing and the Westwooders hung their heads.

'Am I a bogey man?' Dad mocked the movements of a zombie. 'Am I the evil one? Whoooo!'

'We're sorry Dad.' Said Christian speaking for all of them. 'We made a mistake.'

'That's ok guys.' Said Dad settling down. 'Everyone makes mistakes, although come to think of it, I never called my Dad a Druid or a Wizard or whatever.' He said smiling, making them feel even more guilty. 'But I might have thought about it.' He quipped.

'Theres a name for this you know,' he said, 'Apophenia; seeing a connection between random things just because you want to.'

That's the word I was looking for before. Taymi thought.

'I think it might be time to forget about all this and move on.' Mom suggested and began to clear away the crockery. After tidying up Christian, Taymi and Dad were the only ones left sitting at the table.

'Can I ask you something?' Taymi said to Dad who nodded.

'What is the significance in the three rings, on your ring and on the Russian wedding ring.

'No significance really, this Celtic design was given to me by your Mom, the Russian ring is simply a wedding ring.'

'It's usually worn on the right; you wear it on the left.'

'Well in this country you wear it on the left hand.' Taymi decided to drop the enquiry, perhaps this was another case of apophenia.

'Can I ask you something?' Dad asked Taymi now and she shrugged sure.

'You said something about me being in contact with Master Tom. What were you talking about?' Dad appeared genuinely mesmerised by this.

From her folder she produced the folded piece of paper which she had retrieved from the envelope on the Castle and gave it to Dad. He read it studiously.

'This is amazing.' he said, 'A letter from Master Tom.' He set the letter back down and looked up at them.

'This letter was not written to me. I got the envelope of information from Master Tom's son, he told me that his father had previously given the package of information to someone else who was researching the Castle, but he didn't know who that was. This note must have been to that person, I have no idea who it was. I expect it was someone from around here, someone, clearly with an interest in history and this Castle.' Dad pondered for a long moment, there was something else on his mind and he spoke to the two of them in a serious tone.

'Guys, You two are the eldest. I want you to be careful when you are in the woods, and always keep an eye out for the others. That young man that came here one morning, he thought he was among people he knew and trusted. But as you heard, people can do strange things, sometimes with no explanation. He really thought those other boys were going to ……..he thought there were going to kill him!'

XXVII

CALIGA

(Mist)

It was evening of the next day and Lila ran frantically into the project room.

'Something's happening!' she warned alerting the others in a heartbeat. They quickly followed her towards the rear of the house where she pointed out the window. A strange scene had indeed begun to occur; A dense mist had started in the fields at the back of the house and strangely appeared to be lying in the lower depressions of the field, filling them up with pools of swirling grey.

'There's nothing to worry about Lila.' Said Taymi, 'I know it looks odd, but it's just a mist.'

'Is that mist or fog?' asked Morgen.

'I don't know if its *Mister Fog*,' teased Christian, 'but its coming towards *Mister House.*' And they groaned at this weak humour. However the mist *was* coming towards the house, they could almost see it crawling along and it seemed to be spreading wider.

'Run.' Said Lila scared and the others laughed wondering where they were meant to run to. She rushed into the rear hall for another look and they heard her shriek.

'It's getting in!' she cried. The glass on the back door had started to mist up and the others laughed again at Lila's view of the world. The mist was by now creeping into their garden and they noticed how it seemed to snake along the edges before filling in the middle.

'Let's go out and explore it.' said Sophia fascinated with this natural phenomenon. She, Mols and Morgen went out into the garden and walked around. Lila watched from inside the window and Christian and Taymi went back to the project room their amusement waning.

'Why can't you touch the mist?' Asked a frustrated Morgen as he tried in vain to grab some of the evasive substance in his hands.

'This is too spooky,' said Mols, 'I'm going back in.' and off she went. Morgen made his way back into the house too, having reached his boredom threshold.

Sophia stayed outdoors for several more minutes although it was getting darker now. She strayed towards the front of the house and the woods, noticing how eerie everything looked through the thickening mist, even the lights from the house were a blurred glow. She was about to start back for the house when she heard a chilling sound.

Howls!... Long lonesome animal howls that seemed to echo near and far, coming from beyond or within the woods. She shivered with discomfort although it was not unusual to hear night-time howls, she had heard them before and there were lots of dogs living in the vicinity. What happened next though made her forget the howls and run for her life.

A blood curdling scream rose from the woods shocking her to her heart and cutting off her breath.

She ran straight for the house and burst through the front door.

'Whoa! What's wrong?' Urged Dad jumping up to greet a breathless and clearly traumatised Sophia.

'I heard a woman scream,' she gasped trembling, '...Or it could have been a child.' She was shaking with fright and trying to catch her breath back. Dad hugged her tightly to calm her.

'Where?' he urged and she pointed back towards the front door.

'In the Woods.' Everyone had rushed into the room alerted to the sudden commotion.

'Hold on, hold on, let me go see.' Said Dad as Mom took over calming Sophia. Dad went straight out into the garden followed by the others who kept a safe distance well and truly behind him. He walked deep into the mist until they could see only his silhouette, then he stood stock still and listened. The movement of the mist obscured his shadow until they could barely glimpse his whereabouts and they all stood still in the silence wondering if he was still even there. A howl echoed in the far distance. After a little time his voice came back to them.

'I don't hear anything like a scream.' They heard him say. Sophia was by now back standing at the front door again.

'It came from over there.' She pointed directly into the woods and then dropped her arm realising Dad couldn't see her, never mind her gesture. 'It was a loud scream,' she said, 'like someone being...... attacked.'

They listened again for a short while hearing nothing but the stillness of the night with the sound of the neverending waterfall in the distance.

'I think I know what it was.' Came Dads voice as he materialised out of the grey nodding his head in agreement with himself, 'and there's really nothing to worry about.'

'Nothing to worry about?' said Sophia; *Nothing to worry about;* she was absolutely scared rigid!

'I'm almost sure it was.....in fact I'm convinced,' said Dad climbing the porch steps, 'it was a rabbit.'

A rabbit? This seemed to the others a most implausible, harebrained, pardon the pun, explanation for a deathly full bodied scream in the middle of the night that could'nt possibly be countenanced.

'How could it be a *rabbit*?' Sophia most of all couldn't fathom it.

'Believe it or not,' Dad began, causing some disbelief that he was even going to *try* and justify his claim, 'Rabbits can make an extremely high pitched scream. I have heard it before and it sure sends shivers down your spine.' He said noting how they were staring at him now like rabbits in the headlights.

'You probably heard a rabbit being caught by one of those howlers out there or it may have injured itself in some other way. Maybe it sprained its foot.' He declared.

Christian spluttered at the thought of a rabbit spraining its foot and uttering a deathly scream. He was more inclined to believe that someone may be being murdered in the woods or sacrificed by a Druid.

'It's a Rabbit scream I tell you, they scream when in pain.' argued Dad, 'Look it up.' And Mols resolved to do just that.

'Theres only one other thing which it could have been.' Said Dad, 'C'mon, Let's go inside and we can talk there.' They all trooped inside shutting the door tight behind them, leaving the night to the night.

Mom set about making sugary tea for Sophia.

'Are you feeling better now?' Dad asked her and she nodded that she was.

'You said there was something else it could have been?' Taymi said to Dad.

'Like someone dying!' Scowled Christian.

'Not dying, no.' said Dad, 'but close.'

'Someone not dying then?' enquired Taymi.

'Have you ever heard of a Banshee?' Dad said and yes they had heard of a Banshee.

'It's a woman who cries in the night.' Said Taymi.

'And her cry,' said Christian slowly, 'is the warning,' he paused, 'that *someone is going to die.*'

Suddenly Sophia wasn't feeling better again but it was nothing to the feeling that engulfed Christian on hearing these words again, uttered this time from his own mouth.

'It's a myth of course.' said Dad, 'I can guarantee that you heard a rabbit scream, but in past times anyone who heard that scream would have been thinking exactly that; Someone is going to Die.'

Sophia and Mols sat in the project room staring at the screen. They were astonished to discover that Dad was right, a rabbit *can* make a blood curdling scream, just like someone being murdered. It seemed that his impossible theory was plausible after all. Who coulda thunk it.

They had moved on to find out more about the Banshee and discovered that it was a Female Spirit, this much they already knew, an Omen of Death, likewise, but was also a Messenger from the Otherworld.

The name had derived from *Bean Shee*, a Woman of the Fairy mounds. They discovered that there were a people known as the Aos-Si, who were known as Spirits of the Ancestors or sometimes known as Fallen Angels. They were more commonly known as *Fairies*. The girls continued to pick out information.

'They are believed to live in the Fairy mounds or in an invisible world that coexists with our world.'

'Are they good or bad?'

'Not sure, but they walk among the living in their parallel universe. Anyway the Banshee really only cried out for certain families if they were going to lose someone to death. One of these was the O'Neills.'

The O'Neills made them think of the Great Battle led by O'Neill in Clonragget, not far away.

'Any other families mentioned?' Mols was anxious to find out if there was a name closer to home.

'There were only five but our name wasn't among them.'

'Good.'

'But as it turned out, anyone married into any of the five families was also affected.'

Mols thought about it. 'So over the years that probably includes everyone in the whole country then.'

'Probably.'

Morgen entered the room and caught the last piece of the conversation, Sophia recapped for him.

'What did you find out anything about Saint Michael like you said before?' He asked Sophia. She had previously said that she wanted to do some research on the Archangel as he was one of the most prominently named Angels. Morgen liked other people to do his work for him. Sophia grabbed her notebook and flicked back to some scribbling she had prepared.

'He is a messenger from Heaven. There is a special day to commemorate him every year called Michaelmas. In old times it was celebrated with a Goose and rents had to be settled on that day.'

'A Goose,' Said Mols, 'and a tithe.' The goose made her think of the lone goose that she had spotted flying into the woods and the tithe had cropped up in their research before.

'He is usually honoured in high places or mountaintops.' Continued Sophia.

'Like Mont-San-Michel.' Said Morgen.

'Sometimes he is shown in images without a face. The reason for this is because it is thought he may only be seen by those who are dead....'

'I've seen his face in loads of places.' Said Morgen.

'...or those who are about to die.' Sophia finished her sentence, without interruption this time.

'I'm not sure if I really saw it properly.' Morgen reflected more conscientiously.

'He is a protector of the Dark and Administrator of Cosmic Intelligence.'

'And,' said Morgen impressed, 'He always carries a flaming sword or a lance.'

'He saved many who were facing certain death.' Said Sophia. 'And he fought a Dragon, which was supposed to indicate a Serpent or a Demon or a *Devil.*' She told him. Morgen recalled the statue of Michael, ramming the spear into the Dragon's mouth. He pictured Michael striking out at the Devil who had fallen like lightening from Heaven, arch enemies in a battle to the death.

'He is also the Patron Saint of Germany.' Continued Sophia as Taymi popped into the room to see why there was a gathering there.

'He is sometimes known as the Angel of Death.' Sophia continued.
'Who?'

'Saint Michael.'

'I thought he saved people?'

'He was known as the *Good* Angel of Death.' Sophia corrected herself. 'It's because at the hour of death he gives everyone a chance to repent, then he carries their soul to heaven.'

'Or smites them to Hell.' Added Morgen.

'He uses a weighing scales to decide that.' Sophia informed him.

'He is also an Angel of healing and was also thought to have lived on earth as.....wait for it......Adam.'

'Adam? As in Adam and Eve?'

'Yes, Adam from the Garden.'

'But didn't Adam call on Michael for a seed from the Tree of Life?'

'Don't shoot the messenger please.' Sophia referred both to herself and the Archangel. 'It's what it says here.'

'How can one person be two people at the same time?' Morgen asked a particularly twisted question.

'Think Trinity,' said Taymi, 'Three people in one.'

'The Archangel Michael is known as the supreme enemy of Satan and of the Fallen Angels.' Sophia interjected, completed the lesson and then closing her notebook. 'That's everything I have.'

'He is our friend then.' It was Christian who had now entered the room and the conversation.

'If we are living at the Devils Hill, then we might need to call on Archangel Michael for a little help.' Christian was followed at close quarters by Lila.

'What you all talking about?' She asked.

What to say? Thought Christian, *There is a Devil who lives beside our house, who speaks evil through a stone, but that's Ok cause we're gonna call on the Angel of Death to lance him with his flaming sword?*

Sophia rescued the situation,

'Guess what Lila, we found out that there are Fairy People.'

'Are they real?' Lila was excited.

'Hmm Hmm.' nodded Sophia in a non committal sort of a way.

'Yea!' Lila heard what she wanted to hear. 'Can we see them?'

I hope not. Thought Taymi.

'Why not.' Said Sophia.

XXVIII

AMICUS

(Friend)

THEY WERE BACK in the Woods, wishing for inspiration in the pursuit of a precious artefact, or hoping to lay eyes on a Fairy, but more likely perhaps to find a screaming rabbit. They trooped past the place they called *The Drop*.

'Careful, mind that branch.' Called Taymi warning the others of one of the many intrusions on the route. Morgen, as ever, keen to make progress, bent the branch out of his way and then let it go again. Later he claimed that he thought Christian was going to grab it from his hand but that's not what happened. Christian had been looking down, making sure not to loose his footing and when he looked up... TWHACK, the bendy branch flew back, hit him full in the face and sent him reeling backwards... over the edge of the drop.

Taymi caught sight of him tumbling over the sharp edge and screamed. The others shouted and screamed too when they realised what had happened.

Christian plummeted backwards over the edge, his whole body flipped over and slid down the remainder of the steep slope, snagging on brambles, and rolled to a stop near the bottom and close to the river.

Morgen was quickest down the slope to reach him hurtling from branch to tuft as nimbly as a mountain goat. Christian was groaning and trying to sit up. His nose was bleeding and there was dirt all over his face. Taymi descended quickly followed by the others in succession.

'Are you alright?' Everyone was saying at once except Sophia, at the sight of blood she slumped down on her knees with weakness.

'Something's wrong with Sophia.' Said Mols going to assist her sister.

'Owwww' said Christian faintly and Taymi was glad that he was saying something instead of nothing at all. His nose was bleeding profusely and with the muck on his face it made it difficult to see whether he was cut or injured. The situation was mayhem, Lila was frightened and Taymi didn't know where to turn first.

'I'm coming down!' A voice sounded from high above them and Taymi looked up to see a young woman making her way down the steep embankment. Taymi was grateful that someone was there to help for she herself was somewhat panic stricken.

'Are you all Ok? What's happened? I heard the screaming.' said the woman when she reached the children and she immediately began tending to Christian.

'He fell!...down that hill.' Said Taymi comforting Lila now, 'and my sister doesn't feel too good either.' She nodded to Sophia. Christian still felt dazed, he was sticky with blood and the lady helped clean up his face, 'What's your name?' she asked.

'Chridiad.' he replied with his pinched nose.

'Ok Christian, lean forward, pinch here at the soft part of your nose and hold until the bleeding stops, breathe through your mouth.' She issued clear instructions.

'Ok what about you?' she moved over to Sophia who was about to faint. 'What's your name?'

'Sophia.'

'Ok Sophia, lets get you lying down and your sister here can keep your legs raised, this will allow you to get blood to you brain quickly.' She advised. 'You've just fainted.'

Christian was struggling with his breathing following the trauma.

'Breath easily through your mouth, slow deep breaths.' Advised the lady. He was able to control his breathing slightly better. Colour was coming back into Sophia's face and everything was getting back under control. Taymi was glad, she took note of the strangers blond hair and khaki clothes. She was practically dressed but her style was fashionable.

'Thank you.' Taymi said to the lady.

'That's no problem,' said the lady, 'Are you kids from around here?'

'We live very close.' Said Taymi who was detecting a discernable accent that suggested the lady was not from around here.

'What are your names?' she said, 'I already know Sophia… and Christian, that's an intriguing name.'

Taymi introduced the others.

'And I am Anouk.' Said the lady.

'Are you French?' asked Taymi identifying the pronunciation of her name, and the giveaway of course of the name itself.

'Yes indeed, you could say French/Irish, I have lived in both countries.'

Taymi nodded knowingly.

'I am also a small part German and I have a drop of Russian blood.'

Taymi's eyes widened, amazed at this multicultural mix, especially since she was not aware of any exotic connections in her own family tree, they all seemed to have come from the same place.

'I like your name.' said Mols.

'Thank you, it is a variation of the name *Ana* which you may be more familiar with. Actually there are over two hundred variations of that name.' This astonished the Westwooders.

'What are you doing in the Woods today?' Anouk asked them taking a good look at them now, each and every one.

'We are looking for treasure.' Lila said and Christian shook his head in disbelief that Lila would so readily give away their secret.

'That's interesting, said Anouk, 'that's *exactly* what I'm doing too.'

Christian looked up.

'I am working for the mining company, taking soil samples from the surrounding areas. If we can detect the presence of certain minerals in the soil it is a sign that precious metals might be present underneath the ground.' Anouk said.

'What kind of treasure are you looking for?' she asked Lila.

'Gold.' said Lila.

'Same as me then,'said Anouk, 'but if you find any I am afraid you cannot keep it.'

'Why is that?' asked Taymi and Christian looked up again.

'Because anything under the ground belongs to the nation, not to any individual.' She explained. 'If you want to look for something you must have a licence, mining rights and permissions. Even with these rights you have to pay a lot of royalties.'

This disappointed Christian, even if they were to find the stone it would not belong to them and they may not have any claim to it.

'How are you doing?' Anouk asked Sophia who was sitting up now.

'I am feeling better thank you.' Replied Sophia.

'And Christian, how are you.'

Christian sat up straight and stopped pinching his nose. The bleeding had stopped.

'I think I am Ok now.' He said. 'Thank You.' Christian looked a mess with blood and dirt stains on his face. He was wearing a white tee-shirt over a black long sleeve top. The white shirt was saturated with blood stains.

'Mom and Dad will never allow Christian back into the Woods if they hear he has had another incident.' Said Taymi. 'especially if they see the state of him.'

'Oh I am sure that will not happen.' Said Anouk. 'It was merely an accident.'

'Christian suffers from weakness sometimes.' Taymi said by way of explanation.

'Christian is not weak, he is strong, I can tell.' Anouk said looking at Christian. 'Here let me help you get cleaned up. Give me your shirt; I will see what I can do with it.' Christian took off his outer tee-shirt and Anouk took it to the waters edge to wash out as much of the blood as she could.

'See if you can clean your face in the water.' She urged him.

Anouk put the shirt into the water and washed the bloody area. Taymi could see the blood stains create a small cloud in the water before streaming away with the flow.

Bloodstream. She thought.

Anouk wrung out the shirt and gave it to Taymi.

'Pop this in the wash at your house.' She said. 'It might be best if you don't make too much of a fuss about it when you go home.'

Christian was looking much cleaner now and almost back to normal, in fact he was interested in finding out more about the mining exploration that Anouk was involved in.

'How do you know where to look for soil samples?' He asked.

'I will be taking samples from as many locations as I can,' said Anouk, 'I expect to be in the woods for about two weeks collecting small samples, before I go back to France.

'How do you know you haven't already been to a part of the Woods?' he enquired further.

'I have a very detailed set of maps, which I will mark as I go along. I am an excellent map reader and cartographer.'

'What's that?' asked Morgen.

'I know how to prepare maps.' Answered Anouk.

'I am interested in maps.' Christian informed her. 'I'm doing my own map of the woods.'

'That's excellent Christian, perhaps you will have the opportunity to chart new territory.' She said.

'Have you ever been to Mont-san-Michel.' Morgen interrupted, wanting to explore the French connection.

'Yes, I have.' Said Anouk smiling, 'My work takes me to many places and that is one place that is of great interest to me. I have been there many times.'

'Did you go to the top of the island, to the church?' asked Morgen.

'Yes, but did you know that church was once a prison?' Morgen did not know this.

'Also, the church was once almost burned to the ground in a fire that destroyed most of the village,' she told him, 'it was during a bloody battle, a massacare.' she said. Morgen's eyes widened with this information and Lila was impressed too.

'Were you there?' she asked. Anouk laughed a long laugh.

'It was eight hundred years ago.' She advised.

'Did you ever see the Archangel Michael at the top? With his sword? Spiking the demon.' asked Morgen.

'Michael had two sides,' Anouk spoke like she knew the Archangel personally, 'the side that you saw, with the sword, but he had a softer side, it was he that rescued Isaac from certain sacrifice, he's not as tough as he's made out to be you know.'

'I know that story!' Morgen said, 'but I didn't know it was Michael who came to save the day…what if Abraham didn't hear Michael in time.' Anouk laughed.

'Then it would have been a whole different story,' She said. 'And the entire course of history may have been changed.'

'How do you know about all this.' Asked Morgen.

'I have studied in many areas,' said Anouk, 'not just cartography.'

'Sometimes I say a prayer to the Angels.' Said Lila shyly absorbing the discussion about the Archangel.

'You do not need to pray to Angels little one,' said Anouk, 'Angels do not accept worship from humans.' Sophia was intrigued by this strange comment.

'Do you live in France full time?' Taymi knew that the accent was much more rounded than that.

'No I move around a lot, I lived near here for a time. This project was a perfect opportunity to come back for a short visit. I hadn't been back for a few years.' Anouk told her. 'But now I really must go back to where I left my equipment and continue with my work.' She said. 'Else I will have lost my maps and that's not good for a cartographer.'

'Thanks for helping us out.' Christian was truly thankful.

'Its nothing,' said Anouk smiling, 'Perhaps you will do something for me one day.'

'Yes, thank you.' Said Sophia.

'No thanks necessary, I am here to help,' she said, 'just consider me your Guardian Angel.' She smiled at Sophia, Christian and the others.

Anouk made her way back up the steep slope and off into the distance leaving the Westwooders to themselves. They gathered themselves and all their stuff and made their way home, it was enough action for one day and Christian was sore from the fall. They made their way back by the same route they had come, with Sophia tagging along behind still not having fully got over what happened.

When they made it home, Taymi snuck the bloody shirt into the wash disposing of the evidence. Sophia had something else on her mind. She took herself to her room to read some more about Angels whispering softly the words she read.

'Angels are often considered messengers of the Supreme Being and will do required tasks. It is not known if they have their own free will. They are also thought to have been former human beings who continue to take a human shape.' Sophia flicked forward in her reference book to something she has seen about Guardian Angels.

'A *Guardian* Angel is assigned to look after and guide a person. They are considered a tutelary Angel which is an animistic guardian of a person or place. Tutelary spirits existed before Angels such as Diana of Aricia who watched over a sacred grove or Goddess Levana who watched over children. Scriptures suggest that children are understood to be looked after by Guardian Angels.'

Sophia thought of their trouble in the Woods and how Anouk had suddenly appeared to look after them when they needed help. She noticed that the names Di-ana, Lev-ana were some of the many versions of Ana that Anouk had mentioned.

Sophia pondered on the name Anouk and thought to explore it further. She made her way to the project room and typed the name Anouk into a website devoted to the meaning of names.

Anouk was described as a French name meaning *favour and grace.* Sophia felt it was a fitting meaning.

She thought back to the Woods, tagging behind the others thinking about the lady they had met. Anouk had seemed so calm, controlled, assuring....*graceful....Angelic!* There was a mention of an Angel in the verse she remembered but they hadn't been able to figure it out; *Angel peel of the coet,* although she thought now that it could possibly mean that an Angel could come in the form of a disguise under which their true identity could be revealed.

Sophia wasn't sure why she had looked up at that moment, but she did, perhaps to see if it was going to rain, or to see if the sun was going to break through the clouds or because *something* made her.

But *something* was falling softly down to the ground. She picked it up and looked at it closely and then looked back up at the sky through the branches. There was no sign of a bird or even a nest overhead.

She placed the item carefully in her notebook and closed the cover. She was convinced it was a sign, the sign…. of an *Angel.*

It was a single delicate white feather.

Not far away, another pair of eyes saw the feather fall. Saw Sophia collect it, saw them making their way home. He did not like what he saw. The Dark One had work to do.

XXIX

PRISTINUS

(Ancient)

'I'VE GOT AN appointment in Clones tomorrow.' Mom said, 'We can all go if you would like to spend the afternoon somewhere different.' She offered.

'I'd like to go see the new library there,' said Dad, 'you guys should come, it's a beautiful building, state of the art, cost seven million euros, thousands of books more than our town library.' Sophia was immediately interested, but a little confused, she was familiar with the town which lay about twenty miles to the West but....

'Is'nt Clones a much smaller town, why would it have such a big library?' She asked.

'It has the primary library in the region.' Explained Dad, 'in fact for Centuries Clones was the primary *town* in the region... apparently.'

'Yes it was.' said Christian, 'And I know why. It contained the Primary Abbey in all of the country, the Primus Abbus, put there by St.Tiernach. That's why it was so important.'

'Impressive.' nodded Dad.

'Actually, I think it was quite a small Abbey.' Said Christian.

'I meant you.' Said Dad.

Christian smiled humbly, 'That's where Christianus was Primus Abbot, The Abbey still exists, can we go and have a look at it?'

'Of course, if we can find it.'

Everyone was in agreement, a trip to Clones was on the cards. *This is shaping up to be an interesting trip.* Thought Christian. *Perhaps my historical namesake will have left a clue for me about the hiding place of the Golden Stone.*

Most roads into the Clones town lead steeply up into the central town square known as The Diamond.

Dozens of little houses and shops stepped smartly on each side of the street and the town had a comfortable historic feel to it. It was pleasantly busy but it with no particular sense of urgency. They parked right in the centre of town and Mom went off to her appointment leaving the rest of the family to choose which direction they wanted to sojourn.

'Where to start?' said Dad looking this way and that. Their plan was to locate the Abbey and later meet up at the new library.

'What about there?' Morgen pointed. High up in the Diamond was a large stone Celtic Cross, it was as good a starting place as any and they walked towards it.

The Celtic Cross was surrounded by rails and they gathered around to investigate. It was clearly very ancient with a series of carvings cut into its vertical and horizontal sections. An information plaque gave further information.

'This high cross dates from the 9th century depicting images biblical importance.' Read Sophia.

'That's well over a thousand years ago.' Dad pointed out. 'That is a looong time.'

'The bottom panel illustrates Adam and Eve.' Read Sophia.They looked and saw two crude figures, they were difficult to distinguish and some of the detail had worn away over time with weathering, but in addition to the people they could just about make out the serpent.

'Then there is Abrahams sacrifice of Isaac.' Sophia glanced up, interested to see this depiction of a scene which they were by now all familiar with. Again it was a crude image, in this case the boy appeared to be leaning over a stone and his father had the knife raised over his head. What appeared to be an Angel hovered overhead.

'St. Michael.' identified Morgen pleased to see his friend again.

'The top panel is Daniel in the lions den.' Sophia continued.

This too was difficult to see, but it appeared as if Daniel was in the middle and he was surrounded by six hungry lions.

'It reminds me of serving dinner to you guys.' Dad quipped.

'Do you know anything about this story?' Mols asked.

'A little,' said Dad, 'as far as I know Daniel was thrown to the lions, but he survived….that's all.' Mols thought she would like to know more, *especially how he had overcome the Lions.*

'The top side panel is a depiction of Cain killing Abel.' Sophia read.

'Now who would want to do that?' Morgen gesticulated in a strangling motion towards his brother.

They continued to examine the ancient cross, its messages and images spanning generations and centuries keeping the faith, keeping its strength. On the other side of the high cross were images from the New Testament, loaves and fishes, water into wine, the Baptism of Christ.

New Life. Thought Christian. This was not what they had come to see but it had somehow attracted them to it, spoken to them. *Is this what they meant when the said the Golden Stone spoke?* Thought Christian.

Having fully examined the cross they made their way down another street where Dad was confident the old ruins lay. A tall ancient tower came into view, a medieval Round Tower.

'This looks promising.' Said Christian.

'These round towers were used as bell towers and a place to hide in an attack.' Pointed Dad. They made their way towards the tower and discovered it was contained within a walled enclosure.

Christian stretched to look over the wall and Morgen clambered up the side of it to see. It was a Cemetery, gravestones leaned this way and that at odd angles. It was clear that the cemetery was no longer in use and those that lay there had been here many years. There was no indication of any other ruins that could be considered the old Abbey.

'Let me see.' Urged Lila, lifted up by Dad.

'What happened?' she gasped, to her young eyes something terrible had unearthed the monuments.

'Zombies.' Said Morgen.

'Old age.' Said Dad.

'Precisely!' said Morgen.

'There's a gate down there.' Pointed Mols and they made their way to a heavy iron gate, beside which there was an information plaque on the wall. Its opening statement was;

This graveyard contains the sarcophagus of Saint Tiernach.

'Sarcophagus, a Burial Tomb like the Ancient Egyptians.' Said Morgen.

Tiernach. Thought Christian, he hadn't realised that the Saint who had promoted this town was actually buried here. He read further,

'The sarcophagus was originally contained within a church on these grounds which was destroyed during war. A similar fate occurred to the Abbey nearby which was subsequently rebuilt.....Oh, Then this is not the Abbey, its somewhere nearby.'

Sophia gripped the bars of the gate and pulled aggressively. It was stuck fast. She pressed her face between them and peered into the cemetery.

'It's a pity we can't go in there.'

Dad put his hand on the gate and gently pushed it open.

'Oh.' She said.

They made their way though the Cemetery along a gravel pathway towards the Round Tower. Morgen and Lila ran ahead passing numerous crooked gravestones carved with faint wording and names. When they reached the Tower, Lila turned around to see the others coming. Something made her gasp and she grabbed Morgens arm. He looked, he gasped too. They were witnessing a very eerie sight. Lila ran to Dad and grabbed him.

'I don't like it.' She said. The others had by now reached Morgen.

'Look.' He raised his hand pointing, they turned around. At the back of almost every tombstone was a carving of skull and crossbones.

'Yikes.' Said Taymi, 'That's freaky.' It did make for a macabre sight; the cemetery looked entirely different from this angle.

'Why the skull and crossbones?' Christian asked Dad.

'It must have been the tradition at the time.' Dad said, he was comforting Lila.

'Don't worry Lila, there are some pictures of Angels too.' He pointed out. It was true, some of the carvings were Angels, with a solemn face not unlike the skull except that the Angel images had a set of wings. They didn't provide much consolation to Lila.

They stood at the Round Tower and inspected it closely. It had small slot windows, a door about three quarters way up and its conical roof had fallen in. Taymi was looking around for something else.

'That must be the sarcophagus over there.' She pointed out a raised tombstone which appeared to have a simple stone roof. They ran over to it leaving Dad and Lila still admiring the tower. The sarcophagus was constructed in by now very ancient stone and its simple decorations were weather worn. Near it was an independent tombstone carved with a message that caused Taymi's mouth to drop open when she read it.

'Ohmygosh! Look at this,' she called out to the others gesturing wildly for them to hurry.

They were equally astonished at what they read. *What did this mean? Had they somehow come full circle?* They were certainly confused, feeling that they were somehow missing a point somewhere. Christian read the inscription aloud trying to justify it to himself.

'Here lies Tiernach…*Of the House of Oriel*'

The House of Oriel, as in the message in the woods, carved into a tree, in a forgotten language, decades and decades ago. Now here was the same wording carved into an ancient tombstone hundreds, almost thousands of years old. *How could it be?*

What was the connection between the little girl in the Castle, and this figure from ancient history that lay at their feet? They had assumed the House of Oriel to be her house, the Castle, now it seemed that Tiernach, successor to Macartan was *of* the House of Oriel, but how? In what way? It appeared they may have misinterpreted the message in the woods, but if so then how were they to reinterpret it. A whole host of questions opened up. The mystery deepened and widened.

Dad and Lila arrived.

'Whatcha found?' asked Dad.

'This is his tomb alright.' Covered Christian, he read the remaining description.

'Primus Abbot and Bishop of Clogher, 500-548'

'What age was he then?' asked Dad.

'Sixty?' Lila's maths made Dad smile.

'This is quite a significant landmark.' Said Dad, 'We are standing at the burial place of a Saint.'

'Would his body be preserved?' asked Mols thinking of how Pio's body had stayed intact.

'Who knows Mols.' Said Dad, 'possibly.'

'What do you know about Tiernach then?' Dad asked. Christian had promised to find out something about Tiernach since they were going to visit the town. He pulled out a piece of paper on which he had jotted down a few notes.

'His Mom was the daughter of a King.'

'Was she a princess?' Lila wanted to know.

'A princess yes.' Said Dad, 'That means Tiernach was of Royal Blood.'

'I guess.' said Christian. '...and his Godmother was Saint Brigid.'

'Wasn't she...' started Sophia.

'Yes, Macartan's niece.' said Christian, 'Tiernach was educated in a monastery.'

'Why a monastery?' asked Taymi.

'He had appeared to have special powers.'

'What powers?' asked Morgen.

'I don't know ...can I finish this.' Christian was exasperated.

'Go on.' Said Dad.

'He visited Rome and France and came back to Ireland where he could work miracles.' Christian waited for any interruptions but there were none.

'After Macartan, Tiernach became Bishop of Clogher and he moved the seat of power to Clones. He was blind for most of his life. He built the Monastery here at Clones and a small Abbey in which he died. He was known as the Primus Abbas, the most senior Abbot in the land. Later on Christianus got that job and ruled Clones.'

'Good report.' Said Dad.

'Oh and he died of the plague.' Concluded Christian.

They made their way back through the waves of skulls and crossbones and through the seemingly impenetrable black gates. Christian hadn't mentioned about Tiernach being of the House of Oriel, he had only just discovered this and had no idea what it meant. But the discovery weighed heavily on his mind and ticked over in his brain. But now he needed to turn his attention to something else.

'So where is the Abbey?' said Christian.

'Precisely.' Said Dad.

They walked for another short distance along another narrow curved street and arrived at a place not far from the Diamond. In front of them was what appeared to be church ruins. Christian ran up to it and checked the information plaque.

'Yep, this is the Abbey.' He called as the others caught up.

Sophia tried gently pushing the churchyard gate and it swung open freely allowing them to enter. The Abbey was a small building with only one gable at full height; the remaining walls having crumbled to head height. Dad examined the entrance door arch and the formation of a conical arched window.

Christian regarded the small size of the important Abbey, the Primus Abbus. He had thought that Christianus should have been lording over a stately pile, not this little church, it hardly seemed important enough.

The small churchyard contained many old tombstones similar to the type in the tower cemetery. Some had slowly sunken like they were melting into quicksand…except that it was slowsand. One tombstone had fallen almost to the ground but was caught on a twisted bush which seemed to catch the stone and raise it eerily back up again.

'Taymi don't move.' Dad warned suddenly. She stood stock still beside the outside of the wall of the Abbey.

'Beside your head.' He pointed. She flicked beside her ear and leapt away quickly.

'It's not a bug!' he laughed, 'I just noticed this.' It was a small Celtic cross carved into a single stone in the outer wall. 'Fascinating.' He said before moving on leaving Taymi looking incredulous after him.

There were several tall tombstones, several of which were in the shape of a Celtic cross. Taymi read one.

'Here lies Joseph whatshisname, also his grandfather, his brother, his uncle, his cousin, his brother, his uncle *and* his nephew….. Whew,' she said out of breath, 'You couldn't fit any more people into the plot or onto the headstone.' Morgen noticed there was something written on the side of the stone…….

'…and also his Grandmother.' He read.

Christian stood at the gate and looked at the Abbey; he was walking in the steps of his namesake Christianus. It was possible that Christianus was even buried here, but he had been unable to identify his name on any of the stones. From the gate of the Abbey he could see the High Cross in the Diamond. In the other direction he could almost see the Round Tower. His thoughts were interrupted by Dad.

'C'mon guys, Mom just texted, we can go and meet her.'

'Mom just text, not texted.' Taymi corrected Dad who ensued to put up a fierce argument in favour of the word 'texted'.

Christian formulated the locations of the ancient sites in his head and made a mental note of the distinct pattern they made.

'Fascinating.' He repeated Dad's word.

XXX

DISCERE

(Find)

AFTER MEETING UP again with Mom they all made their way to what Dad called the 'Primus Liberus' his made up name for the new Library. It was a stylish modern building of white cuboid formation and expansive glass sections. Inside was an interesting combination of concrete ceiling, white walls and some dark wood panelling. This didn't distract the Westwooders who ran off to get books without giving the walls and panelling a second look, except Dad who deconstructed the ceiling in his mind and then recreated it....except better.

Mols began looking for something that might have read; *How to Fend off Wild Cats; by Daniel.*

Morgen had already found a large book that fascinated him; *Images of a Changing World.*

Sophia was looking for something that might tell her more about Clones, this ancient town.

Mom was perusing the mind body spirit section, Dad sat down to nurture his.

Taymi couldn't decide what to choose to read and she wandered around a little aimlessly. Then it occurred to her and she marched up to the librarian's desk.

'Do you have a copy of the Nuremburg Chronicles please.' The librarian looked at her as thought she had just asked for the Book of Kells.

'We don't have a *copy* of the Nuremburg Chronicles.' she said smartly, 'Copies of that book are very rare in the world and are held in such establishments as the Smithsonian Institution.'

Taymi felt a little foolish, *How was I supposed to know?* she thought and at the same time she realised how precious the copy of the book in the Castle must have been.

'We may have something *about* the Nuremberg Chronicles.' The librarian tapped her keyboard.

'There is lots about the Nuremberg Trials,' she said peeping over her glasses, 'Ahh, here we are, Nuremberg Chronicles.' She wrote down a reference number. 'I'll get it for you.' She smiled.

Taymi settled at a large reading table joining her siblings who were already there, except for Christian.

Mols had found several books on biblical characters.

Morgen was looking at images of scorched earth.

Sophia had found a pictorial history of the town of Clones right there on the table.

Christian was distracted. He was looking at a large photograph of the town of Clones taken from the air which adorned one of the library walls. The picture confirmed something for him which had already been on his mind; the positions of the three ancient monuments in the town and the pattern they formed.

A Trinity! He thought, *Three that become one, three locations become one shape. A shape of three equal length sides. A perfect equilateral triangle.* 'Christianus,' he said to himself, 'I think you may have given me a clue after all.'

'Do me a favour,' said Taymi when Christian came to join them, 'there seems to be something called the Nuremberg Trials, it might be related to this, could you grab something on it.'

'Dang nabbit.' He moaned and trudged to the section on World History where he was surprised by how easily he found something on the Trials and was back in a flash.

Taymi began to review the book about the book.

'The Nuremberg Chronicle was written in Latin and called the Liber Chronicarum or the Book of Chronicles. It was written by a Physician.' She wasn't sure if anyone was listening to her or not and she didn't mind either way.

'The Nuremberg Trials,' read Christian, 'were the court tribunals of prosecution of the Nazis after World War 2, including Hitlers henchmen.'

'Clones,' read Sophia, 'was called Cluain Innis, the island retreat, as the raised town often stood above surrounding waters in times of flooding.'

'Look.' Said Lila, she was drawing a skull and crossbones.

'Look at this too.' said Morgen holding up a page from his book which demonstrated in a series of pictures the devastation caused to the earth by the drying up of a river bed over a one year period.

'Daniel became famous for reading the meaning of dreams.' Mols read out from her biblical book.

'It was printed in 1493, in Nuremberg, one of the earliest printed books.'

'The trials were held at Nuremberg at the Palace of Justice.'

'The Abbey was also known as the retreat and it was burned twice in its history.'

'He had the ability to make predictions.'

'Who?'

'Daniel.'

'The book is a history of the World and its illustrations were unique in that they were hand painted. The World map does not include America because although Columbus made his discovery in the same year, it was too late to be included in the publication.'

'British Prime Minister Winston Churchill had suggested that there should be on the spot executions for some of the war criminals.'

'The holy sites in Clones were granted from the Pope to a Local King and eventually passed down the line until they were owned by the Bishop who had to pay tithes on the properties…there's that word again.' Said Sophia.

'Look.' Said Lila, she had drawn an Angel.

'See.' Said Morgen holding up photographs of depleting ice glaciers, the photos were taken six months apart from each other.

'They primarily documented the six ages of the world, from Creation to the Deluge, from then to Abraham, to David, to the Babylonians, to Christ, to now.….or 1493 at least.' Taymi looked at the six ages. The David referred to was of David and Goliath which meant she knew something about all of the ages except Babylonia.

'Despite the war the Palace of Justice was virtually untouched.' Said Christian. 'Nuremberg was the birthplace of the Nazi's and it was going to be their demise.'

'This historic local town has been written about and been filmed on numerous occasions.' Said Sophia.

'Daniel was a Babylonian from 600BC.' Mols stated. 'Babylon was a holy city, one of the first civilisations.' She informed them and now Taymi knew a little about all of the six ages.

'About 2500 copies of the book were ever made, many have perished in the intervening years.'

'Many of the Nazis were sentenced to Death; the most famous Hermann Goering committed suicide the night before his planned execution.' Christian felt angry that this top Nazi didn't stand up like a man and take his punishment and instead spirited himself away.

'Daniel was precious to the King but the Governors tricked the King into throwing Daniel into the Lions den.'

Morgen held his book up again. 'New Orleans, two days apart.' The destruction of the city after the hurricane and flooding was obvious.

'The book is an incunabulum,' Taymi struggled with the pronunciation, 'its means infant or infancy, in publication anything printed before 1500 is an incun....one of them.'

'The executions were by hanging and the bodies were burned in the furnace, their ashes scattered in a river.'

'When the King went to the Den the next morning he found Daniel alive and well. An Angel had come to keep the Lions at Bay. The King threw his governors in the Den instead.'

Morgen held up his book with another before and after picture, the Twin Towers.

They all looked.

Taymi looked back to her book; she gave a sharp intake of breath.

'There was a Seventh Age!' she gasped. 'The Seventh Age!....in the verse.'

'The *Infant* of the Seventh Age!' Christian nearly choked as he pieced it together. He repeated the words from the verse.

'But I would again spare the infant -Of the Seventh Age'

'It's the book!' Taymi screamed as silently as she could. 'The Gatekeeper was trying to spare the book, not the child, or maybe both.' Now she was confused.

'You said the book was printed in 1493, it was an infant of seven years before the year 1500 turned.' Christian pointed out, 'It was age seven.'

'Somebody wanted the book in the Castle burned, destroyed and they didn't care if people got burned at the same time.' Taymi was aghast.

'What does it say?' Christian gestured at the book. 'The six ages covered the entire history of the World, what is the Seventh Age then? Everyone was all ears; Taymi read;

'The book is completed with a short Seventh Age, which is not a historical account as per the majority of the book. It is a prediction of what is to come.' She read.

'A prediction....wait...' Christian had something, '....an object which predicts the future is called an *Oracle*, ...could this be an

Orical as in *burn the house of Orical?*' They were speechless, it was entirely possible that he was right. Christian nodded to Taymi to carry on with reading and she did.

'The prediction related to the End of the World and The Last Judgement.'

'The End of the World?' Morgen was shocked, Lila was quite displeased. Taymi read more quietly;

'At the end of times it predicted that there will be one who will come to rule and destroy the world. He will emerge by stealth, stealing power and fastening his grip on the destruction of the World. This will be done by setting people against people and country against country, destruction and plagues, it will be known as the *Epoch*.' She whispered the final bit, her voice almost shaking,

'The one who will bring about this destruction is known as Satan, the Anti-Christ.....The *Devil*.' There was an image from the pages of the actual book displayed here, it was the Devil on horseback, a lady assistant with him. Taymi looked up with an almost scared look in her eyes. There was silence around the table inviting her to read on.

'This section of the book was an apocalyptic vision similar to the prediction of the end of the world in other books such as the Bible. An Apocalypse!'

Morgen's book lay open at a page which depicted a single image, a grainy photo of an atomic explosion, the *first* atomic explosion, the beginning of the atomic age which led to Hirosema and Nagasaki, it happened in July 1945, secretly in New Mexico, Mankinds new ability to destroy itself, an *Apocalypse*. During the test, words from Hindu scripture locked themselves into the mind of the Test Operations Director. '*I am become Death, the Destroyer of Worlds*.' Morgen looked at the photo, he looked at its title, as with each test it was given a name, the name of this the first atomic explosion was a name he was familiar with....... He looked at it and read it silently,... '*Trinity*'.

'There's a bit more.' Taymi said but they weren't sure if they could stand it.

'After a period will come The Day of Judgement in which Satan will be destroyed and all those on the side of evil will be judged at the left hand of God while those on his right hand will be saved.' Taymi frowned at the task assigned to the left hand.

'This will occur after the dead have arisen…..'

'Zombies!' Stated Morgen, 'I knew it.'

'….and after the second coming of Christ.' Taymi concluded.

'The second coming of Christ.' Taymi repeated, 'Will he come again, as a child, an infant…of the Seventh Age?'

'But the End of the Seventh Age predicts that Satan will be defeated forever, the verse says the Seventh Age, *The End*.' Christian summarised.

'I suppose so.' said Taymi still digesting what she had read.

'So that's a good thing then.' He said.

'Yes, except it's not that great when you live at the hill of the Devil.' She said.

'Will there be a war?' Morgen asked.

'There are always wars Morgen.' Sophia said, 'Just look at the TV, maybe that what it means when it says the world will be destroyed.'

'But there hasn't been a war around here.' Morgen pointed out.

'Ahem, what about the war that destroyed Clones? The Battle of Clonragget?' Christian asked, 'What about all the fighting there has been in Northern Ireland?'

'Drugs wars, it's all over the newspapers.' Taymi added.

'But at least there was no plague.' Morgen said.

'One hundred thousand people died or emigrated….' Taymi reminded him. '….right here in Clogher, in three years due to hunger, plague and greed.' It was patently obvious that there had been a lot of destruction in just this small area notwithstanding the rest of the World.

'Maybe this is the Seventh Age.' Said Morgen. His words were profound, there was much to indicate that this might be the Seventh Age.

'The book predicts the end of Satan.' Said Christian, 'Is that enough reason to burn down the Castle?'

'Maybe someone doesn't want the Seventh Age to end, they want to wipe out all mention of it.' Said Taymi.. They couldn't be sure either way.

'I've found something here about Cain and Abel.' Sophia said. 'And its got something to do with sacrifice.' She had absentmindedly flicked the pages of one of Mols biblical books and held it opened at a story concerning the two brothers who had cropped up on the ancient stone cross earlier. The others turned their attention to her.

'Both Cain and Abel made a sacrificial offering to God. God accepted Abel's offering but not Cain's. This was because Cain was jealous of Abel and also because it was Satan who had commanded that Cain make an offering. Cain then decided to murder Abel.' Morgen made a mime of raising a knife against Christian before Sophia continued.

'Cain got the idea to bury Abel's body from a Raven who scratched the ground with his claw to indicate burial.'

Mols nodded, this was typical of Ravens.

'Cain was banished to wander the world but if anyone were to try and kill him they would be cursed seven times.'

'Seven, Seven, Seven.' Said Taymi, noticing how the number kept coming up.

'Twenty one.' Said Morgen. Lila smiled upon hearing the significance of seven mentioned again. Taymi looked at her thinking how her age would change within a matter of months, on December 14th,... the date was another multiple of seven, it would be the *end* of Lila's seventh age. But Sophia had not concluded yet,

'His curse was indicated by a mark which is thought to have been the Hebrew letter *vau* which occurs in up to six other alphabets. In many of these it is the sixth letter.'

'Phew,' said Taymi, 'better six than seven.'

'The letter vau,' continued Sophia, 'is in the form of a hook, similar to the shape of the number 7.'

'Dammit.' Said Taymi hearing that number again.

Christian was thinking about the sacrifice. God had rejected it because it was commanded by Satan, and when Cain failed in having it accepted he committed the first murder, the first evil of mankind.

Mols was staring into her book, her eyes grew wide as she read.

'Daniel had a vision about a Golden Stone!' she exclaimed catching their attention instantly.

'Read it!' Directed Taymi.

'In Daniel's vision he saw an idol made of gold, silver and clay stone and its appearance was terrible. In the vision there was another stone, a pure stone that was used to smote the idol.'

'Destroy it,' said Morgen explaining the word smote, 'I heard it on the Simpsons.'

Mols continued. 'The clay and silver and gold broke into pieces and its dust was carried away on the wind so that it could never return.'

'That's what it says in the verse,' Christian said, 'banish the druid by breaking the stone. Here it says by the pure stone, the verse said something about a pure hand.'

Taymi grabbed the book and scanned over the section that Mols had read out to them. There was no more detail regarding the dream but there was a final Chapter which she read to them;

'And wheresoever the children of men, the beasts of the field, and the fowls of the heaven dwell, Hath. He given them into thy hand, and hath made thee to rule over them all; thou art the head of gold'.

'What does that mean?' She said grimly. It wasn't clear what it meant but all the keywords were there, the children, the beasts, the birds, the hand, the Gold!

They pored over the information they had unearthed, Tiernach of the House of Oriel, the Infant of the Seventh Age, Daniel's dream of a Golden Stone.

If it hadn't been for this trip, Christian thought, *we wouldn't have discovered all this….its uncanny.* He thought of how Daniel, a biblical figure from 2,600 years ago had a dream that appeared to be a message to *them* of how to destroy the Golden Stone. It fit right in.

It was overwhelming, a link in history going back thousands of years. He was certain this message was for them, for him and he was going to have to try and figure out how to make sense of it all. It was a thought he carried with him as they made their way from the ancient town, the town which today yielded a few of its many secrets.

As they left Clones, Morgen looked back at the hill rising up to the town square. It reminded him a little of Mon-San-Michel, he could almost picture Archangel Michael at the top defeating a violent writhing dragon with a lance straight through the throat....defeating Satan at the End of Times.

XXXI

NOX NOCTIS

(Night)

LILA WAS FEELING scared; the reason, endless discussions about Devils and Druids.

'There's no reason to be scared Lila.' Mom told her though she was not fully aware of what was causig the problem, 'You're safe and warm.' But Lila still wore a pitiful look.

'Let's say your prayers.' Said Mom, 'You know whenever you feel scared you can say your prayers and they will protect you and make you feel safe.' She assured the little one.

'You can say prayers anytime, anywhere and they will keep you from harm, just like Angels.' Lila felt a little better hearing this and together they started with the Holy Trinity.

'In the name of the Father the Son and the Holy Spirit.' They said her prayers finishing with the *Glory Be*. 'Glory be to the Father and the Son and the Holy Spirit, as it was in the beginning, is now and ever shall be, World Without End, Amen.'

As she settled down, Lila thought about the words in the prayer, *World Without End'*. She believed in a world without end, not the '*end of the world'* that the others had been talking about and she was glad she had prayed for it.

Morgen was in his room but not yet ready for sleep. He was wearing a night vision visor gadget and was watching activity from the window. Work was undergoing in the nearby farmland and all day machinery had been busy pruning and chopping overgrown hedging and bushes. The debris was gathered up into pyres and even though it was now almost dark, the work was continuing into the night. The pyres were being burned and the long arm of the machine in the distance crashed and rooted through more bushes, its spotlight illuminating its work.

But that's not what Morgen saw.

He saw a scene from War of the Worlds, an alien tripod with lazer weapons lurching over the hill and crashing through interruptions, its deathly whine echoing across the landscape, its mechanical limbs flailing through trees, its white death ray seeking out human victims for obliteration. Earths atmosphere was contaminated with an eerie glow and fires burned where the tripods had flung lazer fireballs to the ground. The World was a scene of burning devastation, smoke and fumes mixed with the stench of death and destruction....an *Apocalypse*.

Morgen lowered his the visor on his futuristic lazer device; only one person was in the position to save humanity from this evil, only one person had the tenacity, the charisma and the vision, the night vision, to take on the menacing monsters. He knew this was the moment he had been anticipating for his whole life, he alone must rise to the occasion.

He focused on the alien machine whose objective it was to exterminate humankind.

'Not today brother.' He murmured out of the side of his mouth. He took aim.............

Sophia and Mols talked into the night, they talked about the project, which had turned into a treasure hunt. They talked about all that they had discovered, the mystery, the meanings, the messages.

How will all this end? How did all this start? They didn't have all the answers, but for now, just talking about it was good.

'And why is it that the Golden Stone just happened to be planted right next to our house? Why not somewhere else? Is that not a coincidence?' Mols complained. Sophia thought about that.

'Maybe if the Golden Stone was somewhere else…..we would be somewhere else too.' She ventured.

'You've lost me.' said Mols.

'Antimatter.' said Sophia confusing Mols even more. 'I heard Morgen talking about it; it's like the opposite of something. You said the stone was planted beside us…..' she explained, '…but maybe *we* were planted beside the stone.'

'But we've always lived here.'

'Exactly.' Sophia felt she was onto something. 'Our family have always lived here for as far back as we can remember, as far back as the Strong Man and we don't know how many generations before that. Maybe we are here because the stone is here. Maybe its not coincidence…..perhaps we are here by design!'

'But why?' asked Mols.

'I don't know.' Sighed Sophia. 'I don't know.'

Taymi was at sixes and sevens. She was thinking of all of the references to these numbers. There were six siblings in her family, there were six siblings in Granda's family, his father was one of six siblings. Six, six, six….history was repeating. A thought flew into her mind,

'6,6,6, the number of the beast, from the Bible… the Devil,' she shook her head, 'Apophenia, leave me alone.' She thought again of the prediction of the Nuremburg Chronicles, the Devil fastening his grip on the destruction of the World. She thought of the Golden Stone, if it fell into the wrong hands, its power could be used to further fasten the Devils grip on the World. If they ever did find the stone, it would be their duty to destroy it surely.

The Seventh Age, *Seven*, this number kept turning up repeatedly, it seemed to carry huge significance, everywhere she turned it appeared, she had started to notice it more now, on TV, in the newspaper, a scratch on the table, seven, seven, seven, what other secrets did it conceal?

She turned the numbers over and over and over......

Christian was lying awake. He had been having a recurring thought for days and he was having it again now. The same words were running through his mind and he couldn't do anything to stop them.

'Someone is going to die.'

The words frightened him.

'Someone is going to die.'

There had been so many things, so many symbols and signs, could he ignore them all? There was the spirit that visited him, the scream in the woods, the lone goose, the ravens, Lila and Grandas names carved in stone, Dad pointing out where he will be buried. Mr.Kelly had actually said the words. The weight of history seemed to weigh heavily on him, battles, massacres, sacrifices, the march of time, how many have passed on, who will live.

It could all be over in an instant, a name on a stone, or on a tree.

Who still lives that built the Cathedral? Or who lived in the Castle?

Who remembers the names in the Ancient Graveyard? Or the Gatekeeper?

Someone once told him that lives are like candles, some shorter, some are longer, all will burn out eventually, but no one knows whose candle will be next. No-one can live forever.

He anguished with the questions in his mind and agonized over the answers. He lay there in a cold sweat.

Why is this happening? Why can't it all just go away?

Through it all, those words kept recurring.

'Someone is going to *die*.'

XXXII

AQUA

(Water)

It rained.

It rained so heavily that torrents ran down the roads. It rained so hard that rivers formed where they had never been. It rained so intensely that plants were destroyed, walls were washed away, floods came.

Usually after a torrential rainfall, a small pond would form in the Westwoods garden at its shallowest part, this time however there was a *large* pond and growing larger by the minute. The deluge occurred over the period of about two hours in the evening, Dad was outside inspecting the scene, Mom staying inside trying to maintain calm. The garden flood had become the largest they had ever seen, it covered over half of the area and the Westwooders thought this was.....brilliant!

'We have our own lake.' Sophia squealed.

Lila peeped out from inside the house, she was the only one not happy about it,....except for Dad.

'It's continuing to rain,' he told Mom, 'if this keeps up the water will keep on rising, I don't know where it will stop.'

A Fire Engine, lights flashing passed by their house and stopped just down the road. Dad waded through the now boot deep water in the garden and onto the dry land at the entrance gate and made his way to see what was occurring. He was accompanied by an already drenched and loving it Taymi, together with Christian who, so far, had remained relatively dry.

There was trouble at Brockrady Bridge. The bridge was at the lowest part of the road and the river swept around their neighbour Marc's house before disappearing under the bridge and into the Woods......normally. Now the river had swelled, and was trying to sweep through the house and to take the bridge and everything else with it. The river had become a powerful, relentless, demon, raging and roaring, destroying all in its path.

They looked over the edge of the bridge and watched the river three times wider than normal sweeping a new course into the Woods and flattening the bushes and trees embanked on either side. The water was a silty brown, a mixture of water and soil washed away from the river banks.

'Whew, I wouldn't like to see what the waterfall is like.' Said Dad, meaning he *would* like to see what it was like.

'I haven't seen anything as bad as this as far as I can remember,' he said, 'as long as we have been living in Westwoods anyway and that's almost 20 years.'

The Fire Brigade were pumping the water from Marc's garden with a snakes nest of pipes and pumps but water had already reached his door and was seeping in. There was quite a commotion at the scene, the fire engine with its pulsating lights, firefighters, noise and clatter, the roaring of the river, traffic being directed to turn around and bystanders. It was continuing to rain. Dad spoke to the Marc who thanked him for his concern.

'Well there isn't much I can do.' Shouted Dad. He had to shout due to the sound of the heavy rain, the gush of the river and the Fire Engine intercom system.

'How is your place faring up?' asked Marc.

'I've got a lake in my garden, so long as it doesn't turn into a sea, I might be Ok.'

'It's exactly twenty one years ago since I saw this,' said Marc, confirming the timescale that Dad had mentioned earlier, 'I remember it well, the exact same thing happened.'

The figure was not lost on Taymi, seven, seven, seven, twenty one.

The Fire Chief's jeep had arrived. Dad knew the Fire Chief.

'The same guy who reviews the design of buildings for fire safety.' Dad explained. 'Its how I know him.' Dad spoke to the Fire Chief and asked him if he would take a look at the flooding at Westwoods when he was through at the bridge.

'Yea sure, is the water near your floor level yet?' Dad informed him that it was not yet near the floor.

'Then we will come back to you a little later,' said the Fire Chief, 'we have a situation in the village, some houses are flooding, and on the opposite side of the Woods too.'

'Are you guys able to cope?' Dad enquired.

'Strangely,' said the Fire Chief, 'it's not widespread, the flash flooding is localised to the Castle-Hanes area.'

Dad, Taymi and Christian returned to Westwoods. The water had risen again and was now ebbing towards the bottom of the steps to the house. Their home sat upright on three steps so the water still had some way to go. Dad inspected the drainaway which surrounded the garden, normally flooding waters would run into it and be taken away, now however, the drainaway was full and was emptying water *back* into the garden.

'If it's coming in, its not getting out.' Dad shouted. He marched to the rear of the house and came back with a spade and looked up at the dark evening skies, the rain battering off his face.

Taymi and Christian followed him to the front of the garden and the small woody strip that separated the garden from the road and the woods. There was a large deep gully, which took the flow of water from the drainaway and then through a concrete pipe under the road and away through the woods. The gully was full.

'If this water doesn't get away, the flood will keep rising, our house will be waterlogged.' Dad explained to them. 'There must be something blocking it.' They had seen Dad working in the gully before, clearing it of twigs, leaves and branches that were washed in there stuffing up the pipe. The difference was that before the water in the gully was shallow, now it was the complete opposite.

Dad went to the place where the pipe drained from the gully. He used the spade to poke down into the water as far as he could to try and determine whether debris had blocked the entrance to the pipe.

'I can feel the end of the pipe.' He said and wrangled some more with the spade. 'Theres a lot of stuff in front of it.' He took off his watch, held it in his teeth and reached his arm into the water until it was above his elbow and ground at the 'stuff'. His frustration at working at this impossible angle was obvious.

'There's only one thing for it!' He said withdrawing his hand from the water and his watch from his teeth..

'Here hold this.' He told Taymi and then he jumped feet first into the gully until he was in it to his chest.

'*What are you doing?*' screamed Taymi.

'I've got to clear this or our house will be flooded.' He said, 'Ho-Boy, this is cold!'

'But it's dangerous, wait on the Fire Brigade.'

'You sound like your Mom.... I'll be Ok, I'm standing on top of the pipe.' Said Dad. Christian wasn't too sure if Dad was Ok, but he admired his spirit. Dad used the spade to reach down and hack at the entrance to the pipe.

'There's something big blocking it.' Dad shouted. 'He wrestled for a time but was unable to remove the obstruction.

'I've got to get deeper.' He said.

'No, don't.' said Taymi but it was too late, Dad had stepped down from the top of the pipe and was now up to his neck in stormwater.

'I can reach it better from here.' He said. 'I can feel something moving.'

'Here hold the spade.' He asked Christian who did so.

'Back in a minute.' Said Dad, and with that he ducked his entire head under the water.

'*DON'T!*' screamed Taymi, but Dad was already back up raising with him a large tree branch.

'Here grab this, pull it out, don't let yourself slide in.' he warned and they pulled the hefty branch out of the water. Dad ducked again and emerged seconds later.

'This didn't help.' he said, throwing out an old plastic two litre water bottle. Christian knew that Dad would be mad with finding the bottle, he was always pointing out how some people thought it was ok to throw litter along the roadside.

'There's a large stone jammed in the hole, if I can move it the water will get away much faster. Pass me the spade.' Dad shouted.

'It's too dangerous.' Shouted Taymi. But Dad already had the spade and he was prising at the stone under the water with all of his might.

'Come out!' Taymi shouted, 'the water is rising.' Christian noticed that the water was incrementally higher now than previously. Dad prised again, but shook his head indicating that he wasn't having any success.

'Come out.' Taymi shouted again, 'Please.' Dad struggled in the water. His face grimaced and he pulled aggressively at something.

'I can't get out, my leg is stuck fast.'

Taymi freaked, 'Oh No, Oh No,' Dad struggled again, trying to free his foot from being trapped…. unsuccessfully. He raised the spade and held it with both hands.

'See if you can pull me.' They tried and tried but it was hopeless.

'I've got to try and move the stone.' He shouted, his neck raised now to keep the water from his mouth.

Dad prised again at the stone. It wasn't working. His face was panic stricken. He closed his mouth to prevent the water getting in. He looked at the children as the water washed over his face, he was completely submerged underwater holding his breath. Everything was moving so fast.

'*HE'S GOING TO DIE!*' Taymi screamed, echoing the words of the prophesy that Christian had been repeating.

This can't happen. Christian thought, *It can't.* He watched as bubbles emerged from where Dad was,…. his last breath.

An image flashed into Christians mind, it was the baptism in the river Jordan, the man emerging from beneath the water. That was the picture he had for his Dad, Emergence, Renewal, Born Again, the water of New Life not the water of the last rites. Though he stood there as though frozen in time, he knew he could not allow it happen, he had received the messages, the warnings, it was time for massive action.

Christian sucked up all his breath, leaned over and plunged his head into the water. He blew all his breath into Dads mouth, the breath of life, and came out of the water gasping.

Christian looked around for something, anything, there was nothing……..there was something. He grabbed the plastic bottle and held it down against a rock, grabbed a sharp stone and started cutting at it aggressively until he had removed the base. He quickly unscrewed the lid and covering the opening with his hand, he plunged the bottle into the water and the neck of the bottle into Dads mouth with the now open base pointing up into the open air.

He could hear Dad breath through it.

Dad breathed for his life, he wrenched again at the stone, he forced it with every fibre in his being.

The stone gave, they could hear it instantly, the underground sound of the pipe could be heard gushing, the water immediately began to go down.

The water went down below Dads eyes, below his nose and below his mouth. The water continued to subside and Christian cast the plastic bottle aside. Dad breathed deep gulps of air. As the water lowered, his torso emerged from it.

Taymi was crying. Dad spoke in a freezing stutter.

'If.f I e.e.ever get …the guyy who dropp..eed thaat litter, he'lll bee sorrrry!'

Tears rolled down Christians face.

Dad used the spade to prise away the obstruction at his foot, eventually freeing it and crawling out of the gully onto the slippery and muddy bank with the help of his children. He hugged them both. He gripped Christian's shoulders.

'You saved me.' He said.

'You would've saved me.' Christian told him back, thinking of their discussion in the Cathedral.

'You showed maturity beyond your years.' Dad stressed.

'It was not your time.' Said Christian and his Father found the words to be profound. Dad gripped Taymi's shoulders,

'You saved my watch.'

She managed to deliver a very watery smile as she took out Dad's watch, looked at it and handed it back to him. It must have got some water damage because the digital numbers didn't move. All three walked slowly back to the house, soaking and shivering. The waters were already beginning to recede and it had stopping raining.

Dad was visibly shaken but it was Taymi that was the most pale.

'I thought God wasn't going to send any more floods after Noah.' Dad said.

'Who said God sent it.' Taymi muttered just as the Fire Engine drew up alongside the road, lights flashing.

'It's Ok now.' Dad called across the pond to them, 'I cleared the gully, everything is under control.'

Taymi was'nt so sure about that, in her head she still had a picture of Dad's watch when she had looked at it before handing it back to him. She was sure it was not a coincidence.

The time read 7.17

The date read 17.7

XXXIII

CURSOR

(Messenger)

Mols was awake earlier that most. She was getting some juice from the fridge when she observed, through the kitchen window, the Buzzard, perched stately on top of a telegraph pole. It was observing too, surveying all in its vision, turning its head through 180 degrees and silently scouting for prey and sustenance. Suddenly it swooped down and she momentarily lost sight of it below the line of the bushes, but seconds later it rose up again, like a phoenix from the flames of nature, and resumed its position on its perch. Mols wanted to get closer; she stepped out the back door and deftly darted in the direction of the Buzzard. She could feel the morning dew creeping into her light slippers and the cool air on her face. She made it about halfway across the divide when the Buzzard turned and looked directly at her. She froze.

They each stayed perfectly still looking at each other.

Mr. Kelly had said that it was a biblical messenger.

'What message do you have for me?' Mols whispered.

The Buzzard looked at her long and hard; she felt it might have been trying to tell her something, but what?

They looked at each other for what seemed like an eternal moment before the Buzzard stretched out its magnificent wings and in one fell swoop it was gone.

Following the events of the night before, Dad was having a long lie in. Christian went in to see him.

'You're awake.' Christian said as Dad rolled around to see who had entered the room.

'I am?....I mean I am!' Dad said, 'I don't think I will be going in to work today if you can let the boss know for me.... tell him he's a pain in the butt too.' Christian smiled, Dad worked for himself.

'There will be no Woods today or for a few days,' Dad said, 'the river will be too dangerous and the ground too slippy.' Christian was disappointed.

'Don't worry, you will be too busy bringing me hot drinks.' said Dad.

'I'm glad you're alive.' Christian said before leaving Dad in peace.

'Elvis is alive, we are dead.' It was another of Dads cryptic comments. Christian considered it quizzically.

'Take the name Elvis and see what you can find.' Dad suggested before being swallowed up in the duvet. Christian gently closed the door. He thought about what Dad had said. 'Elvis.... Elvis...Elvis is Alive....Elvis.....Lives!, Elvis *Lives.*' He had rearranged the letters of the name 'Elvis' and created the word 'Lives', a hidden meaning within the name.

'Therefore,' he thought, 'if Elvis Lives, we, the opposite, must be ....the opposite!'

Alive yet Dead, he thought, *Dead yet Alive.*

Mols was hunting a Buzzard ...online. She discovered that the Bible references to Eagles were through the use of the Hebrew word *'Nesher'.* The word meant 'Bird of Prey', it was generally taken to mean Eagle but could equally include the Buzzard or any other bird of prey. She discovered that the Bird of Prey was used in heraldry, it was known as one of the heraldic beasts. She had heard Taymi talk about this, she recalled the words that she had used.

'An Official Messenger, a sign of what is to happen.'

She read how the Bird of Prey is considered to be strong and immortal, it is known as the King of the Air and Messenger of the

Gods. It was also known as a protective spirit, a carrier of prayers, a guardian.

'A guardian Angel?' Mols whispered to herself. There was a reference to St. John and she read it.

'The Eagle is a representation of St. John the Evangelist because of his uplifting gospels and his prophetic messages.' She looked at the last two words. 'What Messages?' She typed in the words *St. John* and began to pore over the information. He was one of the Apostles, the youngest. *The infant?* crossed her mind as she read further.

The Four Gospels of John consist of three Epistels (or letters) and the last book of all the gospels, The Book of Revelation also known as The Apocalypse.

Mols looked at the words, *Revelation*, and *Apocalypse*. Her mind was thrown back to their visit to Clones Library and their discovery of the Seventh Age, the Apocalypse. The words *The Book of Revelation* were a highlighted link, she clicked on it.

The Book of Revelation is a prophesy, a prediction of what is to come. The Apostle John had written it as a statement to Seven Churches of Asia which became known as the Seven Churches of the Apocalypse. The book describes the end of the world, or the end of the age, in which Satan will be destroyed in a great battle.

Mols was agog at the information before her, it was almost identical to what they had read in the Nurmberg Chronicles, a prophesy of the end of times. It was John's message. She thought of the Book of Kells and the Gospels of St. John it contained, the latter part of his writings had been ripped out and were missing, presumed destroyed. Was it the Book of Revelation that had been ripped out from the Book of Kells, she had no way of knowing for sure but she was willing to place a bet on it. It was as though there was a deliberate effort to destroy prophesies of the end of the seventh age, when Satan would be destroyed forever. What was in this message for her? For them? How could they possibly be connected to the prophesy? She felt sure it was the Golden Stone. Should they find it they must certainly destroy it, it was the voice of Satan, a voice that must be silenced.

Mols read how Revelation is divided into seven cycles of events. The number seven appears frequently as a symbol within the text. She was startled at reading that a predicted seven year *Tribulation* would occur which meant a time of trouble during which Christians would be persecuted and martyred. She was conscious of Taymi's concerns about the number seven and now she felt uneasy about that number herself.

There was another number too revealed in the Book of Revelation, the number six, a Trinity of sixes making one number 666. The number of the Beast. She read how the Beast was identified by many as the Roman Emperor Nero. His name when equated with numerical values as used in a system called gematria equalled the number 666. He was an ugly ruler in leadership and in appearance and he slaughtered his own immediate family in order to keep power. His persecution of Christians included them being thrown to the dogs, crucified and burned. His name was closely aligned with the name Neo, a word which meant *new* and which was an anagram for the word *one* suggesting *the one*. This made Mols think of the Neo Druids that she had heard the guys talking about.

Mols closed the computer down; there was much to tell the others, another link in the mystery. She felt uneasy, all of these prophesies, all these messages, were leading to something, it was why the Buzzard was there. Mols stared out through the window and up at the sky, they were there, circling, calling.

'Is this why you came?' Mols asked them through a whisper, 'Is this the time of the Beast?'

XXXIV

REGIUS

(Royal)

IT WAS THE next day, it had taken all that time for the flood waters to go down, it was now possible to drive their car out the avenue and so they had decided to take a little trip later in the day. The flood had become a diminishing lake, it looked serene, almost beautiful, that is, if it were'nt for the worms.

Mols looked at the worms; she had previously taken an interest in the spaghetti like creatures, she recalled some of her findings about them now as she stared at them floating dead on top of the water.

Worms; Parasites considered putrid or corrupted; the word wyrm was used in medieval European lanuages as a name for a Dragon or Demon and by extension for Satan.

Mols turned her back on the Satanic creatures, for the first time in her life she felt that a threatening presence hung over her safe and warm home.

It was a relatively short journey they were undertaking, to the village of Clogher, the small town which where Macartan had founded his Diocese. They drove there in thirty minutes. It was suggested as a trip to see if they could find the grave of Saint Macartan although that was only partly the reason that they wanted to visit this key location. The main reason of course was to see in person the stone idol which was the original Golden Stone, though they hadn't yet informed their parents about this. For Christian this was a visit of necessity, he knew he had to do it, to follow the message from the icon in St.Macartans Cathedral, to go where Macartan went, to see what he saw. Sophia had discovered that there was also an ancient Hillfort nearby and they hoped to get a look at it too, it might give them some clue someway somehow to locating their own fort nearby.

They waited impatiently until Dad had finished off his work before they made the trip. It was evening. Taymi and Christian had brought notes. Taymi read some out on their way there.

'The Cathedral is two hundred years old but was built on the site of the original church founded by Macartan. Inside the Cathedral is a pagan stone.' She didn't elaborate that this was in fact the original Golden Stone, given to Macartan and which once had been adorned with gold and silver coverings.

She didn't elaborate either that the stone was once a speaking stone, an Oracle, Cermand Cestach, a name of Germane extract also known as Kermand Kelstach and that a Demon, a Devil could speak through this stone. She didn't describe the horrors that were attributed to the stone, the stories that they had dug up through their research.

They had sat in their project room beforehand and considered the information that they had found.

'The voice of the stone can speak through a Druid.' Taymi had informed them. She described to them how the Golden Stone was one of the *three* great Oracle stones of Erin, forming a Trinity of oracles. The Golden Stone, The Stone of Destiny/*Lia Fal* on the mighty Hill of Tara and another stone known as the Crooked Black Stone /*Crom Cruach*. The voice of these stones, when worshipped in history, had encouraged War, through whispers to Kings and the overthrowers of Kings.

'The stones were associated with human sacrifice, blood and bones.' Taymi went on. Sophia felt her stomach churn.

The Golden Stone was connected to *Cernunnos* the Horned God and God of the Underworld and this made Mols think of the

Underworld they knew, the murky, uninviting Dark Underworld of the Woods.

'And the Golden stone was linked to *Crom Cruach*, the Crooked Black Stone which was destroyed by Saint Patrick. But it was responsible for the deaths of three quarters of the High Kings army and.....and more.' Morgen tried to picture Patrick destroying the evil stone. 'People called it Jaw Head or Gory Worm' Taymi concluded.

It seemed that the voices of these stones only seemed to encourage war and bloodshed. So Lila let most of this discussion go over her head, it wasn't the type of subject matter she cared for.

Hearing the word Crom, Christian had instantly thought of the historical tyrant Cromwell who wreaked a brutal campaign of atrocities and killing across the landscape much like this Crooked Black Stone. If he wasn't mistaken Cromwell was also responsible for a Regicide.... the killing of a Monarch. Both Cromwell and Crom Cruach seemed cut from the same stone.

'It's no wonder that Macartan hid the Golden Stone.' Christian commented, 'But why didn't he destroy it like Patrick destroyed Crom Cruach?'

'Dunno, must be a reason.' Said Taymi folding away her notes.

'How did Patrick destroy the stone?' Morgen queried.

'He struck it with something, it may have been his crozier and it broke crumbling to dust. After this happened, the Demon image appeared briefly but Patrick cursed it to Hell.' She told him.

'And more what?' Christian asked.

'Huh?' shrugged Taymi.

'You said Crom Cruach destroyed three quarters of the Kings army and .....more?' She hesitated for a long moment before concluding that part of the report.

'...and people were known to kill their *own* children in sacrifice to the stone......their own children.' Her words spoke horror.

Taymi sighed. 'This Golden Stone is supposed to be the secret to great wealth and power. What I can see is that it's the power of war and all the wealth that comes with it. Who wants that?'

'But it is the value of the stone, its gold, its valuable!' said Christian.

'But it speaks evil.' Said Sophia.

'And it does evil.' Said Morgen,

'I say if we find it, we must destroy it.' Mols was thinking the same thing.

Now, having arrived, they were looking at the building that held the original Golden Stone. It was a plain structure with a simple square spire, similar to the spire at Clonraggett. Christian had been expecting a Cathedral of the grandeur of that in Monaghan and was somewhat surprised. They walked up to the Cathedral and stepped inside the porch. A kindly gentleman stood inside the porch and he welcomed them to a choir recital which was about to take place. Mom explained that they were there just to have a quick look around.

'You are in luck,' he said 'normally the Cathedral is locked, this evening there happens to be the recital.' Just inside the porch was the very thing they had come to see, the pagan idol, the original Golden Stone.

It was completely *not* what they expected.

The stone was extremely large. It was taller than any of them, a huge lunk of squared stone, with rudimentary cuts in no particular pattern.

'How did Macartan manage to move the stone here.' Christian muttered.

They stood and looked at the artefact. It had also been known as the Chief Idol of the North. Its macabre stance made them feel uneasy; after all it was responsible for many manovalent happenings, bloodshed, sacrifice, demonic rituals and perhaps war. It had been the voice of the Devil, an Oracle of Evil, a dark force in history.

How many had looked upon this stone and been demented by it, demonised, sacrificed?

How many had heard the voice, seen the evil, worshipped at its feet?

How many had been influenced to take up weapons, to draw blood, to perpetrate evil?

Standing looking at it they knew now that its power was extinguished. As it stood before them, it could not harm them or for that matter speak to them.

Christian examined some grooves in the surface of the stone.

'This must have been the lines of silver and gold.' He pointed out, but any trace of the precious metals had since been removed. From what they had figured out, the silver and gold had been taken and reused in the formation of a replacement Golden Stone, the one that they were now seeking, the one that now held the power, the voice of the Demon, the voice of the Devil.

He turned and looked at the simple Cathedral.

He looked back at the stone, the pagan idol now captive in the house of God, silent, powerless.

He turned her back on the stone and left the building.

Inside the Cathedral the choir recital had begun and solemn music poured through the doors, filling in the space of the quiet evening.

They paced the graveyard looking for the last resting place of Saint Macartan. His grave was presumed to be within the cemetery but its exact whereabouts was unknown. They walked amid the tall gravestones for some time and read many of the inscriptions, but were unable to identify what may have been Macartans grave.

'If its location were known, it would have been signposted.' Dad concluded and they made their way slowly out of the churchyard gate. Sophia was looking out beyond the cemetery and to a hilltop close by the Cathedral.

'I think that's the Hillfort.' She pointed. A large hill rose up close by and was surrounded on the top by a circular arrangement of trees.

'Let's go and have a closer look.' Said Dad. As they exited the churchyard gates, Christian paused, he noticed an engraving atop the curved railing that contained the gates, it was the image of a Bishop. He looked back over the cemetery. Somewhere in here, but he knew not exactly where, lay the remains of the Bishop, the Saint, Macartan. Lying silently in the ground, his work done, his foundations laid; but Christian knew the work never stopped, the building never ended. Christian had hoped to perhaps get some sense of understanding from the visit here as he had at Clones, but apart from having faced the original Golden Stone he had received no clue. No matter, he felt it would come.

'Fortis Et Fidelis friend.' He whispered.

Sophia had brought some findings relating to the Hillfort. She had asked Dad if he would help her research it and she had some printed information which she imparted as they drove the short loop that would bring them around to the hill; to the Fort.

'It's over two thousand years old, it was the capital of the Kingdom of Oriel and this was where the High King of Oriel lived.' She told them. Dad accompanied her with some facts.

'At one time the Kingdom was nicknamed Swordland, and there were a tremendous amount of roman coins and artefacts found here.' He said. *A treasure trove.* Thought Morgen. They parked as close as they were allowed to the Hillfort and found a pedestrian gateway through which they could gain access to the hill..

'Normally you can't get near hillforts.' Commented Dad, 'They are usually inaccessible and hidden.'

Not so in this case, a mown path had been prepared all the way up the hill to the top. As they ascended the steep incline, more and more of an incredible view came into sight, they began to realise the significance of the hill and its dominance over the landscape....and the effort it took to lumber to the top of it.

'This particular hillfort was such an important site,' Dad continued from where he had left off, 'that it was identified on an ancient map as a *Regia* by a guy called Ptolemy......you probably never heard of him.'

'I did!' piped Morgen, 'he's in Stephen Hawkings book. He thought the World was the centre of the Universe and everything circled around it.' Morgen recalled a diagram he had seen in Hawkings book which described Ptolemys theory. He shook his head at how silly a notion it was.

'….Anyone could have made that mistake.' Said Dad in Ptolemy's defence. 'Anyway, Ptolemy was an Egyptian scientist and astronomer from almost two thousand years ago, he produced a World map based on science and numbers ….at the time he thought the world consisted of just Europe.'

'Anyone could have made that mistake.' Quoted Morgen.

'The point is,' said Dad, 'that this exact place was marked on Ptolemy's map, that's how significant this hill was.'

'Whats a Regia then?' Taymi enquired.

'A Regia was a Kings residence, the word normally referred to Roman Monarchy, the original Regia was in Rome.'

They had reached the summit. It was circles by a structured mound surrounding a plateau, and it was lined all around with trees inside of which would have been the Fort; the Kings Castle. There were no remains of a Castle now, only a grassy plain of humps and hollows. When they walked inside what was the Fort, their view was obscured by the trees. Back in time however the Castle would have sat up righteously looking out and above the trees, if indeed the trees were even there at the time.

But what they could see was that the view was incredible and the warm sunny evening was so clear it allowed them to see for up to ten or even twenty miles.

Morgen looked out into the far distance and saw row of huge rotating wind turbines. *Sinister robots with flailing arms marching ominously over the hills and coming to sack the Fort.* He narrowed his eyes to focus on them clearly. There was enough time for him to prepare to defend the Fort; they would not defeat him or his army, *not today brother.*

As they walked around the perimeter trees they saw that the view held in every direction giving the King of Oriel command over the hills and the valleys of a significant portion of his kingdom. He had advance sight of marauding armies advancing and command over his subjects.

'I'm dumbstruck.' Said Taymi, blown away by the awesome view of the Kingdom spread before her.

'Or just dumb!' Deadpanned Christian.

Lila had discovered something of interest. 'Look, a circle.' She ran off to a nearby interesting ground structure. Sophia consulted at her notes.

'That must be the penannular ring barrow.' She said studying it. By now Lila was standing in the middle of the structure, a circular mound with a seperate raised mound circling all around. The low evening sun threw down its shadows painting a striking, haunting image of the circles and the child.

'Whats it for?' Morgen asked.

'It's a burial place,' said Dad, 'Lila is probably standing on top of a body.'

'Why is it called a… Penannular Ring barrow?' Taymi queried, reading the name from Sophia's notes.

'Penannular means a ring but not a fully enclosed ring, a barrow is a burial place.' Taymi now noticed that the circle of the ring barrow did not fully enclose. She was reminded of the annulet, a ring which indicated royalty.

'This would possibly have been the burial place of the King.' Dad concluded.

'Cremated remains were found in a dig of the barrow in the 1960's.' Sophia informed them from her notes.

Christian wandered back into the centre of the Hillfort.

This was where the King of Oriel lived, the Monarcy, the Royalty, the Palace, the Castle.

It was then that it came to him.

'This is the House of Oriel!'

Dad's voice interrupted him, he was following close behind with the others.

'I can tell you something else about this Fort,' Dad said, 'A King called Eochad resided here as King of Oriel, his son Caibre was known as the Little Prince.'

'The little Prince? The Prince who gave the apple to Macartan?' said Morgen. Sophia fluttered through her notes, she didn't remember finding out anything about this.

Christian put it together, Eochad was the King who had at first rejected Macartan, but following the peace offering of an apple from Caibre, Eochad had befriended Macartan and had *given* him the Golden Stone.'

'And whats more,' continued Dad, 'King Enoch had a daughter...'

'A Princess?' piped Lila who had just rejoined them.

'Correct, a Princess, and she in turn had a son, someone you already know....'

'Son of a Princess?...Christians mind was revolving.....he had come across this before.

'Was her son....Tiernach?'

'Yep, Tiernach, he was Enochs grandson, so this was his family home, his house.'

Christians mind was spinning, Eochad was the King who had given the Golden Stone to Macartan;

Tiernach was the Grandson who had been given the seat of power after Macartans death;

Tiernach was 'of the House of Oriel', the Royal House. Christian had researched the House of Oriel previously, after their visit to Clones but had turned up nothing except a few Guest Houses and Hotels of the same name.

He looked around him, this ancestral home was silent now amid the trees but this must once have been a busy place, the centrepoint of the Kingdom. He looked out over the lands that the King commanded.

Only one obstruction stood in the way of an uninhibited 360 degree view, it was the building they had just been to, Clogher Cathedral. His mind was still turning.

Eventually the power of the Kingdom was taken over by the Bishop. *The kingdom changed from the Kingdom of Oriel to the Diosese of Clogher.* He thought. *The seat of power moved from here to there.* He looked at the Cathedral, it was only two fields away.

Its not like Macartan had to transport the stone too far. He thought.

Christian thought now of the Golden Stone, the symbol of the Kingdom, which became the new Christian Kingdom of Clogher. The stone and the power of the Kingdom moved from the Fort to the Cathedral and had remained there. The Cathedral remained standing, the Kingdom and its capital residence destroyed, consigned to history.

Christian noticed Taymi's coming up alongside him.

'The Bishop became the new King of Oriel.' Christian blurted out to her. 'The Bishop of Clogher, the Christian Church became the new House of Oriel. Whoever held the stone held the power.' It took a moment for this to sink in but it began to dawn on Taymi what Christian was spelling out. Christian realised that Tiernachs link was twofold.

'Tiernach became the Bishop of Clogher, he became the leader of the new House of Oriel, the Christian Church.' His mind was flung back to the omen in the Woods, *Burn the House of Oriel.*

'Someone wanted to destroy the Church or Christianity and it looks like someone still wants to.'

'The Druids...' Taymi began, 'or the Neo Druids.' Christian looked at her, he knew she was right.

'The Druids were all but destroyed, first the Kings demoted them and reduced their power.' Taymi continued.

'And gave away their precious Stones.' Added Christian.

'And then Christianity took away their power completely and banished them.' Taymi concluded. 'I don't know who the Druids would have despised more, the Royalty or Christianity.' Christian thought of the House of Oriel, it represented *both* Royalty and Christianity. He thought of the burning of Castle-Hanes Castle, the connection to Aristocracy.

'I would say they despised them both equally.' Christian said. 'Although there are no Kings now in this country.'

'It's why Macartan hid the Golden Stone.' Said Taymi, 'It would be the Druids wish to get their hands on it again.'

'What would happen if they did?'

'They would use it to try and destroy the Christian Church.'

XXXV

NEFAS

(Sin)

THEY WERE BACK in the Woods again. The Woods that they believed held the power of the Golden Stone, the power of Oriel. It felt natural to spend time here; it was their focus point, their hideout, their domain, though they thought of it more as their *Demesne*. It was their first time back since the flood.

As they made their way down the steep slope to the rope swing, Morgan, who was in front stopped, there was something very, very wrong with what he saw. He stared at the view before him.

'It's impossible.' He whispered. The others, coming closely behind, all stopped and stared too.

The full river flowed steadily past the rope swing, the river banks were washed clean and great chunks of the edging had fallen away giving the whole vista a significantly different appearance. But most amazing of all was that the Dam, the huge hulking multi tonne Dam, had completely *disappeared*.

'Where did it go?' Morgan looked all around amazed.

'It must have been swept away.' Taymi answered from behind him. 'The flood destroyed it.' She thought of the power that would have been required to uproot the Dam, it must have been phenomenal, *incomprehensible*. Without the Dam they were not going to be able to cross the river here since the waters were still swelled and strong and with the banks eroded the river was too wide.

'The Rope!' shouted Morgen. They saw that it was gone too, at least the bottom part of it with the seat. The end of the rope dangled over the centre of the fat river.

They made their way back to the track and along the alternative route towards the bridge since this would now be the only way they could safely cross the river.

As they approached the Bridge another shocking sight awaited them. The bridge had been crushed by the force of tonnes of logs and river debris.

'The Dam!' shouted Taymi, 'it ended up here.' The Dam had been washed down the river by the force of the floodwaters gathering additional debris and pace until it hit, with force, an immovable object....the Bridge.

'It must have hit it with massive speed.' Christian gaped at the devastation. There was evidence that the flood waters had swept either side of this new obstruction and washing through the vegetation on either side of the bridge, flattening it.

'We can still cross it.' Morgen pointed. Although the bridge was crushed and buckled, there was just enough room for one person at a time to squeeze along it. So they took it in turns to cross.

Lila was afraid when crossing, due to the hulk of logs piled up and packed against the side of the metal rail. Taymi came closely behind her and fed her through the narrowest part where the spindly fingers of the hulk clawed, trying to inch forward. Taymi came next and as she crossed, the bridge gave a low moan, a metally creak. She froze. Quickly she raced across the remainder of the bridge in case it should collapse under the weight of the Dam and wash her and it away downriver. Thankfully it didn't.

They moved quickly back on the opposite side of the river to the Rope to examine the scene more closely. It was a different place. This was where they had once enjoyed lazy afternoons swinging, walking on the Dam and hanging out. Now it looked desolate and destroyed. The Dam was gone, the rope cut, branches broken, pebbles had been washed away, the bank collapsed and eroded, the ground was damp and dark. There were the burnt remnants of a fire and damaged saplings.

'Those guys did this.' Said Taymi. 'They wrecked it.'

'It will come back.' Said Christian, hoping that with time, nature would restore what she and others had destroyed.

'C'mon.' He said, 'Let's go further.' He started walking again, leading them on, deeper into the Woods, deeper into their mission, with eyes open, searching for something they might have missed previously, a clue, a signal, a guide, something although he wasn't sure what.

Christian had spent the morning researching Clogher and Oriel. The royal site at Clogher, as they had discovered, had been the seat of the King of Oriel created over 2000 years ago. The valley over which it surveyed had been historically described as the fairest and richest in all the land. Clogher had been known too as a Druidic Sanctuary, Druidism had apparently held the country captive until the coming of Patrick and his assistants who dealt the Druids a deadly blow.

Eochad, the reigning King had been the proud owner of the Golden Stone which sat in his courtyard within the Hillfort that they had visited. He had given the Stone to Macartan and the district had in time become known as the Diocese of Oriel and it eventually became the Diocese of Clogher. The Bishop was known as the Bishop of Oriel until the 14th Century.

Christian had discovered another interesting fact, the name Oriel had derived from the ancient Celtic word *Airgialla*, a word which translated to *Hostage of Gold*. He mused over whether this may have been a reference to the Golden Stone, held first in Eochad's courtyard and then taken and silenced by Macartan now hidden in a secret location, a location that he was determined to find. He was keeping his eyes peeled for any further clues which might contribute to their quest. But it was Sophia who spotted something unusual and called the others.

'Come and look at this.' Sophia was standing by a tree and gesturing at something on its bark. They joined her.

'What could have caused that?' Christian was astonished. At about a metre high on the tree were what could only be described as scrapings, gouges and hacking in the bark. Someone had been hacking viciously at the tree with something sharp, an axe, a knife or ….claws.

'It looks like cat scratches.' Taymi pointed out.

'No cat is that big.' Scoffed Morgen. Mols thought otherwise, there was a cat that big but not a domestic cat that Morgen was thinking about. She scanned around, was this evidence of a *big cat*?

'Could it be the Panther?'

'Oh, come on Mols, you can't still be thinking about that.' Taymi was dismissive. Mols looked around at the trees nearby observing whether there were similar markings on any of them, as she looked she noticed something else on a tree close by, something different.

'What's that?' she pointed and they all looked. There was a mark on a tree, something was cut into the wood, a carving. They went over immediately to see more closely. The cutting was at eye level, it was very fresh and could have been done as recently as that day.

It was a simple symbol, the shape of the letter 'S' though not quite so rounded.

'Who did this? What does it mean?'

'It's an 'S'.'

'Yes but why?' Taymi asked. 'What does it stand for?'

'Saturday?' tried Mols.

'Sunday?' said Sophia.

'Sabbath?' said Christian.

'Sophia?' said Sophia suddenly a bit worried.

'Snake.' Said Lila, 'It looks like a snake.' It *did* look like a snake even more that it looked like an 'S'.

'Satan?' Taymi whispered the word low enough that the others couldn't hear it.

'Stongman?' said Christian.

'Seven?' suggested Morgen.

'Seven what?' Taymi queried.

'Seven days, seven years, seven...'

'Silence!' Said Mols interrupting Morgen. They all suddenly stopped and listened cautiously.

'I mean Silence may be what the *S* stands for.' Mols explained and all shoulders relaxed.

'You frightened me.' Said Lila.

'I'm going to look this up when we go home, in case there is something we are not thinking of.' Said Taymi.

'How can you look up *S*?' asked Morgen. They looked at the carving for another short while and examined the surrounding trees for anything similar. There was nothing else of that nature around and so they eventually made their way onwards.

A word popped into Christians head after they had left the scene, it could be the word that the carving represented, a word that had cropped up pretty regularly since they began this project, the word......*Sacrifice.*

At home Taymi flicked on the computer and considering what Morgen had said she simply entered 'S'.

The letter S originally came from a Greek letter 'Sigma' but before that from the Egyptian letter 'djed' meaning Osiris, God of the Afterlife.

'Symbol of the God of the Afterlife?'

In the early 19th century a long 's' was used which looked like the letter 'f'. She knew what this was about, she recalled the extracts from the Lucas family history which used the letter 'f' in the place of an 's'. *A long S?* she thought. Tentatively she entered the single letter 'f' and pressed return. The origin of this letter was the Hebrew letter 'vau' which looked something like a hook.

Taymi knew something else this Hebrew letter represented.

'The mark of Cain!' She turned back to the page on the letter 's'.

The letter S can also be derived from the Semitic alphabet. (from Shem, one of the three sons of Noah) In this alphabet the letter was called Shin or more simply 'Sin'.

'Sin, we didn't think of that word.' Maybe she was getting ahead of herself, after all the carving in the tree was an 's' shape not an

'f' and not a hook in the shape of the number seven as had been suggested as the mark of Cain.

Nonetheless, everything that she had researched in connection with the letter 'S' had given her an ominous feeling. Whatever the carving signified, she was sure it wasn't for good and the same could be said, she was sure, for the person who carved it.

XXXVI

MEDIUS

(Centre)

SOPHIA COULD FEEL the season changing. She had noticed that the garden wildflowers had diminished and it wasn't so bright in the evenings anymore. She had noticed the first of the blackberries and she knew tha this meant late summer. There was a line in a poem by Kavanagh about the blackberries and she had been reading it.

Green grasshoppers on the railway slopes,
The humming of wild bees,
The whole summer during the school holidays
Till the blackberries appeared,.

But she had noticed something else in Kavanagh's writings, something with a darker edge and she was flicking quickly through his book of poems to substanciate her theory.

It was the name *Apollo*. It cropped up in his poems again and again.

…my stumble, Had the poise and stride of Apollo

And elsewhere;

…maybe I'll find in Charity's
Illiterate book of pieties
Apollo's writing in a Christian hand.

And again;

Apollo's unbaptized pagan who can show

To simple eyes what Christians never know-
Was it the unspeakable beauty of hell?

It was the linking of Apollo and Christians that she had noticed. She didn't fully understand the poems but it appeared that Apollo was opposed to or the opposite of Christians in some way. She was sure that she had heard his name crop up somewhere before but she couldn't remember where. She thought she might look it up now.

'What do you know about Apollo?' she asked Christian as she passed him in the kitchen.

'Rocket that went to the Moon.' He answered truthfully.

Sophia discovered Mols in the project room, Mols expressed some interest in Sophia's sideline project.

'Apollo, a Greek God.' Sophia read from the world wide web which went on to tell her that he was the God of light, was worshipped in ancient times and in modern neo-paganism. He could bring ill health and plagues as well as healing.

'Nice mix.' Said Mols.

'Hymns or chants to Apollo were called paeans, they could be bring misfortune or healing.'

'Pagans?'

'No *paeans.*'

'Pagan paeans?'

'Maybe.'

'The Ancient Greeks called him *The Destroyer* - God of the Delphi Oracle!'

'An Oracle!' Mols leaned closer so that she could read at the same time as Sophia.

'It was the most important Oracle in the world. Presided by a Priestess called a Pythia, from the name Python.' Read Sophia.

'Too many P's.' said Mols.

'Gives you a lisp.' Said Sophia adopting a lisp.

'All Oracles in the World took their name from the Delphi Oracle; some of these like in Tibet and Nigeria still have the tradition of the Priestess.'

'There are Oracles all over the World then?' Said Mols.

'But this is the one that was the boss of them all,' Sophia contended, 'Listen to this…'

'All Oracles in the World are thought to have been modelled on or linked to the Oracle at Delphi.'

'Linked to it? How?'

'Don't know, maybe they share power?' Mols pictured a series of lines linking Oracles from all over the World to one central Oracle. They learned that in ancient times leaders from many countries visited the Delphi Oracle to ask for predictions for the outcome of wars or politics. These predictions came in dreams and the rituals often had a sacrifice in thanksgiving.

'Sounds like the Golden Stone Oracle could somehow be linked to this World Oracle.' Said Mols before Sophia continued.

'Delphi was identified as being the precise centre of the Universe in ancient Greek times, this is why Apollo's Oracle was constructed at that exact spot. It is also known as the *Navel of the World* and its guarded by *Navel Stones* called Omphalos.'

'Omphal-ompos?'

'No Omphalos!'

'So at the precise centre of the Universe is a Dark Oracle stone linked to all other Oracle stones?….*including* the Oracle stone that we believe is hidden right beside our house?'

'Hmm.'

'So, *Evil* commands the centre of the Universe.'

'Not quite!…. There is one other location with an Omphalos stone which competes for the title of the centre of the Universe.' Mols craned her neck again to see the screen as Sophia pointed out her findings.

'It is in the Church of the Holy Sepulchre in Jerusalem….. a place thought to be the most important Christian site in the World.'

They sat back and stared at the screen.

'Good versus Evil…' said Sophia, '…in a Battle for the centre of the Universe.'

XXXVII

PERFICIO

(Perfection)

'WE'RE GOING TO walk the Triangle.' Mom called out to Taymi.

This meant that Mom and Dad were going for a walk on a circuit they called the Triangle and Taymi was for a short time, in charge of the house. The Triangle included three sections of roads which linked up and comprised about one mile. One of the roads was relatively new but Dad had told Christian that there had been a previous Triangle before this one.

The Triangle, Christian thought.

'One of the basic shapes of *geometry,*' his Tech Graphics teacher had preached, 'one of the strongest units which can be designed and used in structural elements such as roofs and floors. Triangulation will add strength,' he had said, 'think of the pyramids, an equilateral triangle of the purest form.'

A triangle was Christian knew, a powerful symbol too, symbolising any triad or group of three, or a Trinity.

'A Trinity.' The word flashed across his mind as it had in Clones when he had seen the juxtaposition of the ancient monuments and burial grounds. The word Trinity kept coming up…In Christianity the Trinity was considered the *Greatest Mystery of all Time,* no-one could understand how there could be three persons in one person! But now the Trinity seemed to be the key to this particular mystery.

'Macartans Trinity,' he spoke quietly to himself, 'A Triangle?'

He thought of the three Cathedrals named after St.Macartan. He knew where two of them were located, but where, he now wondered, was the third.

Christian made his way to the computer and sitting down, tapped in *St.Macartans Cathedral, Clogher Diocese*. Lila also in the same room took little note.

The Cathedrals were located in the towns of Clogher and Monaghan, both of which he knew and the third Cathedral was located in the town of Enniskillen. It was a town located about an hour northwest of where he lived and he had been there only a handful of times.

The name of this town came from two meanings; Ceithlenns Island, (Ceithlenn was a mythical prophetess) but also Inniskillings, *the Island of Killings*. It was true that the town had a troubled and bloody past.

Enniskillen's old Cathedral had some of its bells cast from cannons used in the famous Battle of the Boyne. It had an unusual peal of ten full circle bells but these bells had a wider story; a Dean from the area had gone to South Africa to a township called *City of Saints*. He persuaded the townspeople to construct a set of bells identical to Macartans Bells and these became the first set of full circle bells in all of Africa which became copied again and again even up to 1996.

'The year I was born.' Christian read on;

> *The Christian Bells of St.Macartan continue to ring out and grow the Christianity of Africa every day telling news of the Greatest Story ever told.*

Christian was amazed, Macartans influence, his *power*, was still being felt to this day and not alone that, it was *growing*.

He paced quickly to his schoolbag and pulled out his geography book, grateful that it was still in the bag. He opened the page which illustrated the Island of Ireland and began to pencil in locations.

The Three Cathedrals, would they form a triangle? He joined the locations of Monaghan, Clogher and Enniskillen in straight lines, of course it was a triangle, joining any three points would form a triangle unless they were in a straight line.

Interestingly the triangle formed was not just a random shape, it formed the shape of an isosceles triangle, two of its sides were equal, not three as in an equilateral triangle such as he had witnessed in Clones. He thought of the Trinity, three equals become one, all three parts must be equal, it can't be unequal.

Lila was colouring, 'What are you doing?' she asked Christian.

'I'm looking for a triangle.' He answered.

Lila began to draw a triangle.

'It's *not* the Cathedrals,' Christian thought, 'Enniskillen Cathedral didn't exist before the 1600's'

Christian studied the map again. Where did the power lie? The seat of power of the Bishop of Oriel resided in Clogher initially, then Clones and now the denominations seats rested in Clogher and Monaghan. Monaghan Cathedral had not been constructed until the 1800's so why was the seat of power moved there?

'The first Christian settlement.' Monaghan was relatively close to Rockwell. Taking his pencil he drew lines connecting Clones, Clogher and Monaghan. Again it was a triangle, this time it was *almost* an equilateral triangle, *almost but not quite*. If it were to form an equilateral triangle, then the third point should fall more easterly than Monaghan, the third point would be almost directly ....he drew the third point where its geometry took it.

It formed a perfect equilateral triangle, the third position of power. He put his pencil on the third point; it fell directly on Castle-Hanes.

Christian hastily dug out the maps of the Woods that had been given to him by Dad. He cast his eye over the maps again and again. Joining any three points would form a triangle, unless they were in a straight line. He had already done this exercise, joined three points...in a straight line. They need to form a *triangle*! An equilateral triangle, a Trinity. To do this he needed another point, a *fourth* point.

'Is there another holy site?' he said, his finger drawing imaginary triangles on the page.

He allowed his finger to drift over to Clonraggett. The Church was indicated on the map.

'Clonragget is a holy site.' He studied its position in relation to the others. He noticed something. Getting a ruler he drew a line from Rockwell ancient graveyard to the church at Clonraggett. He already knew by looking at it, that it had significance but he measured it anyway.

'It's the same distance from Rockwell to Clonraggett as it is from Rockwell to the Northpoint.'

The next move was obvious, Christian drew a line from Clonraggett to the Northpoint. He had created a perfect equilateral triangle pointing North.

'It's perfect.' He whispered. He noted that the left side of the triangle from Rockwell to Northpoint had the mass rock at its midpoint. He marked the midpoint along the other two sides, Northpoint to Clonraggett and Rockwell to Clonraggett.

'Are any of these of significance?' he cautioned himself. He connected the three midpoints together with lines. They created another triangle, an upside down one.

'The medians.' He joined one corner to the midpoint on the opposite side creating one median. He completed the other two medians, they all joined in the centre. Christian studied the centre point and frowned, through the tracing point he could see that this was not a raised drumlin where he would expect to have found the fort.

'At the left hand.' Christian looked at the left hand side of the triangle. He had already identified this midpoint as being the mass rock. He shook his head in frustration, could the midpoint on either of the other two sides be the place he was looking for? Christian looked at the image he had drawn and he noticed something in its proportions. He slipped his hand into his pocket and withdrew from it a coin, the coin with the image of Vetruvius Man. The coin that had been in his pocket ever since that day in the Cathedral. The coin he had resisted handing over countless times in shops.

He placed the coin beside the maps and picked up his pencil. He joined the mass rock to the midpoint on the right side which became the top of a square symbol the vertical sides of which extended down to the base line.

The square, the simple building block, the symbol of four, the four elements, Christian thought briefly of the four evangelists. He proceeded to draw a circle, touching the mass rock, the right mid point and the middle of the base line.

The circle, never-ending, universal, unity, the sun, the planets, the wheel, family.

He looked at the image and began to draw again, carefully and with as much skill as he could muster he drew the image of the Vetruvian Man within the circle, square and the *triangles*.

It was a perfect fit.

'At the left hand.' Christian whispered, and he held his pencil at the point of the mans raised left hand, the image that he thought looked like Christ. The left hand met the circle, the square and the triangles all at the same point.

'The hand of God?' he whispered.

It was clear to see that this was a point of raised topography as indicated by the contours on the map and this to Christian was clearly the place which he had been looking for.

'The perfection of all things.' He said, 'I have found it.'

Lila had been trying to imitate Christians drawing but had run into trouble after drawing the medians. Seeing his delight made her feel even more frustrated.

'I can't do it!' she complained.

'That's Ok Lila, I'll help you finish it.' Said Christian. 'Actually,' he said, 'I see something even better in your drawing.' He redrew the lower two medians and the base line and added in two more lines.

'It's a star Lila,' he said delighting her '....an upside down star, but that's Ok.' He assured her. He noticed then that the five piece star shape he had drawn also touched the four holy places in his drawing and that the two upper lines aligned with the mans raised limbs.

'You can colour it now Lila.' He said kindly and she set about doing just that.

Christian returned to his map, now he had found what he believed to be the precious location on the map, he was going to have to identify its position on the ground. He already knew that it lay within the more densely forested area of the Woods, an area of difficult terrain that would be arduous to negotiate. He didn't relish the task.

It was appropriate too that it should fall within this area, an area that they knew well, one that they had coined their own name for……the location he was looking at, was directly at the place they called…. *The Dark Underworld.*

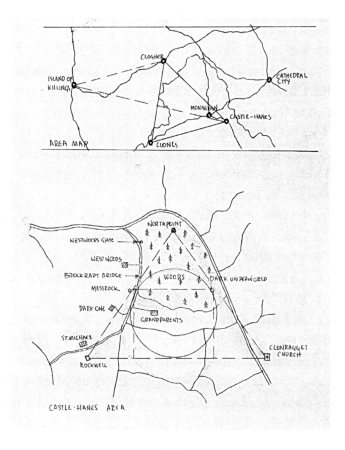

XXXVIII

TYPICUS

(Symbols)

TAYMI WAS READING more on Druids, she was becoming an expert. Christian was planning his attempt to infiltrate the Dark Underworld but he was also listening.

'The Druid could bring about a madness by using horrible incantations. They used it at times of battle to make soldiers excited with fury and horror so that they would move at great speed.' She thought of the great Battle of Clonraggett.

She read more about how Druids could supposedly live on after death, reappearing as other men or animals. Some said it was the Fairies that helped the Druids with their magic gathering at sacred sites like Stonehenge or Wood groves and that they originally came from France or Gaul as it was called. She was taken aback to discover that in the 18th century there was a Druid *revival* led by dark writers like William Blake, a possible Archdruid.

'There were Archdruids?' It was a rethorical question. 'Oh, listen to this,' Taymi sat up, 'Children selected for *sacrifice* were thrown onto a *bonfire!*' She was horrified with what she was reading.

'The Druids called it a *bone-fire* since only the bones were left. The Druid would foretell the future of the village from the dying screams.' She stared at the paragraph. 'That is horrible, evil....its worse than evil...it's even worse than that.' Christian was looking at her in realisation.

'What?' she said looking back at him. Then her face revealed her shock.

'The child! The child in the Castle! Oriel! The Castle was a bonfire! Thank God she escaped.' The alternative didn't bear thinking about.

'The burning was a sacrificial fire.' He said. 'It was to sacrifice the child. But Why?'

'Neo-pagans.' She tapped the book. 'It says here they tried to follow the rituals of the ancient Druids…. And they're still doing it!'

This was not the kind of news Christian wanted to hear.

'They still gather in secret.' She said. 'Sometimes in groups, sometimes alone.'

'Like the one who's been chanting in the Castle.'

'Yea… one of their gatherings was for Imbolg in February at full moon time or where the sun aligned at the midpoint of winter solstice and vernal equinox; that was one of their special times.'

'February,' said Christian, 'that's when the Castle was burned.' It wasn't lost on him either that it was also the month of his birth.

'The Druids demanded that if a leader lost a battle he should turn his sword on himself, a self sacrifice petition to the Gods!'

Self Sacrifice, Christian thought of those Nazi leaders that had turned their metaphorical sword on themselves having lost their battle, he didn't see it as a petition to the Gods, more like an easy way out. He understood that the self sacrifice of suicide was a complex matter, in many cases no one knew why someone took their own life, but he couldn't understand how someone could do it as a petition to the Gods or to outwit the enemy. He couldn't understand how anyone could do it at all, it was something he could not comprehend, it was something he felt he could not and would *never* do.

'Caesar stated that Druids believe that after death the soul passes from one to another. But that does not necessarily mean from one human to another, but to other life forms too such as demons, bulls, ravens and other beasts.' Ravens, the Souls of the Dead, they had heard this before, but bulls and demons?

Taymi flicked past some more pages in her book. Suddenly an image flashed into Christian's mind, something in the book he recognised. He grabbed her hand.

'Go back to that picture!' Taken aback Taymi reversed until Christian told her to stop. As the page fell to the image he saw a diagram that he instantly recognised.

It was a circle within a square within a *triangle*, almost identical to the image he had created using the Vitruvian Man and the triangle. Taymi recognised it too. There was a slight difference in the image from that which Christian drew, the circle fitted fully within the square and the triangle was housed within another all encompassing circle.

Taymi read the accompanying text; 'It's the symbol of Alchemy. These are magical shapes.'

What was it about these shapes that was so special? Christian wondered; but he soon found out.

Alchemy it transpired was the practice of achieving ultimate wisdom and immortality. Alchemists' two main goals were to try and turn lead into gold and seek eternal life.'

'Is this the symbol of eternal life?' Said Christian. If so, it was also the symbol of the perfection of all things.

The Alchemists were actually the first chemists it seemed! And they believed that in the search for eternal life they need to find … guess what? A precious stone! But not a Golden Stone, no, they sought another well known stone *The Philosophers Stone* which had been apparently stolen out of the Garden of Eden by Eve. Christian was captivated by the story of this stone and its power which seemed to mirror the Golden Stone. In the 1800's an occult order known as The Golden Dawn wrote this about the Philosophers Stone;

> *"There exists in nature a force which is immeasurably more powerful than steam, and by means of which a single man, who knows how to adapt and direct it, might upset and alter the face of the world. This force was known to the ancients."*

'A precious stone, with a dark power, capable of upsetting the World....does this sound familiar to you?' Taymi asked Christian.

Yes, this did sound familiar to Christian. A stone of immense power, more power than he could have thought to imagine.

Christian abruptly pointed at another image of the page facing that which they were reading. It was another image that Christian recognised, it was the star that he had helped Lila draw when she was struggling to copy his Vitruvian Man sketch. This image too did not hold any good fortune in its description. Christian read about it aloud;

'The Pentagram, a five sided star. The pentagram is considered a symbol of the five senses, and is a symbol of good, *however*, when inverted it has entirely different meanings, it becomes an image of sinister and evil. The two points in the air represent horns, the side points represent ears and its single point below represents the goat beard of the Devil.'

'The Devil's hill.' Taymi reminded him...like he needed reminding. Two of the symbols he had drawn had evil connotations. The hidden location that Christian had identified was a key point on the Alchemy symbol and also on the horn of the Devil.

Things did not bode well.

XXXIX

RUDIMENTUM

(Trial)

THEY HAD BEGUN their expedition to the place Christian believed they would find the stone. They made their way along the Wood track until such time as he directed that they needed to hike left. They hacked through brambles, long grass and prickly trees until the ground started rising. They were entering the Dark Underworld.

Trickles of water ran between their feet and the branches of the trees were lowhanging and touching the ground. The branches, the ground and the atmosphere were damp, dark and slippy. They picked their way between branches, it was difficult.

'Yuck.' Said Sophia as she tried to grasp a slippy slimy branch. 'Ouch!' she shouted as it broke off rotting in her hand. Mols feet squelched in the damp earth beneath her, it was sticky and wet. Taymi was struggling to help Lila who was getting dirtier and dirtier by the minute.

'We're getting there.' Christian encouraged, but the others could not see any sign of getting anywhere.

Morgen seemed to be the only one who was enjoying himself. He grabbed a large branch which broke off in his hands due to the damp rot. 'See my strength.' He shouted, but he too was struggling to make headway. They were going in different directions. They had spent quite a while trying to make their way and they were beginning to feel tired and bicker.

'I know it's just up ahead.' Protested Christian, 'Just keep with the rising ground.'

'We are not going up, we are going across.' Taymi insisted. The warm damp earth and the cool air was creating a vapour rising from the ground. It was turning into a slight mist. Christian fought his way in front of the others, but he was confused as to which direction he was heading in. The mist was getting heavier and obscuring his view.

'I don't like this.' Taymi called, 'If this mist gets any heavier we will get lost and be stuck here all night.' Christian was frustrated. The expedition had not gone well. This part of the Woods was particularly tricky. He slipped on a branch and his elbow sank into the soft ground. Drips of water came from the mist condensing on the branches. They had been in the Dark Underworld now for more than an hour. They had covered a lot of ground but didn't seem to have got far, there were so many obstructions.

Eventually it was the mist that had finally defeated them.

Christian turned around to look at the others; they had more or less given up.

'We have been here before.' Morgen said.

'What?' said an exasperated Christian. Morgen held up the rotted branch that had broken off in his hand a long time ago. They were back at the same place. Christian felt like he was going mad. It was eerie and quiet.

'Alright let's go home then.' Christian conceded disappointedly. *But I will keep trying until I find it…* he thought, *…that is my vow.*

It was easier to get out of the Dark Underworld than it was to get into it, but by the time they got home they were exhausted, dirty and fed up.

When he arrived home Christian thought more about the mist. He had not noticed any mist along the trail home after they had left the Dark Underworld. He put it to Taymi.

'That's because it is not as damp or as dark there,' she reasoned, 'the mist is trapped among the dampness and can't escape, you should know this geography geek.'

'It's not the damp and it's not the dark,' he said, 'the sun cannot get directly into that area so it can't heat up the ground that much.'

'So what are you saying?'

'I am saying that it is something else which is making the mist.......maybe even some-*one* else.'

'Oh, come on!' she said disbelievingly. 'You *cannot* be serious.' She had heard Dad say this phrase.

'What if it's a Fe-Flada, a Fence of Protection, keeping us from seeing where the Fort is.'

'We were all over that place, perhaps we did'nt see the Fort because perhaps it isn't there. I'm not even sure if I will go back in there again.'

'Well I will be going back...and I'm going back tomorrow....with or without you.' Christian was sure that he could conquer the difficult terrain of the Dark Underworld and that it would all be worth it in the end.

Persistence beats Resistance. He told himself with a steely determination.

XL

OCCULTE

(Secrets)

'WHO'S COMING THEN?' It was the next day and Christian had arranged the second attempt to conquer the Underworld. Interest had waned in the expedition. Mols, Sophia and Lila were not as keen to pick their way through the quagmire of unfriendly branches and sticky mud this time round.

'Just us then.' Christian spoke to Morgen and Taymi. Morgen was still as keen, Taymi less so but Christian had convinced her overnight that they just may be onto something and she was willing to give it one more try. After having made their way via the same route to the Dark Underworld, they hiked around in a large circle in a bid to find a more accommodating way to cut through to the heart of the Underworld however the dark quagmire of growth appeared uninviting from all angles.

'Let's try here.' Christian started to pick his way through the gnarly claws of low hanging branches and slippery blackness. It was cumbersome work. Morgen was a little after him, he had his Rowan lance with him for support, and Taymi trailed further behind. They felt they were making better progress with a smaller more compact group. On several occasions as Christian tried to move forward he was held back by a branch or hook picking the back of his jumper. It was as though the undergrowth was teasing them by impeding their progress. Christian looked back in the direction from which they came, he looked ahead and to each side, everything appeared the same no matter where he looked. He noticed now as he did before that he did not have full clarity of vision and tried to refocus his eyes, there appeared to be a hint of a mist hanging in the air among the branches. The unexplainable mist that was forming all around in every direction. He turned forward to press ahead.

Behing his by several metres to his left was Morgen keeping well within sight. Morgen thought that the branches seemed to twist more tightly together, whichever variance of route he chose seemed to be the more difficult one. He used his lance to hack his way through. They had forced their way deep into the twisted Underworld and it was becoming increasingly difficult to see clearly now. Taymi noticed that the only sound that she could distinguish was the sound of only themselves, there was no other sound of nature, wildlife, water or wind. She looked around wondering why this was.

Christian knew that they should be making their way uphill but he could not tell if they were ascending or descending. He looked around again. Taymi was just catching up. He could barely see Morgen to his left through the dense air but looked over to see how he was managing.

Morgen seemed to be standing still, both hands holding his stick, facing forward; his posture filled Christian with unease. Christian strained to see Morgen's face. At that moment Morgen turned to look directly at Christian. Christian staggered back with horror at what he witnessed.

His brother's face appeared *featureless*, there were no eyes, mouth or nose, his face had melted into a seamless, expressionless façade. Christian collapsed back on top of Taymi, his abrupt action frightening her.

'*What is it?*' she shouted panicking. Christian's horrified face looked back at Morgen, Taymi looked too.

'What is it?' she repeated, not seeing anything strange. The image has disappeared, Christian looked back at his brother who was making his way quickly over towards them, Morgen appeared fine.

'What did you see?' Taymi insisted.

'I ......thought I saw something.' Christian was still staring wide eyed at Morgen who felt more than a little uncomfortable at being stared at.

'What?' persisted Taymi.

'I couldn't see Morgen's face.' He told them. Morgen looked bemused.

'That's because it's too misty.' Taymi didn't find anything too strange about this.

'But I couldn't see his *face*.' Christian insisted.

'Are you feeling Ok?' Taymi asked him, and he noticed that she was looking at him as though he was going a little bit mad. He himself felt that he may be going a little bit mad and he remembered the ability of the Druid to cause madness.

'Yea, I'm Ok.' He said, 'I must have been hallucinating.' He lied, 'Let's keep going. What time is it?' Taymi tapped her watch.

'It's stopped, must need a new battery.' He guessed that they had been searching for over an hour now; if they were to find the Fort amid this dark quagmire it must be very close.

'I saw a light up ahead, that's what I was looking at when I heard Taymi shouting.' Morgen said. They looked in the direction in which Morgen was pointing. There did appear to be a light breaking through the mist.

'C'mon, we're nearly there!' Christian began making his way forward again with the other two following closely behind. He wasn't sure what the light signified but he was sure that it must be good. He forged ahead of the others.

'Hurry up!' he called back to them.

They clambered through the remaining black murky branches, through long grass and briers and burst into the open light. It was ....the place they had been before, almost exactly where they had entered the Underworld. Christian stared.

'Is this the Fort?' asked Morgen before realising that he was back to square one. 'Wait...How did we get back here?' Taymi followed through after the others.

'Oh Great!' She threw up her arms. 'That was a complete waste of time.'

'Maybe it was a worm-hole.' said Morgen a pun linking Hawkings intergalactic time space continuum and the monstrous Devil Crom Cruach. It hadn't been a complete waste of time as far as Christian was concerned, it was a setback, it just proved to him that there was justification for trying again to breech the Dark Underworld, that it had something to hide. Perhaps they needed to use torches or string, something that they could use to help prepare a straight route. He wasn't giving up. All they could do for now was to make their way home again and so they set about their return journey; a dejected little bunch with not much to show for an afternoons work.

After a time, Taymi, who was in front, turned around and signalled to them with her hands to quiet down.

'What is it?' Christian whispered.

'Shhh!' She whispered back, 'There's someone over there, I think....I think it's the Dark One.' They juked down beside Taymi, hidden behind an embankment of earth and leaves and peered over it. They could see him, some distance away, the Dark One seemingly focusing his energy on a tree. He was partly concealed by the tree trunk but he appeared to be scratching or brushing at a section of the trunk.

'What's he doing?' Morgen hoarsely whispered but they didn't reply lest they make too much noise. After a minute or so the Dark One moved away. He walked hurriedly and disappeared quickly out of sight.

'Let's go see.' Urged Taymi and they crept out of their hiding place and made their way towards the tree taking care to ensure that he had completely gone, which he had. When they got to the place where the Dark One had been they were unsure which tree he has been focusing on.

'Look at them all.' Urged Taymi, 'There must be something!' It was Morgen who found it.

'Over here!' he called and the others ran to him. There was a very clear marking cut, *carved* into the tree. A symbol that they had not seen before but were nonetheless familiar with, a symbol which carried a heavyweight of meaning, none of it good. They stared at it without speaking.

If Taymi was uncertain what the 'S' carving represented, she was convinced without doubt of what this carving was and she said it.

'It's the mark of Cain.'

Looking at the carving it was clear to her. It had the shape of a slash, a hook, like a curved number seven.

'Maybe it is a seven?' Morgen said.

'But the mark of Cain looks like a seven.' Taymi pointed out.

'I'm not sure,' said Christian, 'It's too curved, to be a seven or a hook.' To him it looked almost semi circular.

'Maybe he didn't finish it.' Morgen considered.

'As if he is going to come back later and make it into …..a love heart!' Taymi sniffed. 'This is clearly the mark of Cain, it's a curse, just like the one we saw before and it was put here by the Dark One. He's got an agenda and we better find out what it is.' They examined all around the carving and all of the nearby trees for any further or similar markings. They found nothing and so they began again in the direction of home further discussing what they had witnessed.

'He could be a neo-pagan, or a modern Druid.' Taymi insisted.

'Maybe it is just a carving, a wood cutting, no meaning.' Christian wasn't even convinced by his own words, it seemed too coincidental.

'If it is the number seven carved on there, then we better look out for Lila.' Morgen added reminding them about the attempt on the life of Oriel and the words of the journal referring to the seventh age. Taymi thought about it.

'Could this be a repeat of history, after all modern Druids were inclined to repeat the traditions of those that had gone before.' She recollected a line she had read in some of her research on Druids and quoted it as best she could remember.

'Satan, the mastermind behind the Druid rituals, has been repeating the same basic strategies throughout history.'

They stuck closely together on the walk home and agreed between themselves that it would be best if no one venture into the Woods alone.

Everyone was gathered for tea so Taymi used the opportunity to seek out some information.

'We saw the Dark One in the Woods today.' She started.

'Don't call him that, its not nice.' Mom corrected her. She knew who Taymi was talking about.

'How come he wanders around the Woods looking at things?' Taymi continued.

'You wander around the Woods looking at things' Dad pointed out.

'He seems to spend a lot of time at his house, doesn't he work?' She asked.

'I spend a lot of time at my house….*and* I work.' Dad said.

'What does he do then? Wood carvings?' She tried.

'If I told you, you probably wouldn't believe me.' Dad said.

'Go on then.' Taymi felt she was onto something.

'Well…' Dad started, 'I would have to say that he is probably the most creative and talented guy around…………..apart from myself of course!' Taymi almost couldn't believe it.

'At what? Carvings?' she tried again.

'Nope.'

'Painting?' suggested Christian.

'Nope.'

'Dancing?' tried Sophia to which Dad looked at her with raised eyebrow.

'What then?' persisted Taymi.

'He's……how shall I put this,' said Dad, 'He's got his own gothic electro punk band, and they've got quite a large following, sold some singles too.'

Taymi spluttered over her food. 'You mean there's this punk band right beside us and we don't know anything about it?' she was incredulous. '…and the Dark One is in it?' She said.

'Not only is the Dark One in it …he is it.' Said Dad, 'he and his assistant.'

'*Leon*!' Mom was unhappy with Dad referring to their neighbour as the Dark One.

'How come we don't we know about this?' Christian asked.

'It wouldn't be your scene.' Dad pointed out, 'not really mine for that matter, but that doesn't mean I don't respect the music …man!'

'And what kind of a following does he have?' Taymi was still finding it difficult to make the adjustment to understanding that the quiet guy that they had seen only occasionally was in fact a successful recording artist.

'Some of their fans travel a hundred miles to gigs.'

'Gigs? There are gigs?'

'Oh, yes. There could be several hundred at a gig. They've played in several of the local towns.'

'Why is this so low key?' Taymi asked.

'Well I would say that their music is quite selective listening. It's very …Dark,' Dad said. This was one piece of information that Taymi was not surprised at.

'It is founded on Gothic and Dark Pop, not everyone's cup of tea, and often misunderstood.'

'Or understood.' said Taymi.

'So don't judge a book by its cover.' Said Dad.

'Or do.' said Christian.

'And don't expect to see him perform at the local community concert.'

'What's the name of the band?' Taymi's question was going to allow her to do her own research.

'I believe they are called *In Your Gothic Arms*.' Dad advised. And somehow they thought that fitted about right.

The Westwooders were all gathered in the project room. Taymi was leading the foray into the Dark Ones musical identity by googling *In Your Gothic Arms*. She found some music reviews which gave a good account of gigs played by the local ensemble and was still astonished that this should have been going on with her being aware.

Then she found a website in their name, an obscurely referenced site which was as could only be expected....*black*. There were images and photographs, gothic in nature, accompanied with other depictions that were of biblical tones. She noticed a small video panel and clicked on it.

It relayed a video of a live gig in what appeared to be a dark warehouse, a background sign identified the premises as *The Spirit Store*. A dimly lit stage area held the band and it was surrounded by a large amount of revellers punching the air and dancing to the music. The music....it was certainly darkwave, electronic style, deep and repeditive. Taymi turned the sound up so the others could all here and they gathered around to watch.

Through the punching arms and bobbing heads they could see a figure on stage leaning over a microphone and calling out lyrics....even thought the quality of the video was grainy and at times unfocused they could see that it was indeed the Dark One. They listened. The lyrics were like the music and the man...dark. They poor quality of the video make words difficult to distinguish and they could barely pick out phrases. The leaping of the revellers in the spirit store appeared to take on a demonic appearance, clawing at the air, lurching in irregular movements, the intermittent lighting like flames casting odd shadows, hallucinatory visions. The words had a chanting quality...it reminded Christian of the chanting he had heard in the Woods, he looked more closely at the screen.

'There!' Christian pointed at the screen, his mouth open. He saw words he was familiar with, written here in a list along the side of the website... written in a list of songs. It was the words that he had pondered numerous times, the words that had struck darkness into Christian's heart, into his *soul*.

'*Sacrifice of Blood*'.

Taymi clicked on the words. An audio player popped up and the words so familiar to Christian leapt out through the speaker.

'Sacrifice...of blood, Sacrifice...of blood. It was the words; it was the *voice* that they had heard in the Castle Dungeons. Now they knew it was the voice of the Dark One.

'It's the voice from the Dungeon.' Christian confirmed it to the others. Now he witnessed these words being chanted out to clamouring crowd of ecstatic Goths.

Was this simply a song or some sort of voodoo. The evidence was pointing in one direction and one direction only, the Dark One was responsible for some very disturbing behaviour. Taymi pressed on another video clip, it was from the same gig, the same grainy video. More dark music invaded their project room. The Dark One launched into new lyrics.

'Remember the words, Remember the words….of William Blake, of William Blake.' Taymi almost leapt back in her seat….she recognised the name.

'What is it?' Sophia noticed her reaction.

'I've heard that name before, I read about it, somewhere, recently…….it was in my research book, it's the name of ….an Archdruid.' Taymi jumped out of her chair and grabbed the book which had referred to the Archdruid. She found the page that she had previously read.

'Here it is…. *in the 18th century there was a Druid revival led by dark writers like William Blake, a possible Archdruid.*'

'Google it!' she commanded Christian.

'Ok m'lud.' He said and battered it into a new window, and they all scanned over the results.

'William Blake, a great English painter… a prophetic poet… possibly mad.' Taymi looked over Christian's shoulder and read some more out.

'One of seven children …never went to school.…influenced by the Bible.…when drawing in Gothic churches he heard imaginary chanting and saw imaginary monks processions.…Ok, so that's weird.'

Christian continued, 'His work was abstract and violent… ….his paintings were fantasical.….'

There was an image of one of Blake's paintings shown on the website, it was called Helcate, an image of the Greek Goddess of Black Magic and the Underworld. The website told them that Blake on the day of his death worked feverishly on drawings of Hell called Dantes Inferno until the hour of six o' clock when he died; strangly, those present at his death said that it was the death of an Angel.

Christian completed the section. 'He attacked religion but yet did drawing for the Book of Daniel; Daniel from the Bible again!.....he claimed to have visions of Angels and Archangels.....but he also had visions of Ghosts and Demons....one of his most famous artworks was *The Marriage of Heaven and Hell...* He became an Archdruid between 1799 to 1827.'

'Does that mean he's a good guy or a bad guy?' Sophia scrunched up her face.

'If only we knew.' Replied Taymi.

'What does the Dark One mean when he says *Remember the words of William Blake?*' Mols asked.

'Lets see if we can read something that he wrote.' Taymi clicked into a link to *The Marriage of Heaven and Hell.* She read various extracts.

> *Let man wear the fell of the lion, woman the fleece of the sheep.*
> *The eagle never lost so much time, as when he submitted to learn of the crow.*
> *The fox provides for himself, but God provides for the lion*
> *For the cherub with his flaming sword is hereby commanded to leave his guard at tree of life, and when he does, the whole creation will be consumed, and appear infinite, and holy whereas it now appears finite & corrupt.*
> *An Angel came to me and said O pitiable foolish young man! O horrible! O dreadful state! consider the hot burning dungeon thou art preparing for thyself to all eternity, to which thou art going in such career.*

'That's probably enough of that!' Taymi said, she noted that the passages ran into thousands of words. In this one extract alone so many of the words had familiarity to the Westwooder, the Eagle, the Crow, the Fox, the Cherub, the Flaming Sword, the Tree of Life, the Dungeon, but it was the in-between words that cast the darkest shadows.

'Let's go back to the Dark Ones website.' Taymi clicked back in and read through the full catalogue of songs. The theme was similar throughout. One title caught her attention. It was called *Commandoes of the third Secret of Fatima*. This name rang a bell. The secrets of Fatima were given to three young in the village of Fatima, Portugal by the Virgin Mary in an apparition over ninety years ago. There were three secrets given…what were they? She entered the query.

'The Three Secrets of Fatima.' She read.'The first secret was a vision of Hell, Demons and Souls burned like black animals. It included references to wars such as World War One which the Pope described in July 1918 as the suicide of Europe.' The description made them feel uneasy.

'The second secret was a request for the consecration of Russia and for people to turn to good….or else the first secret may come true.' This made them feel even more uneasy.

'The third secret was not released until the year 2000…' started Taymi.

'That's my year.' Cited Morgen as the year he was born.

'…although it was meant to have been released in 1960, it was withheld until a more appropriate time. The secret described an Angel with a flaming sword…'

'That's Archangel Michael!' Morgen interrupted again.

'…and described much trouble in the world. Its meaning has been interpreted many ways but it is assumed to have described the ongoing conflicts between Christianity and those opposed to it and potentially the end of times.'

'And this has *what* to do with the Dark One?' Sophia couldn't piece it together.

'There are two sides to this story,' Taymi turned around, 'the good side… and the bad side…We're on the good side.' It was enough of an explanation to do.

'So what do we conclude now?' Christian asked an open question.

'Well I think we know the Dark One is up to no good. Said Taymi, 'He has left curses in the Woods, we know that he chants for a sacrifice, he follows Druidery, if that is a word, he has many followers.....I would go as far as to say that he is a Neo-Druid and his activities tell us that he is planning something.' No one could argue with her viewpoint, it was all there in black and white.....and mostly black.

'I say that we must remain on red alert.' She said, 'These bad omens seem to revolve totally around the Golden Stone, I think we should keep trying to find it and when we find it .....we *must* destroy it.'

XLI

CAMPANA

(Bells)

TAYMI WAS FLICKING the TV controller. He who has the controller has the power, or she. Morgen waited. She was not really concentrating since she was reflecting on their recent discoveries and trying to make some sense of it all.

'Go back one!' interrupted Dad suddenly usurping the power despite having had the appearance of reading. Taymi flicked back to the fleeting glimpse that had caught Dads interest. It turned out to be a nature programme on the subject of Bats, which were apparently the *only* mammals which can truly fly. A narrator spoke over various images of the nocturnal species in motion telling of the mythology of Bats.

> 'In mythology Bats are Symbolic of the land of the dead, the underworld.
> They also symbolize death and decay.
> Bats were associated by the Ancient Mayans with human skulls and bones due to their night-time flying and penchant for living in dark caves. In one South American cave up to 20 million bats lived squashed together in cramped conditions.
> Mexican depictions show bats with snouts like sacrificial knives.
> Their association with death led their image to be engraved onto funeral urns.

Some bat depictions take on characteristics of other entities
of the night such as the jaguar, and the owl.

Morgen was reminded of the day that a bat had actually got into the house. It was a strange occurance, they had noticed something horrible moving behind the window blind and had ran outside the window to get a look. It was a bat stuck between the glass and the material of the blind. How it got there was a complete mystery but once it was discovered, the house went into complete frenzy. It was as though the Devil himself had arrived. He remembered too how it looked like a rat with wings.

Dad who remained ever calm, rescued the situation and the bat by covering it with a tub and sliding a sheet of cardboard below it. He removed the bat and put it carefully into a small dark outdoor pump shed leaving the door cracked open for it to escape when night came. It had its own little cave and they dared not go near it or peep in lest the bat fly out and clamp itself onto their jugular vein. Morgen wondered if this was the same bat that flapped around Dad at night, his special pet.

Taymi waited for the bat programme to finish so that she could switch to something else but it was not to be. As soon as the credits rolled Dad asked her to leave that station switched on.

'I want to see the news headlines,' he said, 'it starts now at 6 O'Clock.' Taymi flicked the remote to see how long she would have to endure the news. She noticed that the 6 O'Clock news didn't start until one minute past 6 O' Clock.

'Why does it start at 6.01 and not 6.00?'

'There is one minute allowed for the Angelus.'

She had forgotten about that. The Angelus was played on national TV every day at 6 O'Clock, it was a tradition that extended back to the beginning of the broadcast of TV in many countries and continued in some to this day; although there had been some who thought that it should be abandoned.

The Angelus was a one minute prayer under tolling bells which are said to spread goodwill across the World. In the TV version they watch rolling images of people reflecting at the end of day.

'What does Angelus mean?' Taymi asked.

'The word Angelus is Latin for Angels and if you notice the tolling of the bells takes the form of three tolls repeated three times.' Dad informed her. 'In Germany, Holland and France the Angelus bell is actually known as the Peace Bell. I saw a programme on it once, in the Phillipines it's known as the Oracion, it means a repeated recitation. There are many types of Oracion in different countries, some are for healing, some to keep away evil spirits, its quite interesting.'

Taymi let Dad watch the news headlines. They always seemed to be the same to her, doom, gloom, robbery, killing, no wonder they played the Peace Bell beforehand. She remembered Patricks bell that cast out evil demons, birds and snakes. She noticed Dad returning to read his book.

'Would the Castle bell have rung out the Angelus.'

'I would say it would have. Yes, probably.'

'Could it ring out the Angelus now?'

'No, I know the bellcote is not in working order, it hasn't been for a long time, it is very old.'

'Why do you call it the bellcote?'

'That's an architectural term, it's another name for a bell tower or a bell cover.'

Taymi decided not to choose something to watch on TV. Instead she quickly left the room, something was on her mind.

Christian was sitting in the project room reading, minding his own business. Taymi *burst* in, went straight over to him and grabbed him by the shoulders, staring him directly in the eyes.

'I know how to get through the mist.' She informed him decisively.

'You're ......hurting me.' He said quietly and she let go.

'We are so stoopid.' She said sitting down and shaking her head. 'It was right in front of us the whole time.' Christian waited patiently.

'To raise the Fee....from the journal,' she started, 'It means to raise the *Fe*...the *Fe Flada*, the *mist*!'

'Ohhhh!' said Christian, 'how do we do that?'

'By the peal of the Angels Coet... it means Peel of the Angels Cote....the Ring of the Angels Bell!' Her voice was racing, he was unable to keep up.

'The ringing of the Angelus Bell from the BellCote will raise the Fe Flada!' she spelled it out.

'It will life the mist...we will be able to pass through.' Taymi could hardly contain herself.

'The Angelus Bell will raise the Fe-Flada?'

'Yes, remember how Patrick's bell chased away the spirits, and the Angelus is also known as an Oracion which dispells evil spirits.'

'So the Castle bell ringing the Angelus...'

'..at six o clock...'

'...at six o clock, and it will dispell the mist.'

'Yes!'

'So all we've got to do is ring the Castle bell at six o clock.'

'No.'

'No?'

'The Castle bell doesn't work any more.'

'Ohhh!...............Could we ring our own bell?'

'Not sure if that would work....it may not be powerful enough... and it may have to be a consecrated bell.'

'I know!'

'You do?'

'Yes!.....The Cathedral!'

'The Cathedral?'

'The Cathedral bell, when the wind is coming this way we can hear it...it travels for up to ten kilometres, we've heard it before.'

'Would it be strong enough to lift the mist?'

'I guess,' said Christian, 'There's only one way to find out.'

XLII

MOENIA

(Fort)

It was a mission that they all wanted to go on, even Lila. They set off before 5 O'Clock so that they would have plenty of time to be at the appointed place at the appointed time. Morgen brought his metal detector, Christian some digging implements. Before leaving the house Christian had checked the weather conditions, it was clear and dry…. Perfect.

They made their way to the Underworld and began their entry into the craggy darkness. As usual it was difficult and damp, with just the slightest hint of mist. As they forced their way slowly through the knotted growth, they could feel the moist heat rising from the ground; the humidity increased and as before the thickening mist hung in the air.

'What time is it now?' Christian asked Taymi for the umpteenth.

'Two minutes after you last asked me.' She flatly replied. 'It's five to six.'

After another few minutes Christian called on them to stop. He could see the others struggling and he was beginning to have difficulty identifying which direction to go.

'It's almost 6 O'Clock now.' Taymi advised. They stopped and listened…..nothing.

'I can't hear anything.' Said Mols. It was true; there was virtually no sound, not even birdsong. It was like all sound had died and the air was dead too. They all stood there, listening to the silence.

Christian felt something. It was an ever so slight…breeze. He heard something. It was a barely audible ….bell chime. They paused, the breeze paused, the bell paused.

'There!' Christian heard the bell again, louder now and a stronger breeze swept against his face. The bell rang out three times in a waverly tone rippling in the shallow wind. They all felt it, they all heard it. The breeze moved the branches, it cooled the damp humid air, it swirled the mist, weakening it.

Now they could hear it completely, the bell gave its remaining three rings, from the Cathedral, over the hill, carried on the wind, echoing over the lands, calling out for peace, dispelling demons, calling on the Angels. The breeze was sharp, cutting through the damp and mist, clearing the way, the mist could not exist in the breeze, it disappeared as mysteriously as it had arisen, leaving only wisps hanging in the air. The veil was parted, a clear direction ahead was visible and they made for it as quickly as they could.

Was it just a breeze that had cleared the mist and carried the sound of the bell?... or was it the sound of the bell that had dispelled the mist? Either way, they were for once able to make clear progress. Christians heart pounded, they had set out to dispel the mist and now it was happening, they were succeeding.

Christian knew they were ascending, the ground was drier now and there were less rotting branches, it was brighter too and more greenery formed. The undergrowth was just as thick but it was more of what they were accustomed to.

'Come on, keep up.' He checked behind to make sure no one was in difficulty. They were all happy to be out of the gloom.

'I see light ahead.' Morgen pointed and Christian hoped it wasn't going to be a repeat of their last expedition where they had arrived back at the square one. They swept through the remaining bushes arriving at a place of open ground. It was not somewhere they had been before; this was new.

They stood in an oasis in a desert, light flooded into an open plain of about an acre, the size of their garden. The ground was roughed up, layers of brown leaves that had fallen over time mixed with long grass.

There was a large mound in front of them. Christian ran up to it and climbed on top. He could see that this mound continued around encircling the whole central space of the clearing. His heart beat strong, all doubt washed away. This was it, the place they sought; he was sure …..the Fort. Generations had searched among shady groves and dark recesses of the Woods for the mysterious location of the Fort but he believed that it was only they that had figured out its position and the means of access. He savoured this sublime moment.

The others followed him up to the top of the mound.

'Is this it, the Fort?' Sophia wasn't sure, it seemed so basic. She looked around, the clearing was about twice the size of the circular mound and was surrounded on all sides by thick growth and tall trees. There was an ethereal and subdued feeling in the clearing and no wildlife chatter.

'This is the Fort.' Said Taymi, she could feel the history in the ground. People lived here hundreds, no, *thousands* of years ago. There were no remnants of houses or walls or anything else for that matter, just the circular mound, but that was enough to convey the historical feeling.

'Is it the Fairy Fort?' Lila asked.

'Yes,' said Sophia, 'Watch out for Fairies.'

They went on some exploration of the area. Examining the mound walls, walking along the top of them, kicking up leaves. No one had walked along the mound in a long, long time.

'I knew it was here.' Christian was bragging to Mols, 'I knew it all along.' Morgen was already covering ground with his metal detector. He paced about quickly covering as much ground as he could but it was a large area and it would take some time. Christian sat on the perimeter mound thinking about the Golden Stone. *Was this its resting place? Where in the Fort would it be hidden? How big would it be?*

If it was anything like the stone in Clogher Village Cathedral then he had no idea how they could unearth it. *Did it still have any power?*

Despite all they had read and witnessed, deep down Christian felt that the stone was simply a valuable artefact and not something which had a mind of its own or something that could speak. They had promised that if they found it they would destroy it, but Christian was having doubts about that, after all it could be very valuable, but not if it were broken, and what would happen if they destroyed a national treasure? They wouldn't get much thanks for that.

He hadn't forgotten that this place was the horn of the Devil, the Devils hill, it did not have a good reputation, but sitting here now in this peaceful place, he really couldn't see what all the fuss was about.

Mols and Taymi were examining the extremely tall trees that surrounded the clearing. One in particular appeared much taller than the others, it seemed to extend well beyond the others and high into the sky. It had a very wide cracked and weathered trunk.

'I think this might be the King of the Woods.' Taymi was excited. 'Look how much taller it is that the other trees and considering that we are raised on a hill here would put it above anything else in the entire Woods.' Mols had noticed something high up in the tree. She wasn't sure but thought it was what appeared to be quite a large nest. She hardly dared hope, this could be the nesting place.....

Pe...eew

High above the clearing she could see the Buzzards circling, watching. She watched them back. They both circled for some time before swooping down towards the clearing and high into the tree to where she had seen the nest. This was their home, right here overlooking the Fort, a quiet protected area, in the tallest tree in the Woods, grand enough for royalty. She was right and she had finally found their precious place.

'The Buzzards live here at the place of the Devil.' Taymi's views on the birds remained unchanged.

'It's the King of the Woods.' Mols whispered, referring to the bird not the tree.

Morgen had already had a number of false alarms and now his detector was beeping again. He poked at the ground in the Fort finding nothing. The beeper still beeped. He dug a little deeper.

'Christian, how about some help!' They both dug into the ground, the beeping continued. They hit something. It reminded them of the day they had discovered the metal box containing the journal, however this something didn't have a metal sound. Morgen turned off the machine.

'It's stone.' Christian carefully enlarged the hole they were making.

'Why does it beep then?'

They carefully excavated enough of a hole to observe that they had discovered a flat stone. Morgen tapped on it with the handle of a trowel.

'It's hollow, there's a space underneath.'

The girls were gathered around to see. It was a slow process. They dug to expose more of the flat stone until they eventually began to expose its edges. Christian tried to prise it upwards, it needed more freedom so they excavated more space around it. He prised it again. It was lifting, Morgen helped, they all did. They managed to get enough implements beneath it to prise it fully, then Christian gripped it and raised it fully. It revealed a deep hollow core. A crude square hole formed by four stone sides. They craned to look into it. It was empty. They could only see the mud packed base of the hole.

'Is this where the Golden Stone was kept?' Sophia whispered.

'...*was* kept.' Repeated Christian. 'Looks like someone got here before us.'

'But that cover stone hadn't been moved in years.' Taymi pointed out.

'Then maybe it was taken a long time ago,' he sighed, 'or maybe it was never here.'

'But something was here.' She insisted. They all sat around looking at the hole in the ground.

Is that it? Thought Christian, *Someone got here before us?* This was a great disappointment, having eventually found where it was most likely to have been hidden to discover that it was now gone.

'No!' he said suddenly.

'No?' Said Morgen.

'No.' said Christian leaning towads Morgen and snatching his metal detector. He switched it on again. It was beeping like crazy. They looked at each other; Christian looked back into the hole.

'Give me the trowel.'

He reached into the base of the opening and began poking at the mud floor. There was something buried in it. He painstakingly picked at the base of the hole and had to put his entire head in there to see what he was doing. He was exposing a solid object bound in cloth.

'I think I can get it now.' His hollow voice echoed from inside the hole. As he pulled out the object so his siblings pulled him out of the hole. He was holding the object bound in cloth. It was about seven or eight inches long and about four inches wide. He looked at the others. He gasped for breath after having his head buried in the hole.

'Open it.'

He unwrapped it carefully, the cloth was wrapped around at least three times. As the cloth fell away from the item it revealed something which they had only until now known as a legend.

It was a glittering and sparkling stone.....it could only be, and was, at last..... The Golden Stone.

They looked at it without speaking.

It formed a similar shape to the original Golden Stone in Clogher Village Cathedral, a *minute* version of it. Christian was holding the Stone in his hands, for some time he was speechless, he was thinking of something profound to say.

'It's not really that heavy.' He eventually mustered; he had expected a gold artefact to be much heavier. Taymi took it from him. Up close she could see that it was not a solid gold stone but that the gold and silver of the stone were tiny fragments, like metal filings, which were bound up in the stone.

'It's a clay stone.' She deduced for them. 'That's why it's not heavy. The gold and silver filings were mixed up with clay and cast into this shape. The gold and silver go right through every part of the stone.'

'Is it valuable?' Morgen enquired.

'Very valuable.' Taymi confirmed.

They each took it in their hands and examined it closely. The beauty of its gold and silver was countered by its brutish features. It made them feel uneasy. A spot of light which had broken through the tall trees fell on the ground near Sophia's foot. She moved the Golden Stone into the light spot. The light made it glitter, reflecting on her face, it was mesmeric, her eyes glazed over just looking at it.

'Its amazing.' She said and passed it on to Mols who was equally struck with its magnificence.

Christian took the stone off her. Was it now just an artefact? He couldn't see how it could still have any power, despite all that they had been through and all they had witnessed, it seemed far fetched to imagine that this stone could speak and command leaders of armies.

Yet he was aware, they all were, that this was the Golden Stone after which a Kingdom was named, it was one of the three oracles of Erin and a treasure over which battles were won and lost.

'We have to destroy it.' Taymi reminded them.

Christian's grasp on the stone tightened. 'I don't know if that's a good idea.'

'It was your idea!' She wasn't sure whose idea it was except that she had understood their mission to be seek and destroy.

'Imagine the trouble we'll be in if we damage it.' He argued wrapping the stone back in its cloth covering.

'Imagine the trouble we'll be in if we don't.' she argued back.

'I think we should take it home and decide what to do with it then.

'We can't take it home, its an evil stone, anything could happen.'

'No one knows that we found it, nothing can happen.' He stood up and walked towards the perimeter mound with the stone carefully packaged up in his hands. He stopped short of reaching the edge,

'I can't.' he said.

'You can't what?' Taymi asked.

'I can't take it out.' He said.

'Why?'

'I don't know.' Christian seemed confused, at odds with what to do with it and how to do it.

'We better put it back where we got it.' He said.

It seemed like the best idea for now, they couldn't suddenly arrive home with this incredible artefact and start explaining how and why they had found it. Especially with the depth of history and legend that surrounded it. Perhaps it was best to reinstate it where they got it for now. Taymi took the bundle and placed it very carefully back into the hole from where it came. Together they closed the lid and concealed the area where they had been digging.

'We better go back.' Christian felt like getting out of that place. He felt like a black cloud was hovering over him and he was sure that it had physically got darker. Despite being in the outdoors he wanted fresh air.

They went back the way they had come, the underworld was as unwieldy as ever but they appeared to see their route more clearly as they made their way out of it through the darkly murky growth. Christian lagged behind the others contemplating the magnitude of their discovery and wrestling with thoughts of what course of action to take. Morgen turned around to wait on him. As Morgen looked at his approaching brother he saw something strange. A branch just over Christians head appeared to *bend* of its own accord. Christian noticed the look on Morgens face. With horror Morgan realised that the bending branch was not a branch at all but something else lowering itself onto Christian's shoulder, something known not to have existed in the entire country, it was a black and slimy *snake*.

In one swift movement the snake wrapped itself around Christian's neck with a sudden tightening movement. Christian, shocked, tried to prise it off with its hands as it fastened ever tighter. Morgan reacted quickly, fighting back through the rotting wood, a branch broke off in his hand as he wrestled through it, he shouted for help and the others swung around to see what was happening. Christian was fighting for breath, Morgen reached him but didn't know what to do.

'Fort...' gasped Christian. Morgen glanced back towards the Fort, *What did Christian want him to do?*

'Fort...' wheezed Christian urgently, he couldn't squeeze out anything more, his eyes pleaded with Morgen to understand. And Morgen understood.

'Fortis Et Fidelis!' Morgen screamed at the viper. Instantaneously it whipped away from Christians neck and glared at Morgen, tiny fangs appearing in its stretched open mouth. Words sprung into Morgen's mind, words which had been deciphered from many centuries ago, words that the Egyptians had called upon to dismiss the snake's evil, he called on them now.

'Keep away from my house.' He shouted the simple command.

The snake spat a venomous hiss at Morgens face. Morgen swung his arm to protect himself, he was holding his lance. The lance connected fully with the snakes head sending it reeling. Its head smacked sickeningly on a tree trunk, it slithered swiftly away in the filthy ground.

'Get out, Get out!' Taymi was dragging Morgen and Christian through the branches and towards the edge of the underworld, crashing through old branches and tearing through spiky briars. They all broke through the remaining growth until they emerged into the grassy green growth.

'My eyes!' Morgen had been hit with venom in his eyes. 'My eyes are burning.' Mols quickly turned around and grabbed spotted a clump of shamrocks.

'Wipe your eyes with this!' She directed him urgently and he did.

Christian was gasping for breath, Morgen blinked his eyes open, the shamrocks seemed to have taken the sting out of the venom and he was able to see even though his eyes were puffed and red. They made their way quickly away from there and breathed the clear fresh air.

By the time they had arrived home, Christian was able to breathe properly again and Morgen's swelling had died back down. They had stopped by the rivers edge to gain their composure and wash out Morgen's eyes again thought Mols was sure that it was the healing powers of the juices of St Patricks shamrock that had helped restate them to normal.

'We are *never* going in there again!' Taymi was adamant, 'Stone or no Stone!'

And given all that had happened, nobody disagreed with her.

XLIII

FATUM

(Destiny)

IT WAS A restless night for everyone. They thought of the discovery of the Golden Stone and the thought of the attack of the snake, it was difficult to sleep after all that had happened. Eventually however, despite themselves, nature took its course and everyone had fallen into slumber, the moon at full phase shone brightly in the night.

Christian's sleep was interrupted. 'What time is it?' He knew it was still the middle of the night. He crawled out of bed and made his way to his parent's room. He opened the door and padded quietly to his fathers side of the bed.

'Dad.' There was no response.

'Dad?'

'Yes.' Dad stirred from beneath the bedclothes.

'Did you call me?'

'.......No......' Dad checked the time, 'Christian it's the middle of the night?'

'Sorry, I thought I heard you...'

'Go back to bed son....See you in the morning.'

'Ok.' Christian crawled back into bed and slid back to sleep.

'*Christian.*'

Was it minutes later, or an hour? He distinctly heard his name being called, it sounded like his father.

'Dad?'

'What?'

'Did you call me?'

'No Christian I didn't call you…can you go back to sleep.' Then Dad hoisted himself up on one arm, he looked a little concerned.

'Christian,' he chose his words carefully, 'If you hear a call ….you *don't* have to answer it…. Ok?'

'Ok.' Christian went back to bed but this time he did not sleep, he lay awake and listened. There was nothing. Then….

'Chrissstian.'

It was a whisper, a low voice, from where he did not know. He got out of bed and made his way to the door entering onto the landing. The landing window blinds were brightly illuminated by the moon. Christian went to the window and slowly drew the blind up so that he could see out. The Woods stood dark and foreboding, the full moon hung overhead, wisps of clouds drifted across its eerie form, dimming its illumination and then as they moved on revealing again the moons brilliant light.

He was sure he heard his name being called, was it coming from *there*, the Woods? He opened the window slightly and listened carefully. He could hear the shash from the leaves on the trees and the rush of the water over the waterfall. He listened to their repeditiveness. Through the *shushing* sounds he thought he could almost hear his name repeating, *'Chrissst…. Chrissst…'*

He listened carefully to the formation of the sounds ….the sounds of his name….and then…..

'CHRISTIAAAAN!'

He sat bolt upright, *'Lets Rock!...we're going to the Cathedral.'* It was Dad calling. Dad popped his head around Christian's door urging him to wake up and get on with the day.

'Time is of the essence…..didn't you hear me calling you from downstairs?'

Christian sat at the breakfast table, he felt that he was still living last nights dream, he wasn't yet fully engaged with reality. Sophia flipped the Angel calendar and read.

'August 1st, your soul will keep you safe and give you the guidance you seek.' She thought about this in the context of the incident in the Woods and was glad they were all safe.

'In exactly one month we will be back at school.' Mols reminded her.

That's if we can stay alive til then. The morbid thought crossed Christian's mind and he recoiled from himself for thinking it.

'It's a special day for me' said Sophia.

'How so?' asked Mols.

'Because this is the feast day of Saint Sofia, my Patron Saint. I looked it up before, remember I told you.'

'Was that the story of the three daughters.'

'Yes, her daughters were called Faith, Hope and Charity. Three of the seven virtues, Sofia was called Wisdom...just like me.'

'But did'nt they....'

'Yes.' Sophia did'nt wish to go into the rest of the story, it was a cruel story of how the three daughters had survived a fiery furnace only to be martyred later during the persecution of Christians. Their mother had died three days later praying over the graves of her three daughters.

'But did you know,' said Dad about to introduce a piece of bizarre architectural information, '...that the largest Cathedral in the World for over a thousand years was built in her name.....*your* name.'

'No, I did'nt know that.' Sophia was impressed and somewhat proud of her namesakes achievement.

'The Hagia Sofia in Istanbul.' He told her, 'We should look it up later, I think you will be interested.'

And that is what they agreed to do.

They were back in St.Macartan's Cathedral.

Christian couldn't concentrate; it was the dream that bothered him. *Was it a dream?*

He couldn't simply let the Stone just lie there in the Woods. He felt that he needed to hold it one more time, to look on it again, to explore its wealth, its *power*. The thought of it preoccupied him to the point where he remained seated when everyone else stood and remained standing when everyone else sat.

He looked at the images in the Cathedral, those that he could see from his seat. Isacc and Abraham, the Baptism Font, the Macartan tapestry, the Candle, the Carvings, the Stained Glass, the Crucifixion. Their images mixed with the domination of the huge pipe organ and the choirs hymn. His mind swam with his thoughts of the discoveries they had made over the course of the summer, the Ledger, the Silver Shrine, the Book of Angels, the Cemeteries, the Vitruvian Man, the Bell that lifted the Mist and ultimately the Golden Stone, the Stone after which a kingdom was named.

He thought too of the carvings, the dark history they had uncovered, the flood and the snake that had almost choked him. He may have attended mass but he wasn't present.

'Dad and I will be here in the Cathedral later tonight.' Mom reminded them as they exited the building after mass. That evening a special concert, *An Evening of Sacred Music*, was being held in the Cathedral. It was not unusual for the magnificent building to be used as a venue for concert choirs or hymn recitals and its resonance contributed immensely to the sonic effect.

Mom had arranged for herself and Dad to attend the concert. It was a longstanding arrangement and Mom was looking forward to it.

'I'd rather be going to hear U2 in Dublin.' Dad said from the side of his mouth, '…but at least we'll be going on a full stomach.' He had promised to take Mom to dinner prior to the concert.

At home, Sophia, Mols and Dad browsed pictures of the Hagia Sofia, the Cathedral named for St.Sofia. It was a famous Architectural landmark with a huge dome roof. It was one of the first Architectural Masterpieces Dad had studied in College.

'Byzantine Architecture, its design changed the history of Architecture.' He marvelled before leaving the girls to further study one of his favourite buildings.

'Let's switch to You Tube.' Mols instructed the moment Dad had left the room.

'Wait, there's something interesting here.' Said Sophia, picked out something of interest.

'The Wood of the True Cross.......' She pointed to the passage and they both read it quietly to themselves.

A historic custom which venerates the Wood of the True Cross on Aug 1st was begun at the Great Church of Hagia Sofia. On this day a relic of the True Cross is revealed from the imperial treasury and shown to the people.

It was *todays* date, the day in which the Wood of the True Cross was celebrated, *Sofia's day* and it had begun at the Cathedral of Sofia. Not alone that but there was another interesting comment included in the paragraph.

The actual Wood of the True Cross had been found after having been buried for 300 years at the site of the Church of the Holy Sepulchre in Jerusalem.

Sophia knew another incredible claim of the Church of the Holy Sepulchre in Jerusalem, it was known as one of the most important Christian sites in the World, and now she had an idea why.

'The Centre of the Universe.' Whispered Sophia.

'You Tube.' Whispered Mols.

'Sorry guys, but no-one is allowed to go to the Woods today.' Mom reminded them later. She was going to leave Taymi in charge of the house whilst both parents were away and wanted to ensure that no-one took advantage of the eldest sister.

Nobody wanted to go to the Woods anyway, not after the incident with the snake, how did they know there weren't more snakes slithering around in the slimy underworld or in any other part of the Woods for that matter. At lunch they sat around the table and discussed everything except the Golden Stone.

They had gone on a quest to find it and they had found it. Now they felt like it could stay there.

Mom called everyone together and gave clear instructions.

'Taymi is in charge. It's almost 4 O'Clock now, the concert starts at 6. We want to be there early to get good seats but we should be home by half past eight. We've got out mobiles but remember they will be switched off for the concert.'

'You look lovely Mom.' Said Sophia and they all agreed.

'Ahem!' said Dad.

'Your collar is crooked.' Pointed out Mols and helped him fix it.

Their parents drove out the avenue and turned the corner.

Mom and Dad had been gone for a while; everyone was quietly spending the afternoon either in their rooms or watching TV. Taymi looked out the window, there were dark clouds over the Woods and she hoped that it wasn't the formation of a storm. She sat down at the table and looked at the Angel calendar; she re-read the passage that Sophia had mentioned that morning. But there was something else on there, something that Sophia had not read. Taymi picked up the calendar, just under the heading of August 1st and in tiny print was a single word.

It was a word she recognised but it appeared to be used here in a different context. She held the calendar and looked at it, what was the meaning of this word, it had appeared in the register, why was it here? She put the calendar back down; she had some work to do.

Taymi went to the project room and pulled out the register. She pored over it to see if she could again find the word that she had seen in this book and also on the Angel calendar. The word was *Lemass* or as spelled in the calendar, *Lammas*. Her finger ran down the lists of names until she found the word.

The writing was poor, the spelling was not clear, but it was undoubtedly the same word in the register. She had previously thought this was a name, now she was not so sure. A strange foreboding feeling came over her, the name written in the register was the same, but so was the date.... August 1st.....*today*. It was one of the few names in the register with numbers opposite.

She sat back from the register. *What was significant about today? Who or what is Lammas?*

Taymi powered up the pc with a view to finding out.

'Lammas, a festival day,' she spoke to herself, 'to celebrate the harvest, also called the feast of the first fruits.' She glanced at the paragraph.

Lammas is a neo-pagan feast the direct opposite time of year from Imbolg and takes place when the sun in nearest to Leo in the zodiac. Named after the god Lugh and August 1ˢᵗ is in memory of his foster mother. The French town and capital of Gaul, Lyon, was named after Lugh.

'Lammas is the direct opposite of Imbolg?' The pagan feast day which in time became St.Brigid's day. Imbolg had also been listed in the register. Taymi flicked back to that book and found the word *Imbolg*, it too had numbers listed opposite. She returned to the article.

Lammas was known as the last day when tenants had to produce crops for the landlords, and was also known by the name the Gules of August.

'Gules of August?' Taymi knew the meaning of the word Gules, it was the heraldic word she had pursued previously. 'The Blood of August?'

She tapped the words into the computer and read. Morgen wandered into the project room, he was wearing black cheek paint as worn by American footballers and wrestlers.

'Morgen can you get Christian for me please.' She asked him politely.

'Ok.' He wandered off.

Taymi continued tapping; neither Christian nor Morgen came back. She referenced the register again and then reverted to frantic tapping. Morgen wandered past again.

'Get Christian please!' This time it was not so polite. She looked at the screen and did not like what she saw, her heart beat, she felt worried, unsafe. Morgen was at the door, Taymi turned to him.

'WHERES CHRISTIAN!' she virtually screamed at him. Morgen, shocked, held up a small piece of paper, a hastily scribbled note.

'He's gone!'

XLIV

EXITIUM

(Destruction)

CHRISTIAN WAS DEEP in the Woods, close to the place they called the Underworld, the place that led to the Fort, to the Stone. He obscured himself behind a tree. Someone was there, at the place where they had entered, he recognised the figure, it was the Dark One.

He wasn't sure why he had come, he had felt compelled to. It was something to do with the dream, the calling, he felt it had come from the Fort; he knew this was the centre of power. He felt that he needed to get to the stone; he felt that he should have destroyed it yesterday. Why didn't he? He couldn't, there was something about the stone that he knew he couldn't destroy it. But he must try, that was why he was back. He knew that it would be some time before it would be possible to use the Angelus bells to lift the mist but he didn't want to wait.

Now he had seen the Dark One. Was it the Dark One who had called him?

He didn't know what to do, should he confront the Dark One, should he wait until the Dark One went away. He knew that the stone had the potential to manifest evil if it fell into the hands of the Dark One. He felt sure that no-one had held the stone in many, many years because of the way in which it was buried, he wanted to ensure that no one would hold it that would put it to ill use, or use it as an excuse to do so.

He hoped the others wouldn't follow him; he had left them a note, he had told them to ring him on his mobile if necessary, he knew phone reception was impossible in the Woods.

Christian came to a decision; he would walk out there and face down the Dark One. He stepped out from behind the tree and at the exact same time a hand gripped his shoulder.

'What's wrong?' Sophia had arrived to the project room to see what all the shouting was about.

Taymi was reading the note.

'Gone to Woods, ring if you need me.' She read flatly, 'He *knows* there is no phone reception in the Woods, why did he go there?' she implored of the others. They had no idea why he would have done so or why it was of such importance to Taymi.

'He has been acting strangely all day.' Commented Sophia.

'He's in danger.' Said Taymi.

'Maybe the snake is gone,' said Mols,

'It's not that.' Said Taymi, 'Oh what am I to do?' she lamented. She looked at the clock, it was 5.40 exactly. She grabbed her mobile phone.

How could she ring them, how could she even begin to explain to her parents why she was calling, why they had to come home urgently, too much to explain, too little time. She deliberated and then she dialled.

Mom and Dad had taken their place in the Cathedral. It was beginning to fill up but they had managed to get seated in their favourite place, front row centre. In case she forgot, Mom powered off her mobile phone and flashed it at Dad for him to do the same. Taymi got through to Moms answerphone, she couldn't leave a message, it was too complicated, she tried Dad.

Dad slipped his phone back into his pocket, silently, powered off and smiled back at Mom.

'We're going to have to go and get him.' Taymi announced folding up her phone.

'Why? What's happened?' Sophia wanted answers.

'I'll explain on the way.' Taymi commanded, 'Quickly, get ready.'

'But it might be dangerous there.' Mols was still thinking of the snake.

'It might be dangerous here.' Taymi retorted, her tone frightened Mols. Taymi looked at Lila, she was only seven, was she putting her in the way of danger by taking her to the Woods or was she protecting her? She had a decision to make and she decided that it was better if they all stuck together, for better or worse.

Christian spun around to see who it was that had gripped his shoulder and discovered that it was *Anouk*. She had grabbed Christian and pulled him back and out of view from the Dark One.

'Keep away from him.' Anouk whispered, 'He is not safe.' Christian looked at her speechless. By way of explanation she continued,

'He has been following me for weeks, where I go, he goes, he is not to be trusted. You must keep away from him.' It was Christian's sentiments entirely. He nodded.

'Come away from here.' She said and they started to make their way.

Taymi locked the front door of the house behind them.

'Lets go,' she started along the avenue quickly with her startled siblings alongside having had no time to prepare or even understand what this was about, Morgen grabbed his stick, his lance, he still had black paint on his fingers.

'Tell us now.' Insisted Sophia.

'I discovered that this is the day of sacrifice,' Taymi began to explain what her extreme panic was about. 'The first of August is called Lammas, it's also called The Gules of August, which means the Mouth of August or the *Blood* of August, it's a pagan feast and a day of payment, a day of the *tithe*.' She had an attentive audience.

'There are two main days of the year which are most sacred to pagans; Imbolg and Lamass, its on these days that sacrifices are offered. Today is one of those days.'

'How does this affect us?' Sophia persisted.

'It was listed in the register,' said Taymi, 'Lammas on the first of August and Imbolg in February. They are both listed in the register.' She explained. 'Beside each of them were numbers, Imbolg had 06, 20 and 34, Lammas had 13 and 27.'

They hurried through the west wood gate and down the track.

'I figured out that these numbers are years, 1906, 1913, 1920. These pagan festivals were celebrated every seven years, but alternatively.' It still wasn't making any sense to the others.

'Imbolg was *celebrated* by the burning of the Castle in 1920, the attempted sacrifice of the child.'

'And this is a multiple of seven, this very year, and it falls on Lamass, August first.... today.'

'So there is supposed to be a sacrifice today?' Sophia concluded.

'Exactly.' Confirmed Taymi, 'It's what the Druid has been planning, its what the *Dark One* has been planning, that's why the 'S' on the tree, it meant seven, it may even have meant sacrifice. We were wrong about the mark of Cain, it was a seven too and we found it exactly seven days ago.' It was beginning to dawn on the others.

'The Dark One has been preparing for this day, he has been preparing a sacrifice, and now Christian has walked right into it' Taymi told them.

The others were horrified.

'He's following us.' Christian had spotted that the Dark One had noticed or heard them and was pursuing them from some way behind. They stopped and listened.

'Wait here.' Instructed Anouk. 'I will go and see.' She lightly stepped around a tree and disappeared from sight. Christian leaned his head back against the trunk of the tree. He closed his eyes and shook his head. *What had he become involved in? He shouldn't have come here. The Dark One seemed to be pursuing them. What were his intentions?*

Christian heard footsteps rush up behind him but before he could turn he was gripped aggressively around the throat and pulled to the ground.

'But if Christian is in trouble, there is someone who will save him.'

'Who?' Taymi whipped round to see who Sophia meant.

'Anouk!' said Sophia.

'How?' said Mols.

'I've been figuring it out,' said Sophia, 'Anouk means grace, she has been around when we needed her.'

'It doesn't mean she'll be able to help Christian.' Said Morgen.

'I think it was her that appeared in the photo,' It was a plausible suggestion, 'and I think it was her that Taymi saw one day and thought it was me.' Taymi stopped to consider what Sophia had said.

'I believe you are right about that.' She said.

'I've also found a white feather after we had met Anouk and I have been thinking that in some way Anouk might be ....'

'Say it' insisted Taymi.

'...I think she might be ......an Angel, a Guardian Angel.'

Christian came too. He opened his eyes slightly, his vision was blurred, he head hurt, he was regaining consciousness. Someone was there, he tried not to move or alert them that he was conscious.

He realised that he was tied by his hands to a large tree by tightly knotted bonds... *wire?*

It was the Dark One, working at the wires that bound him. Christian was unable to move. He recognised where he was, he was tied to the King of the Woods, at the place of the Fort.

How had the Dark One taken him here? Where was Anouk?

Suddenly he saw hope, Anouk appeared out from behind a nearby tree, silently she approached and deftly lifted a branch as a weapon. She looked at Christian to implore him not to make a sound; he looked at her to implore her to rescue him. She closed up on the Dark One.

The Dark One stopped, he turned his eyes to Christian, and realised that Christian had regained conciousness, at the same moment he noticed in Christians open eyes the reflection of Anouk directly at his back. He made to swing round just as the branch connected with his head.

The Dark One fell to the ground.

'She can't be an Angel, how could that be?' Morgen asked the question but he wasn't entirely sure, there were so many things that seemed out of his control. Mols seemed more receptive to the idea, they had learned so much about Angels and she fully believed that they existed. Lila mouth was wide open at Sophia's declaration. Taymi didn't say anything either way.

'Could it be true?' Mols asked, 'Could Anouk be an Angel.'

Taymi stopped. 'Yes.' She whispered.

'If she is an Angel,' Mols continued, 'then she will protect Christian, she will save him.'

'She's not going to save him.' Said Taymi.

'But if she's an Angel...' Mols continued.

'She *is* an Angel...' Taymi spoke forcibly and then looked around at the others,

'...that's precisely the problem...she's the Angel of *Death*!'

'Thank God.' gasped Christian as Anouk attended to the wires that bound his hands tightly to the tree. 'He might have been going to kill me.' A pain seared into Christian's wrist making him wince. The wires were far too tight. He looked at Anouk. She looked at the wire and saw that it was firm. Anouk stepped back and looked at Christian coldly.

He didn't understand how it had happened but he knew deep in his heart that he had just made the greatest mistake of his life. Anouk looked down at the Dark One who she had struck to the ground. Christian realised now that the Dark One had been trying to *release* him, not tie him. It was Anouk who had put Christian in this position.

'He has been on my trail.' She referred to the Dark One. Christian said nothing, he moved his wrists, they were fastened tight.

'He is a student of the Dark Arts, but his aim is to disrupt, not enhance them.' She looked again at Christian.

'He has learned all about Druidry, symbolism, history, the Castle. But he proclaimed Christianity.'

Christian realised now that it was the Dark One who was the one who had received the package of information from Master Tom and had been studying it. He realised that the words 'Sacrifice of Blood' referred to Christ's blood. He realised that the lyric 'Remember the Words of Williams Blake' was a warning, not a call.

Anouk spoke again. 'He worked out the timing, the location, the markings, but he failed where you succeeded Christian.' Christian knew what she was referring to.

'He failed to access the Fort. Until now. He simply followed the path I made. But he failed to break through himself and he failed to locate the Stone.'

Christian maintained his silence.

'You see a payment must be made.' Anouk continued, 'on this day, fittingly it is the seventh day.'

'Why?' whispered Christian breaking his silence.

'It is commanded, I am obliged to. I have returned here for many years to do the will of the Dark Lord. His voice speaks to me through the stone he inhabits here. Today the tithe is due and I will arrange it. Then I will be gone......' she looked at him, '...and so will you.'

Christian struggled with the bonds that held him.

'You don't have to,' he said quietly, 'you could let me go.' His words triggered a reaction in her, she swept closer to him, strain showed in her face.

'You don't understand, this is not a choice. A payment must be made, a debt paid, it must happen and it will happen. If it is not paid it will be taken, one way or another. It is an eternal bond.' She turned away but kept talking.

'Let you go? Throughout time, throughout history he has been kept alive through the work that he commands and the tithes that are paid.' She flashed around at Christian again.

'Don't you know that you are but a token! You are simply a link, *I* am a link, the oracle is a link, there are many, many links that form a whole.'

Christian struggled for meaning. He was a link? A link in Christianity? Of many faithful and of all those who would do good in the name of God, *one* God. She was a link, a worshipper of evil in a world of evil and madness. The oracle was a link, one of many oracles, through whom the voice spoke of many Devils, of *one* Devil.

Taymi was explaining as she was walking, she recounted how she had stumbled on the truth.

'They just kept coming up.' She was referring to the *women*. Whilst she had been waiting on Morgen to go fetch Christian she had continued searching. The God Lugh, she discovered, had dedicated the feast for three women. It made her think of how often females had come up in their searches, the Nemetom, Diana, Levana, all Godesses. She typed in Goddess;

> *May be associated with Earth, Motherhood, Love, alternatively War, Death, and Destruction.*
> *They had a strong role in neo-paganism, and many believe were replaced by Druidesses.*

Druidess? She typed in the word.

> *Druidesses from the Celtic and Gaul Druids, she was a woman Druid known also in the ancient language as a Ban-Drui.*

The words struck her like a bombshell. It was the equivalent to the words from the ledger, *Ban an Drui*, she realised now that it didn't mean *Banish the Druid* it meant *Woman Druid*. Taymi was reminded now that the Celtic word *Ban* meant *Woman*, she was reminded too that it had another meaning in Irish, -*White*. The White Druid? Could it be a reference to blond hair? She read more.

> *St.Patrick had given a warning to Kings to give no countenance to Pythonesses or Augurers where Pythonesses were understood to be Druidesses. The name Pythoness corresponded with the Irish Ban-Drui with Pythoness being the name of the priestess at the Oracle of Delphi.*

Everything that Taymi read seemed to convince here more and more that the Druid they had been seeking was in fact a Druidess. She continued to read.

> *The Ban-Drui may have given human form to the mythical Ban-Shee.*

She remembers Sophia's research regarding the BanShee, a woman of the fairy mounds, one of the fallen Angels. She typed it in and her eyes picked out sections of relevance.

> *The BanShee may be an older frightening woman, or a younger beautiful woman of any age.*
> *Her mourning call is heard usually at night when someone is about to die. She may take the form of other animals such as a Raven. She is also known as the Woman of the Mist.*
> *Another name for the BanShee is Bean-Nighe which translates to Washer Woman also known as the washer at the ford; she wanders near streams where she chooses those who will die. She does this by washing the blood from the clothes of those she has chosen.*

Taymi gaped stunned at the last passage. She recalled the incident in the Woods where the blood was washed from Christians clothes in the river. He was the one *she* had chosen. *She* was the one they had met that day in the Woods...Anouk. Taymi, in shock, kept reading.

The BanShee was considered one of the Aos-Si, the so called Fallen Angels, also commonly thought of as Fairies with the BanShee equivalent being the Fairy Queen.

Taymi remembered the lore associated with the Fairy Queen, she was obliged to pay *a tithe to hell* every seventh year. She looked at the words Fallen Angels and clicked on it.

An Angel exiled or banished from Heaven. The best known Fallen Angel is Lucifer or Satan. He was banished from Heaven to Hell as the Devil where he now tries to persuade mankind to do wrong in order to compete with God. He is the tempter of humankind and the personification of evil.

The Devil commands a force of evil Angels or Demons which include the Angel of Death.

The Angel of Death, Taymi recalled the Good Angel of Death; *Saint Michael the Archangel.*

Who then was his alterego, his nemesis, the Anti-Michael? She pressed it;

The Angel of Death is Death personified. Perceived in some languages as male and in some as female where that culture sees Death as a woman in white. Considered to be the bringer of death, who causes death but can also be tricked or outwitted in order to retain life.

The Angel of Death goes under many names in various cultures, Hellenic, Slavic, Celtic, Baltic......

She pressed Celtic, the name that flew up hit her instantly. The name that she saw was;

ANKOU.

It was virtually the same name, a slight variation ....of Anouk! She stared at it; a horrible shiver ran through her. Anouk had either fashioned herself as or *was* the Angel of Death.

Ankou, the Breton name for the personification of Death.

She read with horror the traits attributed to the Angel of Death.

The Angel of Death kills off the children of men.
The three primary methods of death attributed to the Angel
of Death being burning, throttling and slaughtering.
The Angel of Death will take on the form or image that
best serves its purpose.

It was enough, everything she had seen had pointed to Anouk. It was Anouk who was the Druid, the *Druidess*! It was she who was the danger, she who had come to wreak havoc and devastation.

She was the combination of the Fairy Queen, the Nemeton, the Pythoness, the BanShee, the Goddess, the Woman of the Mist, the Fallen Angel, Hellcate, the Devils Assistant, the Angel of Death.

They were all representations of the same thing, they were all one and the same being, they were all the same woman, just as the Trinity was comprised of three beings, so the Angel of Death was comprised of different persons; yet all the same…and Taymi had found her.

She feared for Christian, she wanted him to stay safe, not to go near the Woods, where *she* may be, to stay here in the house, just for today, it was he who was the chosen one, chosen for…………

It was at that moment that Morgen had walked in with the note.

Taymi had explained everything to them as they trekked swiftly along. They were shocked at what they had learned. Now they were making their way thought the Woods to the place of evil itself. In a short time they had arrived at the Dark Underworld, the place of the Stone, and in Taymi's view, the place of the intended sacrifice.

Mom and Dad sat comfortably, the Cathedral was in hush. A choir was gathered directly in front of them on the steps of the altar. Candelabra had been set up especially and the light from the candle flames flickered, adding to the serene ambience.

The choir breathed the beautiful air of voice into the sacred space. Their voices rose up in the soft beginning of the hallowed Latin hymn, Ecce Panis Angelorum/ Behold the bread of Angels.

In the background the Cathedral bells began to toll out the Angelus.

Dad checked his watch; *Right on time.*

They had already started their journey into the Underworld and it was already hazy. Taymi stopped to check her watch, she signalled the others to listen. They listened quietly.

'*Please.*' Taymi uttered the tiniest whisper.

A wisp of air moved and then…*dong*, a distant bell toll wavered in the air, *dong*, again, *dong*, a third toll carried on a stronger breeze, a breeze that moved the mist aside.

They began to move again as the toll of the bells continued.

The perfect harmony of the choir raised in vocal strength had a powerful effect on Mom. She sat mesmerised with the beauty of the vocal music and words.

Dad listened attentively, the words were sung in Latin but he knew their meaning, he whispered the translation after each Latin line.

> *Ecce Panis Angelorum / Behold the Bread of Angels*
> *Factus cibus viatorum / Made the Food of Wayfarers*
> *Vere panis filiorum / Truly the Bread of Children*

He looked at the tapestry of Macartan, the one where he created the miracle of the bread.

The kids carved their way through the difficult branches, their way now clear of mist and haze.

> *In figuris praesignatur / Presignified by figure*
> *Cum Isaac immolator / When Isaac was immolated*

*Agnus Paschae deputatur / the Paschal Lamb was
commanded*

Dad looked at the stained glass image of Isacc, prepared for sacrifice by his own father.

Christian twisted his wrists within the bonds but they were tight.

*Tu nos pasce, nos tuere / Feed us, protect us,
Tu nos bona fac videre / Make us to see good things
In terra viventium / In the land of the living*

He looked high above the altar, at the decorated stone supports, the two stones that supported nothing.....*Panthera*. Dad closed his eyes and became at one with the hymn.

A deep and ominous thunder roll echoed across the lands.

'What happened to the gatekeeper?' Christian was still trying to piece things together, trying to buy time. She looked at Christian,
'He stood where you stood now.' She said, 'He betrayed me. He was close to the family; he was supposed to bring the girl.' She was reminiscing now, her eyes distant. 'He failed to go through with it. He betrayed me again by alerting the house to the fire, I could not allow him to betray me a third time.'
'But he did,' Christian reminded her, 'He warned me, he told us how to get to the Fort.'
She smirked and shook her head. 'Then he betrayed you too.'

'Were you going to bring her here?' Christian was asking about the child..
'But for a different reason.' She said cryptically.
'Was the fire set to destroy the book or the girl?' Christian continued talking.

She thought about this. 'It was designed ….to kill two birds with one strike.' She looked above Christian allowing her gaze to continue up the tree, he followed her line of sight. She looked at the buzzards nest, she looked upwards and beyond the top of the tree into the darkening sky.

The night sky lit up with a lightening flash, a thunderous crack erupted. It began to rain lightly.

Christian realised the meaning of what she had said, it was her intension for him. A *lightening strike*, it was bound to hit this, the tallest tree in the Woods. A single strike would take out the buzzards; it would travel down the tree, to where he stood tied to it.

Why had he subjected himself to this? he thought; How would his family find him, what would they think happened to him?

'A freak accident,' she spoke as though she had read his mind, 'Going alone to the Woods in a storm,' she shook her head, '……Misadventure.'

Christian glanced at the Dark One, she read his thoughts on that too, 'He was always hanging out in the Woods,' she mimicked like a nosy neighbour, '…ironic that he should have been accidentally trapped in there…Misadventure.'

She began speaking lowly now, in communication with the storm, or with someone.

'I give so that you may give in return.' He could hear her words.

He tried again to twist his wrists so that they might have loosened, he grimaced as he realised that this only caused them to tighten.

Using a long stick she drew a circle in the dirt around herself. He could hear intermittent words. Her head was bowed, through the rain she seemed to fall into a trance; a cold sweat broke out on her forehead.

'….I call on the power of your voice ……Ancestors, Spirits of the Dead, Earth Spirits…….Gold, Silver, Sacrifice….I am the ultimate sadness…..maintain your temples of worship…..'

The wind was raised, the storm gathering pace. Through the wind, Christian thought he heard a distant and familiar sound, it was ever so faint, not strong enough to have interrupted her, it was the faint ringing of a *bell*.

The Dark One stirred, uttering a low moan, it distracted her. She looked at him, he moved slightly. She continued to chant, more urgently now. The Dark One groaned and moved again clearly a distraction to her. She raised her head to the skies, raising her arms she called out in frenzy.

'I call on the Fire of the Sky....by the hour, unleash thy mighty!'

She looked at Christian, 'It is inevitable.' She said, she looked exhausted. She turned to look at the Fort, the location of the stone.

'Why don't you just take the stone, take it away from here?'

'It can't be taken.' She said,' Not by me.' she turned round to face him, 'Not by you. There is only one who has free will over the stone.'

'I should have broken it when I had it in my hand.' He said.

'The stone is unbreakable, in your hands.' She informed him.

The stone was unbreakable? Then there was no way out of this fix.

'Even if the stone was broken, it couldn't change anything. The stone is a link, there are many links. The debt must still be paid.'

Christian thought of the bell toll, he knew they would come, he *knew* they would come, his eyes flicked around. She noticed.

'There is no way out of this, a sacrifice must be made within the hour, it is your blood that he wants...the blood of your veins.......or that of your brother or your sisters.....'

Christian fixed his eyes on hers.

'.....Let it be *your* choice.' She cautioned.

If they come now, they will be in great danger. Christian thought. He *hoped* they would not come but he *knew* that they would.

'There must be another way?' Christians voice was a plead.

She turned to look at the Fort again. The only sound was the blustery wind, and the distant thunder. She was fixed in a trance, was she communicating with the stone? She turned to look at him again.

'There is only one other possible way.' She took a step closer to him examining his face staring into his eyes. 'I see myself in you.' She said quietly. 'There is only one other possible way.' She hesitated weighing it up. 'You will still suffer, but you will live.........you will *live.*'

He didn't speak, he didn't understand, he waited.

'Commit yourself to him.' She revealed, 'Commit you soul to the stone, to him........and you will live.'

Commit himself to *him*, to Satan. Commit his soul to the Devil, so as to live.

'You will *all* live.' She said.

'You must decide before the strike of seven........It is your choice.' The strike of seven, he knew that she was cross referring the time with the lightening strike that she had called. The Dark One moved again on the ground. She looked at him,

'I must purify the site.' She said urgently and with the strength of an ox she dragged the Dark One away through the trees and out of sight.

A thunder crack jolted him with fear. He knew that a bolt of lightening was destined to strike the tree travelling all the way to the ground electrifying everything along the way. He knew that the strike would definitely come at 7 O'Clock if not before.

What time was it now? He managed to twist his wrist enough to see that it was about 6:20.

He was alone, he looked at the Fort, the stone was there, it was the power to which she obeyed. It could not be broken she said, not by his hands, what did she mean? She said that if it was broken it wouldn't make a difference, then who is it that can break it.

She said she couldn't take it? But he had been in the Fort, he had held the stone in his hands.

She said that if he committed himself...his *soul*...to the Devil, that he would live. He would suffer but he would live, how? How could he survive a lightening strike and live? Was she promising him eternal life? Is that what she meant?

How could he commit himself to the Devil, he was the opposite of that. But he wanted to protect his siblings, he wanted to protect himself. Why was it his blood that they wanted? The blood of him or his brother and sisters. Was it his family blood that they wanted? Why? Because they lived here at the place of the stone. Because of their Christianity? Because of their decendency from the name of Macartan? Christianus? Was it because they had broken the code? Found the location? Because they were a threat to the stone? Was he the chosen one? Was it destiny? The questions swirled in his mind, not enough time to figure it out, not enough time to decide.

What if he did commit to the Devil?

Would he become like her? Indebted? Seeking a sacrifice? Subservient to evil? No free will?

But he would be free to live!

He wanted to live, not to die, he wanted to live and he would do whatever necessary to live.

If this was what he had to do to live, for his family to be safe, he had to consider it, if it was the only possible way.

'*Christian*!' It was Taymi's voice shouting, she had broken through the growth leading to the Fort. They others were emerging directly behind her. Christian looked across at them, he *knew* it, he knew they would come but he didn't want them there, too much was at stake.... their *lives*. They were shocked to see him tied to the tree.

'Don't come near me.' He shouted the instruction before they got too close. 'It's too dangerous.'

'Where is she?' Taymi demanded looking around quickly.

'She will be back...soon.' Christian realised from her question that Taymi may already have figured out who was responsible for this. 'It was...'

'Anouk...I know.' Taymi told him.

'I can release you!' Taymi took a step forward.

'Go back!' Christian shouted, 'I don't want you hurt, any of you, if lightening strikes..... you could all be hit, stay back!'

'But you will be hit......you will be hurt.... you will be killed!' she shouted at him. He shook his head, he didn't know what to tell her.

'If I can get you untied, you will be free.' She called out to him.

He couldn't tell her, if he was free then it may be one of them who would have to pay the price, it was a no-win situation. He was tempted to take the deal, to commit himself to Satan, then he knew that he and they could live.

But was it a trick? Could he trust Anouk? She had already mislead them, mislead *him*, in a confidence trick. Was it a risk he was willing to take? How could he live if one of them were to die?

'I'm going to untie you!' Taymi had made up her mind.

'No!' he shouted, but she was already racing over to him and began immediately grappling with the tight bonds at his wrists. She grit her teeth as she tried hard to loosen them but it was futile, they were wound tight, she looked at the bonds in horror, they had merged into Christians skin, he was fastened to the tree and the only way free would be to cut away the flesh of his wrists. He winced in pain as the bonds became even tighter.

'Go back.' He urged her. She looked in his eyes. 'You must go back.' He said. She ran back the short distance to the others.

'I can't release him.' She said, 'he is stuck fast.'

'Then the stone.' Said Sophia, 'we have to get it, we have to destroy it.'

Christian could hear their words. '*No!*' he shouted. They could only look at him.

The stone may be his only way out of this situation. How could he commit himself to the stone if the stone was destroyed. She had said that even if the stone was broken the debt still had to be paid, someone would have to die. But by keeping the stone intact there was a way out of this, by his commiting to it.

'We have to destroy it.' Shouted Taymi.

'You can't, it is unbreakable.' He shouted.

'We have to try.' She shouted back.

'I need it..' his voice wasn't heard, they had already turned and ran into the Fort and to the place where the stone was hidden.

Together they wrenched the heavy stone lid back, propping it against a hefty root, and Taymi lifted out the wrapped bundle within. She unwrapped the artefact and held it. Christian winced, he almost felt as if the bonds on his wrists tightened.

Taymi felt there was palpable evil emanating from the stone, it scared her. She felt disoriented, she raised the stone so as to strike it against the cover stone but she didn't have the strength to do it. The stone weighted heavy in her hands, she put it down.

'I can't…I haven't got the power to do it.'

Morgen leapt into the fray, he grabbed the stone and tried to do likewise, but he was held in a frozen state, he couldn't strike it, or even move.

'Take it!' he managed to instruct Sophia. She took the stone and immediately dropped it due to what she experienced as an intense heat coming from the stone itself.

Mollie tried to touch the stone but she felt an intense and brittle cold which prevented her hand from touching it. The startling array of sensations frightened them.

'We have to take it to Christian.' Taymi attempted again. She lifted the stone and quickly made her way towards Christian. When she reached the edge of the Fort, the embankment, she couldn't proceed. It was as though there was an invisible wall, a shield through which she could not pass. She looked at Christian.

'I can't take it out of here.' She was apologetic. He knew that the stone had power over them.

Morgen tried to take the stone from the Fort, he met the same problem, at the edge of the Fort there was an impenetrable barrier that he could not see.

There was no way out, the stone and Christian's bonds were unbreakable, the stone could not be taken out of the Fort. They looked at Christian and he looked at them.

They struggled for words, there were none.

Christian wrestled to look at his watch, it read 6:53. He had seven minutes before time ran out.

He tried to figure it out, she had said something, the stone was unbreakable in his hands, therefore not necessarily in everyones hands, she had said something about one who had free will over the stone when he had talked about taking it out of the Fort.

'Give it to Lila.' He shouted to them.

She had said something about bringing the girl, *Oriel*, to the Fort for a different reason. Was it to take the stone out of the Fort? It was the words in the ledger, *only the innocent can retrieve*. It had to be of her own free will....Lila had come here of her own free will, accompanying the others.

It was Anouks voice that spoke next. 'I think you have figured something out here.'

She had appeared from among the trees and stood between Christian and the others in the Fort.

Lila held the stone that Mols had given to her.

'She is still an infant,' Christian pieced together the pieces, 'but she has acquired knowledge of right and wrong and free will.'

Anouk nodded.

'Because she is still innocent she is not capable of using the stone for evil purposes and therefore she can take it from the Fort..... of her own free will.'

Anouk looked at Christian, 'It is your time now, if you are not to die, then you must commit to the stone.' The others didn't understand what was being discussed, there was nothing they could do. Christian closed his eyes, he swallowed hard.

'What have I to do?' he asked her.

'Tell her to deliver the stone to me.' Were the instructions.

Christian fixed his eyes on Lila. 'Lila,' he called, 'you must do exactly what I say, but you must do it of your own choice too, but no matter what, I want you to know that I mean what I say.'

Lila nodded shakily.

'No matter what, Lila,' he urged.

'It's time.' Anouk said and he knew that the time was now, there were no more minutes left.

'Bring me the stone.' She instructed towards Lila.

'Lila,' Christian instructed, 'Break it! Break the stone!'

Christian had figured it out, if Lila had the power of free will to carry the stone out of the Fort, then she had the power of free will to destroy it. It was she that was the child, the pure hand, it was why the Druid had sought out Oriel in prior times but had failed.

Anouk swung around at him, eyes blazing. She turned to Lila.

'If you break it, he will die!'

Lila looked at Christian, he didn't deny it, his eyes told her that with the stone broken there would be no way out.'

'Break it Lila, you must do it now.'

'Give it to me and he will live.'

Lila beleved them both, it was a grave choice. Lila was unable to decide.

The wind had raised and it swept all around Lila aggressively. She remembered Moms words, *When you are scared and unsafe your prayers are like Angels to keep you safe and out of harm.*

Trembling she whispered the words of a prayer.

'Glory be to the Father and to the Son and to the Holy Spirit.' Her words called upon the Holy Trinity.

Anouk screamed, 'Bring the stone now or I will come and get it.' She was making her way towards the Fort.

'As it was in the beginning, it is now and ever shall be.…..' Through the intensity of her prayer Lila could see… *figures*, figures standing at the perimeter of the Fort. In shimmering white they emerged, people, with hands linked, creating a fence around the Fort, young and old persons and they had, they had……*wings*.

Lila knew that Anouk could *never* enter this Fort; it was protected from her, by a ring of Angels, an enclosure that kept evil *out*.

'….a world without end.….. Amen.' Lila finished the words of the prayer.

She raised the Golden Stone and in one swift motion she smashed it on the lid stone.

A frenzied wind whipped around her, and a roar of thunder circled. The stone exploded into thousands of particles of dry dust and gold and silver filings. The tiny fragments circled in the wind and were swept into the image of the Demon, Lucifer, the Devil, *Satan*. For one single instant his golden image existed there amid the thunder and wind and then in the next instant the image was whipped away, the dust blown about and scattered over the entire area of the Fort.

Anouk screamed the scream of a thousand knives, at the same instant, Christian felt the bonds *release* from his skin and he *ran* in the direction of the Fort, he ran for his life, he ran past Anouk.

An almighty explosion ripped through the tree. A lance of fire blitzed from the sky through the trunk, electrifying every branch and spitting out smaller electrical discharges to any nearby conductors, one of which was the person standing closest to the tree….. *Anouk*.

Christian was thrown to the ground. He scrambled up and ran into the Fort where he grabbed Lila in a hug. The others stared at the scene of destruction, parts of the tree were burning, Anouk's body lay on the ground. The Golden Stone was destroyed.

They gathered around Christian, they grabbed him and hugged him.

'You're Ok.' Mols told him.

Christian looked around to where Anouk was struck down, she no longer lay there, she had disappeared, he just caught sight of her lurching away between the trees.

'It not over.' He warned them. He knew that the debt must still be paid, but he didn't know how it was now going to happen. Destroying the stone was a delaying tactic, he knew that he would surely now be dead if he hadn't done it. He had toyed with the idea of handing it over to Anouk, of committing himself to the stone, to Satan, but there was no way in his heart that he could.

But it wasn't over, Anouk had told him that either way, someone had to die, he had to try and figure out a way to avoid that, he had to figure out a way to live.

'We've got to get out of here quickly.' He urged them to move quickly and they followed him out of the Fort, away from the still burning tree and back through the deep growth and branches.

Mols took a last look at the tree, her heart lifted to see the Buzzards high above circling and safe, their nest was destroyed but she knew that they would build a new one.

XLV

BELLUA

(Beast)

As THEY MADE their way back from the Fort, having exited the Dark Underworld, Mols noticed something;

'Shhhh!' she said and the others slowly came to a stop and turned to look at her. They stood there silently, Mols face a picture of concentration, listening.

'I can't hear anything.' Said Taymi.

'Exactly.' Said Mols, 'where have all the animals gone, why have they stopped chattering.'

'It's the storm.' Said Taymi looking above her head and noticing now that the worst of the storm had blown over.

But Mols knew differently. She had mastered her intuition, summoned her sixth sense, her antenna were raised and she knew, she just knew....

'*Somethings coming.*' she whispered, straining to hear, attuning her attention to the sounds of nature. A twig broke, they heard a small rustle, each one of them turned to look in the direction from whence it came, a bush moved ever so slightly. What emerged made their blood run cold, they couldn't move from where they stood, they faced a horror that they could never have imagined.

No, it can't be. The thought raced through Mols mind, her body beginning to tremble with fear.

But it was, she and all of them were standing face to face with a black beast, a killing machine with the strength of ten men, something that should not exist in the northern hemisphere, the fully grown symbol of death, a Black Panther.

Everyone stood rigid, not knowing what to do. The Panther had emerged fully from the bush and was standing menacingly looking at them. Keeping her head turned towards the beast Mols used her eyes only to look around for a place of escape or a cave or a shelter or something. There was nothing.

'Hold my hand Lila.' Taymi whispered to her sister and together they started to slowly back away, the Panther took a step forward.

'Don't run.' Warned Mols, 'It will attack you.' Taymi and Lila stopped dead.

Sohia could not move, think, or take any action whatever, her legs together with her brain had turned to jelly. Morgen was still holding his stick in his hand, the lance. The animal was so strong, so muscular and lithe, Morgen felt the weapon was pathetic in comparison.

Christian stood just to the right of Morgen. *Is this what it is to face death?* He thought, trying to make sense of their situation. He could not see any way out of this, the Panther was taking stock of the situation, analysing each persons position, preparing and capable of lunging at any one of them.

I can't let it happen, it's my fault, I led them here, I put them at risk, I must face it, not them. The thoughts streamed through Christian's mind in rapids, each second standing there felt like a lifetime. *It will give us all a better chance to escape.*

'Give me the lance Morgen.' Christian spoke as calmly as he could, 'I will hold the animal here and I want you guys to go.'

'Christian....' Taymi didn't know how to answer.

The beast took another step towards them and its snarl grew into a deep guttural growl. It was only about six metres away from where they stood.

'Go and get help!.' Christians instructions were firm. 'I will face it alone.'

Morgen held the lance horizontally, like Granda had done when he presented it to him, he reached it over towards his brother, Christian gripped it as he took a step towards the beast, Morgen held tightly to the stick, *stopping* Christian from moving forward.

'Not today brother!' Morgen said, Christian looked at him, Morgens worried face also showed his determination, he knew this was the moment he had been anticipating for his whole life. Morgen, using his knowledge of the beast took command of the situation.

'Everyone get behind me.' Morgen held the lance in its centre and kept it horizontal, the only barrier between them and the beast. The others edged closer together around and behind Morgen.

'We must make ourselves look bigger, like one beast, we can scare the Panther.' He instructed. They were all now gathered around him, feeling a little better for the security of it.

'Move your arms, make noise.' Morgen instructed. The formation of one single entity instead of individuals did seem to confuse the beast.

'Yaaah!' Morgen shouted. 'Yaaah!, Yaaah!' The others joined him.

The beast raised its head and *ROARED* back reminding them of what a perilous position they were in.

Morgen just remembered something, something he had done in preparation for just such an event. He held the stick vertically and then lowered its point in the direction of the beast.

'Hold this.' he said to Christian who did so.

Morgen released the buttons on the front of his shirt and revealed a familiar marking on his chest crudely drawn in the same paint he'd put on his eyes. He'd just managed to have time to do it before they hurriedly left the house. It was an amulet, a protection, a christogram, it was the familiar symbol of the Chi Rho.

Morgen retook the lance and resumed his position, this was his destiny, a soldier, a knight, a jungle warrior, facing down a deadly beast, he roared back at the beast shaking the lance in one hand and his tee-shirt in the other.

'YAAAAAAH!

The beast took a step back, Morgen took a step forward, the others moved with him. The confrontation, the amulet was working.

'Don't corner it,' warned Mols, 'That could make it attack.'

'YAAAAH!' shouted Morgen. The beast took another step back, its tail swishing agressively, touched the bush behind.

'Be careful!' Mols warned but her caution was falling on deaf ears. The beast pawed the ground and flicked the bushes with its tail; it shuffled its hind legs, and lowered itself closer to the ground.

'It's going to attack!' Mols tried to shout but no one heard her ......except Christian.

Christian saw the look in its eyes change, he saw that the shuffling was priming for ground grip, he saw the lowering as a precursor to springing action, he knew it was going to attack before Mols even said it He knew that even with their attempt and Morgen's amulet that this beast was never going to leave without blood, he knew that the beast was not just a rambling lost beast, but the Druid incarnate. The Druid had assumed the hide of the animal, the mantle of the Beast and all its characteristics, instincts and powers, she had become the Beast in all its forms through the migration of the soul from human to animal.....metempsychosis. He understood all of this now because they had read about it, researched it and studied it in preparation for that which he didn't know then was to happen. But now he knew and he knew from the moment he saw it that *Someone is going to die.* And he thought with absolute clarity;

That someone....... is me.

He knew why someone had to die, he knew that all the signs he had seen had been leading to this moment. He knew why it must be him, he had pursued the legend most aggressively, he had led his brother and sisters here, he was the eldest male, he must protect the others so that they may live, he had already saved Dad now he must save them.

Christian felt that it was his greed for wealth that had led them to this difficulty place. It was he that the spirit had appeared in warning to. Now he felt he realised why it had come, it was revealing to him his impending *death*. Two attempts had been made on his life; this was the third, the Trinity.

This is why he lived, he could have died at birth but he didn't, he was honoured in the highest way by the Christian church at his baptism, he was reminded constantly through his asthma that his very breath, the breath of his life, was a gift.

His name alone carried the history of two thousand years of prayer, persecution, betrayal and sacrifice.

He had been chosen, the mark on the tree, it was his vau, a 'C' in reverse, the Anti-*Christian*.

He thought of the Christian martyrs, the shedding of blood for their belief, the slaves fed to the beasts of Rome, they had kept Christianity alive by their selflessness. He thought of his own blood trickling in the water, flowing away, disappearing, he felt bound up in the course of history.

He thought of Isaac, the boy who had looked about the same age as himself, was there any hope that God would send Archangel Michael in a last minute bid to stop *this* bloodletting? Would Michael arrive with his flaming lance and spike the beast? He thought of Daniel too, the Angel had protected him from six beasts. Now there was one beast and six kids. Where was the Angel?

It is in the hand of God, there is always hope. He thought.

He would not let the beast touch the others, he would protect them with his life, it would be his sacrifice, the ultimate sacrifice, it was his choice and he was prepared to make it.

This is why I lived; This is why I must die, My time has come. Fortis Et Fidelis.

When the beast lunged............so did Christian.

Christian threw himself in front of the beast as it sprung on them. He threw himself in front of the girls and Morgen as their protector. He threw himself into the line of fire, the lions den, the oblivion, the apocalypse. He put himself in the way of the Devil, the Demons, those who would do evil and stand in the way of truth. He aligned himself with the aims of Macartan, Patrick and Bridget.

He threw open his arms to shield his siblings in the manner of Vetruvian Man and Christ on the cross.

His eyes looked up to the open heavens beyond the tops of the trees above.

He threw himself at the mercy of God.

The beast hit him like a ton of bricks, landing on him with all its weight in a sickening thud, pinning his outstretched arms to the ground with its powerful paws. The impact had scattered everyone to the ground, Morgen had been knocked violently onto his back, Taymi had tried to protect Lila by shielding her the moment the beast attacked and she hurriedly scrambled them both now back from where the beast landed. Sophia and Mols both screamed and turned to try and run when the beast pounced but its speed and agility was so quick that they too were thrown to the ground and were trying frantically to get on their feet.

Taymi was first to realise that the beast was on Christian. She screamed at the top of her lungs and continued screaming. Realising what was happening Sophia screamed too. 'No, No, No.'

Lila looked at this scene of unmentionable horror but she was unable to comprehend or process the severity of what was happening, she was staring at it but she was shutting it out. Mols had begun to run, but now she stopped and turned around, to witness a scene worse than any nightmare.

Morgen, closest to the beast, picked himself up from the ground dazed, his blurred vision revealing to him what the others were screaming at. The beast had pinned Christian down with its powerful limbs. It was three times his size and many more times powerful. It had its head buried into his neck. He could see its teeth at Christian's throat. Its mouth was wide open and wrapped around his slim neck. Its head jerked aggressively as it uttered a series of frenzied growls.

Blood was coursing from Christian's throat, *too much blood*, it spewed copiously, too much blood to loose for anyone to survive. Christian's eyes were closed, his mouth open, gasping for breath, his face turning blue from suffocation.

Taymi kept screaming, now the scream of a mourning wail, she realised that even if he survived the injury and the asphyxiation, the blood loss was insurmountable.

Morgen managed to stand up, his whole body was trembling, jerking, even his head, he tried to do something, *anything*, but his body wouldn't work, he was still holding the lance, he took it in both his hands in a vain attempt to do something but he realised that it had been broken in the attack, it was useless.

The beast raised its head and roared the death roar, there was blood all over its teeth and mouth and streaming down its neck. It started to back away, its brutal job done, a horrific killing.

Morgen was standing less than two metres from the beast, it turned and looked at him, they looked at each other, the beasts eyes were not the eyes of the hunter he had seen a minute ago, they were the eyes of a killer who was content in the knowledge that it had brought certain death.

The beast backed slowly away, Morgen knew that it wasn't going to attack him, he knew that if it did attack him he would have be unable to do anything, to even move, such was his shock at what had occurred.

The beast backed away considerably now, it turned and walked back into the bushes and out of sight.

Morgen continued to look after it. The girls except for Lila rushed to Christian's body, they were screaming and wailing, he lay there limp and destroyed with blood. There was no pulse, there was no breath.

Lila stayed where she was; she was on her knees looking at the girls urging life back into Christian's lifeless body.

Why didn't the angels come? Lila thought. She had *seen* the angels, she knew they were there; they were close by, at the Fort. *Why didn't they come?*

She still believed in them, she believed they could make things better; she joined her hands together and began to pray for a miracle.

Morgen turned to look at his brother, it was a desperate scene, the girls were screaming and crying over his body, their voices seemed far away, blurred. Taymi leaned down and lifted Christian's head to her shoulder and embraced him. There was blood everywhere, the blood of August. Taymi screamed words which Morgen couldn't understand.'He's dead, he's dead!'

The words seemed like they were coming from somewhere else, they felt like they were coming from the past or the future. It sounded like he was hearing them through water or in a dream; he was *not* going to accept those words.

Morgen looked back in the direction the beast had gone, he tried to process his thoughts, his head and body were still jerking uncontrollably with shock. He had *seen* something. He looked back at his brother, *lifeless*.

'He's ......' Morgen was unable to complete the words.

'He's ......' He couldn't find the words.

'He's ....dead.'

It wasn't right, the words were wrong; this wasn't what he wanted to say.

'He's ....*not* dead.' Morgen whispered.

'He's *not* dead.' He said again. 'He's *not* dead.'

'He is *alive!*'

'HE IS *ALIVE!*' Morgen shouted with all his might and anger. He ran to Christian, he pulled Taymi out of the way and laid Christian's head down on the ground.

'HE IS ALIVE!' He screamed, and making a fist he thumped down onto Christian's chest.

'STOP, STOP' Sophia and Mols screamed.

Morgen continued hitting Christian on the chest aggressively. The girls tried to pull Morgen away.

Lila seeing all of this closed her eyes tightly and prayed more intensely.

They tried to pull Morgen back but he fought them off, he grabbed Christian's throat and wiped at the massive blood loss there. He wiped away as much blood with his hands as he could.

'HE IS ALIVE!'

There was no wound.

There were flesh wounds and ripped skin but it was all superficial, mere scratches, not more than you would receive from the brambles, there was no gaping wound, no bite, no exposed arteries, there was no wound.

Morgen thumped Christian's chest and the girls allowed him to.

The Stigmata! Mols thought of how Pio's stigmata had healed up immediately after his death.

'Breathe damn you, BREATHE!' Morgen shouted at his brother. He moved up to Christian's head and leaned over to give him mouth to mouth resuscitation. Morgen breathed for Christian, he breathed the air of life into Christian's lifeless body. He listened to Christian's mouth.

Nothing.

He breathed and breathed. He listened.

It was a tiny, *tiny* wheeze.

Morgen breathed into him ......Christians chest heaved, his body spasmed and Christian gasped for intake of air, he gasped for his life, his eyes opened and he gasped wildly for oxygen, gripping Morgen's arm on one side and Sophia's on the other.

'CHRISTIAN, CHRISTIAN!' Taymi and Mols screamed.

Lila looked up, her eyes wide, witnessing Christians return to life, she continued to pray, her mouth making the movements of her silent words, she could see the little group around Christian, she could see about *ten or twelve* gathered around him. Her prayers turned to those of faith and thankgiving.

Morgen raised Christian's head up slightly, he was getting his breath back, they gripped him like they would never let him go. They couldn't understand and they didn't want to, they knew that they might never fully understand what had just happened.

It took some time for Christian to recover enough to be able to sit up. They all huddled close together in comfort with one another. Few words were spoken. They gripped each other, all six, silently weeping or just staring.

'How did you know?' Taymi eventually asked Morgen.

'I saw the beast,' Morgen said, '....when it came away from Christian, I saw something. There was something in its mouth. I didn't know what it was, then I realised, it was the top of the lance. The lance spiked the beast through its throat and mouth. It broke off and I was left holding the bottom bit.'

They couldn't believe what they were hearing.

'The beast was unable to close its jaws because the lance was rammed in its mouth holding it open. It couldn't bite into Christian.' He told them.

'But where did all the blood come from, there was so much blood.'

'The lance spiked through the beasts gullet, it must have slashed through its jugular vein, all of the blood was from the beast.' Morgen explained to the others as well as to himself.

'How could it survive that?' Morgen said, 'When it jumped it knocked the lance out of my hand, it fell on the lance, the bottom of the stick drove into the ground and the upper part of it went through its mouth.'

Christian spoke quietly. 'When I was falling, I saw the lance slice into the beast..... I saw a hand holding it steady.' He looked at Morgen, they had differing accounts, Morgen said that he had dropped the lance.

Morgen thought of the statue of St.Michael lancing the demon through the mouth, atop Mont-San-Michel. Was it the hand of

Michael that held the lance as it spiked the beast? Was it the hand of God?

'Saint Michael.' Whispered Morgen.

'Remember the story of the Rowan stick,' said Christian, 'if the Devil comes demanding a soul, touch a witch with a branch from a Rowan tree, the witch would be taken instead.'

They struggled to comprehend what had happened and why.

'The beast is *dead*.' Christian said eventually and the others looked at him.

'Wherever it went to and it can't have been far, it would have bled to death. We are safe now,' He concluded, 'from the beast..... from the Druid.'

After a silence Christian spoke again. 'Part of me thinks that it threw itself on the lance on purpose.'

'Why?' asked Taymi.

'I can't explain, I could see in its eyes, perhaps she saw it as the only way out, the only escape from a life of pain, a life of slavery.' They considered Christian's comment quietly.

'Are you Ok now?' Taymi asked Christian.

'I'm as good as I'm going to be.' He replied trying to stand up amid crippling pain and agony.

'I feel alive.' He said as he arose fully and walked.

'...and I'm Hah, Hah, Aow,...Staying alive!' he struggled with a self depreciating attempt at a joke which was clearly a chip of the old block.

They walked together, slowly, to facilitate Christian, in the direction the beast had gone. There was a heavy trail of blood for quite a distance, then at about fifteen metres away, lurching in the river, they saw its remains. It was not what they expected.

The beast was clearly dead, however it did not have the mass of a carcass, a body. It appeared only as the skin, the hide of the beast, a *cloak*. They could see that its head was intact, eyes glazed over and turning yellow, its teeth still separated by the lance, blood still oozing from the gash in its throat where the lance had entered. The beast held no fear for them now. They were not inclined to go near it.

'Leave it there.' Christian said, 'It will disappear.' He knew that it would, just as the carcass of the deer had disappeared years ago, melting into the forest floor, pickings for the wild animals.

He felt that the remnants of the beast would degenerate more quickly than usual, perhaps it would be washed away down river, he felt there would be nothing left to see by tomorrow.

The rain was falling softly again, washing away the blood on the ground, the blood on the leaves, it created little trickles joining together blood and water which flowed into the river.

The children didn't look back. It was done.

They made their way slowly back through the Woods. Christian led them to where he felt certain the Dark One had been taken. They found him there, tied and bound in one of the narrower Castle dungeons, the entrance closed up with rockfill, *buried alive.* They helped create an opening, untied him.

It was Druidic symbology, the Dark One pointed out, the methods of destruction used by the Druid, the Flood =Water, asphyxiation caused by the Snake =Air, lightening= Fire, burial= Earth….. the four elements.

They walked together home.

XLVI

OTIUM

(Peace)

THE CHILDREN BROKE the entire story to Mom and Dad, it took hours and days to convey the complete history of the quest and there was much hand wringing and investigation by their parents. They took Christian for a full check up at the hospital citing a 'fall'. He was Ok'd and they were thankful that he had no broken bones. Ultimately they all decided that these events must rest with the walls of Westwoods and go no further than that. It was days later before they were able to properly relax and discuss the events objectively and with a little humour.

'I still can't believe that you guys thought that I was the Evil Darkness, or whatever it was you called it.' Said Dad.

He's never going to let us forget that. Sophia thought, *...ever!*

'Do you not know already that I am the immaculate one, the *sinless* one.' Dad said. They knew this already as Dad had insisted on telling them countless times in the past. Dad had been born on the 8th of December, an important date in the Catholic Christian calendar. It was the date that Taymi had previously noticed had been the validation of the will of Francis Lucas. It was the nominated day to celebrate the *Immaculate Conception*, a day which marked the conception of Mary, the mother of Christ, who from the moment of her existence was filled with divine grace and was therefore without original sin. During her lifetime too she accumulated no sins. Every year the day is celebrated in church and also signals the real start of the Christmas season. Dad liked to claim by association that he too could claim to be immaculate and sinless though there was plenty of evidence to the contrary.

'*And* you failed to take into account the meaning of my name.' He insisted.

'We know what it is,' said Taymi, 'Leon, A.K.A. the Lion, the Jungle Beast, the King.'

'That is correct,' said Dad having also often reminded them of his royal inheritance and position within the household.

'But there is another meaning to my name.' Dad grabbed a piece of paper and in capital letters wrote his name on it. LEON

'Here, look at it as a mirror image.' He told Taymi. She swung the page to 180 degrees.

'Not that way Dodo…. in the mirror!' Dad corrected her, 'Women and directions..' he tutted.

Taymi held the page up in front of the Mirror. Accounting for the back to front letters, she read what it said. 'It says NOEL.'

'Correct,' he said, 'and the meaning of Noel is….?'

'Christmas!' said Sophia.

'Yes, it means Christmas, Christ's –Mass, it also means Peace.' Dad said. 'It's my name in reverse, my alterego, my *antimatter* me.' Dad looked at Morgen. 'The Latin origin is *natalis*, which means Birth or Re-Birth.' He continued to tell them more about how great and special he really was and they did their best to ignore him.

The Westwooders were glad that things were returning to normal.

XLVII

NATALIS

(Rebirth)

TAYMI HAD WANTED it to appear that everything was back to normal, but something was troubling her. She had been poring over the detail of the old register. It was her intention to unhook all of the mysteries contained within its pages, but there was one entry that caught her attention....not for the first time.

It was a date entry 17.7. together with the entry of a single name.

Originally when she had looked at this book, these numbers had meant nothing to her, now it was different. It was the date that the great flood had occurred, it was the date that Dad had almost drowned, it was a combination of sevens. She also noticed that all of the other logged dates always had the year attached, except for this one.

There was a single name entry opposite it, which was again slightly unusual in that most often, more than one person would be arriving at the gates and normally listed with the prefix Mr. or Mrs. together with the surname. She had looked at this name before and assumed it to have been a friend of the little girl Oriel.

Taymi was looking at this name again now and upon closer inspection realised that it was *not* spelt as she had first assumed.

The name Taymi was looking at was *Anastasi*.

Taymi closed the register, was she becoming paranoid? Examining every detail, every word, most of it meant little of interest, was this pure coincidence? She looked out of the window, Christian and Morgen were sitting on the fence having an animated conversation about something which involved moving your arms about rapidly and laughing uproariously.

She thought how lucky they were that Christian was alive; now and when he was born. How lucky that Dad was alive, how lucky they all were to be alive and well and safe.

'There is no such thing as luck?'

She momentarily thought of Anouk.

It struck her.

'Anouk, from the name Ann or Anna or *Ana*, there are more than two hundred versions of the name.....Ana-stasi?'

Taymi opened the register and looked at the name again. She turned on the computer, she could barely wait for it to warm up.

'Don't let me down.' She warned.

Google....she typed the word Anastasi...return.

'Building developers....footballers......Cathedral............ *Cathedral!*' She clicked on the entry that mentioned Cathedral.

'Arian Cathedral in Italy called Hagia Anastasi. The Arians were a Christian cult who questioning the whole meaning of the Trinity, so they were condemned.'

There was another entry which caught her attention.

Anastasi —A name for the Saturday before Easter, Prote Anastasi, Holy Saturday.

It was the day that Christian had been baptised, in the Cathedral, in a nighttime vigil, Holy Saturday. Taymi stared at the screen, but not at this entry, it was another entry, directly below which now held her attention.

Anastasi, a Greek word meaning ....

She looked at the next word long and hard before saying it.
'......*Resurrection.*'

She looked out the window at Christian, she thought of his survival from the beast... *Resurrection.*

She thought of Dad emerging from the water on 17.7.... *Resurrection.*

She thought of Anouk......*it wasn't possible?*

There was yet another entry for the same word, another entry that drew her attention swiftly.

Anastasi- Church of the Holy Sepulchre-Jerusalem

She recognised this name, it was the place that Sophia had discovered to be one of the most sacred Christian sites in the World, the place where the Wood of the True cross was discovered, *the Centre of the Universe.* She read,

'The Church of the Resurrection .... in Greek -*Naos tis Anastaseos*......it is located in the old city of Jerusalem.....it is the considered the place of Golgotha and Sepulchre .....the place where Christ died and was buried and the place..... of his Resurrection.'

No wonder the Wood of the Cross was found there, she thought, *it's where the crucifixion took place! ...whats more, it's where the resurrection took place!*

She was drawn to another entry associated with the word Anastasi. It was a name, it was the name that Taymi had first thought of when she had seen the word in the register. She looked at it again now.

'*Anastasia............*It's just a name. Isn't it?' She clicked on it.

'Grand Duchess Anastasia, the youngest daughter of Tsar Nicholas II, the last sovereign of imperial Russia.' Taymi looked at the last word.

'Russia.' She thought of Anouks words, *I have a drop of Russian blood.*

'Royal Blood?' Taymi questioned whether she was becoming too far fetched in her thinking.

She read further.

'All seven members of the family including the child Anastasia were massacred at the hands of the Bolshevik secret police, on the 17th of July 1918.'

Taymi's heart stopped, her hand went to her mouth. It was the date, *the date in the journal*, the 17th of July........*17.7.*

She looked back at the entry in the journal, no, she hadn't made a mistake. Shaking, she returned to the article, taking a closer look at the girl in the picture. She was a blond haired pretty looking girl almost like Sophia. There were seven in the family, all murdered. She returned to reading, still shaking.

'The bodies of the family were recovered except for that of Anastasia and her brother.......the name Anastasia also translates to 'breaker of chains' or 'the prison opener'.....all of the family members were considered martyrs ......she was 17.......many have since claimed to be Anastasia, the most famous of these was Anna Anderson a German who first made the claim in the 1920's.'

'Anna Anderson?' The link to the name Anna Anderson was highlighted in blue.

Taymi hovered for a moment before pressing it. The link opened.

'Anna Anderson ...an imposter who claimed to be the missing Grand Duchess Anastasia ....Anderson had been institutionalized following an attempt to commit suicide....she continued to insist on her association with the Royal.' Taymi scrolled down, there was a picture, a side profile. Taymi's face paled, the face in the picture had dark hair but she bore a striking resemblance to a face that Taymi already knew. It was a face that struck horror into her heart, horror into her very soul.

The face in the picture was unmistakably that of the person she had come to know as........

'.....Anouk.'

XLVIII

Tutela

(Guardian)

CHRISTIAN SAT SILENTLY for what seemed like a long, long time after Taymi had shown him what she had discovered. She sat silently looking at him until he eventually spoke.

'It was suicide. She threw herself on the spike.' He was referring to the beast's impalement in the Woods. 'But she knew that she would live again,' He said stonily, 'in another body, in another place. She will resurrect.' He said looking up now at Taymi.

Taymi felt a fear coursing through her. 'How can she do that?'

'She has Druidic abilities,' he explained, 'She can take the form of another person, or a beast, or even a bird.' He said recalling the information they had previously researched. 'She can do this after Death or at any other time. That is why her body was not there after she died here. She had moved on.' There was a silence before Christian spoke again.

'She lives in a world of Death. She brings about Death.' He said darkly, 'Murder..., Sacrifice,... Massacare,.... Suicide,.... Slaughter.... Martyrdom....If the death is not someone else, then it is her own. If she cannot bring about the required instructions from her master, then she will sacrifice herself.'

Taymi was speechless but she felt that Christian was right in what he was saying.

'But she can never die.' He said now, 'she will always live again. Brought back to life by him, to do his will again. She is Death itself, but she is a slave to Death.......yet she will live forever.' Christian displayed total clarity, total insight, into the workings of the dark side. He realised now that this was the eternal life offered to him, a life of recurring death and rebirth as someone else, a life of pain.

'What if she returns here?' Taymi whispered, 'There are over two hundred names under which she could reappear, that is if she sticks only to the name Ana.'

'She won't return,' Christian assured her, 'there is nothing here for her now, she will never return.' He said the words convincingly enough for Taymi to believe what he said, though he could not decide if he should believe himself. He had no guarantee that she would never return.

Perhaps she will come back, he thought to himself, *in seven years.... maybe later......maybe sooner.*

Christian knew that he must remain alert; he had known that from the moment that the Beast had been defeated. He feared that whoever was responsible for the death of the beast could be cursed seven times; the curse of Cain, he feared that person was him.

He must always remain alert, *always*, as a defender of his family, of himself, a defender of the faith; it was the reason he was born, it may determine the length of the candle that burns for him, this he knew, at last, was the meaning and the purpose of his life.

XLIX

ETERNUS

(Without End)

GRANDA HAD CALLED into Westwoods to say hi on his way to the hardware store. After he chatted to everyone in his usual jovial manner he was left with Dad, both of them sitting at the table. Granda fiddled with a piece of folded paper which was on the table. It was the paper with Dads name on it.

He looked at it.

Dad looked at it too.

Dad thought about the moment when Taymi had mistakenly turned the page around, Dad had seen it, he felt she did too, perhaps at a subconscious level, but she *had* seen it.

In the upside down position, the name looked something like NO37.

By discounting the E, it looked like NO 7,..., Number Seven.

It also read NOE.7

Noe, an anagram of *One*.

He knew the meaning of Noe. It was a name. It had several meanings.

Noe, meaning Peaceful, meaning *Noah*.....

Noah, from the Bible, known as the 'Keeper' or the 'Master of the House'.......
Noah, he predicted the flood / the Day of Judgement.....
Noah, some thought he was the Archangel Michael ....
Noah, he had cursed his own son....

There were Seven Laws of Noah, the laws for all mankind. Those who lived by the laws were known as Children of Noah.

Most of these seven laws had been broken by the Angel of Death.

The first and foremost of these was; *You shall not have any idols before God.*

But it was the seventh law, Noe.7, which was the one he felt had sealed the fate of the Angel of Death;

You shall not eat the flesh of anything still living; animal ...or human!

Dad knew all this already,

'Guilty by Association?' he said looking at Granda,

Granda put his hand on the paper and slowly crumpled it up.

Only one word was spoken before Granda stood up and left the house.

'Inceptum.'

L

ANGELUS

(Angels)

THE WESTWOODERS WERE making their back at the Fort, the place that had almost obliterated them. It was easier to find their way through the Underworld, the ground was drier, there was no mist and air flowed easily among the branches. The Fort was a calm and serene place now. Mols picked at charred debree which had fallen from the King of the Woods. They talked over all the things which had happened over the weeks.

'Now we will never have great wealth and power.' Christian lamented, however he was equally glad not to have the ill-fated wealth and power of the stone and all associated with it.

But Morgen was not to be deterred. He had brought back his metal detector hoping to perhaps detect some flecks of silver or gold clinging to a leaf or nestled on top of the ground. He spent a long time mooching about the fort to no avail. The others took turns too helping him to look but there wasn't a blip from the metal machine. The gold and silver had been scattered, flailing to the four winds. In a last ditch attempt Morgen returned to the hole, the tomb where the stone had lain for centuries, perhaps here there was the possibility of some tiny filings of the precious metals, although when he looked in there wasn't the hint of a glint of it.

Which is why he startled so easily when he switched on the machine and it shrieked its shrill shout of discovery. Everyone looked up with mouths agape and darted to the electronic beacon.

The tomb was empty, but they had been in this place before. The others allowed Christian get down again to examine the earthy recess. He laid on his belly and reached into the hole scuffing and widening the indent that had been left where they had pulled the stone out of the ground before.

And he could feel another cloth. Another protection, a swaddling wrapped around something solid and square. He freed up the bound object and extricated it and himself from the dusty tomb. He sat back and laid it there on top of the cover stone. All eyes watched and wondered, not a word was spoken. Christian looked at each face of caution and then began to unwrap.

He gradually exposed what appeared to be a tarnished metal box, about the size of a pencil case. As the cloth was fully taken away they could see that it was decorated all around its extremities with decorations and carvings, a tree, a cross, other symbols. Though it had nothing of the ornation intricasies of the Silver Shrine yet they were sure it was of a similar age.

Christian lifted the box and held it carefully in his hands. Though he could not have known whether or not it contained anything at all, he was beginning to formulate a thought about what might be in there. Ever so carefully, so slowly, so delicately, he began to prise the top of the ancient artefact using only the grip of his fingers. He could feel no movement at all in the lid but maintained the same pressure all the while until his fingers were white with the effort. A tiny little budge of movement sent little dust particles circulating in the sunlight as the top gave a little breath and came softly away from the sides.

Christian gently lifted the top slightly away, not wanting to allow the sun shine so suddenly into the box lest it disintegrate its most precious cargo. He had a knowledge that he was exposing to light something that had lain in solitude for almost two thousand years. They all leaned in to see, their heads forming a halo through which the sun cast its warmth on a simple wooden shape resting in ancient padding. The wood was dark with age, its rough grain pattern not the work of any skilled joiner. It was crudely fashioned into shape, the unmistakable shape of a cross, a crucifix, but at the intersection, at the place where Christ would be, there was something that further made the connection.

It was a dull jewel, just like the one they had witnessed on the Silver Shrine in the Narional Museum, and it confirmed it for Christian, it confirmed it for them all.

'This is it?' whispered Taymi.

'The Wood of the True Cross.' Said Sophia softly, rediscovering the most precious relic so many years after her namesake St.Sofia had discovered the same relic in distant histories. It was the wood of the cross on which hung the Saviour of the world and they just stared and stared at the wood that had changed the world.

Christian's hands were quivering with emotion, he set down the lid on the tombstone and took the box in his left hand. He moved his right hand over the wood of the crucifix, *the* crucifix, and felt the jewel between his fingers. He gripped it tightly.

'What are you doing?' whispered Morgen, sensing that there was something going on which he didn't understand and yet as he spoke, Christian, in a slow movement, pulled the jewel clean out of the wood...... exposing a small square hole.

Morgen stared at his brother and saw the raw emotion in his eyes, the trembling in his lips and the shake in his hands. Christian raised his hand to his heart and then to his throat and drew from inside his shirt neck his small square crucifix. He looped the cord over his head and lowered the crucifix towards the box. They all stared speechless as he took the well worn heirloom and fit it exactly into the hole reserved in the Wood of the True Cross. No words were spoken, no words were needed.

Lila sat in the centre of the Fort, on a small tree stump, her hands on her knees and her eyes closed, smiling. They had replaced the box back into its tomb and covered over the scene of the opening. It was the best thing to do. It would remain where it had been left in safekeeping. It was the Wood of the True Cross now they realised that had drawn the Angels, the ring of strength and protection through which no evil could penetrate. And that was what had protected the Golden Stone from the wrong hands, the *im*-pure hands. It was a stroke of genuis, a stroke of faith to bury together the artefact of greatest evil and the artefact of greatest good. Though there was much more to contemplate on how they had found themselves here and Christian felt again the crucifix at his throat whilst thinking about it.

Lila opened her eyes now and spoke.
'There are seven types of wealth.' She said.
Christian looked at her, it was a strong sentence for a little girl, what did she mean? The others gathered around.
Lila could see them, she could hear them, they spoke to her......
Angels, beside her and nearby. She repeated their words, the simple words that explained many things.
The others sat around, listening, spellbound. They couldn't see anything but they knew that she was connected somehow, a channel.
Lila spoke eloquently and happily, the words which were whispered in her ear she repeated for the others to hear. The words that should be heard by all, beautiful words, a bright light.
Her siblings sat around her and listened to her as a teacher. Nature was alive, a dragonfly hovered and then settled on Christian's arm, and he let it.
They returned here many times, and through the child many more words were revealed, words which opened their minds and their hearts, words of richness and immense power that had been carried throught time.
They listened and they received that richness and power. For they knew they would need it.... when the time came.

The Gules of August –The Truth

The family in the story do actually live in the townland of Cordevlis which translates to Hill of the Black Fort or The Devils Hill on property owned by ancestors down the years.

Each of the characters of the family are based closely on the actual persons and their characteristics.

They live in the house described at the western edge of the woods in the story and the locations within the woods are based on real places; including the Waterfall, the Rope, the Ledge Walk and the King of the Woods.

The area in the story Castle-Hanes, is a variation of the real name, which translates to the Fort of the Fairies.

Their grandparents live at the location described, in the townland which translates to the Field of the Stone. Generations of the family lived in the ancestral home and surrounding lands.

The majestic Buzzards are real and constantly hover and circle the woods and the family home.

The character Leon is a representation of the author, whose reversal of name is Noel. Born on the same date as the validation on the Lucas family will and the Christian feast of the Immaculate Conception.

The character Christian is based on real life Christian, born on 23rd Feb and baptised in the Holy Saturday Easter Ceremonies in St.Macartan's Cathedral by the Bishop of Clogher. At birth he suffered near asphyxiation as a result of the cord wrapping around his neck. The spectral night visitor is based on an incident that he actually reported and he has been troubled by the asthma and weaknesses described.

He attended St.Macartan's secondary college, described I the story, which has as its motto; Fortis et Fidelis.

The ruined Castle in the woods and the family that inhabited it and their ancestors are accurately described. The cause of the burning of the Castle is unknown however the Lady of the House and her seven year old daughter Oriel, who were the only family occupants of the house at the time, escaped unhurt together with other maids and assistants.

The story by the author of remembering his Grandmother talking about visiting the Castle for garden parties in its heyday is true.

The description of the Castles current state is accurate at time of writing however the remaining walls still continue to slowly crumble. The vaults and underground nooks remain as described. The bellcote still exists together with a walled garden close to the Castle but now on private property.

The described remains of the West-Wood gatelodge was 'discovered' by the family prior to the writing of this book. It is not known how long it lay overgrown and in ruins.

The chance meeting described between the author and Sophia and the real Sir Jack Leslie was an actual occurrence during which Sir Jack told of his memories of the occasion of the burning of the Lucas Castle and the arrival of the fleeing family to the Castle Leslie in the real village of Glaslough. Sir Jack gained certain notoriety for letting slip the secret wedding of Paul McCartney.

The connection of the Leslie family to Winston Churchill is real as is the framed baptism gown kept in Castle Leslie.

The story describes real legends and mythology associated with Fairy Forts.

The unusual story of a Black Beast, a Panther, patrolling the region was reported in local and national media on numerous occasions over a period of years including some video footage of a supposed sighting.

The disappearance of deer from the Woods and the discovery by the family of a large carcass are true. However a sighting of a deer in the Woods after many years was witnessed by the author during the writing of this book.

The ancient language of Ogham was a medieval alphabet sometimes called the 'Celtic Tree Alphabet' thought to have been invented in the 1st Century BC. It is considered to perhaps have been created by Druids as a secret means of communication.

The character known in the story as 'The Dark One' is based on a real person and friend of the family. His dark gothic musical background is true.

The history attributed to and the connections between 'The Golden Stone' and the 'Diocese of Clogher' are real and documented. The actual Golden Stone still exists in St.Macartans Cathedral at Clogher as described in the story and it is said that St.Macartan is buried in the same grounds in an unmarked grave. The visit to the old Cathedral and the nearby Hillfort, the 'Kingdom of Oriel' took place during the writing of the book.

The histories and legends attributed to St.Partick and St.Macartan are based on actual recorded descriptions including the artefact the Silver Shrine which is now kept as described in the National Museum of Ireland and their meeting with the King of Oriel and the Little Prince.

The descriptions of Druidic and Pagan practices together with the mythology associated with Celtic Gods are based on actual recorded documentation. As are the myths and legends associated with the Banshee and other mythical entities.

The area described as Rockwell is based on an actual area of similar name and position which includes the ancient graveyard and St.Michael's school as described. The SchoolMaster is based on the real person and the actual handwritten message signed by him together with a package of information on the Castle was used in the story.

The existence and location of the mass-rock are accurate as described.

The character Auntie Mae is based on the authors real Aunt and her visit with the glove of St.Pio is true. The history attributed to Padre Pio is as documented.

The descriptions of St.Macartans Cathedral in Monaghan are accurate including its artworks and depictions together with the inscription Gilla Chroist. The plaque remembering the 100,000 people affected by the Famine is as described. The description and story of the boy, an uncle of the character Leon James is accurate.

The visit to the historical island of Mont St.Michel as described did actually take place during a family trip to North France.

The exhibitions described in the National Museum are real exhibitions (at the time of writing) including the Silver Shrine. The Book of Kells is kept as described in Trinity College University.

The three cemeteries described and the family connections within are as described in the story.

The Angels calendar and the Little Book of Partick are actual possessions owned by the family.

The newspaper referred to and the article from it read by Taymi relating to the burning of the Castle and the existence of the Nuremburg Chronicles are real. In reality this article opened up the link to the Chronicles.

The wildlife man Mr.Kelly is based on a real person and his wildlife collection and knowledge of all things wildlife are real. The habits and traits associated with all wildlife in the book are as accurate as possible

The area known in the story as Clonraggett is in reality the scene of a great and bloody battle.

The author *did* read 'A Brief History of Time' by Stephen Hawking during the preparation of this book.

The incidents involving the early morning visit of the young man and the bat at night did actually happen.

The visit of the family to the ancient town of Clones is recorded in the story almost identically to how it occurred in reality. Including the discovery of the Celtic Cross and its messages, the finding of the ancient cemetery and its startling message proclaiming Tiernach to be of 'The House of Oriel' and the search for the Abbey. Also the linking of the three sites to each other and the visit to the Library. The connection to Daniel and his vision of a Golden Stone, an actual documented biblical story, came from this visit. Art imitating Life.

The flash flood described actually occurred during the writing of the book and only in the locality as described in the story. The visit of the Fire Brigade, the flooding of the garden and the attempt to clear the drain happened in reality.

The damage to the woods, the river banks and in particular to the bridge occurred during the flood as described in the book.

The geometric positioning of locations are accurate as described in the book.

The character name Anouk was chosen at random, that it so closely aligns to the Breton name for the Angel of Death was entirely coincidental.

The chapter where the parents are attending a function in the Cathedral listening to a rare hymn whilst the children are in danger in the Woods was written on a Saturday morning whilst listening to the hymn playing. In the afternoon the author was asked by chance to administer Eucharist that evening in the Cathedral. He found himself by coincidence back in the Cathedral and listening to this very hymn being sung in a rendition for a particular one off event. Life imitating Art.

The histories attributed to Princess Anastasia and Anna Anderson are based on recorded accounts.

The Author

Noel Murphy is the alter-ego of the character Leon James.
He is a writer, technical architect, occasional artist, sometimes
poet, radio documentary maker, public awareness campaigner
together with many more roles and responsibilities.
His behaviour as the character in the book
is pretty much accurate to life.
If you have read this book then you know
where he lives and all about his family.
This book is dedicated to them.
This is his first book; unless it sells more
than 3 copies it may be his last.

The Author can be contacted at noelgerardmurphy@eircom.net

Lightning Source UK Ltd.
Milton Keynes UK
UKOW02f1524071115

262243UK00003B/68/P